"Tanuja Desai Hidier captures the raw vitality of New York City's club scene without missing a bhangric beat, using it as a context to explore the complexities of multicultural identity and human relationships. *Born Confused*'s female characters and the intensity of their friendships are particularly powerful and have not often enough been explored or written about in this way. I loved the book, and was sad it was over – I want more!"

DJ Rekha

★

"The first-ever Indian American teen girl book: Tanuja Desai Hidier sucked me in with her hilarious situations, larger-than-life characters and unsinkable heart… This book reads like a South Asian American version of a Jennifer Love Hewitt movie and – honestly – I have been waiting for it all my life."

Neela Banerjee, Editor in Chief, *Asian Week*

★

"In this enlightening first novel, Hidier offers readers an engrossing, personal account of the Indian-American experience through the eyes of an insightful narrator… On one level, the book explores the growing pains, rebellious phases, peer pressures, and first love experienced universally by teens. On a deeper level, if celebrates a harmonious blending of cultures as it traces one adolescent's bumpy trek toward self-actualization… The author poetically captures the essence of her characters and the richness of seemingly insignificant moments. Absorbing and intoxicating, this book is sure to leave a lasting impression."

***Publishers Weekly*, starred review**

★

Shashikala K. Desai

Born Confused

TANUJA DESAI HIDIER

SCHOLASTIC
PRESS

Scholastic Children's Books,
Commonwealth House, 1-19 New Oxford Street,
London, WC1A 1NU, UK
a division of Scholastic Ltd
London ~ New York ~ Toronto ~ Sydney ~ Auckland
Mexico City ~ New Delhi ~ Hong Kong

First published in the US by Scholastic Press, a division of Scholastic Inc., 2002
First published in the UK by Scholastic Ltd, 2003

ISBN 0 439 97862 9 (HB)
ISBN 0 439 97360 0 (PB)

Printed and bound by Scandbook AB, Sweden
Printed and bound by Nørhaven Paperback A/S, Denmark

10 9 8 7 6 5 4 3 2 1

For my Jeevansaathi, Bernard
(. . . flap, flap . . .)

Acknowledgments

Immeasurable-and-one thanks to Bapuji and Shashikala Desai, for all that time at the Saraswati. For your bravery, beauty, and superlative sense of humor. For you. You are my first and forever hero and heroine, and I want to be just like you when I grow up. Happy Birthday.

Many mercis to my brother, Rajiv, for all those powwows: fourteen miles around the reservoir and at "the place" and always. You have been my support and inspiration from the day I was AB.

To David Levithan, dream editor and one-in-a-million person, whose belief in this project from its inception and guiding graceful hands were vital to bringing it to fruition. Thank gods we met!

To Liz Szabla, for letting her beautiful eyes fall upon the proposal that day, and linger.

To Laurelyn Douglas, for her perspectives on this project — and so much more: seventeen years of friendship. You make this life a garden.

Big thank you to Jaikumar Ramaswamy. Thanks to Sreenath Sreenivasan and the SAJA Stylebook from the South Asian Journalists Association, http://www.saja.org/stylebook. Also to Nutan Christine Shah (Bollywood ben!), Poonam Ahuja Banerjee, Smita Gadher (wedding makeup and dress); Vena Ramphal, Vanisha Kumar, Dipty "Bhabi" Desai, Karishma Patel

(Bharat Natyam); Shreyas Mavani (tablas); Mike Kobal, Srinivas Kuruganti (photography); and Arvind Devalia (connection).

Muchissimo gracissimos to Sylvia "Chiquita" Alvariño, sister in club crime and DJ inspiration, for being so gorgeous (inside and out).

And, chronologically, to Jennifer Clarke Smith, for putting the cool into high school and ever after; Pamela "Verbatim" Tatum Montemayor, people genius, for all the worlds we made together; Amy Carden Suardi, for dreaming magic slippers and filling the darkness with glitter; and Rekha Malhotra, for blowing my dance world with Basement Bhangra and Mutiny (and waiting till we got there only to play Bally Sagoo and Malkit Singh's "Gur Nalon Ishq Mitha"). Ji!

And last but *never* least—this is for you, New York, New York: Thank you, most beautiful, beloved, *irrepressible* city, for the inspiration, desperation, and invaluable experience. And to equally loved London, your reverse twin, for gifting me the peace of mind to behold you.

Find out more about the author at
www.ThisIsTanuja.com

* * **x** ** *

"Some souls one will never discover, unless one invents them first."
— Friedrich Nietzsche, *Thus Spoke Zarathustra*

I would believe only in a god who could dance.
— *ibid*.

the reincarnation of
dimple rohitbhai lala the last

I guess the whole mess started around my birthday. Amendment: my *first* birthday. I was born turned around, and apparently was holding my head in my hand in such a way that resulted in twelve treacherous hours of painful labor for my mother to eject me.

My mom said she imagined I was trying to sort out some great philosophical quandary, like Rodin's *Thinker* sculpture that she had seen on a trip to Paris in another lifetime. But I think that was just a polite way of saying I looked like I didn't get it. Born backwards and clueless. In other words, born confused.

So I came out the wrong way. And have been getting it all wrong ever since. I wished there was a way to go back and start over. But as my mother says, you can't step in the same river twice.

★   ★   ★

This was going to be the first day of the rest of my life, Gwyn had announced to me on the way to school. After today: long hot months ahead, in which anything could—and would—happen. She said it with that insider wink that made it clear she had something up her sleeve, even though it was too hot for sleeves today and a silver armlet snaked a tantalizingly cool path round her biceps. The way she smiled mysteriously, mischievously at me was a surefire guarantee the heat was on in more ways than one.

And it was true the temperature was rising and there seemed to be no end in sight. By second period, honors history, all my makeup had run off, even the so-called waterproof concealer; by third my thighs were welded to-gether under the cramped desk, and by fourth my perm, which was supposed to have grown out months ago, resurrected itself with a vengeance, sending little ringlets Hula-Hooping out all over my head. There was a line for the fountain, and everyone was insatiable, sucking the water from the source, metal-lipped, which my mother says is unsanitary and very American. In fifth period, all the windows were cracked open to let in no wind, and a bead of sweat glittered on Mr. Linkhaus's nose the entire hour, bobbing, teasing, but never falling.

No one was paying attention anyways. The only physics anyone was thinking about was how quickly a moving body could make it out the front door and into summer vacation. That is, everyone except me.

Now the last bell was ringing and I was staring into the upper shelf of my locker at Chica Tikka, my beloved camera. I was waiting for Gwyn, who'd called a ULP Wow (Urgent Locker Powwow), a little unnecessarily, consid-ering we met up here every day after class; she had news for me, which was usually the case. And I was feeling lost without her, which was usually the case, too.

In our twosome I was "the other one"—you know, the one the boy doesn't remember two seconds after delivering the pizza. The too-curvy, clumsy, camera-clacking wallflower with nothing but questions lately. But I guess you need someone with questions to give the one with all the answers an ear to inform, and maybe that was why we were together.

She had it all, Gwyn. And I had her, which by some sort of transitive theory gave me access to the allness she cupped in the palm of her hand. She even had the majority of my locker space, I realized now that I was un-loading my own books and binders to find they'd taken up minimum inch-age. It was mostly her stuff here; we'd been sharing since I'd ended up with a more central A Hall locker, and in addition to her vinyl-coated books, she kept a makeup kit and hair serum in it. Pinned on the inside of the door, on either side of the black-and-white-and-many-greys image of a snowy peak in Yosemite that my Ketan Kaka had sent me, was a postcard of Marilyn Mon-roe losing her dress over a subway grating, and a calorie chart.

I took out Chica Tikka now, checking the counter. I still had a few shots left on this roll. I'd been taking black and whites all week, staying around late when Gwyn scooted off as usual to meet Dylan Reed, to whom she'd been joined at the lip for the last eternity.

I got disproportionately nostalgic at the end of the school year, not only for the good times but even, perversely, for my own misery, and took snap after shot of the empty hallways, bathrooms, classrooms. But no matter what I was trying to capture on film, if Gwyn was anywhere around, she always jumped in, drawn magnetic to the lens. I half-expected her to do so now, and even took off the lens cap to facilitate her entry, but it was a no-go.

I loaded up my knapsack, wondering if she'd forgotten about our meeting and was with Dylan now. Through my lens I was watching everyone's jubilation, the happy clack of locker doors, the sign-my-yearbooks, the hallway hugs among people who never really seemed to hang before. Everyone was careening out to the buses, high-fiving each other; a few people said bye to me, *have a good one.* Even Jimmy Singh, whose real name was Trilok, nodded discreetly out from under his turban as he shufflingly followed his hawkish nose out.

I didn't have to struggle for spy status. Fortunately I have this gift for invisibility, which comes in handy when you're trying to take sneaky peeks at other people's lives, and which is odd, considering I'm one of only two Indians in the whole school. The other being the above-mentioned Jimmy (Trilok) Singh, who wore his ethnicity so brazenly, in the form of that pupil-shrinking turban and the silver kada bangle on his wrist, I got the feeling many people had stopped noticing that I hailed originally from the same general hood. But I did my best to play it down. After all, the day I wore my hair in braids everyone yelled *Hey, Pocahontas* and did that ahh-baah-baah-baah lip-slap at recess. You would have gotten a perm soon after as well.

Gwyn had gone with me to get the perm; in general, she often acted as my personal stylist, which served to disguise me still further (it was she who'd talked me into buying the too-tight tottery pumps I was now keeling in). In fact, I'd more often been mistaken, heritagically speaking, for Mexican than half-Mumbaite (a geographical personal status formerly known as half-Bombayite). But much as I tried to blend in—and much as I often did, with the wallpaper and floor if not the other kids—I still felt it sometimes, like when my mother came to Open House in that salvar khamees or when I stayed up all night trying to scrub the henna off my palms after Hush-Hush

Aunty's son's wedding because during home ec Mrs. Plumb suspected I had a skin disease and refused to partake of my cinnamon apple crumble. And eating with my hands? I wouldn't even do that at home, alone, and in the dark.

I don't think it was always like this. My gift—or desire—for invisibility. Once again, I suppose it all began around my birthday. Not the one I was about to have in a couple days, my seventeenth, but the last one, when I turned sweet sixteen with no one to kiss because that afternoon Bobby O'Malley swiftly and unceremoniously dumped me on the way out to the late buses. I guess you can't completely blame him; I mean, he'd forgotten it was my birthday, so it wasn't like he did it out of any extraordinary mean streak. Just an ordinary quotidian kind of mean streak. It had been the beginning of a cruel summer, spent with my head in the fridge and my heart in the garbage disposal. And when this year started, I couldn't wait for it to be over, for school to be out so I wouldn't have to see him anymore at all those dances that Gwyn insisted we go to, just to show him, who always ended up showing me by showing up with that batch of new girls, those thinner, prettier, blonder girls who ran their hands through his Irish curls and counted his freckles with their lips and were all hairlessly good in gym. My GPA dropped, mainly due to math, where I was unfortuitously seated next to Bobby (O having ended up next to L for Lala in that sad arrangement), but my Great Pound Average hefted up proportionately, about ten more slabs of flab. Gwyn insisted my scale wasn't working, which was kind of her, but it was a state-of-the-art doctor's scale from my father's office, and I'd tested it against a couple of five-pound dumbbells that were collecting dust under my bed and which I used primarily for this purpose.

That day, I'd walked the final few steps out to the late bus in a daze. Gwyn (shockingly boyless at the time) was holding my seat for me, and I took it and whispered, *Bobby O'Malley just broke up with me.* Her mouth dropped open and I saw the wad of pink gum sunk in the center of her tongue. But she was good at quick saves, and firmly swallowed.

—Dimple Lala, you mark my words, she said. —That is the best birthday present B.O. could possibly have given you.

The rest of the ride she'd ranted out the top 101 reasons why he'd never been good enough for me in the first place (odd numbers are considered auspicious in India, and she'd become an ardent practitioner of that belief). She avoided the one about him secretly crushing on her, which was gracious.

But all I'd been able to think about was our nearly hundred kisses, the first fumbling one across the pond that separated our neighborhoods, in the then-unconstructed neighborhood near the Fields where he pink-cheekedly brown-curledly lived, up to the ninety-eighth under the jungle gym at midnight. And the *I've never felt this way befores*; plenty of those were passed around the playground. And then, at that moment on that late bus, the feeling that forever actually had an expiration date, like a carton of milk, could go sour on you when you were least expecting it.

And since then every expired carton simply served to remind me of other sour times, every ending recalling all the ones before. Which maybe explained my sudden sadness today, the last day of junior year. It had been a particularly tough few terms; I'd had a lot of trouble with everything in the era A.B. (After Bobby) and especially this last year, when my grandfather Dadaji died, before any of us could get to him, freeze-framing my image of India in a fast-escaping, ungrasped past. My mother had returned from Bombay with her accent newly thickened and her feeling that she should have never left as well, a growing desire to see me "settled." I didn't know what she meant, but I had the image of dust collecting pithily on a windowsill.

I had just put my eye to the viewfinder to shoot the inside of the locker door when a voice like blue sky sailed in.

—Is that a supertwin I see on the loose?

Marilyn dropped through the grating as I shifted my camera back out to the hallway. Through the cross of the screen, dead-center and Dylan-less, I now saw my number one diva of the dramatic entrance swinging up, lunchbox purse in one hand, shades atop a shiny blonde chignoned head, and sleek blue mini turning purple as her fishnetted legs slunk around underneath, activating its iridescence. She was in a tight black tank studded with a heart within a heart, and as she reared up she fluttered the air before her with a big silver envelope as if to beat the unremitting heat of the corridor, then handed it to me, pool blue eyes unblinking. It was Magic-Markered *To The Birthday Girl!*

—What is it? I said, fingering the paper tentatively as if it might go off in my hands. I could feel something small and squarish inside, sliding around in all that clean space.

—See for yourself, she said.

I tore it open, half-expecting a letter for a Lilliputian to skid out. But instead, a scant piece of plastic tapped out into my palm. I picked it up—a black strip on one side and a mash of text defining Class D vehicles and an organ donor stamp—and turned it over to come face to face with: myself.

At first I was confused. It was definitely me, yes, appearing as ever the headlit deer. My hair was knitting madly out, brown eyes wide, and a jarringly pale hand seemed to be stroking my chin. I had the initial illogical impression I'd dropped my license somewhere and Gwyn was simply returning it to me. But I didn't even have my license yet; I only had a permit, and my driver's test, which I was already willing to wager I'd fail, was a good couple months away.

Below the image: a signature that looked more like Gwyn's bubbling semi-print script (full-circle dot over the i) than my own microscopic cursive. I scanned the rest of the card. Dimple Rohitbhai Lala. Check. Lancaster Road, Springfield, NJ, and zip. Check. Sex: F. Check. Height: Five foot one—well, one and a half, and I would have preferred rounding up, but good enough. Class D; Social Security number. Birth day (tomorrow), month (this one). Year—year? The year was off by four. This wasn't me but some genetically modified precursor.

—A fake ID! I cried.

Now I recognized the picture as one in the various sets of trilogies we'd taken in the mall photo booth in the corner of the camera store, ages ago it seemed. Gwyn had insisted on making a shop-stop there—as she always did when we passed any photographic medium or even any remotely reflective surface, for that matter. She'd pulled me into her lap suddenly on the last shot, squeezing out of frame and turning my face to the lens with her own hand (hence my fair extremity, I now realized). And she'd insisted on keeping all the pics, since I already had more than enough of my own with Chica Tikka's insatiable appetite.

Gwyn looked abundantly pleased with herself. She sent the purple fringe of her mini flying as she did a little pirouette.

—Courtesy of Dyl, she smiled. —And we're going to use it tomorrow night! We have a lot to celebrate: School's out, a summer in the city lies ahead. And, of course, your *date*.

—My *date*?

She let me suffer a moment, then seemed unable to contain herself any longer.

—Do you remember Julian Rothschild? Dylan's partner in crime here at Lenne Lenape, he graduated the same year?

Did I remember Julian Rothschild? Of course I remembered. The much-coveted, recently collegiate Julian Rothschild to be precise. Girls passed whispering notes about him in study hall, where he'd read books by people with unpronounceable names like Deleuze and Derrida scripted flagrantly across the cover. Julian's hair curled down the nape of his neck, winging out at the bottom, a little shorter than Dylan's. He wore green lizardskin cowboy boots; Dylan wore snake. And he was an atheist, or something cool like that (Dylan was agnostic, which was, of course, cooler, since no one knew exactly what it meant). In general, Julian was Dylan's slightly less-tall, less-cute, less-smart, less-motivated partner in crime—I guess a match made in math for Gwyn's lesser half (me)—but in my eyes he was more like four-fifths of the way to hotness himself and at NYU to top it off. Everybody wanted him. Which was enough of an argument for me.

—Yeah, I think I *vaaaguely* remember, I said, unable to suppress a smile.

—Well, then, I hope you like what you remember—because he's all yours tomorrow night!

—But he doesn't even know who I am, I said.

—Oh, believe me, he knows who you are. I told him you were the *Indian* girl. I mean, *the* Indian girl.

I guess that pretty much narrowed it down.

—Dimple, she said firmly. —It's a new ID. You can be whoever you want to be. You can be, as the army has failed to inform us, all that you can't be.

She left me to mull that over, adjusting her double-looped snake belts to hangle just so off her slight hips. She did have a point, I supposed. It was my opportunity to be the older, wiser, bubblier-scripted, white-armed Dimple Lala. And maybe this Dimple could truly be all I couldn't.

* * 7 * *

—You think it over, she said. —I have to make like tic-tac-toe and exit—Dyl's in idle. You go do your family thing or whatever it is you do. But tomorrow night. Tomorrow night will be ours.

Through my viewfinder she left now, dragging out all the color and speed and life with her like a bridal train that sweeps up any confettied hopes with it on its way to the honeymoon. I clicked and the counter ran to zero. And when I lifted my eyes, she was already gone, leaving in her wake the grey linoleum and steel lockers, starkened still more by the fluorescent dentist-office lights. The opaque classroom windows; a scent of chalk and rubber. My own drab reality fell upon me then; whenever Gwyn made her exit I realized how much I relied on her to bring magic to the picture.

Next year we were going to be seniors—and then what? It was this summer that could make all the difference. I stared down at the new image of me, the plastic fantasy in my hand. This could be my ticket. I could be her.

The corridor clock jumped two minutes forward.

It was the first day of the rest of my life.

CHAPTER 2

third eye

I kicked off my shoes on the porch, then dropped off my books on one of the twin beds. Looking at the second twin I wondered how long it had been since Gwyn had slept over. Felt like ages. Felt like Dylan.

I didn't have too long, but went to leave the roll I'd just finished off in my favorite place in the whole house, perhaps the world: my darkroom. Or, my darkening room, as my mother mistakenly called it. (This had led to much alarm for Meera Maasi—my aunt, her sister—who felt I should instead be coating myself in turmeric, or at least exfoliating on a regular basis to lighten my skin rather than pass too much time in a darkening room; I think she feared we had tanning beds installed in the nether parts of our home.)

Down the stairs, through the basement, and into the small sacred space at the back.

My parents had helped me set it up last year. The room used to be a sort of bathroom area. I think my folks had in mind another bedroom area for the burgeoning family we never ended up being, or that it could be used as spare space if we ever brought Dadaji or any other relative to live with us, which we never ended up doing. And so they figured since no one was using the basement anyways it couldn't hurt if I were to pursue my hobby tucked away in the closet. Which suited me just fine. No one bothered me here; I was in an exclusive club of one, with the only password. And I actually spent more time down here than in my bedroom, beginning pretty much from the moment I'd converted it.

I looked now at the space: my enlarger, protected from sink splash by a sheet of cardboard off the box the household computer had come in. The developer trays. Stop bath and fixer trays, hose coiled up serpentine in the sink; whenever the safelight was on it looked like a tiny anaconda, waiting to strike. The print washing tray lodged by the sink and my paper stash. The focus finders, which made me feel like Nancy Drew hot on a case. Stirrers, squeegee. Masking easel.

And, finally, the pictures on the line.

Everywhere: Gwyn. She was all over the photographs hanging to dry. Gwyn in A Hall, a Beginner's Philosophy book in focus in hand, her partial head blurred like a spinning top. Gwyn in an empty classroom, pledging to the flag with one hand and adjusting her bra strap behind her back with the other. Gwyn giving off double peace signs in a tiny-teed, pleathered pose on the scintillating hood of Dylan's car.

My memory filled in the early sunburn below the pseudo-punk safety-pinned gashes in her white tee, the unabashed red of the pleather, the blinding azure sun of that day and the way it had made her eyes burn like liquid metal. Looking at this black and white of a red, white, and blue moment, Gwyn appeared the very image of the American Dream itself, the blonde-rooted, blonde-haired, blue-eyed Marilyn for the skinny generation. And if I was her reverse twin—the negative to her positive—that made me? The Indian nightmare? The American scream?

She'd told him I was the *Indian* girl. *The* Indian girl. Somehow neither description rang completely true to me in terms of how I felt inside, but the thing was I'd never really consciously thought of myself as American, either. Of course I did the Pledge, too, along with everybody else for years of mornings, but like everyone else I wasn't really thinking about the words. I mean, I definitely wanted liberty, like Gwyn had with the car keys and no curfew, and justice for all would be great, especially in high school where people were definitely not created equal (proof: cheerleaders). But I didn't know if that had so much to do with the stars and stripes; it seemed to be more about the jeans and teams.

So not quite Indian, and not quite American. Usually I felt more along the lines of Alien (however legal, as my Jersey birth certificate attests to). The only times I retreated to one or the other description were when my peers didn't understand me (then I figured it was because I was too Indian) or when my family didn't get it (clearly because I was too American). And in India. Sometimes I was too Indian in America, yes, but in India, I was definitely not Indian enough.

India. I had few memories of the place, but the ones I held were dream clear: Bathing in a bucket as a little girl. The unnerving richness of buffalo milk drunk from a pewter cup. My Dadaji pouring tea into a saucer so it would cool faster, sipping from the edge of the thin dish, never spilling a drop. A whole host of kitchen gods (looking so at home in the undishwashered unmicrowaved room). Meera Maasi crouching on the floor to sift the stones from rice. Cows huddled in the middle of the vegetable market, sparrows nesting on their backs. Hibiscus so brilliant they looked like they'd caught fire. Children with red hair living in tires. A perpetual squint against sun and dust. The most delicious orange soda I'd ever drunk—the cap-split hiss, and then the bubbling jetstream down a parched throat.

But mainly all my memories of India were memories of Dadaji. When he died the entire country seemed to come unhitched, floated off my mental map of the world and fell off the edge, to mean nothing anymore, just a gaping hole fast filling with water. And at the same time the place I had known grew fixed in my imagination, rooted in memory. When my grandfather saw me that last time, he beheld me like he couldn't quite believe his eyes. He called me by my mother's name, Shilpa, and then when she stepped in behind me and it all fell into place, the weight of all those years in between visits was visible in his slumped shoulders. To me he'd looked the same, wearing low over a white lungi a familiar moss-and-maroon plaid shirt that I realized later had been my father's.

In fact all sorts of items that mysteriously disappeared from our Springfield home seemed to pop up all over the little flat where Dadaji had lived with Meera Maasi and Dilip Kaka and my cousins. It had been a fuller household at one time: Dadaji had lit the flame to the pyre for his wife, the grandmother I summoned up only as a warmly glinting climate. Then he had to do the same for his son, Sharad, the Mama uncle I also remembered faintly in physical detail, though lushly in atmosphere: an ashy dusk, the page-turn of wings, half-whistle half-hum. Dadaji made it through all these things still standing, until he slipped on his chappals coming home from the garden with marigold for the morning pooja, falling hard, his hip crushed against the petals; how a tiny thing could still create a big hurt.

My cousins were a little older than me: Sangita, the quiet one, sporting soda-bottle glasses from very early on; her eyes receded behind the thick lenses to rain-stilled crater depths, and the rest of her pretty much vanished behind Kavita. Kavita—the one who was buried in the books at NYU now, making up premed credits in an intensive summer program—used to be pretty boisterous: a chair-tipper, a tree-climber, her whooping laugh shaking the branches as she monkey-jumped about. The two were always dressed in clothes I'd forgotten I had, or that I'd been searching frustratedly for through all the closets of the house.

Meera Maasi called these dresses *frocks*, which sounded like an expletive the way it spat forth from her thin mouth—and which I preferred to the actual expletive it resembled because the F-word still didn't come naturally to me. She put the word to vipid use when she chided me, in my Osh Kosh B'Goshes, for not being properly attired, which I found ironic considering her own daughters were so often to be found garbed in my duds—the dress with the mega-radiied purple polka dots, the blue-jean skirt with the rainbow patterns on the back pockets, stiff pink-and-white taffeta numbers that looked like the result of some inadvisable union between a ballerina's tutu and a first communion dress, the cumulus of fabric floating around my young sister-cousins' rail-thin bodies.

I was the American cousin, the princess, the plumped-up one: Kavita never tired of pinching my cheeks, which I hated; they both giggled even when I'd said nothing funny and hovered around me, serving me first from the pots of fluffy rice and the silver thalis; they were always hungry to hear stories about America. Had I ever been on an escalator? Did girls talk to boys at my school? (Wide eyes when I said yes.) Was it true the stores stayed lit all night and supermarkets had aisles of just one thing and doors that slid miraculously open before you? Had I ever met a cowboy? (Kavita began to call me her cowgirl cousin when I told her I'd once ridden a horse.) They marveled at how much I ate, how quickly I spoke. At night, they gathered with home-made pista kulfi and the rest of the household to watch reruns of I Love Lucy on the remote-uncontrolled television (which also looked vaguely familiar to me), laughing uproariously and slapping their knees at things I found cheesy at best. They sang "I Want to Live in America" from *West Side Story*—well, just that one line, over and over, but with surprisingly authentic Spanish accents. They begged me to teach them new songs.

Dadaji could sit for hours listening to me, too, but I didn't feel like such a circus freak around him, even though—or perhaps because—he didn't understand a word of English. And me and Marathi—well, I didn't know enough to get me to the other side of the room; sure, when I was a baby those few months in India I'd spoken it in jigsaw pieces with him. But not since America, where I must have checked any memory of the language at customs. This was Dadaji's constant sore point with my parents: Aaray Ram, Krishna, and anyone else who cared to listen, how could they have been so cruel as to cut off their own flesh and blood from one another through this ultimate act of linguistic negligence?

—This America you speak of is like a dream, he told me one time, Kavita casually translating. —I am too old to travel. And it breaks my heart I cannot picture your life there. Make it real to me, rani.

Rani, I understood; he was the one in the world who called me this. My princess, my queen. I'd been lying next to him on the bed, drifting into jet-lagged sleep. Gusts of sweet tobacco-smelling air skimmed my dreams. When I opened my eyes later, disoriented and dazed, I could hear the slap of wet laundry on concrete in the other room and Kavita's high merry voice, teasing someone as usual. Out the slatted window, children were playing cricket and making cricket noises; sparrows convened noisily in the grill. And next to me, in a faded pair of my father's pajamas, was Dadaji; I realized then he'd stayed beside me the whole time, his hand inches from my forehead, waving the flies from my face before they touched down so I could sleep undisturbed. He was watching me with eyes full of questions.

When I got back to America I started taking photographs for him. He was my number one fan: eager, insatiable. And he responded to everything, often with sketches and shots of his own, the pale blue airmail stationery addressed in his tiny slanty script turning the inside of our mailbox azure with a faraway sky. We were going to get around this language thing! It seemed so simple: We'd use pictures to talk. So I sent him pictures of any and everything. Even the most inconsequential snap (i.e., my locker door) he would gobble up as if it were straight off the wall of a museum.

After Bobby O'Malley broke up with me, I sent Dadaji pictures of the street-in-progress where we'd pulled our first kisses from each other, a lone lamp burning in the distance. They were all dark, grainy, a little underexposed; I think I'd used the wrong ASA. I'd labeled them: *Some shots of the neighborhood.* When he wrote back, his reply was: *You don't need him. You just need a better camera. Focus on the light next time.* I couldn't figure out how he'd known. My parents asked me about that one when they'd translated the letter, but I played dumb at the time; the last thing I'd wanted to do then was talk about Bobby O'Malley.

In the same letter, Dadaji sent a money order to my parents, the equivalent of too many rupees, with the specific instructions that it was to be used only for the purchase of a "serious" camera for my birthday.

And that's how I got her, my third eye, which is why I call her Chica Tikka, for the powder my mother keeps in a little pot in the kitchen temple—the scarlet dust her own mother pressed between her brows the morning she left for America. Chica Tikka, I imagined, could see far far away, even to where Dadaji was now. Whenever I took a shot, loaded a roll, I felt that hand inches from my face, safeguarding the dream. Whenever I peered through the lens I could nearly see him looking back at me from the other end—from a lamppost, a flowerbed, even Gwyn's ever-ready grin—and with so much love in his eyes I had to click to keep the tears from coming.

I haven't gone back to India so I haven't really seen the way in which he is not there, how that singing space has surely taken on his shape. All I knew was the pale blue letters stopped coming to me, though there seemed to be more from Meera Maasi to my mother now, especially since Sangita's wedding preparations began. I missed the letters, but I had the camera. No one truly understood why I was so attached to it, or why I liked spending so much time in the darkening room. But it was in this world where chemicals collided to coax images suddenly up out of sheer darkness that I felt most he was just beside me, abeyant, and all it would take to bring him out of shadow would be a single moment of the right chemistry.

* .* *14* *.* *

—Beta! Your father's home! my mother called. —Are you ready, birth-day girl?

I stepped out of darkness. My eyes always throbbed when I did this too abruptly; maybe that's why babies keep theirs squeezed shut for a while after entering the world. Too much light.

—Coming, I said.

the wish in your mouth

The birthday shopping thing had been a ritual ever since I crash-landed into puberty. Basically, what would happen was my parents would take me to the mall and let me pick out a few of my own presents, and then they'd make me not look while they purchased some of these items, which would then mysteriously appear wrapped in oddly shaped boxes and last year's Christmas paper on my actual birthday.

It wasn't really a statement of my newfound independence, my crossing that department store boundary from the child to adult section, this choosing-for-myself-since-puberty deal. This was simply around the time my parents stopped understanding what I wanted and I stopped understanding what they wanted me to want.

The ritual usually worked according to an unspoken barter system: one proper item for every errant-ways one. For example, last year I'd received a "nice" dress (white, long sleeves, with a sort of pinafore that seemed ideal for bobbing for apples) and a pair of hip-hugger bell bottoms that my mother told me made me look like those hippy-hop boys who's dhugrees are always sneaking up on them.

The mall ritual usually followed the same pattern, and today was no different. When we got there, following my mom's instructions, my dad spent an enormous amount of time circling around the parking lot trying to get a spot two inches away from Macy's, even though half the lot was empty just a little farther back.

(I should mention that my mother didn't like for me to drive when she was in the car. She said she didn't have the stomach for it—this coming from a woman who'd worked the intensive-care unit and delivered babies, but it was true: The few times she'd been in this unfortunate scenario she'd gripped the edge of the seat so hard her knuckles blanched like almonds, and began invoking gods from all sorts of religions under her breath. *Hare Ram, Allah, Jesus.* Calling upon other faiths was something she did only when she was *very* nervous.)

My father's reverse parking job was followed by a stroll through Macy's complete with my mother aaraying and ahhing with equal enthusiasm at anything diamond or cubic zirconia, and graciously accepting every scent sample that fluttered her way from the perfectly eye-lined girls swaying around beachily on high heels; she would thank them with a girlish giggle, as if they spritzed for her alone. By the time we exited the cosmetics department she smelled of Obsession on her left wrist (even though she owned it, fittingly, she could never resist), Trésor on her right, and Samsara on her neck—a discordant bouquet coming together to create something more along the lines of *eau de nail polish remover* than anything else.

On to clothing, where my dad pointed out what he considered to be a "pleasant" nightgown for me (a Victorian contraption that even Jane Eyre might find constraining). Meanwhile, I was longingly eyeing two-sizes-too-small jeans on mannequins with impossibly slim, nippleless bodies that had nothing to do with my own. By which point my father was already bored and took off to check out spy gadgets, with a plan to meet us in forty-five minutes by the potted palms—thereby liberating me to manipulate my mother, by now woozy and pliable from inhaling all those fumes, into going places she wouldn't have dared moments before.

—Ma? I said. We were passing the one way-out store in the mall, which sold T-shirts with Bob Marley pictures on them and incense like we bought in India but much more expensive.

—I suppose you want to go look at the camera schamera business now? she said.

—Well, actually I wanted to know if we can go to Style Child.

That was Gwyn's favorite store; it had just opened, and there was even a Manhattan branch in one of the Villages, so it had to be cool.

My mother's face lit up.

—Clothes! she said. —Now that is the normal teenage girl thing. Let's go find you a nice outfit!

The moment we approached Style Child, with its androgynous pink-haired punk rock mannequins reining in (and stepping on) stuffed Dalmatian puppies with snake belt leashes, my mother's face fell.

—Are you sure this is where you want to look? she said. —How about somewhere feminine, like the Ann Taylor or Laura Ashley?

—I'm sure, I said.

One mannequin was in a white mini with zips all the way up both sides. A studded metallic belt that was itself half the width of the mini (we were getting into nano-fractions here) slunk anglingly down the front. The top was a white skintight one-shoulder-bare deal with a single sleeve. It was the kind of outfit Gwyn could pull off sans problem but that set alarm bells off through my head.

One step into Style Child and everything changed. My alarm bells were drowned out by the music blaring from the speakers and the general disco inferno ambiance. And I lost all sense; it was a doomed visit from there. I don't know what it was but when I was in a brightly lit storeroom with a techno soundtrack pumping I felt several sizes smaller than I really was. I began scooping up tiny tees, body-hugger boot-cut jeans, and bustiers with reckless abandon, acting like I was Gwyn. When my mom and I were finally standing with the maximum-allowed five items each (really twelve; I'd sneaked a skimpy crochet halter in my pile and a faux fur tube top in hers) she glanced at the goods.

—Have you checked the sizes, beta? she asked, lifting and dangling the halter off her finger as if it were a steeped tea bag.

—What are you implying? I said, already upset. The music wasn't so loud in here, and a herd of multiply pierced salesgirls was staring at me menacingly, as if they knew there were six items in my hands and none would fit.

—I am not implying anything, beta, but if you insist on trying on these naggudy-faggudy things you might as well get the right size rather than try to be . . . I don't know . . . Gwyn.

—I'm not trying to be Gwyn! I picked these because I like them! All by myself! Come on, give me a little credit. I'm almost seventeen already, hello.

—But they're not your size.

—But I refuse to fit in a bigger size than that, I said with end-of-discussion authority.

By this point we were in the dressing room. At the entrance to our changing stall, the salesgirl, a frizzy-haired, twiggy creature with Taffy on her nametag, hung all the clothes on the hook after asking if we'd be going in together. She had a low-tying halter on and the bones of her back stuck out and rippled as she moved. When she was finished, she turned and gave me the once-over, then the clothes, then me again.

—These are for you? she asked. I nodded warily. —Looks like you need a bigger size.

—In what?

—In everything.

—How do you know? I said, trying to remain calm. Hadn't she read the salesgirl handbook? *Never* tell a potential customer *bigger*. In fact, delete word from vocabulary entirely.

—I can tell just looking at you. The ones you have are way wrong. Want me to switch 'em?

—This is the size I want, I said slowly. —I'll fit in it.

—What*ever*, she said, snapping her gum and strutting off. She called back over her shoulder. —Don't say I didn't warn you.

The room was inhospitably adorned with a massive three-way mirror. Before I even embarked on my Olympian quest to lose weight in the next two minutes, I scanned the glass to see if it was a skinny mirror. I still looked sufficiently harpoonable, so I figured (and prayed) it was not. My mom sat on the bench, exhausted. And I set to work.

The jeans didn't make it past the knees. I could see my butt poking lavishly out of my underwear in the three-way. Frock, I could make granny panties look like a G-string!

—It's just a number, no one can see it, said my mother. —It doesn't mean anything.

—Yeah, said Taffy, popping her head over the stall. —The numbers really don't mean a thing.

That was a relief!

They all read lower anyway, she added.

—*Lower?* I cried in horror. In the mirror I could see my mother waving frantically at her to shut the frock up. But it was too late.

—Yeah, we've done some studies and, you know, they sell way better that way. So we've knocked everything down a couple sizes. Like, you know, normally I'm a zero, but in Style Child sizes, that would be a negative four. It's really boosted sales.

—I need to fit into these, I whispered desperately. Didn't anyone get that I was going to be hanging with an NYU filmmaker in a few short hours?

—Well, in any case, those hot pink militia pants look really great. You should *definitely* get them.

—How do you know? They're not even on.

—Well, I can see them, can't I? And I've got a pair and they're jammin'. Anyways, your top is way fab. You should *totally* get it.

—Uh, this is my bra, I said.

—See? said my mother. —Even *she* does not know the difference.

Taffy's head was perched perfectly on top of our dressing room door as if it had found just where it belonged in this wacky world. I didn't get this thing with salesgirls. They always stuck their head right in before you'd even changed, like you didn't need to be alone to endure what you were about to endure—even when you were trying on bikinis, which could be a very emotional experience, bringing up all sorts of memories (like kids who insulted you on the playground twelve years before). And then they'd tell you everything looked great with about as much conviction as a nonbeliever with a wafer in her mouth.

—So are you gonna *get* them? whined Taffy. She had a spot of lipstick smack in the middle of her front tooth. I decided not to tell her.

My mother was patiently folding and hanging things that had fallen from my fists to the floor. I burst into tears.

—What do *you* think? I said.

—Go, my mother told her. —Go fold something. We need our privacy. Haven't you done enough damage already?

Taffy's mouth dropped open like a fish in a tank with a leak. Once she'd huffily retreated my mother turned to me.

—Dimple, she said. —You are a beautiful girl. You have hips. They're not going anywhere. This is the Indian body. We are not like these straight curveless Americans.

—Mom, I *am* American.

—Dimple, no matter how much you try you cannot change your bones. Your body is your temple; your body is your home. It tells you where you are from.

—My body's the whole country's home! I sniffed. —Look at it! All these hips, boobs, butts. Why can't I just be normal?

—Normal? Dimple Rohitbhai Lala, when you insult yourself, you insult me. Now, you don't want to be insulting your mother, do you?

—Of course not. But Ma, on you all that stuff looks great. You're a mom. You're *supposed* to have curves. But on me it just doesn't work. Why couldn't I have taken after Dad?

—Then you'd have a bald spot on top of all these other so-called problems.

—He has a bald spot? I said, intrigued. —I didn't know.

—Even he does not know yet, said my mother in a hushed voice, leaning in. —I see it when he is sleeping; it is growing, spreading, soon it will take over.

She straightened up and resumed her normal voice.

—Dimple, beta. Stop trying to be something you are not.

Then, as if she'd heard her own words, she curved both hands on my shoulders and kissed my forehead.

—Come on, she sighed. —Let's go to the camera store.

★   ★   ★

After checking out the photographic goods with my parents, they left me by the fountain where the little kids threw pennies and the old couples sat together in potted-plant silence gripping cups of tea from the coffee company. This was also part of the birthday ritual: making myself scarce and all of us pretending I had no idea what the gift was. And truth was, this year I didn't. I really couldn't imagine my parents actually purchasing any of the wish items I'd just indicated, nearly swooning in my relief to be in a store that was all about looking anywhere but me. Especially since my father had just lectured me on why did I insist on taking black-and-white pictures when the world was not black and white, indicating as his idea of the real thing the super-glossy photos of puppies and brides and babies that came with the frames for sale on the display rack. I looked down to the fountain bottom, to all the pennies rippling there. So many wishes. I didn't have a cent on me and wasn't sure it counted if I wished on someone else's but it still felt like a powerful place to be, a mall fountain blinking with so many underwater copper eyes, with so much wanting.

I pictured my dad flipping a coin at the camera counter, against his better judgment.

My parents never seemed to mind my taking pictures until recently. I mean, at birthdays and get-togethers or Christmas (which we all loved, closet Christians that we were) they'd always pose and preen and say jalfreezi for the Instamatic, counting out the *ek, do, teen* alongside my *one, two, three*. Our home was different than lots of homes in this sense: If you looked through recent family albums it was I, not my father, who was most often missing from the pictures, as I was most often the one snapping away.

To be honest I preferred it that way. The less evidence of my ungraceful plummet into adolescence, the better for posterity, if I ever had one. And my parents were not only closet Christians, they were closet Hollywood stars, too (it was in the genes, India being the number one producer of movies in the world, as my father had told me 353 times): As soon as my zoom was on my father would slap on the smile he saved especially for it. It stretched a little too wide across his teeth, his panicked eyes belying the huge grin; he really was a shy man. My mother would turn at some astronomer's angle to show her good side, which changed from photo to photo depending on her mood, gazing at some invisible object with the vacant spectral intensity of a cat. She always pointed one foot out slightly in front of the other as if about to plunge into a curtsy, and smiled with a bit of her lip curled up.

But once I started treating my SLR like more than just a toy, my folks weren't so pleased. Looking at the water-wavery coins, I remembered last year, when my father blew out the candles on his birthday and I took a close-up of his face in the moment of wishing, eyes squeezed shut, holding his breath. When I developed it, I was so excited—it was one of the first times there was a coincidence between what I'd hoped to capture and what actually came out: It was as if you could see the wish in his mouth, like it was too big, about to push out his teeth and burst forth, and he glowed like a little walnut Buddha in the blurred fallen halo of all the candles' light that formed the photo's bottom frame. But when my father saw it, he wasn't so impressed.

—What is it you are doing here, Dimple? No cake? The whole point is to be taking the cake—do you know how long your mother spent on it?

—She bought it, Dad.

—But still—the time to go to the baker's, park the car. And you are making me look like a constipated chipmunk.

—I wanted to get the wish in your mouth.

—The wish in my what? The only wish I have is that you take a nice photo for once!

Then he saw how his own words hung heavily in the air and he felt bad and clipped his mouth tight and hugged me quickly as if I were going to slip away any second, too.

—I'm sorry, he said. —I'm sorry. I'm just afraid. I don't understand you anymore, Dimple. You are my own daughter and I don't understand you.

I knew he was fighting tears because his mouth turned down scowlwards, which it never did except when he was sleeping. My mother said that was where most all the stress of his day came out: in his sleep. He was a very gentle man.

—It's okay, Daddy, I said. —Even I don't understand me anymore.

—Chipmunks are sweet, my mother said, rushing to my defense from an unexpected angle.

Later I asked him what he'd really wished for. I had to know—the expression on his face had been so full of hope and so drained of it at the same time, like he'd already had his cake and was still trying to chew.

—Too much, he'd said quietly. —Too much.

★   ★   ★

When I got to Friendly's, my father was already seated, looking squashed even though it was a booth for four and he had no bags or boxes with him. My heart sank a little. He didn't like this Friendly's too much because the dirty dishes were stacked and burgers flipped in plain view in the middle section (witnessing the behind-the-scenes of restaurants wasn't exactly his idea of an appetizer). He brightened when he saw me.

—Come, bacchoodi, he said, indicating the seat facing him. He liked having me and my mother across from him so he could look at us.

—Mom's not here? I said, mildly alarmed. Our father-daughter moments were rare, and I didn't really know what to say to him sometimes when we were on our own. I don't know when it happened—maybe around the Bobby era. And it made me sad, because I really did love my dad and whenever we had to write Hero papers I wrote about him and how no matter how hard he was working at the hospital he always had time to show me how to draw a face in proportion or solve an equation or hear all the details about my day. And he'd always tucked me in. But somehow whenever the two of us were out alone now we ended up working each other's nerves.

—She's taking a very long time, isn't she? my father tittered. —And it is worrying, as she most certainly has the American Express with her.

We both knew my mother liked to gaze into the glass cases at jewelry stores, and even sometimes have the salespeople unlock them so she could try on the flashing bracelets, the blinding rings. But if she liked something she usually made a mental note of the design and had a version of it created in India for a fraction of the price. She really wasn't dangerous with a credit card—it was just an easy thing to say, like, *Can you believe this heat?* to a stranger in an elevator. It made me sad that my dad and I talked as if we were in an elevator.

—Are you hungry? he said now, rubbing his right arm. —We can order for her. She'll be here any minute, I'm sure.

That was at least something to do.

I'd drunk half of the coffee ice cream concoction we'd ordered for my mom (as well as my own) by the time she suddenly burst upon us, face flaming with excitement.

—Where were you? asked my dad a little petulantly.

—You'll never believe whom I just saw! my mother cried, squeezing in next to me.

—Who?

—Radha Kapoor!

—Who's Radha Kapoor? I asked.

—*Radha* Radha? said my father, a tiny fried clam dropping out the corner of his stunned mouth.

—Yes! I tried to convince her to join us, but she was parked illegally and had to go.

—That's Radha! I'm happy to see she hasn't changed in all this time. Ram, it's been years since I've seen that woman.

—Who's Radha Kapoor? I repeated.

—Radha was one of my dearest friends in college and med school in Bombay, said my mother. —I knew her even before your father, and she met her husband around the same time I met Daddy. It was on a double date—we were supposed to be chaperoning them! Radha and I did everything together. She was like . . . she was like my Gwyn.

—Really? I said, interested at the mention of Gwyn.

—What on earth is she doing here? my father asked.

—She's just moved to the area and set up an ob-gyn practice in the Manhattan. And you'll never believe where she's living—that last house on Lake View!

—Aaray baapray! exclaimed my father. —It will be wonderful to see her! And Samish was with her?

—No, she said something about business in India. He must be tying up loose ends. But . . .

My mother looked at us slyly.

—She *is* here with her son.

—Son?

My dad's interest perked. It was as discernible as a coffee machine clicking on.

—Son. Who happens to be just a bit older than Dimple.

—A bit older than Dimple, said my father, ever the apt English pupil.

—Who is studying at the NYU. Computer engineering and Sanskrit.

—And Sanskrit.

—Who is single, said my mother, sitting down satisfied and punching open her straw on the last syllable.

—Single! Dimple, did you hear that?

—I'm sitting right here, I said.

—We'll have to have them over for chai! said my father. —What do you think, Dimple?

Uh oh—I didn't like where this conversation was heading one bit. The matchmaking was definitely on. Ever since my folks got the news that Sangita was having her marriage arranged by Meera Maasi and Dilip Kaka back in India they'd been dropping hints galore (about how wonderful it was that she was keeping up with tradition, how nice it would be to have a suitable Indian boy in the family) and suddenly, it seemed, ringing all their friends with sons just to say hello. So far nothing had come of it. The sons were either married or out walking the dog during these calls and I'd always had school and fictitious extracurriculars as an excuse to occupy my time. But now it was summertime. Little did my folks know that tomorrow I would be doing my utmost to make Julian mine; I had even more motivation now.

—I'm only sixteen, I reminded them.

—A half-hour ago in the Style Child you were already seventeen, *hello*, my mother reminded me back. —Anyways, there's no drinking age for tea. I think you can handle it. It can't hurt to meet Radha.

—Just have Radha over then, I said. —And anyways, if she's like your Gwyn how come you never talked about her before?

—Oh, I don't know. We lost touch over the years. She got busy in India, and I got busy with, well, America.

She said America like it was an intensive glass-blowing class.

—And India began to seem very far away, she went on. —Or, I don't know, maybe I pushed it before it could push me.

My mother laughed quietly here, but I didn't think she saw what was funny either.

—But somehow we find ourselves together again. And to think she was in America for so much of this time!

—Gwyn and I will never get too busy for each other, I said. But they weren't paying attention anymore.

—Radha Kapoor, my dad was saying.

—Radha Kapoor, my mom nodded. They stared smiling and shaking their heads at each other and I wasn't a part of it. I wished I had my camera, but I had a feeling even the greatest camera in the world couldn't look where they were looking.

CHAPTER 4

sugar and spice

By the time I got out of the shower in the morning, Gwyn was over. Not only over, but she'd already emptied out the contents of my closet on both beds and was scratching her head, pacing around and looking from the duds to the Madonna posters that covered most of the Pepto-Bismol–colored paint and back.

—Gwynnie! I cried. —I thought you were in New York.

To tell the truth, I was relieved to see her. It reminded me that I was not in on tonight's escapade all alone.

She threw up her arms in a ta-da and flashed her pearly whites.

—I'm here for inspiration. Dyl texted me that he was stuck in traffic so I thought I'd pop by and do a little EFC. Or Consoling, considering the state of your closet.

Gwyn's version of Emergency Fashion Counseling usually amounted to her snagging my stuff for her own emergencies, but tonight I would say I had a legit emergency of my own. She was now back at the beds, putting the final touches on a complex mix-and-match maze. Most intriguing was a strip of black fabric that looked vaguely familiar paired bandeau-like with a long denim skirt. I cricked my head.

—That's not a tube top, Gwyn, I said. —It's a neck muffler.

—Only if it's on your neck, she replied matter-of-factly.

One Indian outfit was in the mix too, a gaudy chaniya choli in cartoon colors that she would have had to have reached into the deepest recesses of my closet to find.

She narrowed it down to four outfits and glided around them pointing out their merits as if selling me my own wardrobe. But truth was, I'd never seen these combos before. One was the muffler/skirt mix for that Chaste Yet Naked look, she explained. One was a crisp oxford on a pair of striped red tights—long underwear for skiing, I realized—for that Accessible Schoolgirl (formerly known as Britney) look. Then the alibi Indian outfit. And finally, the dupatta from it, which she'd set up as a sort of wraparound top on black capris that I never wore because they made me look even shorter.

Gwyn had her hand plunked on her hip and stood slinkily surveying her work, slouching in that way that only works on thin sure girls. She seemed quite pleased.

—Gwyn, I said, truthfully. —These would all no doubt go great on you—not great; supercalifragilistic, in fact. But all I'm going to achieve with any of them is that something quite atrocious.

—Dimps, come on—didn't you know Marilyn Monroe was, like, a size fourteen? And you're not about to tell me *she* wasn't pretty perfect.

—Gwynnie, I just don't think it'll work.

—Oh, dear, I was afraid this would happen, she mock-sighed. —Unhappy with your own duds? Well, then, good thing I brought you . . .

She bent down now to drag a snazzy neon familiar-looking bag out from under the bed.

—. . . your birthday present! Straight from the East Village.

—Oh Gwyn, you shouldn't have!

—But I did. Go on, open it.

It was the Style Child outfit. You know, the one in the window I could never pull off? I stared at the white mini, fingered the zippers. Turned out you could actually unzip the thing and split it off into two scant pieces of stiff white vinyl. I couldn't imagine getting it around one leg, let alone my entire pelvic continent.

—Oh Gwyn, I said again. —You *really* shouldn't have.

—Isn't it fabbadabbadoo? said Gwyn. —I liked it so much I got me one, too. I figured it would be perfect for you to make a first impression.

I didn't know what to say.

—I took the train back especially to get it to you on time, she added.

She looked sincerely disappointed at my lack of excitement. And I felt like such an ingrate. She'd actually un-superglued herself from Dylan to get me all dressed up *and* a place to go to boot. And here I was whining. I never used to do that.

—I'm sorry, Gwynner, I said. —I love it. Thank you.

—Then you'll wear it?

—I'll wear it, I sighed.

She threw her arms around me.

—That's my girl! she said, satisfied.

After we'd figured out shoes (she opted for the pumps I'd worn to school yesterday) her attention flitted elsewhere, to the top undergarment for the chaniya choli, a deep pomegranate deal that was poking out on the pillow of the spare bed.

—This tiny top is totally excellent, Dimps! she cried.

—It's not a tiny top; it's like a bra, I said. —It goes under the sari.

Well, if you're not using it, mind if I do?

—Well, if you're not using it, do you mind if I—?

—Go ahead, I said.

Once she'd finished replenishing her Indian underwear supply, she glanced at her watch.

—I've got just enough time to do accessories with you, she concluded. —Before I've got to make like a tree and leave. Whaddaya got for me?

—They're all in the top drawer. Still.

I sat down on the edge of my bed, worn out for some reason, and Gwyn went over and opened the drawer. In the huge dresser top mirror, the sandalwood frame carved with a myriad of deities and elephant trunks, I watched her face, saw how it lit up like she'd just opened a suitcase stacked with gold coins or gift certificates to Claire's Accessories.

—Wow! Dimple! You didn't show me all this new loot—what, did your mom bring it back from India this last time?

—Yeah, I said. —She picked up a bunch of stuff for me when they were shopping for my cousin's wedding. Wishful thinking, I guess.

I went over to look in the drawer. To be honest, I had forgotten what I'd dumped in there.

Stacks of plastic bangles in jellybean colors, silver ones with tiny diamonds and hearts embedded in glistening green and red, thick tarnished chunky numbers, jingle-bell anklets, moderately noisy anklets, silent anklets, pairs of toe rings and thumb rings and armlets, and dangly earrings like ornate jade and gold chandeliers that slipped back to clip into the hair. Sheets of bindis, from simple red velvet circles to glitzy studded curlicues, like penny candy for royalty. Chokers spilling out of soft cloth pouches. My drawers were overflowing with goods, from costume to valuable. All this atop stacks of hand-beaded and gold-threaded sari fabric. My mother always got carried away when she shopped in India, or even Queens and Edison; it seemed she was trying to bring back the whole country with her in her suitcase. I liked one of the simplest jingly anklets a lot and always kept it on; I didn't even know it was meant to be worn in a pair until the last time I was in India, when a troop of village girls with shafts of red desert light in their dry wild pony manes approached me and, pointing down, solemnly declared in voices buttery and fragile as puri rising,

—Excusing us please, lady, but you are having lost your other.

I'd meant to pair up the two halves after that trip, but I could never find the matching anklet. And as far as the rest of the goods went, they felt like a little too much to wear—too over-the-top, too princessy. Or maybe I just didn't feel enough of a rani to carry it off.

Gwyn was digging into the drawer, gleefully pulling out items like a kid in a candy store. Her fist closed around something and she yanked it out with a squeal of excitement.

—Oh my *Claude!*

She was already working whatever it was onto her wrists. In the mirror light flashed and refracted, serrating her face, as if she were turning a knife slowly in her hands. She was mesmerized. I came closer and looked down to her wrist on which two rakhis were now tied in fiery flowery metallic glory.

Rakhis are these bracelets that usually consist of colored thread adorned with red and pink and orange woven flowers set in metallic foil leaves. They're used for Rakshabandhan, the holiday where sisters celebrate their brothers; the sister ties a rakhi on her brother's wrist and in return the brother offers to protect her forever, which nowadays often amounts to his handing her anywhere from one to one hundred and one dollars.

My mother always got really sad around Rakshabandhan because she had that brother who died when I was young, my Sharad Mama. But she still collected the rakhis and saved one to take to temple—she didn't go so often (my father and I didn't really go at all; he had his temple at home, and I wasn't so interested) but she did for this, every year on the holiday, which was around mid-August. When I was little I loved the rakhis, loved to tie them on my fingers and in my braids and, most of all, onto an imaginary brother (usually my stuffed monkey, Coconut, or Ketan Kaka when he was staying with us). Which maybe made my mom sad, too. The last couple of years when she'd given them to me I'd just left them in my drawer.

I told Gwyn all this, except the last part about my imaginary brother and my mom being sad.

—Wow, said Gwyn stretching out her arm and staring at the starry double bouquet on her wrist. —That's so cool, sisters celebrating brothers—I always wanted a brother. Funny, but it feels like one's holding my hand when I wear this—do you think that's how your mom feels, too? You know, about your uncle.

—Maybe, I said. I'd never really thought of it that way; it was strange that Gwyn, who barely even talked about her own family, had.

—You know, I can't believe all this stuff just sits around in your room, Dimple. If I were you I'd just go on and wrap myself in the Indian flag and go to school—I'm serious! Put a little magic in lame old Springfield.

She touched one of the flowers gently, as if it might break.

—And plus, they're so beautiful. Oh, pretty please can I borrow them to go with my top—you know, the Indian thing? They go so perfectly.

Her top? It had been mine just a few moments before!

—I don't know if my mom . . .

But just then my mom was in the doorway. She looked at Gwyn standing there, luminous in all the bangles and chokers and fabrics.

—I was just wondering if you two would like to have some lunch, she said. —I made tuna and mint chutney sandwiches. With Cape Cod chips.

Her eyes fell on Gwyn's wrist.

—Um, I, I hope you don't mind, Mrs. Lala, said Gwyn, almost shyly. —It's just. They were so beautiful it seemed a shame to leave them in the drawer. And, I don't know, they make me feel like I've got a brother.

—Yes, they make me feel that way, too, I suppose, said my mother, and she smiled a little sadly. So Gwyn had been right. I felt ashamed.

—I'll put them back, said Gwyn, hurriedly unknotting the red threads. But then very gently my mother touched her wrist.

—No, leave them on, she said. —You're right. They shouldn't be in a drawer. Take them; they look lovely on you. I'm glad someone appreciates them.

I know this is going to sound crazy, but I wanted them now. *I* wanted to appreciate them. Gwyn was already hugging my mom.

—And have fun tonight, said my mother. —How sweet, a slumber party. Just like when you were little girls.

She looked deeply moved for some reason and I had a mea culpa moment considering the outright mendacity of our alibi: This was hardly a girls-only get-together, and slumber was perhaps last on the list of priorities.

My mother seemed to have come to, and was now contemplating the fashion spread on my bed.

—And Dimple, please clean up that mess—what is the point of having closets if you're unloading everything into plain view?

Gwyn giggled.

—Yeah, Dimple, she said.

After my mom turned back down the hall. Gwyn collected her things and I walked her to the door. On the porch, she stepped into her beaded clogs (whenever she remembered, she tried to participate in our habit of leaving our shoes outside, though when she forgot—like if she was particularly excited about a new pair—or when any non-Indian forgot, in fact, my mother didn't seem to mind so much). And finally I asked her the question whose answer I dreaded most:

—Gwyn, how do you know he's even going to like me?

—He'll like you, she said firmly. —Be yourself and you'll be fine.

She hopped off the porch and turned round again.

—But wear a bindi, she advised. —He's into the Indian thing.

—But that's so not me!

—Of course that's you. You're Indian, are you not? And above all do not forget your new little laminated self—you'll be needing it tonight, I guarantee you.

★ ★* **32** *★ ★

And then she was gone. Her exits were always quick and tidy like this, like an expert criminal's; her entries, as sudden and inexplicable as an angel's. Like the first time I met her, all those Christmases ago.

★   ★   ★

When we were real little and Mr. Sexton was still "participating" in the household, Gwyn's family was pretty famous in town. And this was due in no small part to the spectacle they put on at Christmas every year.

I mean, we got into the holiday spirit, too, particularly the light-twining, trying out all sorts of annual sound and light experiments (for some reason Indians really like Christmas decor, and not just at Christmas, the more garish the better. Take a look at any Indian restaurant on Sixth Street in Manhattan.). But while the rest of us were pegging multicolored bulbs from Woolworth's around the house and hanging wreaths—ours fake, "so we wouldn't have to be killing a real live wreath," according to my mother—and maybe posing giddy little Mr. and Mrs. Kriss Kringle couples on the porch, the Sextons set up and spotlit massive statues of Joseph, Mary, Jesus, and the whole holy crew, creating a real-life-sized Nativity scene across their front yard, the three wise men positioned as if they'd just hopped up off the curb and under the weeping cherry. People would drive up and down from all over the county to check out the sight.

My first memory of Gwyn was during a winter like this. It had been soon after we'd moved here, and I'd gone over with my parents to see what all the fuss was about. My folks were fascinated by the sheer immensity and extravagance of the scene. We'd stayed, staring like the converted, long after the last car had pulled out and night fell heavy and dark as a winter coat upon us. The lights were all off inside the big house, showing off even more the spotlit production on the lawn, the Special Dolls in their yuletiddian Disneyland.

When we'd turned to go, my father lifted me into his arms; I gazed over his shoulder back at the lawn, mesmerized by all these beautiful dolls, bigger than even me at the time. And just then something stirred, a small but mighty shadow by Mary Dolly's genuflecting self. A tiny figure crawled noiselessly out of the manger and stood, shaking off shards of snow like a cold-bathed puppy. It was unmistakably a little girl, pastel pajamas rolled up to the knees, her icy white mass of curls springing out in every direction. A little girl, probably my age.

She had no shoes on and stood perfectly still, staring at me with that extraterrestrial-recognizing-extraterrestrial fascination of children discovering each other. Then, she lifted her hand to blow me a kiss. Nobody saw this. It all happened in a heartbeat. Her feet were bare and I wanted to give her my shoes—they were so warm and fluffy inside with fake pink fur, little igloos in non-igloo colors.

But she was already on her porch and did something that puzzled me. She took something from around her neck—I thought it was a necklace, maybe, like my mother's glittering maharani chokers. Then she unlocked the door with it and let herself in.

I don't know why I didn't say anything to my parents. But that kiss had been just for me and I savored it, like a secret on the tip of my tongue. We walked slowly, zigzaggily, over the ice patches back home, my father gripping me safe in one arm, his other wrapped around my mother's waist so she wouldn't slip.

But when we got back to our dead end I couldn't keep it in.

—What is it, bacchoodi? said my father, alarmed, his forefingers gently collecting my tears in their tracks.

—I wanted to give her my shoes, I sobbed. —I should have given her my shoes. Can we go back?

—Who, beta? my mother asked.

—That little girl!

—What little girl? said my father.

—Don't worry, beta, my mother said. —Her feet aren't cold. It's just a statue.

—No, no, there was a little girl. She came out into the yard.

—You must be imagining things, bacchoodi.

My mother felt my head for fever.

—No parents would let their little girl out in the cold like that, she said. —And alone at this hour, too.

★　★　★

So did she live all by herself in the big double-drived house, and bake sheets of gingerbread cookies for breakfast, and talk to animals like an American Pippi Longstocking? The world behind those double doors titillated my imagination with its magical possibilities. Soon after the first Gwyn sighting I met her for real and discovered the truth: Gwyndolyne Baxter Sexton *did* have parents, two for many years that I could remember, years counted in front-yard Nativities. And then suddenly there was no more Jesus, Mary, or holy crew. And round about the same time there was no more Mr. Sexton. Not that I had ever seen much of him anyways. Just usually Mrs. Sexton splayed out coltish on one of the divans, the television tuned into something with a laugh track, an invisible audience chortling menacingly in the otherwise dark room. Her face was always lit by blue TV screen light, swording so many emotions from the lofty cheekbones and tweezed brows, plucking the skidding stars from the bottle by her side, the fat goblets, the cut glass ashtray glowing with embers like a distant UFO parking lot.

We had to cross this room to get to most anywhere in the house and I always felt terrified in that two-second passage, the pull to something sweet and dark that I worried we would not be able to escape or resist. But we always made it through, and usually ended up out back in the playhouse, in our own wooded universe, making up passwords and stories, imagining movie kisses by rolling our tongues back upon themselves, learning the constellations of each other's birthmarks and beauty spots. In India, the latter were believed to be protection against the evil eye; Gwyn had one, fierce and solitary, freckling a place that I would stop seeing around the time when boys would begin to.

Then just as suddenly as she'd appeared on the lawn that day, Gwyn disappeared, moved away. And for what felt like an eternity, I was Gwynless, which turned out to be an awful thing to be after spending so many hours in her light. I was a sick weed, growing needlessly and clumsily. And out there on that other coast, she was blossoming like a wild rose. I heard the rumors: She and her dad were off living in L.A. Mrs. Sexton was too unfit to take care of her (that was before she did the rehab thing, though the effects of that were obviously temporary, something I didn't bother mentioning to my parents). I got Hollywood postcards from Gwyn occasionally, with pictures of Mann's Chinese Theater and the Walk of Fame and lots of Marilyn Monroes and too many exclamation points but no return address. Even Mrs. Sexton didn't seem to know what it was.

—Last I heard they were on Venice Beach, she said, looking right through me the one time I mustered up my nerve to go over and ask. It sounded so exotic. I imagined Gwyn drifting slowly in gondolas (or dancing around, more likely, like in that old Madonna video). I imagined her crossing the Bridge of Sighs with shadowy men who spoke in delicious, disturbing accents.

And then just as abruptly as she'd come and gone, Gwyn reappeared after junior high, back to live with her mother.

I remember seeing her that first day in earth science, the same old Gwyn but her legs had gone all long and she stretched them out from her desk to right under Tony Mahoney's seat in front of her. She leaned back lazily as if it were Club Med and not room 104 where owlish Mr. Witherspoon worked himself into conniptions over igneous rock and made us believe the collision of the very tectonic plates we were riding upon was imminent.

I can see it well, as if I'd photographed it: She stuck a blow pop in her mouth, crunching immediately through to the gummy center (an old habit). I had a sort of back and side angle view of her. Her hair was more gold than white now, flaxen, and twirled up in about a dozen braids, wound and pinned so the nape of her long neck showed clearly, unadorned. Then she turned towards me—I'd been staring, stunned, wondering whether I'd misjudged the back of the head—and blew a huge grape bubble and popped it. She sucked in the strands (none caught on her gloss), winked at me, and grinned the Gwyn grin.

—Hey, Boopster, she said. —Remember me?

I nearly leapt out of my chair to bear hug her, then remembered: We were in high school now, you weren't supposed to do that to your girlfriends. So I stayed put.

—Rabbit? I said in my best James Bond. —Veronica Rabbit?

And then she jumped up and wrapped me in her arms, closer than a papoose.

★   ★   ★

As children, Gwyn and I grew into a friendship made up of silences and secret stares, one that can happen only between two people who don't fit in — in our case, the rich little girl who lived like an orphan and the brown little girl who existed as if she were still umbilically attached to her parents. But we could look each other in the eye, go porous in our created world, sliding easily from one to the other. Many times I didn't know where Gwyn left off and I began. But from high school on there were a few differences, of course: Puberty had gone all out in the interim of our friendship and now neither of us fit too well in our seats. My hips had erupted lavalike from the waist and there had been much volcanic activity in my chest as well, which I downplayed with plaid shirts and big sweaters — you know, fat clothes. I had, in other words, been branching out into new areas horizontally while Gwyn had gone vertical. But the two of us still fit. And from that moment, we were inseparable again. We never talked about those years in between, just carried on until they became a mere blip on the radar. Our plates came together and we were on the same planet again; seamless.

But now that Dylan had arrived on the scene, I could feel a tiny crack forming, still invisible, but still spreading along the length of the island that was us. I only hoped Julian could mend it. Or give me something to swim towards should I find myself splintered off in strange waters.

Julian. Frock. I had to get ready.

seeing double

I could barely move, let alone breathe, by the time I'd squeezed, squinched, and prodded myself into the Style Child ensemble. I must have looked like a preview for yet another *Mission: Impossible* in the process, but fortunately no one was watching but me. I zipped myself up in a coverall coat before stepping out the door: There was no way my parents would buy the movies-with-Gwyn story if they saw this outfit.

My mother stared at me a long moment with a half-quizzical, half-knowing look on her face. Did my own read night-of-debauchery-and-potential-liplocking ahead? Oh, no—it was the coat. It had to be the coat that'd tipped her off.

—What is it? I said nervously.

—It's just that. I don't know. You're wearing a bindi. I'm just a little surprised.

Frock! She was definitely on to me.

—That Gwyn is such a good influence on you, she said. Then she brushed my hair out of my eyes, ruining an hour's worth of carefully choreographed facial coverage.

—You look just beautiful, she smiled. —You shouldn't hide your face.

—What's so great about my face?

— Beta, when you insult yourself you insult me.

She tried to look cross, but only half meant it.

—No, I don't.

—So—you're beautiful. Now say it.

—You're beautiful, I said. She gave me an *and you're impossible* look, but she was still smiling.

—Oh go on. Have a good time. I love you.

—Love you, too, Ma, I said, air-kissing her to leave my gloss intact.

She kept watching from the screen door as my father and I swapped places and I got in the driver's seat, her hand frozen in a Queen of England salute, as if I were going far far away, to a place from where no one would ever be able to retrieve me. She'd been doing this since I started high school. And tonight part of me hoped she was right. And I tried to ignore the other part, the part that wanted to run back to her, leap into her open arms and never leave them.

★   ★   ★

The sweat was spouting down my face the second I got behind the wheel.

—Don't forget to check all the mirrors, my father said.

Don't worry. I was checking them. Did I have too much makeup on? Now, in real daylight, I looked far faker than I'd intended. My dad started looking at me funny, too, which only made the base pour down harder.

—What? I said.

—I don't know, he said. —It's just, you look so uncomfortable. Why don't you take off your coat? Why are you even wearing a coat in this heat?

—I'm really cold.

—Look at you, you're sweating. How can you be cold?

—I just am!

—How?

—It's a woman thing, I said.

He clammed up, lifting his hands as if to say *sorry I went there*. I used his shyness mercilessly against him.

I was already feeling thoroughly exhausted and he tense and sheepish and we hadn't even exited the driveway yet.

I turned the key and checked for my blind spot, which I was convinced was a moving thing, tracking me just about everywhere I went from every conceivable angle, and not necessarily limited to the automotive sphere. Then we were off like a turd of hurdles, my spindly heels tripping me off the gas and brakes in turn.

As we curved up the road and out to the main street, I started to look for a sign from the gods that everything was going to be okay. I decided red was good, and was encouraged by several auspicious sightings: a kid's wagon in a driveway, a brick house, a red-skirted woman unloading groceries from her trunk, and scores of American flags star-spangling the rooftops. Hinduism had its advantages; with its many deities there was bound to be one who would be in the office.

★   ★   ★

By the time I was actually careening down the grim aisle of the dim mall, my feet were throbbing and I was sure I'd sweat an actual hole through my shirt pits. A college boy. What was I going to talk about with a college boy? And in a white vinyl miniskirt, too.

Julian Rothschild was hanging alone by the potted plants, fists in the pockets of his pleather pants and chestnut hair curling rock-star-esque down the nape of his neck. He made being alone look cool.

And when I saw how, well, how *Julian* he looked, even in the sickly mall light, my stomach did the watusi. Where were Gwyn and Dylan? Now I wished I'd insisted she ride over with me. Julian's gaze turned towards me, no visible shift on his face. My stomach queased: I was going to have to introduce myself. I felt like a consummate idiot and ducked behind a potted palm.

This was probably not the best move if avoiding attention was the goal. Julian was looking right at me now, the truth dawning on him.

—That you? he said, tentatively approaching my fronded hideout. He walked like a movie image, a reservoir dog moving speedily in slow motion: swaggering.

—Yes.

—I'm sorry, I just didn't recognize you. It's been a while, I guess, since we've spoken.

Just short of seventeen years, give or take a few hours, to be precise.

—Where's Gwyn? I asked, trying to emerge as gracefully as possible from the foliage.

—Dillweed beeped me. They're running a little late.

Base sludged down my face; I could feel it. I wondered why the sample colors on the drugstore swatches never matched the shade inside when it came to makeup.

—Why?

Julian gave me a duh look.

—Let's just say they're getting to know each other better. Anyways, as it turns out, they're going to meet us straight at Chimi's to get a guzzle before the movie—so we can try out your new ID, according to Gwyndolyne. We could head on over, if you're ready.

Chimichanga's was a Tex-Mex restaurant smack between the Chinese one and a used car dealer's across the street from the mall. They were particularly famous for a Shoot the Worm drink, and people went there to get plastered before the movies. Therefore it was always packed at six and eight. And therefore there was also a lot of audience participation at the seven and nine o'clock shows.

The walk to the mall exit, which really wasn't so far in the normal world, seemed excruciatingly long in the doped-up universe where a girl like me was hanging with a guy like him.

—You look hot, Julian said suddenly.

I was taken aback and hope illogical went off like a flash inside me.

—Well, thanks, I said, smiling goofily.

—No, I mean . . .

He gestured. I realized he was referring to my arctic number.

—Uh, no, I'm fine.

(Then why are you in a winter coat, stupid?)

—I mean, I'm really cold.

(Now he'll think I'm hypothermic.)

—I mean I *have* a cold.

(Even worse—now he'll think I'm contagious!)

—Not a cold but it's a little chilly, I concluded; blame it on forces beyond my control.

We stepped outside into the 101 degree weather and sweat immediately steeped my face.

—Whatever, said Julian.

I was burning up. And I had no idea what to talk about all the interminable way through the parking lot and across the street to Chimi's.

—So, uh, how's film school?

—You couldn't *imagine*. To be immersed in your métier 24/7, to be liaisoning with people of nearly equal artistic aptitude—it takes rad to a whole new level.

He pronounced métier and liaisoning and, oddly, aptitude, as if he were speaking French. I didn't think he was French though, not even French-Canadian. What the frock was I saying? He was from Jersey.

Inside Chimi's, it was all nighttime ambiance even though the sun was unbudgeably out outside. And also inside Chimi's—swigging with Dylan in the overflowing bar area and waving around the beeper that flashed when your seat was ready—I could make out that reverse mirror image of myself. Except instead of all the black parts being white and white being black as usual, today our second skins were the same shade.

It was Gwyn all right—and in the exact same outfit I was in! She caught sight of me just then and shook the beeper like a maraca. She looked phenomenal, the dream girl straight out of a boy band video. There was no way my coat was coming off this century.

—Hey, birthday girl! she yelped, wiggling up and flinging her arms around me, spilling in the process.

—Hi, Gwynnie, I said, hugging her back as Julian and Dylan high-fived each other. They seemed to be laughing at their own private joke.

—Here, let's get you two a drink, cried Gwyn breaking into their bandedness. —I'm having a Virgin Mary—gotta start slow.

She turned to Dylan.

—But by the end of the night I'll be onto something else, she smiled.

Dylan looked very pleased, and for some reason high-fived Julian again. They were reminding me of something, but I couldn't quite put my finger on what.

—Actually, why don't *you* go for it, Dimple? she now suggested. —You can try out your new toy.

I was nervous, and to be honest the card had been in my fist since we'd entered the outskirts of illegal that was the parking lot. But I was also relieved at the idea of getting away from the boys for a mo. I knew it was only the beginning of the date, but I was already spent.

—Come with me? I said.

Gwyn gave Dylan a kiss that would have lasted a sailor out to sea for a year, then joined me at the end of the bar, where I took a breath and then ordered a round from a redhead who looked like she'd heard it all and even done some of it. Much to my chagrin, she didn't ask for ID. I was about to flash the flimflam anyways but Gwyn slapped my hand down.

—Don't make a point of showing it! she whispered. —That'd be proof it's a fake.

I was wondering how I was in fact going to use this piece of plastic, but Gwyn was off the topic.

—So how's it going? she asked excitedly as our drinks magically appeared one by one.

—All right, I said.

—Don't worry, it's going to be just fine, I promise you.

Like she'd promised she wouldn't be late?

—Why didn't you meet us at the mall, Gwyn?

—I figured you and Julian could use some time together, she smiled. —And Dilly and I, I thought we were gonna be late but we . . . wrapped up sooner than I'd thought. I'm getting good!

—At what?

—Oh, Dimple, she sighed, and she sounded tipsy, which seemed strange if she was on the virgins. —You stick with Julian, and maybe one of these days you'll get it.

—That's encouraging, I said. —So you're in the same, um, outfit as me.

—Isn't it excellent? she grinned, twirling like a machine ballerina. —Now we can be real supertwins!

She began to coax me back towards Julian and Dylan.

—Take off that coat, Dimple, and strut your stuff!

But I wasn't going to be parting with it so easily now.

When we were all equally daiquiried she beamed at the boys.

—So, she said. —What have you two been talking about?

—Well, the film, of course, said Julian. —That's number one prio at the moment.

—Yeah, well, you and Dimple have a lot in common then, said Gwyn. His film was my priority?

—What, Dimple goes to movies? he smirked.

—No, silly! Dimple is an artist—she takes *pictures*, said Gwyn. She put a finger to the top of her straw then pulled it up, sucking out the drink from the other end. —They're really good. She just took a bunch of me at school, in the halls—tell him, Dimps!

—I just took a bunch of her at school, I said dully. The drink was sweet, and had to be virgin, too, since I could taste nothing but strawberries on ice.

—Well, they must be good if you're in them, babe, said Dylan, his hand gripping the small of Gwyn's waist like a possessive goatherd.

—Who are your influences? asked Julian suspiciously.

—I don't know, I said, even though I did.

—There must be someone.

—Ansel Adams, I blurted, almost to get it over with. It sounded funny saying it outside my head.

—Ansel Adams is your influence? said Julian. —Wow. But, uh, how do you apply that to shots of Gwyn in a Lenne Lenape High hallway?

I couldn't figure out what was up with this pop quiz. I felt like I was being held up to a meter I could never measure up to and the result was my coming up with a total blank even though I knew I had my reasons usually, at least somewhere inside me.

—They're black and white, I said. —And Ansel Adams's photos are . . . well. Black and white.

A pause hunched before us then sprang into trolling laughter.

—Good one, dude! Julian sniggered. Why was I dude and Gwyn babe?

—And both have breathtaking natural scenery as their focus, said Dylan, running his hand through Gwyn's hair. She never let people touch her hair (too many hidden bobby pins, which she was now rearranging); all her exes had been denied this right. —That's why I'm going to make Gwyneth Sexton a star one day.

Her name was Gwyndolyne, but no one objected, including the lady in question. Was this a parallel universe?

An alarm bell went off in my head, and so did the beeper.

As Dylan and Julian jawed on about *films*—which were, apparently, not to be confused with *movies*—Gwyn watched attentively from our side of the table, a fixed smile on her face. And I drank and stuffed my face, and drank some more, till tipping time.

Life upright was revelatory, and walking was more like swimming. Everything seemed louder as we left Chimichanga's, as if the sounds were all emanating from within my ears instead of coming into them from the outside. I was beginning to wonder what exactly had been in those strawberries. But it wasn't an unpleasant feeling, in fact it was a tingly wingy feeling, and when we got out to the lot something about the bright blue sunshine made it all seem quite normal. We piled into Dylan's Mustang, Julian and me in back and Gwyn up front. The wind blew in, gusting hair across my face, and Julian smiled at me, his chestnut eyes gone Nutella now.

—You look sexy like that, he said. —Windblown, wild. Like a wild animal.

I didn't know what to say. I think I mostly liked what he'd said but it didn't seem to match the curtains in the usual (tiny) room where I stored compliments in my head for future emergencies. Still, it felt soft and fuzzy, so I folded it and put it in a corner for the winter.

—*Grrr*, I said—did I?—and burst out laughing. He smiled at me, nodding to a slow beat as if a metronome, or bomb, were ticking somewhere in the car.

★　★　★

By the time we walked into the cinema they were on the last preview and the only seats left were the ones front and side, where you had to crane your neck and the actors stretched out on the edges like in a close shot accidentally set to panoramic.

As soon as we were seated, Dylan took back the duffel he'd given Gwyn to carry in. Unzipping it, he now produced several bottles, cups, and cans—and even an aluminum-foiled lemon! In the light of the screen I saw a rum label in the mix. The bottle belonging to which he now unscrewed and, in the darkness of the night scene unfolding above us, tipped generously into the cups.

—To putting the sin into cinema! whispered Dylan, initiating a knee-level toast. He gave us the nod and we all took a sip. Gwyn leaned around him and winked at me. Julian took a slurp then held out his cup, which seemed unnecessary since I had my own. But I drank. It tasted pretty much like Coke, which I normally don't like but which felt good on top of all those nachos and margaritas and that one clincher tequila shot.

And then the movie began. Or at least it began for us. But it was tough concentrating. I was all too aware of Dylan bumping rhythmically against my right shoulder as he made out with Gwyn; he was turned all the way in her direction and she'd disappeared save for an occasional flash of gold hair in his grasp. And on my left, at regular intervals, the plastic cup materialized and Julian nodded, abundantly pleased as I abundantly gulped. And I don't know why, but I wanted to please him.

I took deeper and longer swills so he could love me more and more. And actually, the more that went in the more I in fact began to feel beautiful. Maybe it was because it was dark, which is where I felt best, like in my darkening room, but also, I suddenly realized, I was a seventeen-year-old budding photographer influenced by Ansel Adams and I was at a movie that might even be a film, and all this with a college boy no less, a college *man*, and an executive film producer to top it off! Little matter that this was for, as far as I could see, a so far nonexistent film; invisible things were life's most precious. Wasn't there a saying like that? Or money can't buy invisible things? What did love look like? Inspiration? Elucidation? It was the thought that was counting, as my father said. And the thought of my parents counted, made me smile in spite of myself. They were so *on*: How could I think they didn't understand me? They so *did*. Now I couldn't remember why we were so often shifty and edgy around each other. I was going soft and the corners whittled gone and so much love was filling my heart I felt it was too small to hold it.

And that love Slinky was springing out in every direction and I had an epiphany. I knew what the secret to world peace was (father, hallway, prayer): It resided in a plastic red cup with a swirly-whirly strip in the front row of a theaterful of pixilated people and a boy everyone wanted watching you—of all people, of all things—swallow. And Gwyn, maybe she'd just arrived at that epiphany a little earlier than me, but I could catch up, it was still a relay, and that's what part of growing up was—having too much emotion and not knowing what to do with it and pouring it on everyone and everything, the way the night liquid drenched the ice in my cup, almost spilling over it was, and everything was just a moment away from good things, you just needed that right balance of . . . of Bacardi to Coke, if you will.

I would definitely keep drinking. I must always drink.

—Why are you rocking back and forth like that? whispered Julian.

I was?

His arm was around me now and it felt nice, having a college film producer boy's arm around me in a movie-maybe-film.

We were one and we were all, I thought, happily crunching on my ice.

—You know what *that* means, said Julian. —*Frustrated.*

—Oh, I'm not frustrated, I said. —I'm just having an epiphany.

—You are?

—You're not?

—Well, maybe I'm about to, said Julian, and his face was coming closer like the actors' faces and my neck was craning back like he was the image, unpeeling off the screen, and a split second before his lips were on mine, I knew we were about to kiss and a thrill frilled my neck—I felt like I was in the movie, in the picture—and then a split second after his lips were in use, his tongue was, too, checking out the place where my wisdom teeth used to be.

Actually, it was kind of slimy. After a little while my neck started to hurt, rather impertinently piercing a leak into my floatingly numb reverie. And I couldn't breathe; even my nose was squashed, nostrils flattened to buttonhole slits. So I pulled away to take a gulp of air. But for some reason I think that stricken gasp convinced Julian that whatever he was doing was working and he dug farther, archaeologically, into my mouth. I tried to remember that I was in fact enjoying this, but the convivial buzzy feeling I'd been having was fast evaporating off me.

I came up for oxygen again, and there was a name that could have been a (distant) uncle's on the final credits.

—Look—it's an Indian director! I cried.

—Yeah, he said squeezing my shoulder. —Yeah, I think he is. Or Jewish. M. Night Shyamalan. What does it matter?

—Well, you know, I'm Indian, I said. I vaguely recalled the Cherokee jokes I'd been subjected to in middle school and added: —*Indian* Indian. *Bindian* Indian.

—Kama Sutra Indian.

—What's Kama Sutra Indian?

Julian was giving me this knowing look. I tried to smile back knowingly, too, even though I was growing more and more convinced that what I really knew was very little if anything about what he was talking about.

It did ring a tinkerbell; I mean, I had seen the pocket version the big chain bookstores sold, but they were always chockful of sweatless pretzeling blondes. What did that have to do with me?

—Oh come on, don't play all innocent with me, he said, his hand beginning to dangle off my shoulder and fiddle with the fabric where pit met chest. —Kama Sutra, you know—it's all about the ancient art of love in India.

He leaned in closer.

—Art of sex, he gnatted in my ear.

Sex! I wanted to laugh out loud. Indian people didn't have sex. I was still convinced I was the second Immaculate Conception, not the Son-of-god part but in terms of my parents, who, of course, didn't do It. They were like brother and sister, an affable duo; they even called each other Mummy and Daddy and they never even kissed or held hands, lived, in fact, PDA-free—which used to make me wonder if that meant they might divorce, but Indians don't do that either. It was amazing how many stereotypes he had about the place!

—Indians don't have sex, I whispered back.

—Oh, I know that, said Julian. —They don't have mere *sex*: They have a kamasutronic experience—which is like god or . . . or OD-ing and surviving! And you want to know what I think?

I shook my head side to side and then back and forth, unsure.

—I think you're just born with it in India.

—I was born in the USA, I said.

—It doesn't matter. It's genetic. It's coded in your DNA: You know how to please a man.

He gazed into my eyes.

—Now you can show me some moves, my little Indian love goddess, he whispered.

The lights went on.

And I showed him some moves all right. No sooner had I stood than all that sin-in-cine-magic went to my head in a rush I can only compare to the wave at football games—when first one part of the crowd rises with their hands in the air, then the next, then the next, till the very bleachers seem to be undulating—except what was undulating was my inside. I tripped over my own pumps and landed in the aisle, my view shifting like the world through a camera falling off a tripod. The room tilted at a precarious angle, and I was on the floor in broken geometry, in the middle of an array of pretty puffy white and yellow clouds.

I was on the verge of laughing but it wasn't such a pleasant feeling, any facial motion riding an acidic deluge right up my throat and into my mouth nearly, like a film in rewind of a girl drinking far beyond her capacity. I will never drink again.

—Oh Maude, Dimple, are you all right?

A pair of strappy sandals was inches away and then two knees knocked down and the friendly moon of Gwyn's face worried my own. Her eyes fell on the bottle tipped at my side.

—*Christ*, how much did you drink?

The moon tilted upwards, crescenting.

—You guys gave her all that Bacardi? I mean, she's a novice!

Muffled noncommittal noise from the other two satellites orbiting farther away into the black hole.

—Do you want to go to the bathroom? Dimple, come on—swashbuckle up and hold my arm.

By this point only the popcorn guy was still around, sweeping up, and he was aisles away. My coat was gone somewhere and I watched my legs straighten out below me like a lifted rag doll and then I was upright, well, at a sort of oblique angle in Gwyn's firm grip. The Dudes were keeping their distance, spinning around me in click-clack freeze-frame as if through a slow-moving shutter, nearly blending into a two-headed entity.

—Come on, keep moving. Just act cool for the popcorn people. We're almost there.

—Hey, popcorn peeps! I hollered, waving excitedly, and I immediately dropped down again, my eyes so close to the carpet the pattern jumbled; I looked up to stare down the strip of floor between aisles. I wished I'd brought Chica Tikka; it was actually quite beautiful, the tumbled boxes stripily spilling more white and yellow clouds and gleaming soda cans, the crinkled candy bar wrappers like stars crumpled in a hand and tossed, all glowing astronomically against the dull red deep of the rug and seat backs.

I was up again, and we were ascending the aisle, which made the nachos rise farther but somehow helped abate the spinning; whenever we halted, the nausea went down and the merry-go-round switched to high speed. Not to mention that I was starting to feel low number-two rumblings in my nether regions. To poop or to puke? *That* was the question.

—Keep moving, Dimps, you can do it.

She was swinging me away from a long centipedal line of twitching women and in through a door with no human barricade.

Then we were in the bathroom, and paradise *was* a bathroom, shining and empty. Gwyn led me into a stall where I promptly fell to my knees, the upper ring clattering back down to the lower with the force of my landing.

—I don't feel so good, Gwynnie.

—No kidding? she said. —It's all that grease—you should never mix nachos and rum.

—I'll never eat nachos again, I vowed.

—Honey, just hurl 'em up and let's get out of here before any guys come in.

She was behind me, steadying my head and pulling my hair into, I suspected from the nimble finger motions, a chignon. I gazed into the white scoop bowl, at the shallow-end pool of water there. I could feel it all nearing my mouth and my head was beating hard now.

—Come on, Dimps. Just think of something that grosses you out—like that bugger that was stuck in Mr. Witherspoon's nose all day during the lava lecture, or diarrhea, or, I don't know, kissing Jimmy Singh.

I considered this last option, and pictured him now, silver kada sliding as he unwrapped his Ziplocked pakoras at lunch, reviewing class notes and (copyrighted) business plans on a Palm Pilot all alone at his cafeteria table-for-two.

I often spied on him from my own Sloppy-Joed arena—where usually Gwyn was lecturing stalwarts like Maria Theresa Montana and Shoshannah

Lieberman, and even pudgy pudding-fiend Franklyn Thomas Porter the Fourth on how to lose a pound a week through creative visualization. Jimmy's lunch was always tidily packed, but he was not. Even under that turban I knew lay a jungle of unwashed hair, and maybe even a knife, if you listened to some of the aunties' tales about those warrior Sikhs. So I didn't talk to him much. No one did. Plus, he kind of smelled. It was a smell I'd gotten whiff of sometimes when we had relatives or Indian friends over—coconut hair oil and cumin and slept-on pillows, sandalwood and sweat. In our house it seemed normal; in the school cafeteria, however, the odor made me ashamed—which made me even more ashamed. I carried a tiny pink bottle of Love's Baby Soft in my purse and spritzed it on frequently between classes and under desks. My parents had told me how bathing really was an Indian art, how the British had been taken aback by the cleanliness of the Indian people and the number of baths they took a day, when they were so foul-toothedly colonizing us all those years ago. But you could never be too safe.

—Gym teachers. Think gym teachers.

Ooh, that was good. And that was it: The whole Noahic nacho flood had its second world premiere, splattering the bowl, and flying off—and again. And once more. Was giving birth more embarrassing than this? I lay my head on the toilet rim (hoping no one would tell my mother I hadn't covered it in a foot-thick layer of toilet paper first).

—Oh god, Gwyn, I said, and I broke into a sob of relief. —What would I do without you?

—You'll never be without me, she said.

CHAPTER 6

the house of eternal diwali

As we bumped through the sometimes slick, sometimes rubbled streets of Springfield, I thought about that last trip to India, how my stomach kept rolling long after the hitchka had stopped. Despite avoiding unpeelable fruit, unboiled water, and the crackling pani puri stands of Juhu Beach I'd been constantly nauseous. But somehow I'd managed to keep my inner organs intact until the second to last day at, of all places, the Taj Hotel; shortly after lunch, even the five-star rating couldn't outdazzle the explosive effect on my being that an innocuous-looking shrimp salad was having. The next day I could hardly keep my seat belt on the whole fourteen-hour ride back on the plane. The slightest sign of turbulence elicited unsolicited bits and pieces of the irrepressible shellfish throatwards, and I spent the entire flight panicking not only about dozing off and drooling on the shoulder of the kind-faced Walkmanned stranger beside me, but that I would toss my crustacea on his freshly pressed Nehru jacket as well.

This car ride was a lot like that.

Julian was leaning way over with his head out the window, sniffing the breeze like a Labrador out on the town. But I knew he was just trying to manage his risks, what with me sitting next to him and all. I tried counting sheep to take my mind off my stomach, but math always makes me ill, so that wasn't such a good idea. Then I thought of snow, that particular silence of its falling, blanketing. The whole forked street in white star-crusted stillness. This was a good thought, snow, the way it powdered up and caked onto the edge of a ski braking and in your ears wind and whistle and the almost indiscernible scratch of the pole tapping you into a turn. It worked a while.

But fact was, the AC was broken, the roof was open, and we were in the middle of a heat wave. By this point my skirt had ridden up (a feat I'd hardly thought possible, considering it had never gotten that far down in the first place) and I was shamelessly exhibiting the two tanned beached whales that were my thighs. My coat was off, stiffly crumpled and creating a sort of hurl barrier between Julian and me. And it was still really hot.

I tried to sink deeper into snow. Last year we had so much of the stuff that for a while people were cross-country skiing down Fifth Avenue in the city; I saw it on the news, but by the time my mother and I went into Manhattan to get her visa for India it was all ashen slush, and everyone was slipping at the traffic lights in expensive shoes and getting cranky. We dropped off the passport at the embassy and were told to come back to pick it up stamped later that afternoon. So we went to lunch at a place that wasn't Indian but had things like elderberry chutney and mango coulis (which the waitress pronounced "coolie" to my mother's perturbation) and charged a lot for a salad with leaves called endives that were so bitter I nearly spit my first and last bite out. We left vastly unsatisfied and bought chestnuts from the Indian guy on the corner and went to Bloomingdale's, which still looked decorated for Christmas even though Christmas was long over.

And then we took a walk, clinging to hot chocolates from the diner on the corner. They had marshmallows and everything, but somehow we couldn't get warm. We were sitting on a bench when my mother started shaking, and the hot chocolate grew stormy, the brown liquid spattering the slush caking around her feet, marshmallows flopping out over the brim. She couldn't stop shivering, and at first I thought she was really cold, and I reached over to put my mittens on her bare blue-veined hands and squeezed them and looked at her. But she kept shaking.

—Mom? Mom, what is it? Do you want to go back and wait inside?

—It's too late.

—I'm sure it's still open, Ma.

—No, no, no it's too late—he's going, he's going. I can feel it. I'm not going to make it in time.

And then she was sobbing, and she let me hold her like a child.

—Come on, Mom, don't worry. You're just stressed. You'll make it. It's all going to be all right. Let's walk a little, you'll feel better.

I said it for myself as much as her; I was terrified. We were by Central Park, and the icicles were just beginning to melt, the delicate drops making little plink-plink sounds if you listened close, and my mother's breathing slowly grew even.

And she was right. She didn't make it to India on time. And this idea that you could feel when a person was slipping away to the other side, the way she felt it so viscerally despite the 10,000-mile difference, this terrified me, too. Because I hadn't felt a thing. Even when it was my own Dadaji, who was quite easily my favorite person on the face of this planet or any other. And if people were leaving and I had no clue, how was I going to keep track of them? I'd had a deep and sudden apprehension: *That could be me years from now, getting a chill on a park bench and just knowing.* But I couldn't finish the thought. I had the chill already.

★   ★   ★

We were gliding down the slope of Lancaster Road and branching right towards Gwyn's dead end, which forked off from my own not taken.

Julian was hanging almost entirely out the window now, singing the song on the radio really loudly, guitar riffs included, as if sheer volume could block out my presence. Well before we zigzagged up Gwyn's double drive, he was over me. I guess he'd been hoping for action of another genre than nonstop ralphing; I was definitely not smooch material this evening.

All the lights were off as was often the case in Gwyn's home. This was not an indication of anything in particular. It could mean Mrs. Sexton was out on the town with her latest flame (this one a theater director from the community college); it could just as easily mean she was passed out in the den in the back, semiconsciously watching reruns of *Family Ties*. In any case, Gwyn—much to my envy—could operate as if she weren't home. And tonight, as it turned out, Mrs. Sexton actually was in absentia.

Before Dylan had even pulled the emergency brake, Julian was out the door.

—Hey, man, he said. —I'm gonna book. Mind if I use the wheels to get back?

—Leaving already? said Gwyn. —But I've got wine, and beer, and

★ ₊* 54 ₊* ★

those big Pepperidge Farm cookies, the soft ones with the white chocolate chunks . . .

—Thanks, doll, but I've got to go home and watch my plants grow. Dillweed?

—Sure, dude, take 'em, said Dylan, tossing the keys over. He slung an arm low on Gwyn's hips and drew her against him. —Just swing by tomorrow—not *too* early—so we can get all the shit moved on time. I won't be needing to get home tonight anyways, right babe?

—Uh, right, said Gwyn. —Jules, are you sober enough to go?

—Believe me, I'm sober now.

We were all out of the car and Julian was in, revving the motor. Gwyn had one arm around me and the other around Dylan.

—Later, said Dylan, throwing out a rock 'n' roll devil's horn with his free hand.

—Later, said Gwyn. —But I hope sooner.

Personally, I had a feeling Julian was thinking more along the lines of never. I still managed a halfhearted *Later*. But by the time I said it he was already out the drive, taillights streaking red like a gash in the night, and then vanishing around the bend.

In another place and time and body this sort of exchange might have bummed me out big-time. And I did feel a dull stab, like when the nitrous oxide started to wear off that time I got my wisdom teeth pulled. But Julian's swift departure was more than anything a relief after all the humiliation of the evening.

—Don't worry, honey, said Gwyn, squeezing my shoulders. —He'll be back.

Those skidmarks didn't look like the sign of someone in a hurry to do a U-turn, but I nodded dumbly anyways.

—I think I'll be heading, too, Gwyn, I said. —Thanks for everything.

—Oh *noooo*, Dimple! Stay just a little longer! *Please!*

—Come on, Gwyn, who needs a third wheel?

Dylan gave her a pointed look that said, *Heads up, she might have a point.*

—Dimps! Plenty of things need a third wheel, said Gwyn, pushing my hair out of my eyes and gazing into them. —A tricycle, for example.

But I knew I'd only have a contraceptive presence if I stayed.

—Well, then, I'm gonna ride, I said. —Call me?

—Call you, she said.

And I wiggled my sack onto my back and walked on.

I was dying to sleep in my own bed and forget any of this ever happened, but figured I'd better work off the wooziness first. So I went in the direction opposite from home, towards the strip of woods bordering Gwyn's yard. I crunched through twigs and fallen branches past the silent playhouse, the windows caked with dust as if the children had long ago vanished. I supposed they had. From there it was a hop, scrunch, and plunk to cut out to Mirror Lake. I stood on the edge of the three-holed concrete bridge that traversed it; on one side water gushed into a low-level creek with stones pitted for crossing. On the other was the pond itself in all its quasi-octagonal tadpoled-and-minnowed glory.

Once I had caught a rainbow that began in my own backyard; I followed it out to this bridge and saw how it stretched all the way to the other side of the pond, as far as India perhaps, I thought then, disappearing into what was then still forest, before all the construction began. The rainbow reflected so clearly in the water it went nearly full circle, like a Ferris wheel whirling with sheer speed into simple circumferences of vivid color. It was gone by the time I got home, blown away by the sun-dried wind. I'd always wondered where it had ended on the other side.

Now the clouds glowed opaquely with the force of the moon behind them. A raft with a diving board swanned through the water, scepterlike. I stood on the bridge a moment and stared down, imagined diving. What it must feel like to turn your world upside down, let go, give yourself up to something. Fortunately I wasn't wasted enough to try it, being more a practitioner of the belly-flop, the slamming-against-the-world way of navigating it, than anything so graceful as a dive. I'd once known how to take the plunge when I was younger, but the more my brain started breaking down this concept of putting your head where your feet were supposed to be and vice versa, the more blocked I became.

I crossed over, mounted the strip of woods where Bobby and I used to meet, and came out on the other side. It felt cooler here. To the right was the Fields, with not a field in sight, a neighborhood named, I suppose, for what it had knocked down to go up. That's where Bobby lived and lusted. To the left, where once had been forest, were the newer streets, a neighborhood called Lake View. It was a bit of a misnomer, considering Mirror Lake was actually a pond, small and man-made, and unless you had eyes that could permeate bark, Pine View was much more along the lines of what you'd be buying into.

I guess it was somewhat surprising I'd spent a sizeable amount of time in New York City already considering I hardly ever even crossed over to the other side of the pond. I hadn't been here since a couple of years ago, in the beginning with Bobby, when the streets were all new, not even the house foundations down yet. One night, after hours of furtive first-basing, Bobby took a stick and carved our names in the still soft tar: *Bobby O + Dimple Lala*. It was juvenile, maybe, but strangely reassuring to have it there in writing. Like I really was someone. It wasn't the same seeing my name on pop quizzes and report cards, even in the yearbook below my usually mortified face and overly sprayed hair; in these cases it seemed random, and if I stared too long the words started to sound funny in my head and lose their sense (not that my name makes much sense to begin with—I don't even have a dimple). But here, paired up with someone else's, my own appellation looked rock-solid. Like it had been picked for a team. It didn't even bother me that night the way Bobby did his L's like small h's so that in the end it read more like *Bobby O + Dimple haha*, or that it never equaled anything.

I'd gone far enough.

I don't know why, but I was sobbing the whole way home, and my stomach climbed into my throat all over again. I rounded the dead end, being careful not to set foot on the curbside sand. (When I was little I thought it was called a dead end because the sand was actually cremated bodies, and I guess the myth stuck.)

At my house, a single light still burned. The house of eternal Diwali: That was the symbolic bulb, the vigil we left on in the study to deter burglars when we were out, and, I guess, when we were in, too. Amazed at my sudden onslaught of lucidity I managed to dig the key out of the hippo planter on the porch. I opened the door just enough to push through, catching it with my hand before the mini bang. I tiptoed through the kitchen, which at this hour was filled with strange, shifty shadows—I must have been quite buzzed still, because I couldn't even identify to what objects these belonged. The shadows bumped and swung all along my swaying path; I even thought I felt one glistening a cool knobby shoulder against my burning back.

Stepping over the weak fourth floorboard, I made my ungraceful moonshine way to the downstairs toilet, where I genuflected like a Nativity statue before the already pushed-up seat (thanks, Dad) and made an extra-spicy nacho prayer to the white porcelain god. At least I figured it was that—but what was I even throwing up at this point?

To flush or not to flush? That was the question. Not to flush was to leave a spectacular proof in the pot for all to see and send to the lab for testing. To flush risked my mother's thinking it was a burglar. But then again, my father's snoring would be louder in her ear than a momentary hallway rumble. So I pushed the lever.

The mechanism went off like Niagara Falls in my ear. From inside the barrel. I guess it was pretty loud because I didn't hear the fourth floorboard creak; I didn't even hear the slight whine of the door. But I did see the lights flick on again. And when I turned, there in the doorway was my mother. She was staring at me with an expression I had never seen before on her face, and for a moment I felt I was dreaming it looked so unlike her.

It occurred to me that I wasn't even supposed to be home tonight. So much for lucidity. Frock, now I was really going to get it.

But it was even worse than that.

—Happy birthday, Dimple, she said in a voice as lifeless as a sold house. Then she turned and walked away. I heard her climb the stairs. I heard the door shut.

And I knew what the look on her face had been: disappointment.

It wasn't until I stepped into the now lit hall that I realized what all those shifting shadows in the kitchen had been. The entire room was decked out in pink and red and orange balloons, translucent and gleaming, and dreamily floating streamers. I could see which parts my mother had done (left wall, lower down and straining to be higher) and which my father had hung up (not much higher). There was even Christmas tinsel on the plants. And on the table, a litter of packages, big and small, wrapped and ribboned in gilded colors. Through the loosening corner of one of the bigger ones I could just see the familiar smiley face logo from the camera store.

I felt something rise in my throat, but it wasn't something that would come out even if pushed, even if I drank myself to drowning; it was full of tears and shame and life and it was my heart. I looked to the cereal shelf Saraswati, but she was lost in shadow. Krishna, too. Even Ganesha. I looked to the kitchen clock. 12:01 A.M.

I was seventeen.

CHAPTER 7

born yesterday

Well, things were definitely getting worse before they got worse. If I thought I was illing last night—my room did spins like a windmill on a merry-go-round balanced just barely on a top—waking up this morning made all that seem like a day at the beach. Seventeen was off to a scary start indeed: An entire construction team was at work in my head, and a funky rhythm hammered on behind my right eye, turning blinking into an Olympic sport. I took a very long shower, downed a liter of water from the spout, and brushed my teeth repeatedly, but I could still taste the hootch.

I'll never drink again.

When I finally exited my room, my brain was pounding so hard I was sure everyone could hear it in the pin-drop silence of the house. My heart was still firmly lodged in my throat as I turned the corner and came into the kitchen.

The party was not only clearly over—it had never begun. The balloons were already deflating, floating halfheartedly off the streams of crepe paper, which now sagged wearily in the middle. My mother was standing before the stove, stirring a huge pot. From the milky-sweet newborn scent I knew it was kheer—my favorite Indian dessert, I suppose because it was so American: rice pudding, basically, with saffron and cardamom, a pistachio crown.

—Good morning, Ma, I said. Her shoulders stiffened but she didn't turn around.

My father was beside her, praying to Saraswati. That was my goddess, the one he focused on to make his prayer for me. (He'd organized all the deities like this; being in the medical profession he was a practitioner of specialization.) His bare toes curled up and down on the tiles. I usually didn't talk while he was praying, and now I kidded myself that this was what all the silence was about. But I knew the DL: Zilch rules regarding silence-during-worship existed in our house—India was a hustle-bustle place, my mother always said, you couldn't just sit around forever waiting for a quiet moment to crop up to meditate. It worked the other way around: You found your peace though prayer.

I sat down at the table, chair squeaking against the floor. Sunlight flooded the room, flashing off the glitzy wrapping paper on all the presents; I felt guilty just looking at them. My father was still standing before the Saraswati. Was I imagining it or was he praying even longer than unusual? It made me nervous.

I didn't remember my father ever praying when I was little, but out of nowhere the gods seemed to have sprung up all over our house: in the kitchen alone, the ivory Krishna in the temple (formerly the cabinet that held the can opener and blender, its door now removed), a bright orange trunk-smiling Titwala Ganesha sweetly removing obstacles from the stove top, and the jamming sandalwood cereal-shelf Saraswati, goddess of knowledge and music, strumming blithely away on her veena over myriad boxes of Cream of Wheat and cornflakes. My father paused before each of them for a couple of minutes at a time after his morning shower, waltzing through a prayer circuit that led him through the various rooms of the house with intent glowing eyes and clasped hands, like an enlighted ballroom-dancing real estate agent.

My mother, on the other hand, had stopped praying at about the same time my father had begun. It was as if they were taking shifts: *I'll cover the nineties, then you go.*

When I was much younger she'd meditated every day, going so still I'd get frightened. This daily ritual of hers made me intensely lonely, and I was always relieved when she'd finished. She would clutch a fake ruby rosary in her hands, sitting quietly, eyes closed, in the dining room corner for what seemed like hours. No one actually ever dined in our dining room, though my mother's sewing machine was located there in what Gwyn, years ago, had at first believed to be a liquor cabinet ("Just like the Lillian's!") and I'd often bundled up under the table in games of hide-and-seek, staring at the dizzying patterns on the Persian carpet till my eyes ached and I realized Gwyn had given up looking and was most likely sifting through my elephant collection upstairs (from ceramic bookends to fist-fitting quartz to the miniature myriad ivory flecks that tumbled out of iris-sized apples, turning to tuskers under the alchemical eye of a magnifying glass). Once, from under the table, I watched as my mother entered the room, slipped out of her house chappals, and sat softly with her beads. I could see her bare feet, callused talc white on the bottom, slowly settle out of their twitching and come to rest peacefully, one atop the other. When I emerged from under the cloth she'd opened her eyes, very calmly, and looked right at me. But it was strange, it was as if she didn't see me, or thought I was someone else. I'd felt like the floor was going to drop out from under my feet and swallow up the world as I knew it. And then she'd smiled. *My beta,* she'd said.

But now she had stopped praying, entering the dining room only occasionally to sew a hem or water the palm plant. I'd never thought much about it, figuring it meant she'd gotten everything she'd wanted. But now, it occurred to me, maybe it meant she'd given up hope.

Finally, after what seemed an eternity, my father moved beside my mother, to pray to the Ganesha keeping watch over the kheer. This was the area he used for extended family, like Sangita and Kavita, and Ketan Kaka out in California with his Route One motel, always filled with Harley Davidson gangs and trekkers who'd underestimated the distance to the next Big Sur campsite. From behind it looked like a postcard for Domestic Blissville: man and wife collaborating, choreographed, over the stove together. The two were engaged in a wordless dance; without a glance they gracefully sashayed and sidestepped one another as if at a hoedown till my father padded on into the hallway to finish up with Kashmir and the West Bank. (My parents were very into world peace—sincerely so.)

My dad had only spent a few seconds at the Ganesha. I timed it on the kitchen clock. And he'd definitely committed a good fiver to me via the veena'd one, and god time is kind of like dog years—much longer than, say, the same number of minutes on the phone with Gwyn. I didn't think I was being paranoid, but how did that saying go again? You're only paranoid if they're *not* spending too much time at your cereal-shelf Saraswati?

—Good morning, Ma, I tried again.

—Morning? Your cousin will be here in just a few hours for your birth-day dinner and you call this morning? Where are you living, in the L.A.?

I'd completely spaced on the fact Kavita was coming over. Brillo—now they could compare me to her. Another Hindi-, Gujarati-, and Marathi-speaking doctor in the making. And better yet, they could also line me up next to Sangita, who I was sure would be with us in prenuptial spirit, for a little round of do's and don'ts (guess who'd symbolize which one) for How to Get Your Daughter Married to the Indian Man of Your Dreams.

—Thanks for all the balloons, I said lamely.

—We thought we'd surprise you when you came home from your *slumber* party, said my mother. —But I think it is we who have been being surprised.

—Yeah, uh. Well, happy birthday, I said.

—Happy schmappy, she said.

—Well, I've got to give you the credit, right?

I was reaching for anything.

—We should really be celebrating you, right? You're the one who did all the work—the labor, the delivery, all that. You had me.

—That was the easy part, she said. —It is now that I am needing the epidural.

I noticed her accent had thickened slightly; she was definitely pissed.

—Anyways, stop trying to ghee me up, my mom continued. —You and I both know exactly what is happening here. I wasn't born yesterday.

—I nearly was! I said, trying to make a joke.

—That is very ha-ha. You should be a comedian, did you know that, like that Leno Schmeno gandoo.

My father had returned and was now doing a second round at the Saraswati. The goddess smiled benevolently upon me, looking a little like she was stifling a giggle. Frock, it was going to be bad. He never did second rounds—he was a very efficient man. I lurched forth for a glass of water and retreated back to the table.

My father and mother formed a united front in showing me their backs. I wished they would at least look at me. This was bad invisible.

—Thank Ram Kavita is coming, the back of my mother's head commented. —Enough with these hanky-panky friendships of yours. I thought more of Gwyn.

—Mom, it's not Gwyn's fault. She didn't hold a gun to my head and make me do funnel shots or anything.

For some reason this got their attention. My mother turned away from her kheer—something she never does, usually holding vigil over each grain of rice through the entire one-hour-plus process—and my father unnamasted his hands.

—What's a funnel shot? asked my mother.

—Who has a gun? said my dad.

At least I could succeed in the Q&A portion of the afternoon. Funnel shots happened all the time in the parking lot at school dances, and were apparently big at college, too, according to Dylan.

—A funnel shot—no, it has nothing to do with guns. It's when you sit with your head back, like at the dentist, and they pour alcohol through a funnel and it goes straight down your throat.

—Why would a person be doing this? cried my mother.

—So more alcohol goes in faster, I explained. As soon as I said it I realized my feet were both securely in my mouth, rainbow laces and all.

—Oh Bhagvan! my mother cried, pulling out a chair and collapsing into it. —My daughter is an alcoholic!

—Don't worry, Mummy, my father said as he yanked out a chair beside her and wrapped his arms around her. —We will get through this. There are groups who can help, like the AAA.

Was I here? My parents had launched into that third-person thing again, when I was in fact a third person only a few feet away in the same room. Trouble.

—It's AA, I said.

—Oh! So you already know this organization, is it? my father asked.

—What did I do wrong in this life?

My mother's head was in her hands, and she rocked it like a baby.

—I have a J. Lo–dressing, single, alcoholic, *photographer* who has completely lost touch with her Indianness for my only daughter! It is all my fault. Prabhu, what did I do?

My mom sounded as if she were composing a negative of one of those marital ads in the back of the Indian papers she brought home sometimes from the Bangladeshi grocer's. Most of the ones for the girls started out "Homely girl seeking . . ." At first I couldn't understand how anyone in their right mind could use this to market their product, until my mother explained that homely here meant domestic, homemaker, home-stayer. Like someone who needed to get out more, in my opinion.

And, did you notice? She said *photographer* as if it were the worst of all! She had to be kidding.

—Ha, that's funny, Ma, I said, forcing a grin and hoping we'd soon be slapping our knees, laughing the whole thing off. But not even the faintest sign of a snicker was to be found in her face. She was glowering at me like a sulky child.

—Daddy, I tried, but that was a no-go, too. He avoided my eyes, developing an abrupt fascination with our floor.

—See? he told the tiles. —Now are you happy? Why are you having to torment your poor mother like this? Do you like seeing her cry?

—Of course I don't. And Dad, come on, she's not even crying.

I could do the third-person thing too. But suddenly he wasn't having any of that.

—Inside, said my father emphatically. —She is crying.

He turned to my mother with a pained expression on his face.

—Aaray, Ram, why does she refer to you like you're not here?

—Look, don't you guys think you're overreacting? I sighed. —I just had . . . one. One glass doesn't make me an alcoholic.

—Depends how many times you are filling it, said my father.

—One what? Tank? Reservoir? said my mother, feisting up and tossing her head back. —You smelled like a brewery last night.

She pinched her nose as if to prove it.

—I could get drunken just breathing the air around you, my dad added.

—You should put yourself in a bottle and sell yourself at Ciccone Liquors.

Now they were on a roll.

—Good one, Mummy! my dad cried. She was pleased, and forgot to look mad for a second. They loved making each other laugh. I loved to, too, and really wished I could but doubted they were in my demographic at the moment. I hated when they were mad at me. And it seemed I never knew the right thing to say; what could I say, really? Did I mention that I'd never drink again?

—Mom, Dad, please, I now told the floor. —I'm really, really sorry.

I was, too. Not only about the alcohol. But about being the kind of daughter who made her mother want an epidural seventeen years after giving birth and who made her father talk to tile and disrupted his neatly organized praying pattern.

—I didn't know how strong it was, I told my parents now. This was true. —I just suddenly got kind of . . . dizzy.

—Did they slip that pill in your drink? my mother whispered, scooting her chair closer to mine. —I hope at least you didn't leave your drink unattended. I have been reading how these sick people use this special pill to take the advantage. It puts girls in an amorous state.

—Comatose state, said my father. I think he was correcting her, but my mother now pounced on him.

—I have been telling you and telling. Now do you believe me? Does it have to happen to your own daughter before you will listen? Oh, my beta . . .

All of a sudden my father was the enemy and my mother had thrown her arms around me in a suffocating hug. She smelled of If You Like Chanel No. 5 You'll Love and gentle-on-the-hands dishwashing liquid and spices and I loved her so much and was really sad that I made her worry.

—No, my drink was definitely never unattended, I told her in what I hoped was a reassuring voice. This was technically true, too, and a silence ensued as they processed whether that was a good thing or not.

—And where were you? Who were these hooligans who made you do this? asked my father. —How do we even know you were with Gwyn?

—I promise I was with Gwyn.

Promises are a big thing in our house.

—And only Gwyn? verified my mother, narrowing her eyes at me.

—No. . . . And some of her friends.

—Boys friends or girls friends?

—Boy friends.

—You were with boyfriends? Was it this Bobby Schmobby hanky-panky character? How dare you go out with him!

—He broke up with me ages ago, Ma.

—My god! she cried. —How dare he break up with you! What, he is too good for you? What is wrong with *you*? You are a homely, lovely, multilingual honors student coming from a good family! No crimes, no history of schizophrenia. What is he looking for anyways, the little bastard?

—Something taller and thinner and blonder, I think.

My mother made a disgusted noise.

—It doesn't matter, it's old news, I said. —Anyways, Gwyn was with her boyfriend and a friend of his, yeah, but I assure you I wasn't with mine and I do not have one. And we really did go to her house after the movie.

—Promise?

—Yes.

—Remember what Harish Chandra teaches about keeping your word?

—Yeah, I remember.

I didn't recall the exact quote, but the gist of it was: Keep your word.

—And you still promise.

I showed my fingers and everything.

—I was not plundered. No one sneaked anything into my anywhere. Gwyn didn't make me do anything, no one made me do anything—I didn't, she didn't, you didn't.

I conjugated the whole verb of Not Doing.

—I promise. And I remember what he said.

There was a silence as my parents digested all this. Then:

—That's my girl! said my father proudly. —Thank god we have such an honest daughter. Quoting Harish Chandra and everything.

My mother signaled to my father with a slight squint-wink of an eye that they weren't done being mad at me yet.

—Why did you come home then? she asked.

Because I was so blitzed I forgot I wasn't supposed to and Gwyn was macking by the microwave.

—Because I wanted to wake up at home on my birthday, I said.

This seemed to be the correct response. My mother sighed, and I heard her weaken. She stared deep into my eyes and it was the first time she'd really looked at me this whole morning, but instead of relief I felt even worse. Her eyes were so sad and so honestly uncomprehending as she asked me:

—Beta, why did you have to do this?

—We didn't think you'd have to be like them, said my father quietly.

I didn't know how to tell them: Of *course* I had to be like them. But how was I ever *going* to be like them? That was more than half the problem. I was born different—it started from the skin and seeped all the way in, till nothing matched.

—I'm sorry, was all I could say.

My mother always looked for an excuse to get mad, but she also always looked for an excuse to get unmad, too, and today was no different. She now shifted her worries onto someone else in order to do so.

—I didn't know Gwyn was an alcoholic, she said sadly. —She'll probably end up on a talk show or in a lawsuit with her mother. These American kids always take their parents to court.

—Poor beta, sighed my father. —This whole California-one-day-New-Jersey-next business is too much for a delicate creature like her.

—Did her boyfriend make her do it? my mother suddenly asked.

It? Of course Gwyn hadn't done It—she was saving herself for the Big Love. I was about to attest to her virginity, but quickly realized what my mother meant.

—No, but he was drinking.

—I knew it was his fault, my mother tongue-clucked. She was speaking firmly, but her eyes had gone all gentle again. —These altoo faltoo Western Heston boys corrupt good girls like you two. Dimple, you must develop a stronger will. Now would you jump off a bridge just because all your friends were doing it?

No, but I might anyways at this rate. I never understood how this completely implausible scenario could ever hit home with anyone. Why did everybody keep using it? How did it get passed around like that? I mean, it had been around since before e-mail chain letters.

I shook my head; the inside of it still swung around like a gong.

—But I know it is not just your fault, she continued. —It is this America—you cannot escape it, like those golden arches everywhere you turn. It is hard to resist it. But if I'd known the price we'd have to pay for this land of opportunity was our own daughter, I might never have left. I wonder whether Meeratai did right to stay behind with Kavita and Sangita. Ever since I ran into Radha, it's brought up so many memories all over again. It's really made me wonder. I did tell you I ran into my old school chum, Radha Kapoor?

—Yes, at Friendly's, I was there.

—She has a son.

—I know, I know: computer engineering, NYU, all that.

—So you were listening! That's my dikree, said my mother. —Well, anyways, I've invited them over for chai.

Rewind.

—You *what?*

—While you were—*recovering*—all morning, your father and I got to thinking. Frankly, there is no time to waste.

—This is an emergency of the most serious nature, my father nodded.

—You need a nice Indian boy, my mother concluded. —Someone to be a good influence, to keep you on track. He will appreciate you. He will not be too good for you like some other useless characters.

But I didn't want an Indian boy to appreciate me. What did being appreciated by a geek, or by someone who looked more like a cousin or brother, mean anyway? I could handle nerddom all by myself, thank you. What I wanted was even half a glance by someone cool, someone who played the guitar or made movies or had long hair, or even—jackpot!—all three. Someone who all the girls stared at but who turned and peered out over a slick pair of sunglasses at me, with all of them there, watching. I didn't want, I worried, someone who was not too good for me. I wanted, in short, someone who would never give me the time of day. But I was really in no position to argue.

—When are they coming? I asked slowly.

—Next week, my father informed me. —And they can't wait to meet you.

I could sense the storm ahead. It was going to be a tough one with my parents in matchmaker mode—but how could I refuse? I wasn't exactly all the way over on their good side at the moment. And it wasn't as if I had another option. Unless I could win back Julian, it occurred to me. My head ached with wondering how this would be possible; I realized I was perspiring. The heat was on even more than I'd realized.

In more ways than one: In the not so far kitchen distance, I suddenly noticed a white mass of bubbling froth like a hot snow lava cloud hissing up from the metal cauldron.

—Ma! The kheer!

We all leaped up to stop the overbrewed milk from splattering to the floor. I got there first, scooped up the mitts, and lugged the pot over to safety one range over.

My mother fluttered her hand in front of her chest.

—I don't know where my mind is these days, she gasped. —Thank you, Dimple. I'll just finish up and then . . . and then maybe we can open your presents.

★   ★   ★

They had bought me the color processor from the camera store! And the color head for my enlarger, the chemicals, the paper—right down to the print drum! I couldn't believe it—I hadn't seen the boxes or anything. Granted, they had also purchased a couple of those frames for me: one a gold-plated cheesefest with a matching grinning retriever hugged by a Pampers-perfect boy advertising it; a groom lifting a bride's veil in the heart-shaped second one, sun dipping behind and plunging them into silhouette. I doubted it was about the frames; I had a feeling it was my parents' way of justifying the other purchases, their little P.S. to remind me of what kinds of pictures I was to be taking exactly with these new toys. Their positioning them now on the foyer shelf, halfway between the front and basement doors, confirmed this; they'd be unmissable while entering and exiting both the house and the darkroom.

But I could hardly complain. Thanks to their overwhelming magnanimity, I now had pretty much everything I needed to try out color.

Finally, I tore open the package they made me save for last. Inside, padded carefully between layers of tissue, was an unbelievably resounding salvar khamees, one of those Indian outfits consisting of loose-fitting pants with a long top and scarf, or dupatta. The deep crimson fabric screamed sanguinely open. A river of nearly neon gold dye wound noisily through its length. The salvar was ornately embroidered with gold and silver and garnet beads and little bells that made a racket even as I lifted it out of the box. All in all it was, in fact, so loud I could hear it. Heavy, too—funny how all those little driblets could add up. It looked nothing short of a wedding combo: red, the color of fertility, was the bridal hue in most Indian unions (white, the color without color, being that of mourning).

—It's even more expensive than Sangita's, said my mother, as if she'd heard me. —Now maybe you can model it for us.

I was still staring dumbly at the roaring combo, wondering where my shades were when I needed them.

—Now, said my mother.

★ ★ ★

I returned to the room feeling a fool in the blaring outfit. The dupatta was sheer, gold, gewgawed, and enormous—I hadn't known what to do with it, and now it trailed behind me like a glitzy, gory bridal train. I was about to trip on all the fabric. My folks had certainly themed the presents well this year: I would definitely be needing my brand-new camera kit if I ever put these duds to film; frock, they could turn black and white to color!

But one look at my parents and there was no way I could complain just yet. They were beaming at me as if I were walking down the very aisle (even though Hindu ceremonies involved going in circles, which was much more my forte).

—Baapray, beta, you look . . . why, you look just like your mother did on our wedding day! my dad proclaimed, visibly moved. He turned to my mom and smiled. —Ketli sunder chhokri chhe.

Nil chance I could diss my new look now. My mother was busy draping the dupatta till it formed a crisscross across my body, like a Miss America banner. She stood back to survey her work, clearly pleased.

The two gazed at me now not only approvingly but adoringly. I realized then that my father's comment, coupled with this outfit, had transformed me in their eyes. They weren't seeing the hungover bad girl who felt dressed like a circus attraction; before them was the good Indian daughter, kheer-saver and homely girl, demurely previewing her wedding day duds. In other words, they weren't seeing me at all.

om on the range

—Beta, come up! I heard the car! my father called, slicing a shaft of light into the darkroom with his voice. I'd been so lost in my thoughts (and in setting up my guilt-giving gifts) that I hadn't heard a thing. Reluctantly I exited. And he was right. No sooner had I mounted the stairs than the bell rang.

—Now you be nice to your cousin, whispered my mother, nodding me towards the door. As if I were planning to throw spitballs the second she entered. —She's only coming because it's your birthday, you know.

I mustered up whatever enthusiasm I could—considering that I was at a negative level, I did to my credit manage to bring up my lack of joy (at the idea of spending a migrainous night being compared to and jeered at by my Bombay-bred cousin) to level zero.

So I yanked the door open. And for a second I couldn't believe my eyes. Someone was standing on the porch, all right. But not at all the someone I'd been expecting.

She was a sight, a jovial and superlatively radiant brown angel landed on the front steps. And it wasn't those terra-cotta bronzing blocks that I don't need but use anyways sometimes to capture that special glow. She didn't seem to have any makeup on, save for a thick stroke of kajal on the upper lid of each mischievous eye, extending out slightly and up, Cleopatra style.

Gone was the rail-track girl floating in stiff taffeta hand-me-downs and knees poking out. Undone the two tight plaits of hair like heavy black ropes dragging blood from her temples, which had always lent her a frenetic appearance, even with her eyes closed, even asleep. Everything had seemed too big on Kavita when we were little, from the dresses to her facial expressions;

her features took up so much space it was as if they would devour her very visage. And she'd been thin; when she moved, her bones shifted beneath her skin translucent like fish sliding under water. But now it was as if the rest of her had grown up to accommodate the huge eyes, the angling nose, in the left nostril of which a once chunky diamond now twinkled tinily like a caught star.

—Howdy, our dear cowgirl cousin! she giggled. Her mouth was a laughing mouth, as if it had just heard or said the funniest thing ever, and it was open wide in a toothy grin. —Many happy returns, old lady!

That was the same. The grin, that chuckle. I'd always found it taunting, like she was enjoying some private prank against me every time she spoke.

—Hey, Kavita, I said. —Thanks for coming.

—Are you joking? I couldn't miss this most auspicious of occasions! And you, dear Uncle and Aunty, are looking in the pink of health!

She talked like she wrote in her letters.

—Thank you, beta, said my father, peering over her shoulder at the slunked-over bottle-green VW parked in our drive. —So you are owning a car now?

—It's Sabina's, she said. She must have sensed our collective question mark. —My roommate. It's a cutie, heh?

She was gazing lovingly at the Bug. Her hair was a spun jungle in this heat, spiraling from her shoulders down her back in Magic Marker curls. I'd never even realized it was curly, as it had always been in braids when I'd seen her. Now, it was gorgeously wild, as if she'd been racing horses across the Mongolian plains or, even more unlikely for her, windily kissing all night in the bleachers. Actually it was a lot like mine, but on her it looked good, on me just unkempt.

—Dimple, aren't you going to take your cousin's bag? said my mother, indicating the shopping sack in Kavita's arms.

—Oh, I've got it, Maasi, she said hurriedly. —Though it *is* for the birthday girl!

Taxi! With that Hindi label and all those curlicue peacock designs it was sure to be yet another salvar khamees to jazz up my prehistoric look.

—Well, you've come a long way, beta.

—Not so long, just NYU, Kavita grinned, voicing my grumpy inner thoughts exactly. She kicked off her chappals and stepped inside, blinking twice, befuddledly, at the photo-frame photos on the shelf before passing. —Though I guess you're used to thinking of me as far away.

As we walked through the house, Kavita exclaimed delightedly at all sorts of things I'd long stopped noticing: a thigh-high vase blinking with peacock feathers in the foyer, the sandalwood chariot with the miniature Krishna and Arjuna, the Mexican birds my mother had attached to a houseplant via those twistie things that seal bread wrappers. She stopped at the edge of a handwoven rug, rolling over the corner where I could now see thick black script.

—Baapray! I remember when you bought this—you signed it here, the Kashmiri storekeeper's way of assuring you the rug later shipped was indeed the one chosen. And after—after he drank with us to celebrate the deal, isn't it? Hot tea in glasses, with nuts at the bottom.

Her voice rang through the house like a bell, water spilling over stones, and I felt a great weight lift off me in spite of myself. Glorious sound after all the silence today.

My parents looked relieved, too. Here was a grinning cotton kurta'd direct line back to the motherland. And what a timely entrance, considering how far I'd strayed in their eyes since the innocent age of sixteen.

—It is so good to have you here, Kavita. For a while I had the impression you were still in India, we heard so rarely from you, sighed my mother. —We haven't seen you practically since you started the NYU!

—Yes, I know, ji, said Kavita. She was beside the shut jet-black piano I hadn't touched since I'd quit lessons with powdery Mrs. Lamour. —I'm so sorry—I've just been in over my head from day one.

Ji is the suffix denoting respect in India. I knew this because I did a report on Gandhi and his philosophy of satyagraha and passive resistance in junior high and a lot of our books on the subject refer to him as Gandhiji, or Mahatmaji, or Bapuji (bapu meaning father).

—Well I hope all that studying has worked up your appetite, said my dad. —Your aunty has cooked up a wedding's worth of food.

—Oh, I have an appetite all right, Kaka, Kavita laughed, patting her belly. I noticed then that it was straining the fabric. She never used to eat much; I remembered how self-conscious I'd felt in India reaching for my second butter naan when she'd torn off only an economical edge to pinch up her entire meal's worth of bhaji.

—You *have* put on a lot of weight, said my father, nodding approvingly. I couldn't believe he'd told her what we were all surely thinking—but a moment later I was even more stunned by her response.

—Thank you, ji, said Kavita merrily, running her finger along the dusty piano lid then pushing it open to reveal the keys. They shone like beast teeth in a night forest.

—Dimple, why don't you show your cousin her room? I'll just go check the gosht, said my mother. "Your cousin"; sometimes she said "your father," even "your mother." I wasn't sure why she felt this need to confirm our particular positioning on the family tree.

I must have been just standing there pondering this, because she added:

—Dimple had a little bit of an adventure last night, Kavita. Killed a few brain cells. Apparently the ones needed to listen to her mother. Sorry if she's a bit slow.

—An adventure! cried Kavita. —Ooh! Do tell!

I went promptly into toe-scrutiny mode.

—Okay, maybe not on an empty stomach, Kavita said quickly.

—Oh, I think Dimple's stomach is empty all right, my mother snorted. Kavita looked at her, then at me.

—Shall we check out your digs, then, cowgirl?

I nodded theatrically; I was ready to exit this conversation, and Kavita slipped her arm through mine as we went to my room. She always leaned in conspiratorially, which made me a little uncomfortable. And this close she smelled like nuts, the sweet kind my mother and I bought off the stand from the Indian guy on the Upper East Side that time we went to New York for the visa (she'd insisted he was Pakistani, but to be honest I couldn't see the difference).

Kavita set her bags by the entry to my room.

—Dimple, she said, smiling happily into my eyes. —It is so good to see you. You haven't changed a bit!

—I haven't? I said glumly. I was hoping I had. —Well, you look different. I mean, *good* different.

—I feel different, said Kavita. —It took a long time to get to this place and now I don't ever want to leave it.

—Yeah, well, you're always welcome.

—No, silly, she giggled. —That's not what I meant. I meant, just. Well, you know I was very depressed after Dadaji passed on. It was awful. Going back and not seeing him. In a way I envy your being able to go on, pretending he's there—I mean, you haven't been to India and seen the hole in the house. And to think I didn't get back in time because no one wanted me to miss an exam. How absurd is that? And now I will never see him again. I have to say, it really taught me what it means to seize the day and know what is important. Life is too too short, Dimple.

It was funny—most times my own seemed to be dragging on and on in no direction whatsoever.

—Well, there's always reincarnation, I said, trying to cheer her up. —Maybe we have nine lives.

She looked at me intently, and it was funny, but her mouth unchuckled.

—But this may still be the last one, she said.

★　★　★

All day the house had smelled of spices, and now before our eyes lay the resulting combustion of all that kitchen chemistry. The feast my mother had conjured up was extravagant, and I realized how hungry I was; I wasn't a big fan of Indian food, at least not on a daily basis, but today the sight of it was sheer poetry.

Brown sugar roti and cloud-puff puris just itching to be popped. Coconut rice fluffed up over the silver pot like a sweet smelling pillow. Samosas transparent, peas bundling just below the surface. Spinach with nymph-finger cloves of garlic that sank like butter on the tongue. A vat of cucumber raita, the two-percent yogurt thickened with sour cream (which my mom added when we had guests, though she denied it when asked; I'd seen the empty carton, not a kitten lick left). And the centerpiece: a deep serving dish of lamb curry, the pieces melting tenderly off the bone.

Oh, and of course, small but deep bowls of kheer, coronated with crushed pistachios and strands of saffron, vermillion like tiny cuts in the foamy surface.

The table exploded with food, creaked with the weight of it. Everything was laid out all together, sweet and salty side by side, Indian style. (I'd never quite realized this was an Indian thing till that time the other kids looked on with desire and disgust as I ate my Hostess cupcake alongside my tuna fish-and-chutney sandwich in the cafeteria.)

When Kavita entered, her hair now number-two-penciled into an already unraveling bun, she stopped dead in her tracks at the sight.

—Baapray! she cried, unfreezing and scrambling into her seat. —Aunty, I feel like it's *my* birthday, being included in this!

—Oh, it's nothing, really, beta, said my mother. —I just whipped it up before you got here.

I suppose yesterday does technically count as "before you got here." My mother had begun the lamb last night (it was day-after food, even more succulent after hours of marinating in her fresh ginger garlic sauce), and she must have been up at the crack of dawn to get the samosa crust so thinly rolled. My father and I looked at each other but kept mum as my mother now insisted to Kavita that she sit at the head of the table.

—Oh no, Aunty, she said. —The cuisine queen should sit facing her king.

—Oh, don't worry, beta, my mother said. —I don't usually sit much during a meal.

It was true. Often we didn't need even three seats; when my father was on call or late coming home from the hospital there would be two dinnertimes in our household: one where I contentedly chowed down spaghetti or peanut butter and mango jam sandwiches among my schoolbooks, and one where my father sat down to his khichdi kadhi, my mom munching on bits of both in between. When we were all three there, or at home with guests, my mother usually spent the entire meal on her feet, keeping the naan warm and refilling water glasses, ladling into our plates for the fifth time "just one more spoon, there's only a little left, think of all the starving people in India" despite satiated groans of protest. She never even let me help, except with loading the dishwasher after. But Kavita wasn't having any of this.

—No, Aunty, she said firmly. —Despite the fact that I am dying to throw myself headfirst into that gosht, I refuse to eat until you sit with us.

My mother looked around helplessly then up at the stove top Ganesha as if for authorization from a greater force. She glanced shiftily back at us, and my father raised his eyebrows and did that Indian side-to-side head tilt that served as a yes in the East but looked more like a moment of indecision (or hinge gone loose) in the West. We were both overwhelmed by the concept. It had never occurred to me to do what Kavita had just done, and I felt ashamed. The extent of my mother's efforts hit me like a brick in the belly.

—Yeah, come on, Ma, I said, trying to act like I thought of it, did it all the time.

She laughed shyly as she pulled out her seat, as if the most popular boy in school had just asked her to slow dance in the school gym. Then she put her elbows on the bamboo mat, clasped her hands, and set her chin nervously on them, like a china cup on a steeple tip, a pose of studied relaxation. I had an urge to say grace.

—So, what can I get you to drink? asked my father. —Kavita, beta?

—Oh, I wouldn't mind a glass of wine, said Kavita. I nearly choked on my tonsils.

—You . . . wouldn't? asked my father, glancing at my mother. I knew he'd been thinking more along the lines of ginger ale, cranberry juice, or water. He was particularly big on the benefits of cranberry juice.

My mother glanced back at my father. I looked down so I wouldn't laugh. Here was an unexpected twist!

—Uh . . . said my mother. —I don't think we have any. . . .

—Sure we do, I said, still checking out my lap. Being the alcoholic in the family, I had to live up to expectations now. —You know, all those Christmas gifts in the Christmas gift closet in the study. I can go get it if you want.

—No, no, I'll go, said my father, who liked to avoid awkward situations by plunging right on into them when they arose.

We had quite an alcohol stash for a nearly teetotaling family. All the doctors at the hospital gave us bottles of Johnny Walker and wine, Black Label and cognac at Christmas. The only bottle open was Bailey's, which my mother liked to put in milk at the holidays, but then she usually suffered a headache and intense longing for her childhood in Kolhapur for three days after.

After some cartoonish gymnastics, my father finally got the cork out of the Beaujolais Nouveau (I wasn't sure how Nouveau it was at this point, but the label was convincing) and splashed out the wine, filling all the glasses, though in mine he let runneth exactly one droppeth, which, today, was fineth by me. His own glass was burgundy to the rim; to be honest, he probably needed a drink at this point, after all the events of the A.M.

—So, said my mother, in her cocktail party voice. —Since when did you become a drinker, Kavita?

—Oh, I wouldn't say I'm a drinker, per se, said Kavita. —But a glass of wine with a meal as fantastic as this one would serve as quite a lovely complement.

Who said flattery got you nowhere? Flattery could take my mom from Kuala Lumpur to Rio in a nanosecond.

—Do you really think it looks fantastic? she asked, coy-eyed. —I mean, Meeratai must cook like this all the time at home.

—Are you kidding? Mummy can't cook to save her life! It's Papaji who's got the gift.

—You call him Papaji? my father said, evidently moved. —This is so touching. I myself always called my father Bapuji. So much nicer, so much more respect than Dad or Pop like they do here. Back when there was respect for the parents.

He sighed dramatically, gazing morosely into his glass, like the last man at the bar at closing time, or a Turkish coffee-cup reader with unpleasant news. But my mother had latched onto the alternative detail.

—No, you can't mean that! she said. —Meera can't cook to save her life?

She looked a little pleased but was trying very hard to appear stunned. Like that time the salesclerk told her, *Oh you couldn't be her mother! I thought you were her older sister!*

—Believe me, said Kavita, winking at my mother. —This is a real treat. And regarding the wine, frankly Mummy is so stressed with the wedding and all, I think it would do her good to have a little nip now and then. But you didn't hear that from me.

My mother placed her hand to her ear, smiling.

—Hear what? she said.

Kavita raised her glass.

—To a very special occasion!

—Yes, said my mother, raising her own. —To Sangita's wedding!

—Oh, that, too, said Kavita. —But I meant Dimple's birthday.

—Oh, yes, to Dimple's birthday, said my father.

—To Dimple's birthday, said my mother. —Anyways, so, beta, how is Sangita doing? She must be just thrilled with all the hubbub. I imagine there's a lot to prepare by November.

That's when Sangita's wedding was to be. Which was a long engagement in proportion to how long it took her and Deepak to get engaged: exactly one week from the day they met—and that only because their astrological charts had to be cross-checked for potential turbulence and all the sires, too, via a collective meal including both chicken chat and chitchat about politics, and, more hazardously, cricket.

—Well, there's not much to prepare really, heh? said Kavita. —It has all been written, Maasi, isn't it?

—Well, yes, said my mother, approvingly.

—And Sangita, she is quite happy about it, no? said my father. —At least from Meeratai's letters it seems that way.

—Well she should be, ji? said Kavita. —I mean he is a suitable boy, correct, from a good family, good business prospects, their stars match, five foot eight. Which is tall in India, isn't it?

She had that same tone of voice she'd had as a child, but now I couldn't tell if it really was taunting after all. I wasn't sure if she was questioning my mother, or herself, or his height.

—But what I don't understand, and maybe you can explain this to me, is how come no one is saying what a catch Sangita is? I mean, she is just lovely. I know she is my sister. But it's the truth. She feels so *lucky* to have Deepak.

—Oh, we are so happy for her! my mother nodded.

—No, no, Aunty: I mean, *too* lucky. He's the lucky one if you ask me.

Her wineglass was half full now, and a flush was centering in her high cheeks.

—If Dadaji were here, he would never stand for it, she added.

My mother looked as if she'd been slapped. Her eyes smarted and she even took a sip from her glass. She must have forgotten it was wine, because she immediately made a citric face.

—Well, yes, of course he's very lucky, said my father, diplomatically. He rubbed his thigh anxiously. —Sangita is a wonderful girl. Roti, anyone?

—We must live every moment fully, said Kavita.

—Be productive, nodded my father through a mouthful of molasses, eager to change the subject. —So, Kavita, been doing a lot of thinking the deep thoughts at the NYU?

—Yes, said Kavita. —I've been doing a lot of thinking, that's true.

—Why don't you show Dimple around sometime? It's never too early to start thinking about colleges, beta.

—Oh, I would *love* to—it's a *maaagical* school, Dimple! Full of incredible people. And all of New York is the campus—which feels like all the world. In fact there is quite a large South Asian community there.

—South Asian? said my mother. —You mean Indian?

I was wondering as well; for some reason it was bringing to mind Cambodia.

—Indians included, smiled Kavita. —Thanks to Sabina, I've gotten very involved in the South Asian scene. In fact, we've been helping to organize a convention on South Asian identity; the kickoff party's coming up in just a couple of weeks.

—South Asian identity? asked my dad.

—South Asian scene? I said. What scene? I usually felt like the only Indian on the planet, when I felt Indian at all.

—That sounds like it might be a good thing for you to attend, Dimple, said my mother.

—Ma . . .

—Especially after the events of this morning, young lady, she said firmly.
—Can anyone go, Kavita?

—The more the merrier!

—Do you know by any chance . . . said my mom now, too casually, twiddling the Bounty roll napkin in her hand, — . . . a boy named Karsh?

Oh no, here we go . . .

—Karsh Kapoor? Oh yes, of course—he's very involved in the South Asian scene, too.

Nerd alert! Why wasn't an alarm going off?

—I knew it, said my mother proudly, as if she had something to do with it. I rolled my eyes.

Kavita glanced at me. And—as usual with her lips-up bones-high flower-cheeked face that smiled even when she wasn't smiling—it was hard to read her.

By the time Kavita washed up and came into the room I was truly ready to call it a day. I lay spread-eagle under the sheet; it was hot still, but somehow I always felt safer with a cover of some sort.

—Good night, Kavita, I said. —And thanks again for coming to see me.

I figured she must be exhausted, too; there was something sort of somnambulist about the way she was moving, the loose-fitting nightgown drifting languidly around her calves. Me, I could barely keep my lids up; they kept gliding down like loose panes.

—No mention, she said reaching for the light.

Turning off the lamp was tantamount to turning on the moon, which now poured through the window, a smaller satellite than last night's, but still plump with light. I could see the outline of Kavita's body through the muslin. I expected her to lie down then but she just kept hugging her knees to her chest, the nightgown creating a filmy mountain, her hair a craggy escalade down the back of it, cascading a coromandel shadow all the way to the sheets as she stared up at the ceiling. She was gazing so intently I wondered if she'd discovered a fault line ominously emerging, an upside-down earthquake. I asked her if she was all right.

—I guess all that talk about the wedding just made me a little sad, she said softly. —My life is so unlike Sangita's.

Was she jealous of her sister? I could imagine that. When Gwyn and Dylan first got together I was really happy for her, but when I realized that I was going to be the one left out of the loop, try as I might I found it kind of difficult to share her enthusiasm. I mean, my birthday was almost officially over and she hadn't even called. She'd never forgotten before.

—Yeah, I said. —I can definitely relate.

—Yes? I just worry sometimes that my sister has a lot of pressure on her because of my behavior.

—What's your behavior? I said, up on an elbow now. —Premed, good school, Indian crowd—Kavita, you are a dream child. My parents would swap in a second.

—Don't talk rubbish, said Kavita. —In any case, it's still not staying in India and meeting a nice boy and not getting too overqualified to be a perfect wife. Which is exactly what Sangita's doing: settling in Mumbai and giving up on half her interests. It's funny how history seems to repeat itself.

—What do you mean?

—Like our mummies, for example. Yours went off to have the adventure; mine stayed at home to be the good girl. And now look at them—they can hardly discuss the weather without measuring themselves against each other! They've lost a bit of their capacity to simply *enjoy* anything, because there's always this invisible scoreboard they're watching.

I'd never really thought of it that way, and I wasn't sure I wanted to.

—And I don't want that to happen with me and Sangita.

—Well, does she love him? I asked.

—She's showing all the symptoms of love. Or faking them, like a flu when you don't want to go to school. But how would she know? She's only seen him twice, and that surrounded by other people.

—Twice? I cried.

—That's how this kind of marriage works, Dimple.

—And Maasi and Kaka are making her marry him? I'm sorry, but that's barbaric!

—I don't know if it's barbaric. I've seen cases where it works out, though I suppose you never really know; the divorce rate is low in India, but so is the speaking-up rate when it comes to women. In any case, they're not taking out the talwar or anything. But Mummy—I've just never seen her so nervous. I mean, to put out an ad!

—Ad?

—Yes, said Kavita, sounding surprised. —You didn't know?

—Like that "homely girl seeking" stuff?

—Exactly. Except Mummy of course neglected to mention that Sangita is thin, dark, and astigmatic, like our Mama uncle was.

And this was a bad thing? Astigmatic, okay—but the rest?

—None being such good selling points in the marriage market, Kavita explained.

—Frock, I said. —Here she'd be a supermodel!

—Well of course she won't come here now. The girl has no confidence after all that's happened.

—What happened?

—Well, the first meeting—you know, after my parents already went with my Rahul cousin to investigate the family—she cannot even get by the mother because of her height.

—The mother was tall?

—No, no! Sangita wasn't tall *enough*. The mother of course, chutia that she is, is a good inch shorter, and was in some fancy imported shoes as well, whereas Sangz was just in chappals.

Kavita was up on her knees now.

—The meeting with boy two seems to go well, but at the last minute his family makes the condition that she must have eye surgery before anything is officialized. You know, get rid of the glasses. And—imagine this!—they suggest she use a pumice to lighten up her skin.

Was that why Meera Maasi was so wary of the darkening room? I was sitting up now, too.

—So they give up on the entire advertising method and go to this sort of singles night for CKPs—you know, our mothers' caste, Kshatriya. Okay, I suppose you do not know. Basically, a group of boys and girls are in a big room. All of them have a number. The girls sit on one side of a table. And then the boys line up each before a girl and present a card with their details on it.

—Like their e-mail?

—No, no—their birth sign, salary, number of brothers and sisters. Each pair has a few minutes to talk until someone rings a bell, and then the boys have to all move one over to the next girl. Now, everything being on IST as usual . . .

—IST?

—Indian Standard Time. You know—late. Being late as usual, the rental on the room is nearly over and they have to speed things up, so the bell is ringing faster and faster, till the last boys in line have less than a minute each. So of course, up strolls Deepak. And after a thirty-second conversation that consists of him asking Sangz why she's still staring at the guy who's gone just before—my sister picks him.

—You did *not* just say that! So she tells him right then and there? Wait'll Gwyn heard this!

—No, no. What you do at the end is write down the numbers of the boys who have interested you, and they do the same. Wherever there is a match both parties are notified and it goes from there. So she picked Deepak, and Deepak picked her.

—That sounds almost romantic.

Frock, if the boys I crushed on ever crushed back on me, we'd be in business!

—Well, I should also mention that of course, after what happened, Sangita wasn't wearing her glasses at this meeting. Which is not, if you ask me, the best way to go about choosing a husband.

—Or it's the only way, I said, imagining the dork density of the place with all those computer programmers in one room.

Kavita laughed sadly.

—It really is quite awful, she said.

—So you're not going to have an arranged marriage, Kavity? I asked.

—No, I'm not, she said.   I'm as Indian, if you will, as the rest of them. But I'll arrange my marriage myself, thank you.

—They'll let you do that in India?

—I'm not going back to India.

She sat up even straighter, all silhouette. She was gazing out the window.

—You know, Dimple, they say in the East you love the person you marry and in the West you marry the person you love. But maybe it's a lot simpler than that. Maybe you just love the person you love.

A long silence ensued. My lids began drifting despite myself, but through my lashes she was luminous in the near dark, moon-bathing. And so natural. I wondered suddenly through the heaviness of approaching sleep whether she had an American boyfriend. This kind of mixed-couple thing happened all the time—I'd heard my parents' friends complaining about it at poker parties: how their own flesh and blood had fallen into the grip of Western corruption. (And this during poker parties.)

I'd never felt the way she looked now about Julian, or even Bobby: easily taking up space, loose with her voice, moonlit. I'd always felt tight, fat, clueless. In the dark. Maybe I'd never been in love. I wondered whether she was.

—Yes, very much, she answered.

I hadn't realized I'd asked out loud.

—With an Indian?

—With an ABCD! Funny, isn't it.

I could hear her smile.

—ABCD?

—You've never heard this? It's a term we have in India for second-generation South Asians from the States. It stands for American Born Confused Desi.

—They see what?

—Not *they see*, she said. —*Desi*. Desh meaning country in Hindi. It's a person who comes from South Asia, ancestrally at least. The alphabet goes all the way to Z—not always a nice alphabet, but there you have it.

I couldn't believe it. Someone had made an alphabet about that? I was wired again.

—So you're in love with an American Born Confused Desi?

—Well, an American Born Desi, at least.

She flopped back like she was falling into a pool.

—That wine must have gone to my head! I feel like I've been talking nonstop.

And turned away from me, seashelling up on the sheet.

—It is good to be with you again, Dimple, she said. Her voice sounded far away now. —I'm sorry I've been so out of touch. It was a really tough year. But you know I've always thought of you as my little sister. Even though you're not so little now.

For some reason, I didn't think she meant fat.

—Dream sweet, she said.

Her curls skidded off her shoulder and fanned out over the pillow. It was then that I saw something on the nape of her neck, dark like dried blood, but not accidental; there was a pattern to it. I squinted. I couldn't tell what it was, this strange flower.

It was the last thing I saw before I sandmanned into sleep.

★   ★   ★

Kavita was gone by the time I woke up (I was still on *the L.A. time*, apparently). Her bed was perfectly made up, dime-bounceable, with the cover turned down and tucked in to expose the pillow. A fresh glass of Sprite sparkled on my nightstand through a partly drawn shade (hangover helper, she'd informed me when she inkled out what my infamous "adventure" had been). I hadn't heard her leave, but I vaguely recalled someone pulling the sheet to my chin. The shimmer-clank of bangles as a hand lay gently on my forehead. A scent of caramel and cashew and salted skin that still lingered.

Now that she'd been there and was gone I had a funny feeling. Empty. It had been nice having her in the room, like when Gwyn used to sleep over, before Dylan entered the picture.

I sat up. And there at the foot of my bed I saw the Hindi-scripted shopping bag, which she must have forgotten. But poking out the edge of it was an undulating tide of ribbon, which made me look again. A big blue box lay inside, elaborately frescoed with paper roses, the stem edges likely pulled with a scissor's edge till they rippled. My second salvar, I thought, reaching over to open it; a folded paper fell off as I did. My hands tangled in all the bows, but after that it was easy: She'd wrapped the lid separately from the bottom, and I lifted it off now and peered inside.

At first I didn't know what I was looking at, the gibbous nest of black-and-yellow tubes in magenta tissue, dozens of them, the bright labels. And then it hit me and tears sprang to my eyes. I pried a lid off one of the tubes. Shook out the contents. The perfect weight, the curling edge like a mischievous smile, of a roll of film in my hand.

But that wasn't all. As my hand dug through the 200s and 400s and colors and black-and-whites, it hit upon something hard and flat on the box bottom. I pulled that something out.

In my hands was a heavy black book, the word *Memories* printed simply in gold lettering on the cover. An album to use once I'd gone through all the film, I guessed, carefully turning the leather cover.

But, no, it was already full, this book. Plastered on its pages were not only photographs, tons of them, but scraps of paper, too, sometimes decked with green and red type and stars, sometimes slanting in a very familiar cursive.

Pressed down next to a photo of a sandbox cut off at the corners: *Dear Dadaji, This is where Kevin Dunst told me I was the color of dog doo and Gwyn stuffed his mouth full with dirt.* Below a picture of a street under construction, the street where Bobby and I had shared our first kiss, a caption: *Some shots of the neighborhood.*

I turned the pages, astounded. The pages of the book of all the letters and photos I'd sent to Dadaji over the years. He'd saved it all. And she'd put it together. She must have collected the pieces in India and then assembled it all here, judging from the American label on the album, sitting and cutting and pasting even in the middle of all her busyness. I didn't know how I would ever thank her.

And then I realized: I'd always thought we had nothing in common, Kavita and me. But we had an enormous, immeasurably precious thing in common: Dadaji. It was strange thinking of her as his granddaughter. I thought of Dadaji as all mine, I suppose because I was here and they were there and our letters created a private universe of two between us. But it was true—Kavita and Sangita did live with him, they did know him on a daily basis. A different kind of knowing, but maybe they shared moments as sacred as our letters, as telling as these pictures.

I picked up the page I'd pulled off with the ribbons and flowers; it had been torn from a notebook, the edge still fringed. On it, in a small bubbly script:

I didn't want to give this to you in front of Aunty. It might make her too sad. But many happy returns, cowgirl. He loved you very much. As do I. Yours fondly, Kavita.

I slipped the book under my pillow and crawled back into bed and got all the way under the sheets and cried longer and harder than I ever had for losing Dadaji. And for always having had Kavita, and never realizing it.

On the back of the envelope, in the same champagne script, a P.S. F.Y.I.

American Born Confused Desi Emigrated From Gujarat House In Jersey Keeping Lotsa Motels Named Omkarnath Patel Quickly Reaching Success Through Underhanded Vicious Ways Xenophobic Yet Zestful
or
American Born Confused Desi Emigrated From Gujarat House In Jersey Kids Learning Medicine Now Owning Property Quite Reasonable Salary Two Uncles Visiting White Xenophobia Yet Zestful

Now you know your ABCDs.

★   ★   ★

So I was an ABCD. Why hadn't anyone told me? Why didn't they put this in those spots where they say race doesn't matter but please check one of the following? Growing up, I was always exing Asian/Pacific Islander, even though I didn't understand why they were treated as the same thing. It would have been so much easier to check an ABCD slot.

American Born Confused Desi. So was I not alone in my confusion? Admittedly, my own C was a capital one at this point. Kavita had surprised me, made me think about my parents, my home, everything all over again—even myself. And of course, she'd made me do a double take on her as well.

Were hers taunting eyes, or just not afraid of looking? Was that a giggle that ridiculed or rather the ballad of uninhibited pleasure? Like me, Kavita ended all her sentences in a question mark, but unlike me, it still sounded as if she knew all the answers and was just acting like she was asking so you wouldn't feel too clueless. Which I definitely did. I got so much wrong these days, it seemed. I wondered if I'd ever be an ABD, like her secret boyfriend.

But for now I was an ABCD. I didn't really know what that meant. But I suppose that was the point.

CHAPTER 9

chicken chat

The next day the sun suffused my room as usual, the automatic sprinkler system rainbowed the air, and the moment I emerged to put the water on my mother chided me for sleeping so late. As if it was life as usual, a typical morning. But not for a House In Jersey girl in my condition.

I awoke with the conviction that my new status as ABCD showed, the same way they say your walk goes funny after you lose it. And frankly, I was overwhelmed. Kavita's gift had turned me to jelly and this fact combined with my parents' suddenly going cupid on me had reduced me to a quivering state of capital C. Was I really so hopeless a case that they were going to have to arrange my love life for me?

But there was one thing I knew even in the midst of all this confusion. No matter what else had changed, one thing had not: Gwyn was the one who would understand, the only one with a comeback in crisis.

So as soon as I got a moment solo I rang up on her cell. But it was only after a couple hours of going directly into voice mail that I finally heard her breathy hello sift through the telephone holes.

—Gwyn! I cried. —Are you all right? Where have you been?

—Oh, I'm sorry, honey, she said giddily. —Manicure. Reverse French, and confetti tips—I just had to run by to show Dyl before my shift! He loves when I go glam—he told me I put the Joy into Joysey. Isn't that sweet?

I couldn't tell if it was sweet, but I could tell she was smiling just thinking about it.

—Gwyn—frock! Why didn't you call me?

—I just explained, I was—

—No, I mean, you know, on my birthday. I really wanted to talk to you.

—Oh, I'm sorry, Dimps. I must have spaced. Anyways, I knew you were doing the family thing, so I hardly thought you'd mind. I guess Dyl and I just got wrapped up in. Things.

—Things?

I shouldn't have asked. I (and probably the rest of the entire staff of the Springfield Starbucks where Gwyn syruped and steamed part-time) then received a little more information than I needed, about how she and Dylan had bumped around like amorous amusement park cars in her basement that night.

—Thanks for sharing, I mumbled.

—Well, if you're going to be that way about it, I suppose I shouldn't have, she said a little testily. I realized then how much I was misdirecting my bad mood, and promptly burst into tears.

—I'm sorry, Rabbit, I sobbed. —It's not that.

Gwyn's voice came undone with concern.

—Hey-hey, honey, are you okay?

—I don't know, Gwyn, I'm just feeling so *emotional*.

—Are you PMSing?

Pre, Post, and Pretty Much always.

—My father, I whispered, even though my mom was out, making a trip to the Jain grocer's and then Shop Rite. — He organized a meeting for me.

—Like for a job?

—More like to make sure I never get a job in my life! A meeting with a *man*, if you know what I mean.

This got her attention.

—*Your father's pimping you out?*

—No, no—a meeting with someone who could maybe be a good husband for me!

—You mean a meeting with, like, a suitable boy?

Finally, she was getting it.

—Yes!

—Wow! Gwyn squealed. —Is he cute?

—What? I said, stunned. —Is he cute? Gwyn, I have no intention of meeting him!

—Excuse me? she cried. —Are you out of your mind? You're a free woman—what the hello's holding you back?

I was dismayed. I knew I was a free woman, but it didn't fill me with a sense of gratitude to the fighters of the revolution or anything; it made me feel like a class A zero. The energy drained out of me like a punctured tea bag and I gave in to the call of the couch, slumping back with a soft thud.

—So you're on his side, I sighed.

—I'm not on his side, honey, she said. —You know you're my number one funky diva. But let's just say I'm on his *wavelength*. And if you ask me, you should hop on, too. Don't you see how perfect this is?

I didn't know what to say, and she began to zealously fill up my blank.

—Dimple, what's the harm in any of it, honestly? If I were you I'd be jumping at the opportunity. Claude, I can barely even imagine it in my situation—the Lillian would be far more likely to hit on my man than introduce me to one.

This was probably true of her mother, but that didn't seem like an argument to head *to* the motherland.

—I know it's a nontraditional way to go about it, Gwyn continued. —Or, I guess, a traditional way, depending on how you look at it—but don't you see? Your parents would never choose someone who could hurt you—there's nothing to be scared of. And bonus: You won't even have to go through the whole meet-the-'rents ordeal! Even *better*, you'll get to connect with your culture. You're so lucky you even have one—all those beautiful things in your house, those princess dresses. I don't know why you don't wear them more.

—Princess? I said. That word hardly seemed like it belonged in the same zip code as me.

—Princess, Gwyn said firmly. —Dimple, you know when we were little, just after I met you, I used to stare for hours at our atlas and where you came from, your family, halfway across the world. I couldn't believe my luck—or maybe your lack of it—that you ended up in plain old Springfield despite all those mountains and oceans and unpronounceable places in between. You're so lucky that you have more than one part of the map that means something to you. I wish I had something like that. A culture, a country.

I was amazed. She was the uncontested queen of any place she walked into, as far as I was concerned.

—Are you kidding? You have Gwyndom!

—No, no. All kidding aside, Dimple. You've got choices.

—Choices? To do what?

—To be traditional or not to be, said Gwyn.

That seemed an easy pick. Who wanted traditional? First of all, if my parents approved of Karsh, there was already something wrong, wasn't there? If there was nothing to disapprove of in a boy then what was there to approve of? Just look at Dylan. And Julian. Who I now thought of with a pang. I didn't want to be with someone who would probably remind me more of the brother I never had than a love object. Half the fun in being with a guy was talking to Gwyn about it. If I were with a suitable boy, what would there ever be to talk about?

—You see, Gwyn said slowly, reverse-twinning my thoughts. —With an Indian boy maybe you can, you know, explore all that stuff. Go kamasutronic, so to speak.

I nodded, but I was feeling battle fatigue and was now thinking the tip of another thought: Or maybe an Indian boy would get that most of us don't know that stuff. That it was a lot of hype. It was the bindi blondes who were all over this scene, not the holelessly nosed Indian girls. Maybe with an Indian boy we could stay at home and eat smelly samosas without Love's Baby Soft and draw moustaches on the milky-skinned girls in the pictures of the pocket Kama Sutra. I could wear chappals instead of pumps and my feet wouldn't hurt anymore. And more than anything, he would understand my photographs, why it was so much easier to make the world black and white than brown. In fact, maybe with an Indian boy nothing would hurt anymore.

But then why did even the thought of it hurt so much? Frock, I wasn't ready for either option. Stuck in the middle with me seemed to be more like where I was at.

—Let me put it this way, Dimpledom, she concluded. —You've got nothing to lose.

I didn't know whether that was a good thing or news to make me seek a hole to crawl into and crunch up in forever. It was probably better to think of it as a good thing, I figured. To be an optimist. After all, though my Earl Grey was three-quarters empty, I could always think of that as being one-quarter full.

Gwyn had shut up, I guess to let the full effect of her advice sink in, but even through the wire I could feel her blue eyes like a new sky on me.

CHAPTER 10

the most unsuitable suitable boy between the hudson and the ganges

You know how sometimes you're having a nightmare that's so real you actually feel the brick grate against your skin as you fall from edge to pavement? You open your mouth to scream, lungs heaving against the thin barrier of skin that separates you from that treacherous world and the waking one, but nothing comes out; you try to run but the sidewalk quicksands, suctioning you heel first. And then—you jolt awake. Reality settles upon you like a comforter and you breathe a sigh of relief as it dawns on you that it was all just a bad dream.

It was precisely like this on the morning of my meeting with The Boy. Except without the waking-up-and-realizing-it-was-all-just-a-bad-dream part.

When I went back to my room from my shower (I'd used only Ivory; The Boy didn't deserve the loofah), laid out on my now-made bed was the dreaded birthday khamees, shamelessly spangling morning all over the room.

So my mother wanted me to wear this? Immediately flinging open my closet I put on the pair of secondhand jeans that Gwyn insisted I buy to wear during the SATs (since all college kids wore them, which would positively affect my test scores) and that I once caught my parents, in a rare act of creative collaboration, attempting to burn. (My father: *Aaray, why are you paying more to be in something somebody else has worn?* My mother: *You do not know where they've been, what things they have been doing in it, what kind of karma they are having! And people will call in for child abuse, saying we are not properly clothing our only daughter!*) My folks loathed these jeans with a passion;

to them they symbolized all that was backwards and unethically casual and mo' money mo' problem about Western culture. I completed my pay-to-look-poor look with a My Parents Went to Cancun and All I Got Was This Lousy T-Shirt (my parents had never been to Cancun, but Bobby's had, which had led to several after-school kissing sessions on his Ping-Pong table and an attempt at below-the-bra-ing that turned into a push-you-pull-me session of not-quite-past-the-ribs-ing). Thus attired for combat, I tentatively opened the door, expecting a bomb to go off as I did.

I could smell the vapors before I even followed my nose into the hallway. Chemical warfare was in full force already: a pungent mix of turmeric and onions and pine-scented cleaners missiled up my nostrils. It was war, I had to remember, and all in war was fair, even more so if love was being so unfair. My ears tintinnabulated with the wall of sound that had slammed me in the face as soon as I'd opened my door. And what met my eyes was nearly a battlefield.

A tornado was wending pell-mellingly through the room. And at its epicenter, whirling madly with the vacuum cleaner in a dervish of such pulsating energy that I was left unclear as to who exactly was leading whom: my mother. The cappuccino peacocks on her housedress tangoed tempestuously around her legs, the trim of tiny bells tinkering in vain against the thunderous roar of the Hoover, like a dropped tea party. Most oddly, her head was wrapped in a plastic bag, all her hair sheathed. Her face bunched, a large brain nervy with stress and excitement.

She was so occupied with taming the bucking vacuum, giddyupping in her domestic rodeo, that she hardly noticed me. When she finally stamped the pedal and looked up, she squinted and put a hand to her lower back and rubbed.

—You're not going out like that, are you? she asked, all *of course, you and I both know this is a joke*. The machine made sybaritic sounds as it purred into submission.

—I'm not even going out, I reminded her. —In case you've forgotten.

—Well, you're not staying *in* like that, I hope.

—Well, are you staying in like *that*?

I hated when I got like this, but I couldn't stop myself. In my head sometimes when I was talking to my parents this weird thing happened where I'd be telling myself to *shutupshutupshutup*, but my mouth would meanwhile connect to a power source all its own and run with it, shorting all my better, kinder impulses.

—Like what? my mother said.

—I mean, what's with the Saran Wrap hat?

My mother touched her head, like people touch their earlobes when you compliment their earrings and they've forgotten which ones they're wearing. Her eyes clacked open.

—Oh! Thanks for reminding me—I've got to go rinse the dye out.

—Dye? Mom, you never dye your hair!

—I know, but there was a two-for-one on L'Oréal and the girl on the package was looking so lovely—such wonderful skin and perfect teeth. I'll show you the box later.

She started scuttling to the bedroom, then turned and eyed me sideways, still moving, like a beach crab.

—I'll be back. Can you turn the stove to low? And for goodness sake, please do me one thing in this life and go change out of those dirty shirty artsy wartsy clothes!

What was up with my mother? Since when did she color her hair? I didn't know if she even had any grey hairs, and certainly not enough to warrant a box of dye. Wasn't she overdoing it just a tad?

Well, if I thought the cleaning was on the overdone side, wait till I got to the kitchen. On the four-range stove at least six pots clamored for attention. An economy bottle of Mazola corn oil—one that could be confused sizewise with a tank of super-unleaded—irradiated to the side, perilously lidless. A high pile of pakoras lay cooling, oil drenching the paper towels between them and plate; in close proximity, a billiard of balls of sesame-flecked kachori awaited the same deep-fried fate. The dubba, the round tin with its heady autumnal rainbow of spices all arranged in doll-sized stainless steel thali dishes, was out and open. A jar of chevda—a sort of Indian trail mix of fried lentil and chickpea crisps mingled with Froot Loops and golden raisins (at least in our home)—had been refilled to the brim. And paper boxes flowery with crimson Hindi script strained at the seams like tight bras, overflowing with laddoos and coconut cutlets from the Jain grocer two towns away.

And I thought this was for "just a cup of tea, nothing fancy schmancy."

I tracked my father down and out in the garden, only to find him in a similar state of hyperbole, though his target was of a horticultural nature: He was pulling weeds with a nearly religious fervor, as if a sack of doubloons was to be found beneath their insidious roots. He wove madly among the marigolds and roses, the gladiolas and geraniums. The first were my mother's favorite; she told me they reminded her of childhood walks with Dadaji to pick fresh flowers for the temple, flowers that had to remain unsmelled until they were offered to the gods in the morning pooja. When she'd place them in the kitchen temple in Bombay (not yet Mumbai), they left a brilliant powdery stain on her hands, as if a butterfly had been caught and clasped there.

Only problem was, in my father's fervor, he was plucking the beloved blooms alongside the weeds. In fact, his overly eager hands were heading towards one unsuspecting petal head right now.

—Daddy, watch it! I cried, with an urgency that surprised me, as if an eighteen-wheeler were headed fast in his direction.

Shaken out of his reverie a moment too late, my father blinked twice at the plucked flower in his hands and suddenly seemed to come to his senses.

—Bacchoodi, he said. —I believe your mother is contagious. I, too, am losing my mind.

★   ★   ★

The marigold wound up floating in a shallow bowl of water on the kitchen counter, where my father was now mixing the spices for the tea masala. He had that exacting scientific expression on his face that was a sure sign whatever he was doing was totally random. But tea was the point, the pretext, after all; it played a principal role in the Indian social ceremony and what would happen during it, and I now eyed the cayenne pepper powder in the dubba and wondered if there was any way I could casually tip it into The Boy's cup, and his mother's, too.

By the time my own mother emerged from her cosmetic experimentations to join us, her hair had taken on a vibrant copper hue. That model must have had *really* good skin for her to choose this titian shade. I figured she didn't even know, since the lighting in her bathroom was more appropriate for outings of a vampiric nature than a light-of-day rendezvous, and I chose not to say anything. I knew my father had some questions of his own; his mouth dropped open, but I think he thought better of letting anything come out of it. My mother seemed pleased; she must have figured we were speechless with amazement, which was true in a sense.

—So, what do you think? she said, doing a demiturn and running a confident hand through her auburn locks. —Do I look all right?

Did *she* look all right? Whose date was this anyways? My father and I nodded dumbly. She looked more than all right. But she was hardly recognizable. The 'do wasn't the only new element to her look: She was definitely wearing base, though in a shade fortuitously closer to her skin tone than the dye was to her hair; it was probably my base, come to think of it. Her lips were lined and lipsticked. A scent of one of her If You Like Gio You'll Love perfumes filled the air. Diamonds flashed like rock candy in her ears; her forearms were gold-plated with bangles, seven to a side. And she was dressed to the T in, nonplussingly, some kind of slinky black wraparound skirt-and-top combo. She looked like a divorcee who'd just gotten her second wind, but my father was beside her, which was reassuring. He opened his mouth again.

—What? she said in a tone that made him shut it.

—Nothing, nothing, he said wisely. —It's just. It's different, that's all.

—What's different?

—Just . . . your . . . *way*.

—I don't get it, I whined. —You get to wear that, but I have to dress like some leftover from the Stone Age?

—Dimple, one day you will understand, said my mother. But I wasn't so sure. When was this much-talked-about day when the flash would suddenly go off in my head and I would say, *Ah! This is why I eat all my vegetables, eschew secondhand clothes, and don't talk to strangers!*

—So I'm looking that good, heh? she grinned.

—Yes! I said. —It's embarrassing. Why do I have to look all traditional and you get to be so modern? I mean, come on, isn't it the other way around?

Then I got it. Sort of. I had a feeling my answer was in my question, though I didn't know quite how to explain it.

—Enough yak-yak, said my mom. —Now please give me a pleasure in this life and get changed. It is such a lovely khamees—Japanese fabric, of course, and all the fashionable girls will be wearing it at Garbha this year; the salesgirl told me herself.

I didn't move. But she did, plunking her fists into her wraparounded hips.

—Dimple Rohitbhai Lala, she said, dropping the sales pitch. —Just put the damn thing on.

My mother seemed a formidable opponent with her new Goth look. And I was exhausted. So I did as I was told. In any case, they could dress me up, but they were definitely not making us go out.

★ ★ ★

Of course, everything was ready well ahead of schedule, so we retired to the living room. My father was now in the rather maroon and certainly daring suit he wore to give speeches at the hospital, no tie—"to keep it casually elegant," said my mother, something she'd seen on a wedding invitation once (not an Indian wedding, that was for sure). The three of us sat stiffly as if we'd been starched and then slipped into our outfits. As if for a portrait. I felt ridiculous in my Arabian Nights getup—like I was about to embark on an all-trick no-treat Halloween.

Let me tell you something about our living room. This term was false advertising taken to the max. I didn't understand why it was called this, as (a) we never went in it, and therefore it was far from "living," and (b) with the nearly ninety percent of all our Indian possessions that had taken up residence there, it was jam-packed (as in, no "room"). These lived together in not so perfect harmony with a few American items, such as the faux leather couches creating a corner at the rosewood statue of an Indian classical dancer in a jiglike pose, part of her shoulder chipped from shipping, breasts honey-dewed over the protruding belly. A pastel painting of boats in a Cape Cod harbor—which my father bought because it was so "pleasant"—stared a hand-sewn Rajasthani mirrored wall hanging in the face with quiet menace, the kind implemented in TV commercials for female douching products. On the elaborately carved writing desk serving and lobbying tennis player figurines proclaimed World's #1 Dad and World's Greatest Tennis Player (Father's Day gifts from me when I was little); the cut-blood green-stippled ashtray I made and glazed in art one year, even though smoking is anathema in the house (or out), teetered on the edge of a teak table inlaid with ele-

** 100 **

phants entwining trunks. And dizzyingly the partially glass-encased sandal-wood chariot with Krishna explaining the Gita to Arjuna perfumed the air beside the wildly untuned piano.

My mother was squinting at my face now, as if my eyebrows had disappeared or something. She snapped her fingers.

—I know what's missing, beta! Why don't you put a bindi on?

—Mom! Why would I put a bindi on? Aren't I looking B.C. enough?

—Why do you put it for artsy wartsy boys and not for a nice Indian boy? she said.

She had me there.

—What did he ever do to you? she continued, striving to look wounded.

He did nothing *for* me already, and he wasn't even here yet. And he would certainly never do anything *to* me, I was about to retort when the bell rang, firing off like the start to a boxing match. In one swift move my mother unpeeled her bindi from her forehead and pressed it smack in the middle of my own.

By swipe two/ring two a dupatta unraveled on my shoulders and my mother was wrapping it around me. By ring three my father was already ushering our guests in the door, and I could hear a woman's voice smoky like a shot cannon.

—Bloody bollocks it's good to see you, Rohitbhai! Getting a bit paunchy around the middle, old fellow, but as adorable as ever! How long has it been? No, don't tell me.

A muffled exchange followed; I couldn't hear my father's response to this astoundingly indelicate greeting. Then I could see them, shadowly approaching in the hallway. I tensed, preparing myself.

In walked The Boy. My mother lunged forward to greet him and for a moment I worried that she would tackle him and pin him to the ground and make him swear never to leave us. But she restrained herself at the last moment, like a car suddenly braking, and lunged back, extending her hand in greeting.

—And you must be Karsh! It is such a pleasure to meet you.

And he—get this!—put his two hands together and said, in a faintly accented voice:

—Namaste, ji.

Eek! That was about as far from a *Whassup* as you could get on the audible greeting spectrum.

My mother had told me namaste means *my respect to you*. But my father said it was just easier to put your hands together than always having to remember to shake only with the right in India (the left was used in place of the Charmin, or, as he put it, "for daily ablutions"). His translation of the prayering palms: You don't touch my hands, I won't touch yours, and everyone will be happy.

And I was certainly going nowhere near this boy's hands, or any other part. He was nothing to write home about (we were home already, but still): He was tallish for an Indian guy, but pretty average for an American. He wore a pair of chinos (pleated!) and a loose white shirt that had definitely been made in India. If he had a marital ad, it would have said this: Strikingly average guy seeks fashion consultant. Average height, average weight, average features (save the brows, which were bushy and close to his eyes, giving him a glowering look). Average style sense—okay, the Nikes were slightly on the cool side of average, being the ones with the boingg and a racy red, but I quickly wrote that off as trying too hard.

Vaguely more interesting was the woman beside him. Dun-colored flats. A pair of crisp khakis (what was it with these people and khaki?), belted in tight around a dragonfly waist. Pinstriped oxford, behind which a string of brown acornlike beads hung. Bob of black hair gone wack with double cowlicks. One cowlick was almost working for her, though, and swung a solidly silver chunk of hair across a side of her roundish face, which was balanced on a surprisingly delicate chin. Her eyes were as merrily intent as the squirrel with the nut. And she was now focusing them on me.

—Dimple, I'd like you to meet Radha, said my mother. —Radha, this is our daughter, Dimple.

No namaste for me; I made a point to shake Radha's hand. Her grip was swift and strong and she pumped my hand once as if drawing water from a well. Her nails were unpainted and tidy, the whites beginning low down on the pinks, a sure sign of a one-time biter. This detail pleased me for some reason.

—Dimple, it is a most wonderful pleasure! she smiled brightly. —And this is my son, Karsh.

—Hi, I said, shoving my hands quickly into my pockets. Karsh had extended one of his, and it hung now uselessly in the air before finding its way back into his own pocket, where it dug deep. Then he pulled it out in a quick fist and said:

—Once, twice, three—shoot!

Dork! I just stared at him.

—Well, hi, Dimple, he said, finally. One side of his mouth was up in a smile, as if he wasn't really sure how he felt.

—Hey, I said.

—Dimple, aren't you going to show everyone in? said my mother, which seemed odd, considering we were all in by now, crowding the entry to the living room as if blocked by an invisible bouncer.

—Well, here we are, I said.

—Great place, said Radha.

—Come in, come in, said my father. —Make yourself at the home.

My mother made a great show of taking off her shoes before stepping back into the living room (though they'd been on a moment before), which she does sometimes to encourage non-Western guests to do the same. But there was no need to hint with these people. Karsh had already boingged out of his sneaks and Radha kicked off her mules. My father placed all the footwear on the porch with ours, and then we were all barefoot and stagnant in the living room.

My parents sat on the sofa, coy at opposite ends, politely leaving room in the middle for whoever dared join them. Nobody did. I took the loveseat, then immediately regretted it, wrought as it was with implications, but much to my relief, Radha bounded over and joined me. Karsh headed towards the piano.

—Oh, no! my mother cried. —Not the bench for you, Karsh—please, come sit here and be comfortable.

—I'm fine, Aunty, said Karsh, straightening his spine as if to prove it.

—No, no, I will not have this. You know the guest is god in an Indian household. I insist.

Karsh smiled that half-smile again, where I couldn't tell if he was pleased or teasing, and went over and sat between them. My parents must have been about to pee in their pants for joy: Here I was, cozily sardined in beside my future mother-in-law; there he was with his future folks. And the two of us, face to face over a replete table. It couldn't have been more perfectly orchestrated if there had been place settings.

A small silence rose up into the room, which my mother immediately and nervously broke.

—Eat, eat! she cried, leaping up and whirling around the table as if casting a spell. She carefully chose the fattest juiciest pakoras for Karsh, scooting them onto his plate, and the next best for Radha, and then whatever might be left over for my father and me. Finally, the overfrieds went into her own dish.

—Sit down already, Shilpz, said Radha. —We're not invalids, my dear, we can help ourselves. This is just a casual little *snack*, right? Nothing fancy schmancy—you said so yourself.

My mother thunked down sheepishly, looking uncomfortable, as usual, being still. Her hands twisted in her lap as if she were knitting.

—Now that's better! said Radha. —I can take a good look at you!

She cocked her head.

—Did you change your hair or something?

—No, said my mother too quickly.

—It looks . . . reddish.

—It's always been like that, said my mother.

—I never noticed back home, said Radha.

—The summer sun here brings it out, said my mom. —Karsh, beta, kachori?

—Versus the sun in India? said Radha. —I must be going color-blind. I didn't even notice in CVS the other day. In any case, it looks smashing.

—Um, thanks, said my mother. She was looking a lot less Goth. She gestured now to Radha's silver chunk. —And *your* hair's changed, too.

—Indeed, I'm going grey as a geezer, said Radha. —But I quite like it. My son here refuses to let me dye it.

—It shows off her tan, said Karsh smiling. —And the blessed day it goes all white maybe people will stop confusing her for my sister. It gets kind of embarrassing when we hang out at NYU.

—They confuse you for his sister? said my mother.

You guys hang out at NYU? I thought, but what I said was:

—They do that all the time with us, too.

Silence the sequel ensued, which made my father scratch his leg.

—So! he said.

—So! said Radha.

—So, said my mother.

It sounded like part of a rap. I nearly wanted to join in with a *So! Yo! Ho!*

—So tell us what you've been up to, Shilpa! It's been a long time.

—No, no, you tell me what *you've* been up to, Radha! said my mother with exactly the same intonation. She had on that fixed smile that made the words whittle through her teeth.

—Oh, you know, same old ob-gyn deal. I've delivered so many grandchildren at this point—maybe one of these days I'll have my own?

She looked twinklingly at Karsh, who rolled his eyes.

—And I'm doing some volunteer work with Shakti—that New York shelter for Asian women who are victims of domestic violence. It's really a fantastic group.

My mother nodded politely. Radha leaned back and popped an entire pakora in her mouth.

—And you? she said in the middle of full-on mastication.

—Oh, you know, said my mother, tittering nervously. —Keeping busy. This and that. I don't know where my day goes, I seem to always have so much to do.

She had a funny tight look on her face, like when we run into the neighbors in the supermarket, or see friends with not-so-cute babies.

—But enough about me. And anyways, Dimple keeps me busy, don't you, beta? You know what it's like with a daughter.

—No, I don't, said Radha, swallowing the last morsel and smiling broadly. —But bloody hell, I would very much like to.

She stage-winked me, biting down on an imaginary carrot on the winking-eye side of her face. Then she picked up the tray and handed it to me.

—Laddoo?

I took one, just to have something to hold onto. The milk sweet rolled heavily, smoothly in my palms.

—So I understand your field of study is the computers, Karsh? said my father. Karsh nodded, confirming his status as Strikingly Average Boy Who Is Also Computer Geek.

—Is it the software you are doing? my mother joined in, venturing into unknown territory.

—I do 3D renderings and graphics. And I'm trying to squeeze in as much time as possible on midi and sound production, too.

My parents nodded as if they got it. Me, I'd dropped the compass.

—So far so good—I'm really enjoying it all, he went on, like I really gave a frock. —There's still time to change my mind, but I doubt I will. Technically, I don't have to decide till next year.

—By which time I will have lost my baby to New York City, sighed Radha dramatically. —In just a couple months, in fact.

—You'll never lose me, said Strikingly Average Boy Who Is Computer Geek And Mama's Boy To Top It Off. —I'm just moving across the river, not across the country. And even then.

—Aaray, how sweet. Dimple, did you hear that?

—I'm only across the room, Ma, not across the country, I said.

Karsh grinned.

—And Dimple, what are you thinking? said Radha.

—You'll never lose him, I said, hoping the sinister implication that things would never work out between us was coming through static-free. But my voice ended in a question mark, as usual.

—No, no! Radha said. —What are you considering *doing*. You'll be finished with high school soon, right? You must be thinking a little about what you want?

—Oh, I don't know about that.

—You mean you haven't figured your whole life out yet?

Her eyes jingled with laughter, but I didn't know if she was laughing at, with, or just very near me.

—Well, I . . . I'm trying to work on my, well, photography this summer, I blurted out.

—Dimple is an honors student, my mother hastily added.

—So is that what you want to be, then, a photographer? Radha asked, her regard focused keenly on me.

—I like taking pictures, if that's what you mean, I said, fidgeting nervously. Why was Karsh staring at me like that? I passed the coconut cutlets to him to give him something else to look at, and he promptly got up and brought them to my mother, who now accepted her first one, everyone else having had two already. —But I don't know if I could make a living—

—So you're doing what you like and liking what you do, Radha interrupted. —Well, that's the first step, and the last step, and all the steps in between for the road to real happiness. It has very little to do with the money, Dimple—it's just how seriously you take it.

—Baapray, all this talk, said my mother, on the verge of biting down on the syrupy pink-swirled sweet. She looked annoyed, but more at Radha than me for some reason. —It's just a phase, isn't it, beta.

And one that like a tiny benign tumor would probably go away with time, was the implication. My mother's voice was nearly pleading, and I felt bad, so I nodded.

—Is it just a phase? said Radha, this time watching my mother. —Like you and your dancing, Shilpa?

My mother's eyes widened but she caught herself in time.

—Yes, she said firmly. She put the cutlet down, unbitten. —That was just a phase. What I wanted to do was medicine. So I did. I *chose* to do that.

—It's a shame you gave up medicine then, said Radha. —Bloody hell, you were such a goddamn good dancer, Shilpz! I was so surprised you didn't continue with it.

—How could I when I came here? said my mother. —There were no teachers, no schools.

—You could have taught, you were so good, Radha insisted. —High hell, even I still dance—for myself, really—but I was never as talented as you.

My mother looked pleased and panicky at the same time, like someone getting an award with no speech prepared. And I, who'd never seen her do much more than occasionally tap her foot to the beat, was doing a major rewind.

—Mom, you were a dancer?

She didn't say anything.

—Did she dance? Radha snorted. —Did she *dance*? Dimple, my dear, your mother was a serious sole-stomping prizewinning Bharat Natyam babe back in the day!

—Indian stuff?

—Not just Indian stuff. The foxtrot, ballroom. You name it. But yes, above all, Indian stuff.

—Prizewinning? I cried.

—Multiple, nodded Radha.

—Dad, did you know this?

—Of course! How do you think I fell for this woman in the first place?

—Well, why doesn't anyone talk about it?

—Oh, it's not worth talking about, said my mother. —It's been too many years.

—It's never too late, said Radha. —Not for someone as gifted as you.

—Sometimes it is, Radha, said my mother in a way that made Radha bite her tongue.

My mother was now clearly and completely panicking for some reason. Her eyes fell, as they often did in this sort of social situation, on the piano. And then it was my turn to sweat.

My parents always used the piano to fill the silence, sometimes even when it was just the three of us. But with the way I played, you'd soon be wishing for silence again. Admittedly, I could do a mean version of "Chopsticks," the bottom part to "Heart and Soul," and the right hand to most anything without the black keys. But that was about it.

Everyone followed my mother's gaze, and then the dreaded question was asked.

—Do you play, Dimple? asked Strikingly Average Computer Geek/ Mama's Boy With Amazing Ability To Say Just The Right Thing. He got up and went to sit at the piano. I realized then the lid was still up from when Kavita had been over; it had been a long time since the keys had been in view.

—Yes, said my mother, grasping at a straw, at the same time that I cried:

—No!

—Of course you do, said my mother. —All that money we spent on Mrs. Lamour. Go on, why don't you play us something.

Sweat pooled in the hollows above my nostrils. I'd taken piano lessons for two years exactly. Five years ago. Mrs. Lamour had one eye and her husband was constantly raking; I could see him out the window when I did my scales. Mrs. Lamour was, however, more concerned with the state of my curtsy than that of my chords prior to my first recital. I was to perform a simplified version of "Für Elise." And the day of the performance, I sat at the piano and froze. My mind: blank as a weekend chalkboard. Then I jumped up and did what I did best: ran to the corner edge of the stage and dove into an impassioned knee-splitting curtsy. A little too impassioned, I suppose, as I promptly fell off the stage. Luckily, "stage" was a grand term for what would probably be more accurately described as a slight modulation in the floor plane, and there was no external damage other than a scraped knee. But my ego had suffered third-degree burns; I didn't think I'd yet recovered from them.

—I love that one, "Free Elise," my father piped up.

—I really don't think I should, I said, enunciating each word carefully in case they didn't understand English all of a sudden, which happened sometimes in conversations like these (they never forgot how to speak it, just how to hear it). I could feel the terror mounting up the hole in my spine, like a malevolent rock climber. This was worse than those getting-caught-naked-in-class dreams—and when it was my chubster body we were talking about, that was saying something.

—Oh, come on, Dimple, be a sport, said my father. —What were all those piano lessons for?

—For learning a well-executed curtsy, I said, then prayed he wouldn't ask me to at least do that, then.

I thought I heard a snort. Was Babe the Pig in the room? Both Karsh and Radha burst out laughing.

—I really don't remember it, I said.

—Well, isn't the music in the seat? said my mother. —Karsh, can you take a look, beta?

Karsh got up and opened the bench a crack and peered in. He furrowed his already furrowed brow.

—No, he said, sighing. —Bummer. It's empty.

—Empty? Are you sure?

—With a capital M, he said, setting the lid carefully down then sitting on it. Whew!

—You must have put them all in the study, said my mother accusingly to my father, who, whether he'd done them or not, readily admitted to things when blamed.

—Well, in any case, there's no fear of falling from there, I said.

—At Dimple's first recital she, er, panicked and fell from the stage, my mother responded to Radha's upraised brows.

—Then why the bloody bollocks are you asking her to play, yaar? cried Radha. I liked this woman. Could I just take her for a mother-in-law and skip the son part?—Still a perfectionist as ever!

—She only scraped her knee a little, my mother said, pouting.

—Oh, never mind, no biggie, said Karsh. —I just asked 'cause I've always loved the piano.

—Do you know how to play? my father inquired.

—I'm not sure, said Karsh.

—Excuse me?

—Well, I've never really tried, so I don't know whether I can play or not.

Strikingly Average Smart Aleck. But the heat was off me, so I'd let this one go.

—Karsh does not play the piano, said Radha. —Yet. But he plays the tablas and harmonium and flute and a little bass, don't you, rajah? He has trained on tablas for—how many years now? I can hardly remember. When he was still very small he was taken in under the tutelage of Zakir Mehra, who happened upon him helping cook dinner one night—you know we always had these sorts of people over because of my husband's involvement in the entertainment world. Zack told Karsh that he chopped baingan like a true percussionist.

Now it was Karsh's turn to have a *Mom, puh-leeze* look on his face. But when he said the mother part, it wasn't really bitter, more like a gentle protest. Passive resistance?

—You may be vying with them for his attention, Dimple, said Radha in an amped whisper. —He's very passionate about his drums.

—Mother! Karsh said now; he still didn't seem angry but he did a side-to-side with his head, then lifted his hands in a surrender.

—I've heard of Zakir Mehra, said my father. —He is a classical player, no? So Karsh is classically trained?

—That's right, Radha beamed.

Classically trained? The next thing you knew he'd be telling us he listened to Lata Mangeshkar! She was this really annoying Indian singer with a voice so shrill it could double-pierce your ears and leave hoops hanging.

—The next thing you will be saying is you like Lata Mangeshkar! said my father excitedly. What did I tell you?

The only reason I knew about Lata Mangeshkar was, well, she was one of the only two crooners to know about, apparently. I was under the impression that she and her stridently similar sister Asha Bhonsle had a monopoly over all the songs in the Indian movie industry (either that or all the female singers were trained by the same whinging voice coach). They also had a monopoly on my father's record collection and video bootlegs from Jackson Heights.

—Gotta love Lata, said Karsh perking up. —But I'm equal for Asha —she rocks!

Rocks. Not the word I would have chosen, but hey, liberty for all. So he loved Sister Squawk. No, not Madonna or U2 or something cool—even the Beatles, who everyone pretended to be so over but then sang along to, even the "Hey Jude" outro intact, when they happened to strum up on the radio or in an elevator. But Lata and Asha. My father had already darted out of the room, no doubt to rouse them. Frock, Kavita wasn't kidding when she said Karsh was involved in the Indian community! I mean, *South Asian*.

—He listens to all my records, Radha announced. —And I have a sneaking suspicion that when he moves out next semester, I might find more than a few empty slots on the rack.

Hello? So the Strikingly Average Boy listened to his mother's records?

—For me nothing beats the excitement of the needle touching down, Karsh went on. —All that fizz and dust and then—bam! Music!

Then date your stereo, I thought.

—I didn't know Lata Mangeshkar was even still moving, I said now, wondering whether we should phone a paleontologist, quick.

—In this case, what you don't know *can* hurt you, Karsh replied. Add Smug and Self-Satisfied to that list.

My mother and Radha were looking left, right, left, watching us as if we were the Wimbledon semifinals incarnate. Luckily, just then my father came staggering back into the room with a colossal cardboard box.

—This is wonderful! he said, struggling slightly to keep his grip. —I rustled up my records. Would you like to see them? Imports, exports. Deports.

—Are you kidding? I'd love to! said Karsh, jumping to it to help him.

The two sat down cross-legged on the floor. My father suddenly looked twenty years younger, his spine unfolding like a ladder up a building. What ensued was an enthusiastic conversation about which tunes (if that's what you call a gnat on helium in your ear, except with a chorus) they liked best, which movies ("fill-ums" as my father called them) they rated at the top. That they could tell them apart stunned me; I'd drifted off to sleep and back the last time we were on a flight to India, and for the life of me I hadn't been able to tell if the actresses leaping around palm trees in the Ooty rain (and seconds later, pyramids in the Egyptian sun) were part of the same interminable fill-um or whether I was watching something else altogether. And the fact Karsh got my dad's inscrutable references wigged me out even more.

But, as it turned out, Karsh owned pretty much all the same music as my father.

His toes curled up and down while he talked, like my father's did when he prayed. I couldn't believe what a loser this guy was. I mean, he was chilling with my dad! Wasn't he supposed to be paying attention to me?

My father was flushed and nearly breathless by the time they lifted their heads from the LPs and CDs, like two divers coming up for air.

—Well, this is just terrific. I would call this a cause to celebrate. Would anyone like a drink?

—No thanks, said Karsh. Figured. —I'm going to be driving back later.

My mother nodded approvingly.

—Whaddaya got? said Radha.

—We've got water, ginger ale, cranberry juice, or . . . —here my father took a deep breath. —Red wine.

My mother looked at my father. He stared pointedly up at the boats sailing off the coast of the Cape.

—It's already open, he told a commodious pastel yacht. —From Kavita's visit.

—Hellfire and spitstone, I'd love a glass, Radha declared. —We don't want it to go to waste. Like I always say, think of all the sober people in India, goddammit!

My mother almost forgot to look horrified, but caught her giggle just in time, using it to purse her lips instead.

—I'll go get it!

My father jumped with his newfound energy and was off.

—Oh come on, Shilpz, lighten up! cried Radha. —Haven't you read the studies? They found the French are even healthier from drinking a glass of wine now and then.

—We're not French.

—And you're just now realizing this? Blustery bollocks! Then you definitely need a drink, Shilpoo!

This time my mother unpursed a millisecond.

My father was already filling the glasses—milk glasses, but that was cool; it meant they'd hold more. He even put a toast-adequate serving in Karsh's and in mine. And when he raised his glass—

To the beginning of a beautiful old friendship!

—even my mother took a sip.

CHAPTER 11

the world isn't black and white

Then an interesting thing happened. A full-on trip down memory lane ensued, filled with remember-the-times and whatever-happened-to-so-and-sos. The emptier the glasses got, the further they went, the more visibly relaxed my mother became—and the less I knew what the frock they were talking about. This was also due to the fact that more and more Hindi and Marathi and Gujarati words began to nest in the conversation, like lost birds migrating home, until there was hardly any English left.

It felt strange listening to them, like they'd all shared another time, another planet, and you really had to have been there to get it. They were nearly giddy, in fact, all three of them. When they laughed it was together now. It was gut-clutch laughter. It almost reminded me of Gwyn and me.

Their voices became a constant comforting drone in my ears, like a fridge in a room when you're just getting hungry or the whirring summer night itself, now beginning to unleash its insect orchestra. But Karsh was watching them intently, drinking up every word. And I was watching Karsh. He was so interested in them and everything they were saying he almost didn't look average anymore. There was a flame in his face.

He must have felt my eyes on him because he looked up at me and smiled, rolling his own eyes in the reminiscers' direction. But I knew he wasn't really making fun of them. And I rolled my eyes back, but I wasn't really making fun of him. And he didn't look away. I wasn't used to being stared at, except by myself, critically, in the mirror. He wasn't looking at me critically, though. I don't know how he was looking at me, but it didn't make me feel bad. It made me feel funny, but it didn't make me feel bad.

The grandfather clock chimed nine. For a day I wished had never begun, it suddenly seemed it had all gone by too fast.

—Blistering brimstone, look at the time! Radha cried, stretching her arms, then following them up. She got halfway there before slumping back onto the couch. On a re-try she made it to vertical (well, seventy-five degrees). —All that wine. All those memories. And all that *wine*. Bloody hell, I definitely need a smoke now.

Smoke? I couldn't believe it. It was just one thing after another with these people. Smoking was a sin more dire than premarital—or even marital—sex in our home.

—Oh, I'm sorry, Radha, this is a nonsmoking house, said my mother.

—No don't worry, Shilpz, I remember your bidi policies, Radha said, her words sluicing off the edge of her smile. —Though unless I am going senile there *was* a time you were a bit more lenient now and again . . .

She chortled, sluggishly big-winking my mother, a strange thing to see at this speed; she already had a cigarette in her wavering hand, unlit. My mother looked startled.

—In any case, we've got to hit the road, *Jack*. But thank you once more—this has been bloody *fantastic*. Seeing you two again, and meeting you at last, Dimple—that was the *pista* on my *kulfi*, the *keshar* in my *lussi*, the—

—Come on, Ma, said Karsh, laughing and putting an arm around her to steady her. —What's say we get your *head* on the *pillow*.

In the foyer, as they were saying their aawjos, Karsh's eyes fell upon the gruesomely exhibited display-rack photos. For an unblinking moment it seemed he was contemplating the sheer horror of it all, and my spirits lifted. So maybe there was *one* thing we could have in common—and actually, this was a pretty important one. Perhaps *the* most important, as far as I was concerned.

—Now *that*, he said finally, lifting his palms and gesturing at the shelf. —*That's* what I call a picture, Dimple.

—How *sweeeet*, yaar, Radha slurred, taking a stumbling peek over his shoulder. —Puppies and babies and husbands with wives. Aaray, Baba—if only the world were like *this*.

She looked alarmingly close to tears, and Karsh gripped her more strongly.

The golden retriever nearly woofed. The bride and groom came close to consummation. And I was about to spew my vital organs. Could it get any worse?

No. This time, it really couldn't.

Of course my parents, triumphantly nudging each other, looked inordinately pleased at these shiny happy people we didn't know and dog we didn't own brightening up our home, casting an auspicious glow on the events of today's tea.

—Yes! my father cried. —Karsh, you are making my day. I told Dimple myself, the same very thing—now *that's* what I call a picture. Enough with the black-and-white kachra—the world isn't black and white.

—I'd have to agree there, said Karsh. He was now so far into the negative pointage I couldn't keep up. Or down.

—Yeah, who needs Ansel Adams, right? I said caustically.

—That's right! Karsh concurred, quite forcefully. —Who needs Ansel Adams?

For some reason, this really depressed me.

—Yes, you see? my mother piped in. —See how pleasing this is to the eye? Pictures with colors in them. Pictures with *people* in them. *Glossy* pictures. Not like that matte splat tomfoolery with the heads chopped off—and they wonder why there is so much violence in this society!

This was an unmistakable reference to that shot of Gwyn and the philosophy book. ("Even when you have the beautiful Gwyndolyne in your photograph you focus on the book—I just don't get it.")

Now I was on the verge of tears.

When they were on the porch, sneaked and muled up, Karsh did his yogic thing again, clasping his hands together.

—Aunty and Uncle, the pleasure was all mine, he said. —And that goes for you, too, Ms. Lala.

—Did you *really* and *truly* like those photographs? I said, nearly pleadingly. I needed to know the entire world was not insane.

He looked me in the eyes, then gave me the sure staccato nod that sent my heart plummeting.

—Loved them, he said.

My parents waved them off. I watched through the screen as a little way down the path—to the rhythm of my mother's tongue-clucking *And a doctor, too! She should know better by now*—they stopped and Karsh pulled out a matchbook with one hand, the other still in his pocket, and in a two-fingered flick of the stick into flame lit Radha's cigarette for her. I couldn't believe it. This was taking mother/son bonding too far. Granted, that two-finger flick could have been pretty cool if, say, Julian did it. Julian was an artist. He knew the difference between a film and a movie. He appreciated Ansel Adams. And therefore he had had the potential to appreciate, if not the whole, at least a smidgenny modicum of me.

In theory.

They were in the car. And then—in a puff of smoke and sputter—they were gone.

★   ★   ★

It was only after they'd left and the three of us went into the kitchen that we saw all the cups on the counter, raring to go.

—Oh no, my mother said.

We'd never drunk the tea.

And then my parents did something they never did at moments like this: They burst out laughing. My mother even laughed so hard she started crying. So much so that I went over and hugged her, and then my father came and took us both in his arms, so that we were like a football huddle before the big game. And she just kept crying like this, her laughter hiccupping out through her tears, a smell of salt and sadness and faraway places mixing with the perfume of the marigold, fully open, unafraid, blazing a small fire on our kitchen counter.

durga rising

I was itching to declare the all-cons no-pros mental list I'd now compiled to anyone who cared to listen to make clear beyond unreasonable doubt that there was no way in hello I'd ever date Karsh. But after the utterly unsuitable boy and the whimsical woman who birthed him left, my father was in his own impenetrable world; he had returned to the living room with the remainder of the Beaujolais and was blasting Lata after Lata through the house like a rebellious teenager—except the rebellion was, in American terms, more Gilbert and Sullivan than thrash. And in the kitchen a tangible sense of gloom settled over my mother like a thickening layer of dust after a desert windstorm; it was a mood she seemed to guard carefully. At first I figured she was just exhausted from all her frying and trying, and the crying, but she even refused to let me help her clean up.

—No, no, Dimple, it will be more efficient if I do it alone. You don't even know where half the things go.

—Of course I do, Ma! Why don't you take a break and hang out with Daddy? You must be spent.

She looked it; her skin was almost pale, wet sand gone dry.

—Just . . . I need to be alone a minute. Can I please be alone a minute?

A shrill voice seemed to echo my mother's request, translating it into a squall of sitar-studded veena-thrummed Hindi accompanied by a drumbeat like a cloudburst window. My mother threw her hands over her ears, the way Hear No Evil Uncle, an old friend of the family from Bangalore, did whenever Hush-Hush Aunty (that one-woman information superhighway) gave my mother the scoop on the neighborhood.

—That music is giving me a migraine. Could you go tell your father to turn it down? And please just stay out of my way. I have a lot to do.

So I stayed out of her way. I went into the living room, wondering what she was so upset about. Shouldn't she have been on cloud nine? Her dream guests had come over, her cooking had been a hit, and as far as she knew I wasn't internally hurling at the thought of hooking up with Karsh. She did often stress when we had visitors over, as if they might hold a smudge on the bathroom mirror against us, but this was extreme.

It saddened me, how unreachable she could suddenly become; it was like those times she reverted to Marathi when shouting to be heard through the wire to the family in India. Sometimes she used Hindi or Gujarati with my father, too, though usually only when it was serious business that needed discussing, like when Dadaji fell. At these moments I felt she was leaving me, tongue first—not only leaving me, but that perhaps she had never fully been with me in the first place. And the times we couldn't seem to connect even in English were the worst by far. They reminded me of how when things got bad with Bobby it had been more lonely in his arms than when I was all by myself.

My father was lying feet up on the tasseled armrest of the sofa, lids down, face loose in a good dream. His expression floated just above the skin. I tiptoed to the stereo to lower the volume. The second I did, he opened his eyes with a start.

—Sorry, Dad, I said.

—Oh, no worries, bacchoodi, he sighed, stretching like a cat who's slept in a warm place. —I wasn't asleep— I was just enjoying the afternoon all over again in my mind. That Karsh is simply fantastic, don't you think?

—Oh, Daddy, don't get started, okay, I said. —I agreed to meet him, I met him, and now my duty's done, right? Wasn't that the deal?

—Deal? You talk about it like this is some kind of Brando-Pacino arrangement. There is no Indian mafia. Well, at least not in New Jersey.

As far as I could see the Indian Marriage Mafia—that chain of garishly attired aunties and uncles who placed ads in insider papers and gathered at weddings, holding up tiny Instamatics and aiming just past the bride and groom to their single siblings and cohorts—was alive and kicking, spreading the word nationwide and 24/7 through a fastidiously organized network of cab drivers and poojas, newspaper kiosks and Garbhas. Information was encoded everywhere: trapped in the airy center of the puri, the photocopied cover of a bootleg Bollywood video, the proportion of spices in the pot of masala tea—and sent to every end of America and India, resulting in all sorts of so-called destined unions, including the recent mysterious reunion of a mother with a single son and med school friends with a single daughter in a small New Jersey town just after said daughter was caught nacho-handed in her first full-on hangover.

Coincidence? I thought not. It was definitely a conspiracy.

The music ended and hissed in that secret space between song and needle lift; the arm settled into place and the record spun slowly to a stop, like a tire on a fallen bicycle.

I needed to talk to Gwyn pronto—once she heard all the grisly details she'd hardly be into Project Motherland anymore. But when I left the room, unspiraling the cord straight into the hallway and called her, the phone just kept ringing and even the machine with her breathy Marilyn message didn't click on. Incommunicado. Maybe she was on call waiting and not picking up (something I'd gotten used to relatively recently; Dylan apparently didn't like to be interrupted when he was talking to her—time was money and money was scarce enough, yadda ya).

It was difficult to breathe in the bristling quiet of the house, a silence more acute after having had Radha and Karsh over. So I took a walk around the block to Gwyn's, but no lights there, the double drive doubly empty.

I didn't feel like going home just yet, so I crossed through the strip of pine and fern and went out to the bridge and sat down, dangling my legs off the edge. It felt funny being back here; after my crazy afternoon, the world on the other side seemed miles away. The day was closing down now; a sliver of it danced on the water and I could see the raft, board bobbing as if someone had just dived off. But I waited and waited and no one came up for air.

I guess I'd have to wait till tomorrow to talk to her.

When I got home there was just that one light burning in the study. I kicked off my shoes and went inside. In the family room a laundry basket of ghostly white handkerchiefs and undershirts banked silently high as night snow.

My father had moved out of the living room, no doubt with my mother's sure hand guiding his somnolent steps back to the bedroom, where he probably now lay snoring his deep hoarse birdsong into her feathery sleep. I moved quietly past and on towards the study to switch off the light. But a slight movement, a muted sound, made me soften my step still more. I hung back at the doorway and peered inside.

In the burning halo of the single bulb was my mother, kneeling in her brown-peacocked nightdress before one of the buckling blue trunks. It was open, the weak-hinged lid angling back against the bookshelves for support, and she was staring deep into it, her hands moving over something and body gently swaying. She was singing softly under her breath, a muffled melody, the words turning husky on the high notes, gravelly on the low. She had a sad happy look gazing into the big blue box and with the hum and the sway and the hour it was as if there might be a baby there, a child having trouble sleeping, who she was whispering into the rocking arms of a lullaby.

I slipped deeper into the passage shadows and waited. She seemed so alone, like that time in Central Park; I felt afraid to disturb her. It was almost as if she were having a vision and a word from our ordinary world might break the concentration required to hold it.

My mother's voice was as sweet and faint as a memory of a song. The melody seemed familiar even to me, and I waited till finally her breath ran out on a note and did not begin again, till I heard the creak of the trunk lidding down. I turned into the bathroom. Till the click of the lights off and the fading footsteps. When she was upstairs and the tooth-brush face-wash water sounds had subsided and I was sure her ear was to my father's nighttime warble, I shifted into the study and switched the light back on.

My heart pounded in my throat as I lifted the lid of the trunk, going slowly so it wouldn't squeal. When I looked inside, I saw fabric, a blue-violet sea swaddling high of it, and when I ran my hands through it, they caught in bells and jingly things. A blood orange top, which seemed a sari garment for a svelte person, lay unhooked under the indigo furl, and then a piece that creased softly open like a fan; almost everything carried a rich gold brocade, save for a pair of leggings. I lifted the silken sheets and the bells shimmered fairy rain in my ear. A scent of must and tea rose and, with a soft clang: bangles, armlets, a pouch of rings; heavily jutting choker and longly tangled gold chain; a headpiece made of precious metal and stone, and two open pendants, one a circle, the other a crescent; swung amulet earrings with thin chains ending in hairpins, and what looked like a massive medieval belt that sank silver into the folds in the trunk still.

Digging deeper I came across what seemed to be the primary source of the enchanted broken-ballerina music: Two short thick stretches of dark brown fabric lay flat on the bottom of all that treasure, every inch stitched up with thumbelina gold bells.

I had never seen these before, any of it, in fact, even when I was little and would spend hours playing with my mother's jewelry box, hiding in the special part of her closet among the salvars and saris and satin skirts. The jewelry here was almost like that of the dancing girl statue in the living room, carved in painstaking detail on her bare rosewood body. And when I made this connection I made another one and realized what it was, what it had to be: the costume my mother must have worn as a young woman in India, when she and Radha were sole-stomping, prizewinning Bharat Natyam dancing girls. When her belly was still flat and she had never dreamed of leaving. When it wasn't too late and the music was just beginning.

CHAPTER 13

queens for a day

I was nearly unhemming out my skin wanting to talk to Gwyn about my close brush with geekdom (AKA Karsh). She'd left me a message instructing me to meet her at the Astor Place Starbucks (a few blocks from Dylan's new pad) at 10 A.M. sharp. She had a day off—I suppose from Dylan as much as her own coffee shop gig—and inspired by the rakhis, which had received two thumbs up from the critics ("kamasutronic," per Julian; "puts the In in Indian," according to Dylan), wanted to drag me along to shop for more "exotic" goods. Normally this wouldn't have been my cup of chai, if you will, but getting Gwyn to myself was such a rarity, and I had so much to tell her, that I nearly had the butterflies waiting. However, my hopes were swatted down as ten o'clock came and went, and then eleven, and then even half past.

Her cell was going directly into voice mail, too. I was contemplating how to find Dylan's apartment; I had no idea where it was, and even if I did, wasn't sure I was up for the possible reunion with Julian going there might entail.

I had just returned from the pay phones when the Gwynster herself catapulted into the room, landing in a fell swoop in the seat across from me, all aflutter. Her cheeks were pink as in a little kid's drawing and her hair was turbaned in white fabric. It was a Bad Hair Day trick—in fact inspired by Jimmy (Trilok) Singh—that made it look to all observers as if she were having a Cutting Edge one. From underneath the frayed edge I could see her goldilocks frizzing frenetically; she'd had no time to smooth in her special serum from roots to ends. She'd clearly been in a rush, though probably only I could tell: Her lips were glossed instead of lined and painted; a dash of glitter winked on her brow bone, but not a stroke of mascara to her lashes.

She was in a pair of slightly too big jeans that she'd rolled up to just above her plastic-flower–fronted flip flops, and a slightly too loose I Love New York T-shirt that she'd pulled through the neck hole to turn into a kind of urban-Western halter.

—Sorry I'm late, Boopster, she panted cloyingly. The rakhis flashed upon one wrist as she pointed out the other on which her Swatch boldly and erroneously declared 8:15 A.M. —My watch stopped.

So I could sue Swatch instead. I tried to quell my annoyance.

—Well, let's not lose any more time, I said, standing. She saluted me.

—On to Exotica Central! she proclaimed.

Outside, Gwyn took my arm when I turned towards the train.

—What are you doing, honey? We can walk to SoHo from here.

—SoHo? I said. —That's not where the stuff is.

My bedroom drawer was where it was, or had been at least. West of Houston. Way West. Woe-Ho. But there were other branches open. Gwyn was watching me quizzically.

—Jackson Heights, I said. —That's where my mom goes.

—Well, mother knows best. Gwyn grinned, pulling out her Metrocard.

—At least, yours does.

★ ★ ★

As the train pulled up to the platform Gwyn took off her watch (which now read, interestingly, 8:24 A.M.) and matched it to the clock behind the ticket vendor's head.

—Your watch stopped? I said suspiciously as we boarded.

—Well, I stopped watching *it*, she said, commencing a wink then thinking better of it. She'd pulled her tube of waterproof sweatproof mascara out and was applying away—easier said than done since we were hurtling into the gaping mouth of the subway tunnel. —I can't believe Dyl had this T-shirt. I nearly died when I saw it! But my other duds were just way too skanky.

Frock, was that all she ever thought about? She nodded, but she was staring at herself in her compact mirror, at the results of her fault-free makeup job. She hadn't even bothered to ask me about the suitable boy meeting.

—Where is he anyways? I snuffled. —I figured you two were joined at the hip by now.

—Oh, he had to rush off to school; he's auditioning some actresses for his movie.

—I thought you were going to star in it.

—Of course I am! said Gwyn. —But he has to have a supporting cast, right? Anyways, this project means everything to him, and I've got to be there for him. That's what relationships are all about, Dimple. You'll see.

Secrets played upon her now lined and lipsticked lips. Suddenly my Karsh story seemed pretty lame next to her own private theater.

We bumped along. Relationship. What did that mean, anyways? When she'd started up with Dylan, she'd said she was "seeing him"—as if she were having visions or something. And now they were "in a relationship." That seemed pretty vague to me. I mean, you have a relationship with everyone and anything, don't you? From the ottoman to the person in front of you on the subway. They are in *front* of you; that is their *relationship* to you. "Boyfriend" seemed a lot more uncomplicated a word, but she never used that with Dylan after he graduated.

Maybe I was just jealous; after all, "relationship" sounded so grown-up, so complicated and exciting, insinuating all sorts of lascivious behavior, whereas "boyfriend" was so legit, so PG-13. In any case, I didn't seem to be even remotely in the radii of either.

—Listen, Dimple, I know I spend a lot of time with Dyl. But things are getting really serious. They're. We're. Well, Dylan is really, you know—he's got a lot of experience, and I have to play my cards right. I mean, he's a college boy. A *man*. I've got to hold on to him.

—Well, just use a condom.

She tilted her compact and studied me in it.

—*That's* your reaction?

—Isn't that what we're talking about?

—You think that's where all my value is? she said, snapping the pressed powder shut. My reflection slapped closed with it. —In whether I'm sleeping with him or not? You don't think I can, like, have an intellectual conversation with him or . . . or . . . entertain him otherwise?

—That's not what I meant, I said. It really wasn't, but my foot seemed to have quite a penchant for rubbing up against my larynx lately.

—Well, you should listen to yourself sometimes, said Gwyn. —'Cause that's sure what it sounded like.

The rest of the subway ride was spent in silence. Gwyn was right next to me but I felt something rise up between us, a partition, transparent and thin, but impermeable.

When the train lurched to a halt at our stop, I couldn't take it any longer.

—Come on, I'm sorry, Gwyn, I said. —Let's not mess up the whole day—we're together at last. That's what counts, right?

—You're right, you're right, she sighed. —No, I'm the one who's sorry. I guess I've just been a little edgy lately. Can we make a deal, though?

—Whatever you want.

We were standing below the tracks. An American flag waved languidly on the corner. Every time a train rattled by a trill of birds rushed out from the rails where they'd been roosting, retreating to invisibility in the quiet moments between.

—Let's just not talk about guys, period, for a while, okay?

—Okay, I said. My story had waited; it could wait a little longer. Now I could show Gwyn my part of town.

★ ★ ★

But after a good hour wandering around the Greek neighborhood where everyone assumed I was Greek and then the Dominican one where everyone thought I was Puerto Rican, I still couldn't find it.

—It seemed so easy that time with my mother, I lamented.

—Should we call her? said Gwyn, handing me a minuscule cell phone. —I upgraded. And look—I even programmed you in.

—You did? I said, pleased.

—See? You just push five and send.

Who were one through four? I wondered.

—So your mom's one and then?

—Well, actually, one is messages, two is Dyl's cell, three's his apartment, and then four's his parents' place in Jersey, then you, then work, then the Lillian.

If I had a cell, Gwyn would be my number one button. Well, okay, maybe my parents would be first, but she'd be two at the latest. I tried to imagine feeling about someone the way she evidently did about Dylan—enough to program in a Secret Service roster's worth of coordinates for him—but came up blank. Meanwhile Gwyn had gone telephonic with my mother.

—Hi, Mrs. Lala—guess where I brought your daughter! Queens! Yeah, to check out the Indian neighborhood! I've been thinking lately she should get a little more into her Indian self. Only prob is we can't find it. Look to her heart? No—no, I mean the Indian hood. We can't find the Indian hood.

She passed me the phone.

—Hi, Ma, I said.

—Go inside a deli or store, my mother was saying sagely, like it was all coming to her in a telepathic flash; she spoke as if she were leaving a message and was shouting as if the answering machine were in India. I held the phone an inch off my ear. —And find out from a Greek or Puerto Rican how to get there. But *inside* the store only. Don't ask any altoo faltoo people hanging around on the street in the middle of the day—they are obviously not aware of how to go anywhere fast. I love you and am very excited you are in Jackson Heights.

—I love you, too, Ma, I said.

—Whatever you do, do not pay the full price, she said, sounding like a cookie fortune. —And stress your Marathi side—we have more star appeal. And please don't be too late tonight; your father is trying to switch his call if Dr. Stuttgarden will get off the toilet so we can all eat together like a real family.

We clicked off.

—You're all having dinner tonight? said Gwyn, tucking her phone away.

—Yeah, you heard her. Like a real family.

—Yeah, well, the Lillian and I have a family thing tonight, too.

—You do?

—I told her about you and your family things and said I wanted us to do that, too.

—That's excellent, Gwyn! I said. I was surprised—not only that Mrs.

Sexton would oblige, but that Gwyn would even want her to in the first place—but this was great news.

We set out to follow through with my mother's instructions and, true enough, after we quizzed an Athenian diner owner we got a set of directions that landed us smack in the middle of the Indian neighborhood, no passport required.

The area was like a blast of Bombay parachute-dropped and landed not only miraculously intact but burgeoning, undulating in the heat like a street-to-sky mirage. We began to weave as if drunk in and out doorways and on and off curbs as we shifted into full-on exploring mode, Gwyn turning heads all the way.

As in India, there were people, people everywhere: women in brilliant saris and yellow gold with thin knit cardigans and sometimes socks stuffed into toe-looped chappals, shuffling flashily like deposed queens through the supermarket aisles, half–bag lady half-genie, plucking up half-price jars of ghee and even frozen food (I was amazed at all of the idlee and dosa TV dinners you could find here). Men and boys blended, "hanging around" in loudmouthed clusters; young girls with demure faces and platform shoes whooshed and stomped gigglingly by them. Indians everywhere—save for a few hip-hoppy boys with turned-round baseball caps who must have been Dominican. They cruised occasionally through in beat-up cars with the windows rolled down, pumping thumping beats that mingled nearly seamlessly with the shrill Hindi film music thrusting open the doorways of the numerous bootleg video and tape sellers on the sidewalk.

Streaks of restaurants lit up as if it were never too early to start your Christmas decorating, lights blinking even in the sun. Alleys hectic with Hindi movie posters, the long-haired, elaborately dressed actresses half-heartedly running from men at their sari tails, brusque modern skylines oddly backdropping lush hilly foregrounds, sun and rain, all types of weather and foliage coexisting in cinematic harmony with close-up shots of the cast. A paan maker with black teeth rolling the icy thandak in betelnut leaves that my mother said my father used to hoard in his mouth like a hamster in India. Chai vendors ladling Styrofoam cups smoky with masala tea. Sweetshops smelling like nurseries with all the milk-based confections; in the windows pink mounds of coconut cutlets, iceberg slabs of burfee, and sticky sun bright coils of jalebi, a nearly glow-in-the-dark fried dough that your teeth would crack into, releasing impossible quantities of rosewater syrup; I could taste it through the window. I'd suckled on it in India, where it was one of the few things I could enjoy worry-free because it was so deep-fried no bug could survive the cooking process. I wondered for some reason if Karsh liked jalebi, too.

On a stretch of sidewalk with cheap giddy accessories and tops, Gwyn started snagging up goods left and right. And then I couldn't hold back any longer, either—there was something here I wanted for myself. If I couldn't learn to develop color with the vibrant scene before my eyes nothing would teach me.

At this point Chica Tikka was attached to my face like a new feature. And no sooner did she come on full force than the proof that Bollywood is in the blood did as well: An entire brood of wannabe film stars detached themselves from table and lamppost and brick and leaped, landing in dra-matic poses in my viewfinder—these were mostly men, and sometimes they even blocked Gwyn out, unbeknownst to them (though they usually stood back in awe when they saw her, looking like some hallucinatory ivory-turbaned goddess).

We were now on a strip that must have been the somewhat more expen-sive stores (gone were the socks-in-chappals, replaced by bronze and silver sandals). Gold stores raucous with thumb-smudged cases of bright yellow chains and earrings and black-and-gold mangal sutras, the marriage neck-lace, and with women already so adorned, nevertheless gasping deprivedly and crowing down prices like thrifty birds in a gilded nest, a few men waiting outwitted with their wallets outside.

Sari stores shimmered with silks the sheen of fish skin, bird wing, petal wet, crying iris, broken yolk, brushed tooth, oil slick. Men eagerly unfurled them from banners to display like enormous flags of unimaginable nations to the salivating clientele . . . then rolled them up, annoyed upon the "just look-ing only"s.

We ducked into one of these stores, one that seemed slightly funkier, not least due to the heavily hennaed salesgirl. Her hightop ponytail bobbed as she scooted around in her salvar khamees, but this one with great gaps in the fabric, revealing sorrel stripes of skin all across her back and midriff. Gwyn went to town, trying on all sorts of combinations and doing some serious strutting for my Chica. The salesgirl, Ajanta (so her tag claimed) even got into it, and helped her go Bollywood with her poses. I have to say, I was having oodles of fun—Gwyn was a real entertainer and the film would certainly be thanking me later. With my camera loaded up and in my hands and all this confusion of color and odor and touch around me I was just beginning to feel at home. This could be my place if I let it.

It was when we went outside that I noticed. I don't know how I had missed them before, but now I stopped short when I saw the window mannequins. What was shocking was not the clothes they were adorned in, which were the choicest of the lot, rivaling even my birthday khamees in beaded and baubled embellishment. Nor were their poses unsettling— these were fairly typical: strutting girls clustering in towards each other in self-conscious configurations, all too aware of being looked at, like pretty girls at parties. Nor the expected bindi and bangle, the slim smiles.

What was incredible and across the board with this flock of Indian-attired coquettes, these women dressed straight off my mother's dream runway—was the fact that they weren't Indian at all! Arms ivory as cameo pendants bent and beckoned, creasing into milky fists just a hair off scant hips. Lemonade locks, champagne curls, and on occasion V-8 manes hung in stiff styles of beyond-round-brushable perfection, framing the fair insouciant faces, the enormous vacant blue eyes. It was as if they'd been cast from a Gwyn mold. Even here. In Jackson Heights, Queens.

No one would believe it; I hardly did myself. I turned off the flash, switched to panoramic, and snapped a stretch of vitrine after vitrine and, between the last two encased mannequins, Gwyn, in nearly the same pose as one of them, hip out, fist on it, neck stretched like a proud inquisitive bird, other hand casually curled round the nape of her neck. She wasn't mimicking them. It was one of her natural positions—the way her bones fell together when she relaxed. She owned it. Looking at her through the viewfinder I realized: In fact, she owned the whole place. There was only one queen here, and it was her.

When I turned a small crowd of onlookers had gathered around me, gazing at my object of focus, mostly men, though a few girls who might have been our age and a couple older women hung back, faces twisted in a tangy mix of disapproval, curiosity, and craving. But this time no one dared enter the frame of vision.

—Ye kya model hai! one of the Dominican hip-hop boys declared, catching me off guard. That certainly didn't sound like Spanish. A Dominican boy fluent in Hindi? The world really was becoming a global village.

—You could say so, I said.

—I am knowing it! cried a grandfatherly man with admirable prowess through a sticky mouthful of paan. —I am seeing her in *Sports Illustrating* swimming suits!

—They think you're a model, Rabbit, I called out grinning. —Give 'em what they want.

And in so doing she gave me what I wanted, too. Through the lens it was a joy to see her pleasure; it lit up the place like a halogen. As soon as she noticed her audience she dropped her bags and did what Gwyn could do: Rather than come clean, deny it, tell us to talk to the hand, she began to vamp it up in her brand-new bangles and scarves and I Love New York T-shirt, posing, preening, voguing. The street music created the soundtrack and I clicked away, even getting on my knees for a couple shots. In this little neighborhood it was as if we were hitting the big time; I felt like a pro and liked how it felt.

It took a while to lose our entourage after that, but following a zigzaggy route back to the train we managed to leap unadorned onto the express. Gwyn looked radiant, taking up an entire bench with her bags and parcels.

—Wait till Dilly sees me, she said. —I can be the Indian bride of his dreams.

—Wait till he sees you, I said. —The man is too lucky.

—Speaking of which! she said suddenly. —How was the meeting with your future husband?

—Frock, I thought you'd never ask, I smiled. But to be honest I'd forgotten all about it those moments with my camera.

—Well, why didn't you say something then instead of just sitting there? she chided me. —So was he dishy?

—Total goober, I said. —In fact, I think the candy was named after him.

—I like Goobers. Come on—give me the d's.

—Well, first of all he listens to the same music as my parents. In fact he and my dad own the same records.

—Your parents are even hipper than I thought, Dimps!

—No, no, no! I'm talking the Ice Age Top Forty. And he's totally tight with his mom—he hugs her in public and didn't seem in the least upset about her trying to organize his love life. He still *lives* with her—not like in the Village or anything cool like that.

Not like Julian, I was thinking.

—He even hangs out at NYU with her! I added when I got no appalled response from Gwyn.

—That's *sweet*, Dimple!

—What's sweet about it? Wouldn't you just shrivel up and die? I mean, at *college*, where everyone's so independent?

—If I could be seen in public with the Lillian to that extent I'd thank my lucky star. Where's his father, by the way?

—Finishing up business in India or something.

—So he's being the man of house. That's chivalrous.

This was turning into a battle to make her see my point.

—Okay. Check this: He doesn't drink when offered.

—Look at the pro talking! Come on—it's a good move for scoring points with the 'rents. And better for performance, if you ever get that far: one less cup, faster up.

Gwyn began to sift through her purchases.

—On the aesthetic front? she asked, now mooning over a teal angel-sleeved raw silk shirt. —Style?

—Zilch. Geeky. Chinos.

Gwyn wrinkled her nose.

—*Pleated*, I added dramatically.

—Oh, I see what you mean. This could be a prob.

She contemplated a sheet of bindis.

—But nothing a makeover can't take care of, she concluded, sticking one on. —Is he tall at least?

—Tall for an Indian. But not tall for a Dylan.

—At least your kids will have a chance at seeing over the counter.

—Kids? Gwyn, my eggs crack at the thought of him. Don't you get it?

We have nothing in common. It's doomed. It's like *Titanic*. Without the romance.

—I thought we agreed there was nothing to lose.

—Nothing to lose, yeah, except my mind. Let me put it this way: It was not a kamasutronic experience. I'd rather pick the lint out of my belly button than go through it again.

Gwyn giggled.

—Well then, she said. —Since your Bombay boy is out of the picture maybe I should mention someone who might be back in. Does the name Julian Rothschild mean anything to you these days?

—Julian? What about Julian? I said hopefully.

—Headline news: He told me just last night that he's actually been feeling really bad about the whole Chimi's thing, just bailing on you like that.

—He did *not!*

—I swear on the Madonna de el ciudad de New York, she said, crossing her heart, and no fingers crossed.

Gwyn repacked her bags and slumped back against the slippery cushion of them. She sighed so contentedly I was surprised; she seemed so truly happy for me, for my renewed future with the filmic one. She closed her eyes, a little smile dancing on her lips.

—Did they really think I was a model? she asked.

CHAPTER 14

twice chai

We decided to stop for a mochafrappafiesta before jumping on the train and heading home. Gwyn went off to order and I sat guard.

She returned, setting down two mysteriously foamless cups.

—Chai, she explained. —I'm feeling inspired.

—You are such a suitable girl, I grinned. —Karsh would be proud.

—Karsh? she said, sipping through her teeth to keep her lipstick intact. —Oh, is that his name?

—Yeah. It's Karsh. Um. Karsh Kapoor, I said. For some reason I lowered my voice. You never know who might be watching. Or perhaps, I thought, the nape of my neck prickling—it was because I actually *was* being watched. I looked up. Affirmative. Isn't it funny how you can feel it? A certain someone was looking in this general direction. There on the sidewalk, navigating the yappy sea of dog walkers and scooterers and baby girls in high-tech strollers and fast approaching . . . was Julian.

I was getting all fireworked when I saw the specimen accompanying him and Dylan, who I now made out curbside: a honey-long glidey girl, an absolute stunner. Even from here I could see that: Fresh-tressed cornrows swung to her shoulders, a few magenta strands mixed in with the deep brown-black. She gleamed like polished onyx and a red denim minidress clung defiantly to her curvy compact figure. So Julian had already replaced me! Julian, who, unfortunately, was looking poker-hot. At least everyone else would say so.

—I thought he was solo, I whispered, hunching way down in my seat. Of all the Starbucks in the city, nearly two to a block these days, why did he have to pick this one? I'd never imagined we'd run into the Rudes here, but I should have realized that in New York City starving artists are at least two to a block as well.

—So did I! Gwyn replied. —I'm so sorry, Dimple. But don't worry—just play it cool. You have nothing to be embarrassed about.

I heard the heavy push of the door opening and felt the heat skulk in, letting a slice of fresh, expensive air-conditioned air thunk out onto Seventh Avenue. From below my downcast lids I watched Julian amble on in. I contemplated the exit signs, but it was too late. He was waving.

—Hey, Gwyn! Fancy meeting you here at Fourbucks!

His voice was silly with surprise, even though I was pretty sure he'd seen us, or at least her, through the glass. And then, at last, he turned to me. His smile stuck on a little too long, strained his cheeks. I could feel my blackheads biggen and was certain a pimple was forming volcanically on the tip of my nose, that Rudolph the Red-Nosed stress spot always curdling just below the surface.

—Oh, uh, hey, Dimple, he said finally, going all fidgety for some reason. —How's your stomach doing these days?

Was he going to humiliate me in front of his new flame, who was just pocketing her change from their cab driver and entering a step behind Dylan? Oddly, though, he actually looked like he gave a frock. But then, I suppose love can put anyone in a good mood.

—Uh, hi, I said. —Yeah, it's all right, thanks for asking.

—I should have asked a long time ago, he said.

These dynamics were a little bizarre. I looked to Gwyn for a filler, but she'd already hopped up grinning and I could see she was about to do the salty pretzel around Dylan. But then a very perplexing thing happened. Julian's love interest leaned in alarmingly close to Dylan, her hand slithering with an almost audible hiss up into his hair to rake it. Her blue-black eyes went cagey on Gwyn and even her razzle-dazzle nose ring seemed to flare. Gwyn stared from one to the other, confused as I was, hanging back and trying to look as if she'd meant to hop up for another reason, like her chair was on fire.

—Hey, Dilly, long time no see! she managed. She nudged him, sustaining a funny little smile in the midst of her befuddlement, upper lip sliding out slightly over lower; her happiness at seeing him was still palpable, and embarrassing for some reason.

Dylan looked like it had been such a long time, in fact, he still didn't see. He was giving Gwyn a Queens mannequin look, staring out vacantly from his model-mold face, and it was beginning to give me a very unpleasant feeling in the intestinal region.

—Who's the little girl? said the cornrowed one in a husky voice. —*Dilly?*

—Oh, this is just a friend. From my high school.

—Just a friend! cried Gwyn, trying to laugh, but the chortle abruptly cut off, sounding more like a choked cough. —You're funny.

—Well, we're friends, aren't we? said Dylan, giving her a pseudo-friendly pseudo-punch in the shoulder. —And it *has* been a while! *Hasn't it.* Good to see you, Gwyneth. How's Joysey?

—Gwyndolyne, said Gwyn.

It had been a while? But she'd been at Astor Place this morning. I didn't know what make of watch he was using.

—Gwyn—that rings a dingaling. Oh, is this that girl who follows you around, the one you can't get rid of? said Cornrow coolly.—The one who puts the zzzs in Jersey?

She scanned Gwyn from top to toe.

—Nice fashion statement, by the way. You got any wine to go with that cheese?

It suddenly didn't look so cool to be in a tee that screamed tourist. But still.

—It's his shirt! I said.

—Uh, right, said Dylan.

—It is, Gwyn pouted.

—Yeah, actually it is, said Julian, surprisingly. But Dylan ignored him.

—Gwyn, Gwyn, he sighed now, shaking his head as if to say *You really shouldn't have skipped your medication.*

—By the way, honey, said Cornrow, who was fast becoming Corn-ho. —*Everybody* loves New York.

—Uh, this is Kashmere, D and G—she's the lead in our film, said Julian quickly, as if an introduction at this point would smooth things over.

—D and G? Looks a little more B and T to me, the strangely named one said. —I guess you weren't kidding when you said you were slumming all those years without me, Dyl!

This was fast turning into a most cringeworthy scenario.

—Excuse me! I said, before I could stop myself. —Like you guys aren't Bridge and Tunnel yourself?

—Kashmere is strictly two-one-two material, said, startlingly, Kashmere. —Even switched back from six-four-six.

She shot us another nasty look before turning back to Dylan.

—Now Dyl, baby, enough Kashmere stories, she said. —Why don't we move on out of the children's department. You get the table, I'll get the java. How do my men want it?

—Uh, I've kind of lost my appetite, said Julian.

—I'll take mine black, said Dylan.

—I love you, too, honey, she said, and then she gave him a kiss that convinced me she was the leading lady—and not just onscreen. It lingered, like in sugarless gum commercials, and there were tongue cameos and everything. I think she was overdoing it on purpose; no one macks like that—it was closer to chewing than necking. And then she stepped off, swiggling away to the queued-up coffee counter.

—You know this is your shirt! Gwyn fumed. —I can't believe you acted like it wasn't!

Dylan didn't say anything. Julian began to whistle a little tune and check out the ceiling like he was considering building a skylight.

—So none of that meant anything to you?

—I meant to tell you, Dylan said. —I'm seeing someone else.

Duh! I joined Julian on the ceiling. Both of us sort of hovered about, I suppose in case backup forces were needed, but trying to be as plainclothes as possible.

—Sorry I didn't return your beeps, Dylan added, as if this was the obvious focus for the apology.

—Meant to tell me when? cried Gwyn. —Last night in the bathroom? This morning in the hallway? No wonder you were in such a rush to get to school. Fuck, Dylan, are you even *making* a movie?

—Sex didn't seem like the right time to mention it.

Wha—? So they had? In an eye blink I went through a hasty hierarchy of emotions: First I was really hurt that she hadn't told me, then I realized that was a little megalo, and then I was left just shocked. But I guess if she hadn't talked to me about it, I couldn't really bring it up. And then I was hurt all over again that she hadn't told me. But I tried to stay composed; frock, it wouldn't help much if I acted out of the loop.

—You wouldn't have even mentioned it at all! Are you trying to tell me you had some psychic flash that I would be here right now and came on down to have a heart to heart?

—I told you this would happen, mumbled Julian. —I told you you should tell her.

—It's just we're not in Joysey anymore, Dylan said, ignoring him.

Thanks for the geography lesson, Columbus.

—It's time I started, you know, breaking out into other ethnicities, other cultures, he went on. —Something I seriously doubt would be of any interest to you. How can I fulfill my artistic calling if my entire world revolves around Springfield? Even him—

Here he indicated Julian.

—Even he can be kind of provincial in his outlook, and he's at least an artist.

Julian squinted at Dylan, as if he were hoping not to recognize him; his entire face smarted. We both promptly pretended to be immersed in the homes and gardens section of the magazine rack.

—You think I don't have enough, what, culture? cried Gwyn.

—You wouldn't want to go anywhere without a mall in a five-mile radius, Gwyn! Dylan retorted, irritated. —I need a girl who knows about the world. And that's not you.

Now we were all speechless.

—It's all here in New York, he added. —It's in New York where you can lose your barriers, lose yourself into life.

—Where I can lose you, at least, said Gwyn quietly. —So I'm a friend, huh?

Dylan shrugged and nodded.

—Well, let me tell you something, Dylan Reed, she said, rallying momentarily. —Friends don't treat friends like that. I mean, with a friend like you . . .

She turned away, deflating.

—I thought I didn't need any other ones, she whispered.

—Sorry, my baby.

—You know what, Dylan? she said, but her voice remained quiet. —I'm not yours. And I'm not a baby. I suddenly feel all grown up, to tell you the truth.

But she didn't look all grown up, there in her I Love New York T-shirt, and there was something really heartbreaking about it.

—You'll get over me, said Dylan, consoling her and now superlatively pushing my buttons. —It will take time, but you will. And one day you'll meet someone else.

I couldn't take it. I knew I could be cranky with Gwyn sometimes, but I couldn't stand it when anyone else treated her with even a modicum of meanness. I nudged her foot and spoke.

—Are you dense? She already has! Haven't you, Gwyn?

—Uh, yeah, said Gwyn, not so convincingly.

—She was *meaning to tell you*, I said.

—Oh yeah? he said condescendingly. —Who?

—You don't know him, said Gwyn.

—So, an invisible friend. What, he has no name?

—Of course he has a name! It's Karsh . . . um . . .

She turned to me.

—Karsh*um?* quizzed a dubious Dylan.

—Kapoor, I said.

—Karshum Kapoor! she said. —That's his name. And thanks for introducing me to NYU, Dylan, because that's where I met him.

—When?

—Oh, you know. One of those nights you were *editing*.

At first I'd thought this was a pretty lame cover-up, but Dylan did look a little razzed, and as Gwyn went on I could see what there might be for him to be jealous of.

—He's a tall, beautiful computer genius . . .

—Drummer, I said. —And drummer. In fact, Zakir Mehra—you *have* heard of Zakir Mehra?

—Uh . . . obviously, said Dylan.

—Well, he was taught by Zakir Mehra himself.

—Wow, said Julian. —He sounds really cool.

He did sound really cool, actually. And to top it off: It was all true! I considered adding that he was nice to his mother, too, but figured I'd bring out my inner Seinfeld and quit while I was ahead.

—Yeah, right, said Dylan snottily. —As if a guy like that even exists. And if he did, as if he would ever go out with—

Gwyn's mouth tremored, and she suddenly shot off in the direction of the bathroom. I was about to follow but I still had something to say.

—Don't ever come near her again, I hissed. —You think you're so hot? You don't even reach the soles of her feet. If you mean lack of class, you know there's only one Bridge and Tunneler here.

—I wouldn't talk, Donna.

—Is that a promise? I said, too heated up to even correct him. —You're so condescending just because you're in film school—but where's the film, Spielberg? Sounds to me like you're just spending money to jerk off. But I guess it's fitting—you're definitely the biggest jerk I've ever met.

—You *are* kind of condescending, Julian ventured.

—Shut your trap, Julian, what do you know? Dylan snapped. —You're just the producer.

—And Gwyn should branch out into other ethnicities? I continued, on a roll now. —Hello? She just spent her day in Jackson Heights, Queens —where everyone thought she was a supermodel, by the way. And New Jersey's not multiculti enough for you? I'm Indian, you creep!

—And kamasutronic, Julian added.

—You better go drink your coffee before it goes frappe in that ice queen's hands, I said. —And no point waiting around for Gwyn, in case you were—she's on her way to Karsh, Karshum now. Why do you think she ran off like that? Oh, and I forgot—not only is he a tall, gorgeous, brilliant, full-scholarship computer genius Indian drummer, but he's a *total* expert on Lata.

I added that last on purpose.

—Lata?

—Lata Mangeshkar. You've never heard of him?

—Of course I have, Dylan snooted.

—Well, he's a *she*, bozo—the top-selling musical artist of all time. Gotcha! You know, maybe you should be exposing yourself to more cultures, Dylan, more *ethnicities*. Get out of the house more. Or, I take that back: *Stay in.*

I couldn't believe I'd said all that. It was as if I'd been possessed by—me. The expression on his face had been well worth it, as if he'd been ambushed in a paint-gun attack, naked. I picked up our stuff and turned to go now, and Julian stared at me as I passed, eyes wide in something that looked a lot like admiration.

—Dimple, he said, almost to himself. —Dimple Lala.

★　★　★

In the bathroom all was silent, then a muffled sound, and more silence.

—Gwynnie?

I peered under the stalls, bunching up my hair so it wouldn't drag on the floor. No shoes, and again. And then in the last stall, that beloved pair of size seven feet curling up out of sight a second too late.

I tapped the door.

—Gwynnie? It's just me.

There was no reply and I pushed. To my surprise it gave, and I could see now, hunched on the stool like a tiny New York–loving garden gnome, my Rabbit.

I was swept over with so many emotions, not least of them regret and sadness. Secretly, I had wanted them to break up for so long but now that it had actually happened it didn't feel so good. It wasn't how I'd pictured it at all—I'd always envisioned Gwyn coming out on top, in form, leaving a trail of broken heart bits in her glittery wake. To see her hurt like this was deeply upsetting.

I wanted to take her in my arms but I didn't want to topple her, so I ended up giving her a clumsy sort of shoulder hug.

—Frock, Gwyn, I said. —This reminds me so much of that time in fourth grade when you came looking for me after Kevin Dunst told me I was the color of dog doo and I ran off and hid. Remember that?

She nodded.

—Well, I think I forgot to say thanks.

—Anytime, she said laughing. But it wasn't long before the laughter squelched into a strangled sob and we had our arms all the way around each other. She smelled like when she was a little girl, the sweet condensed-milk scent of her skin mixing with the salt of her tears.

—Don't cry, please don't cry, I said. —It's going to be all right.

—Get exposed to other cultures, she fumed. —I mean, duh, my best friend is Indian!

—That's what I told him.

—You did?

—I did.

—And not to mention my imaginary boyfriend.

—I told him that, too, I said, stroking her hair. —I think I gave him the beginning of an idea of what an asshole he is. But not enough for you to ever give him a passing glance again!

Gwyn looked up at me. Her passing glance now included deep liquid bruises under her eyes where the mascara had run.

—You really are my supertwin, she whispered, voice breaking. She stared down at herself. —I can't believe I'm in this cheesy shirt. You know, right now I hate New York.

—Yeah, I said. —But it's one bad apple in the Big Apple, you've got to remember that.

I took her hands and coaxed her up.

—Come on now, swashbuckle up—you better stop crying or you'll make me cry. And that could get ugly.

She nodded shakily, trying a smile on for size, trooper that she was, and reached up a hand to wipe her face. When she pulled it away, she stared a moment, her fingers gone violet where she'd touched her cheek tops.

—Stupid mascara, she said, shaking her head. —It said it was water-proof, sweatproof, sportproof.

—Don't worry, I said. —You won't need tearproof anymore.

I helped her up, and we wound together to the sinks, close as the Siamese twins we'd played one Halloween. After she washed up she turned to me.

—Geez, Dimple, I've had about all I can take, she said. —Why don't you just find me a suitable boy while you're at it?

surya namaskar a

On the way home, Gwyn kept her shades on and didn't say much. She became so suddenly withdrawn it frightened me. I tried to distract her a few times but celebrity gossip only goes so far in terms of healing power. To be honest, I wasn't too good at comforting her in a post-jettisoned state—after all, she'd never been dumped before!

—Gwyn, you don't need him, I finally said.

—I know, Dimple, she said. —I don't need anything, right? I'm an independent woman.

She looked at me a moment as if she wanted to say something, but didn't, simply turned and leaned her head against the pane.

—Oh, what would you know about it, she sighed.

★   ★   ★

I still felt the sting of her dismissal as we neared home. We walked down Lancaster Road in an unshared silence, passing the houses of people we'd known since we'd had memories nearly, but they didn't bring us back to each other.

We turned right at the fork in the road by the Bad Luck House (which was always for sale) and went by her place first. The panes gaped, dilated, and the driveway cut an uninterrupted arc in the grass, bleeding darkly as the day flushed into descent.

—Are you sure you and your mom are meeting tonight? I said.

—She put it in her calendar and everything, said Gwyn. It was a relief to hear her voice again, even stung with sarcasm. —Of course she never *reads* her calendar—it reminds her of all the things she doesn't want to deal with. Well, anyways, maybe she's just late. Come on, I'll walk you home.

—I can wait here with you if you want, I said.

—No, it's fine. By the time I get back she'll be here. I'm sure.

When we got to my driveway a familiar green candy-shell car bubbled over there. Gwyn lit up.

—New wheels, Dimps?

—No, no—I guess my cousin's here.

—The geekster one you told me always makes fun of you? *In America the girls are talking to the boys in your school, is it?*

She said it in the mock Indian accent we put on to imitate my parents sometimes; to tell you the truth, they didn't even really speak like that, but using it was sometimes somehow still satisfying to me. It bugged me a little whenever Gwyn did it, but then, I had started the whole thing, and it did make me feel she was on my side if, for example, I was complaining about some grievous injustice they'd committed (trying to burn my vintage jeans that time, for example). But right now it just made me feel bad. I'd imitated Kavita in the past, but it didn't seem so funny anymore. I hadn't told Gwyn about the photo album or how close to her I'd felt when I called to thank her. We'd spoken over an hour, I don't even know about what, but when we hung up, the telephone had burned as much as when I used to talk to Gwyn like that, and I felt the hearth of it warming me well after.

—No, not that one, I said. —This one's really cool.

—So not the premed one, said Gwyn. —Can I meet her? I could use a really cool cousin tonight.

Well, if I couldn't be of service, maybe Kavita could. We stepped into the house and were turning into the kitchen when a baffling sight met my eyes: My mother was on the counter in lotus position, still-startling titian hair bristling with static electricity, and was looking ovenwards, throwing out incomprehensible orders with grand flourishes of her arm like a kitchen conductor.

Farther in the room the objects of her commands were two rear ends protruding skyward to high heaven. I couldn't see the attached persons angling in a downward V to the ground; their faces were blocked behind shuddery thighs, feet and hands flat on the floor in a sinuous sea of spilled dupatta.

I gestured for Gwyn to be quiet. I wanted to see how far they would go with this unusual ceremony. We watched in amazement as my mother commanded them through a full circuit that involved jumping their feet to their hands, doing some kind of bird swoop up with their arms, then going through another squat and jump-back that landed Kavita flat and histrionically on her belly and her black-satined partner shakily holding in an impressively low push-up position.

—Baapray, yaar, how are you keeping it so long? exclaimed Kavita, rolling onto her side and poking at the tremulous human plank just inches off the floor beside her.

—Stop it! the plank gasped.

—Kavita, that's cheating, scolded my mother.

Finally the plank landed with a gah-lump and the two of them flumped over onto their backs on the tiles, Kavita clutching her stomach.

—Now *that*, said my mother, evidently pleased with herself. —Is a real surya namaskar. Just repeat those twelve moves for about an hour and you'll be on your way to a true asana.

—They never do it like that at Crunch, grumbled the plank.

—Why howdy, cowgirl cousin! cried Kavita, finally noticing us. I was really happy to see her, standing now, one leg making a number four with the other and hands in prayer position. A warm feeling filled me like tea.

—It is about time, said my mother. —It's too bad you weren't here earlier. I don't think I've had this much fun in—well, I don't know, really—but we are having fun is what I am saying, heh! Well, hello there, Gwyn—nice to have you home again.

—Ah! The famous Gwyn! cried Kavita, extending her hand and falling promptly out of position.

—You've heard of me? Gwyn said, giving me an *awww* look.

—If memory serves me correctly, Dimple told me you were like her Sabina. Who is right beside me in tree pose, by the way, putting me to shame!

I gave the arboreal one a quick once-over. She had blue-black hair, layers just going shaggy on her long neck and sideburns swirling alongside multiple hoop earrings. A few punky chunks stuck straight up, as if she'd either just woken up or plugged them in, and a ridge of hacked bangs crossed choppily high her forehead, endowing her with an irked look. She was wearing narrow bookish glasses with rectangular frames; they were a little fogged up, wiped out her eyes.

I namasted her back and she smiled slightly now, mouth delicately lipping nearly up to her beakish nose. Everything about her was thin, save for the mole orbiting above her upper lip: Her batik shirt hung loose upon her, her skirt just below her belly button around which bloomed a deep red tattoo of a lotus, rippling open and closed as she inhaled and exhaled, like a looped time-lapse photograph. Kavita had draped her dupatta around her and she looked like a stern and exquisite bird.

—We've heard a lot about you, I said.

—You have?

She was clearly pleased, though it showed less on her minimalist features than it had on Gwyn's lush expressive face.

—I thought I was going to be kept tucked away in the cupboard forever, she said, with no accent. —I've been dying to meet you and Aunty. And too bad Uncle couldn't switch his call; I was hoping to say hello to him as well.

—You're Dimps's cousin, too? asked Gwyn.

—No, no, I explained. —In India we call everybody aunty and uncle, all friends of the family.

It was actually a wonderful cover-up in case you forgot which ones were related.

—Are you the one having the arranged marriage? Gwyn now blurted out to Kavita, staring at her in fascination.

—No, said Sabina before Kavita's lips had parted. —That would be her sister being sold off like cattle to the supposed superhero.

—The cow is sacred in India, said my mother solemnly.

—The zero was invented in India, too, said Sabina.

Gwyn broke out laughing.

—No, seriously, said Sabina, poker-faced. —The zero *was* invented in India.

—Well, in any case, said Gwyn. —The way things are going for me, I wish *my* parents would arrange my marriage—but they only specialize in deranged marriages.

—Is there any other kind? Sabina nodded sympathetically, branching out of tree pose and dropping into a chair. —No offense, Aunty.

—Yeah, tell me about it, Gwyn replied, pulling up a chair beside her. She'd sprung back to life and now proceeded to relay the events of the afternoon to her audience, up to and including the part about pretending that Karsh was her new honeypot, which my mother did not seem to find particularly amusing.

—Yes, you need a good Indian boy, she declared from her haughty perch. —Not *Karsh*, mind you. But a good Indian boy nonetheless.

—It's not true, of course, the part about Karsh, said Gwyn hurriedly, noting my mother's furrowing brow. —I think it's *great* about Karsh, the whole meeting thing and all.

—Karsh *is* pretty great, Kavita agreed.

—Whatever, I said. —Even if it were true, it's fine by me.

—Why can't you be as receptive as our dear Gwyn here? sighed my mother. —Honest to Prabhu, Gwyn, you are such a good influence on my Dimple.

—Being receptive is good to a point, said Sabina as my mother refurrowed in my direction. —But not when it slips over into being passive. You can't just sit there and take whatever comes your way. What you need to do first, Gwyn, is address the issue of what kind of people you're dating and why, instead of accepting the role of victim.

She peered over her glasses, piercing Gwyn's mesmerized eyes with the pupils that swallowed up almost all of her own iris.

—You have to figure out what you want, set your sights on it, and conquer. We have been oppressed too long. Don't let anything stand in your way.

—You're right, I never thought of it that way, said Gwyn finally. —How'd you get so smart? I mean, the way Dimple talks about it, seems people don't even date in India.

—We're not in India.

—You're a genius, Sabz. You must have the coolest boyfriend.

—Well, no, said Sabina, and I couldn't tell whether it was a sheepish or irritated look that sprouted like a rash on her face. For some reason she burned her eyes into Kavita now and Kavita stared down into her lap. If you ask me it sounded more like she'd just been dumped to have developed such a philosophy. But I wasn't about to tell her that.

—Well, don't worry, said Gwyn, leaning over and smoothing one of Sabina's electrified locks. —I'm sure there's someone fabulous just around the corner.

—Oh, I'm sure, said Sabina, pulling the chunk out again. She abruptly stood, hauling up Kavita as if the two were soldered together.

—Anyways, sorry to run out on you women, she said. —But I think Kavita and I really need to push off back to the city. We have a sitar lesson tonight.

—We do? said Kavita. —Oh, we do. But we'll see you at the Desicreate kickoff next week, no?

—What desecrate kickoff? Gywn asked.

—Dimple didn't tell you? The NYU party?

—Wow, I completely forgot about it, I said truthfully. It occurred to me that I'd rather stay home and contemplate the missing socks in the dryer than hit the town for a supposedly wild night out (not) with what was sure to be a bunch of aunties and uncles.

—Am I going to have to lasso you in? Kavita grinned. She snapped the dupatta out towards me but Sabina intercepted, hands winged with silk as she caught it and wrapped it around Kavita, pulling the ends around her own back.

—Seems it's easier to catch the Indian, she said. —Than the cowgirl.

—Don't you mean South Asian? I said. I wasn't sure whether I liked Sabina or not. I suppose I did, but she made me edgy. She was a little bossy, but the way her philtrum vanished when she smiled almost made up for it. I'd never seen such short hair on an Indian girl before.

—I like you already, Dimple, said Sabina, as if in reply to my thoughts.

Gwyn and I went out to the driveway to see them off.

—Just one last question! Gwyn cried out as they were unlocking the car. —Is your nose really pierced or is that one of those magnet things?

—You'll have to come to NYU and stay with us to find out! smiled Kavita, slamming the door shut.

And they horsepowered off, reversing into the sunset.

Gwyn lingered in the driveway and then suddenly turned to me.

—Can I stay over tonight, Dimple? she asked.

—Won't your mother . . . ?

—She's not home.

—But I thought . . . ?

—Can I stay over?

—Of course you can stay, I said. She'd been in such a good mood the last couple of hours I'd nearly forgotten what she'd gone through today. — Should we go to your house and get your stuff?

—I don't want to go there, she said quickly. —It's so dark, I don't know. It'll seem so empty after all the fun we just had. Can't I just borrow something?

If I had anything too tight or too long, she'd already taken it. But that wasn't what mattered tonight.

—No worries, I said. —I think we can definitely rustle something up.

—Thank you, Dimple, she said, putting her arms around me. Her hug had changed, it seemed, gone slower and closer; it was a hug for a boy, and I could smell her fresh-scent deodorant. —It'll be just like old times.

★   ★   ★

It was and it wasn't. It was nice, Gwyn sleeping in the twin bed again. But it was strange, too, to have her back so suddenly. To have her available. I switched off the light, but I knew she was still awake. I could hear her staring up at the ceiling.

—I can't believe you've been hiding her so long, she said finally.

—Kavita? I haven't been hiding her, I said. —I only just got back in touch with her myself.

—They're like princesses, she sighed. —So beautiful, so bright. Did you see how they were all dressed up? Why were they all dressed up?

—That's just how they dress, I said.

—It was inspiring, I tell you. I'm going to be a princess, too. That's got to be the secret. How else can you find a prince? I keep ending up with skanks like Dylan. But now I'm going to go out and conquer, like Sabz says. Nothing will stand in my way. *Nothing.*

She paused.

—That Karsh guy sounds real nice, actually. I don't get why you didn't like him—seems like everyone else does.

—Well, then, take him, he's yours, I said, and rolled over. I didn't want to have this conversation again and I pretended to be asleep. It seemed like old times, but I knew better. She'd gone through something, Gwyn. Without me. Whether or not things with Dylan had worked out wasn't the point; she'd emerged with a focus. I couldn't figure out what she was focusing on—it was intangible but rising out of the dark, impending, imminent, the silver crystals changed by chemistry and the latent image there, the one you can't see till the film is developed, till it's too late to turn away.

★ ★ ★ CHAPTER 16 ★ ★ ★

chord change

The night before the party I was unable to sleep. I don't know why. It wasn't like it was going to be a visit to thrillsville, this hangout sesh with the aunties and uncles and the rest of the Indian Marriage Mafia on a night that potentially could have been spent at home dividing pi. But still—it was New York City, and a real club, and a roomful of strangers. I stared at the beam over my head, a butterfly unwrapping from my belly and fluttering frenetically up into my throat.

Outside my window a lightning storm had started up. Tonight the rain was far; a fair gap ensued between flash and boom. It reminded me of the woman I watched from the top of a Rajasthani fortress beating her clothes clean in the lip of a river below, how the ponderous wet slap traveled to me slowly through the moondust pink air, arriving well after the act.

I counted the space between lightning and thunder in Mississippis, but still found the crash catching me off guard. So I got up to get a glass of milk (meaning: a plate of cookies).

As I was crossing back to my room a particularly brilliant flash of lightning went off and the keys of the piano went phosphorescent. I sat and skimmed my fingers over them; it had been so long I didn't know where to begin. I pretended I was playing the thunder, flourishing my hands like I'd seen Mrs. Lamour do all those years ago. The keys felt cool and dewy, inviting to the touch.

I stood and opened the bench; if this thunder hadn't woken anyone up yet I doubted a few moments of pedalless playing would. I could just make out the familiar stack of sheet music, untouched for so long. I pulled off the top set. Another flash of lightning and I saw the title.

I sat there, dumbly leafing through the pages. The words were bold and big as a Broadway marquee on the cover sheet. I didn't get it. Was he blind? Had he taken the muddled name of the song my father had requested literally? But no: He'd said the bench was empty, with a capital M. Did he really like only Indian music—so much so that he didn't even want to hear this piece?

But I had a feeling it wasn't any of that.

Would he be there tomorrow night?

I felt tense, the feathery pages of "Für Elise" strangely weighty in my hands. I wished it would rain, just make up its mind.

in which the aunties and uncles throw it down

The moment the doors of the subway hissed open, spilling a drunken sea of love-hungry people onto the steaming platform, you could hear the music. The swung thump of the bass, like the heart of an enormous, waiting beast—the heart of the very city—and scattered over it, the shimmering artery of a melody line, a voice far and felt as memory.

It was all wide angle at first. And then it was only Gwyn. I turned to her and she was so beautiful, just standing there on the sea-bream smeared-dream tiles of the platform, perfectly poised in her impossibly slopey heels, as elegant as if it were the end of a catwalk. Twilight wound round her waist in the hues of the dupatta, sewn over so many days by twenty stitching fingers and straining eyes somewhere in Jaipur. She flung a twist of it back now, sari-like, over the pomegranate "tiny top," sending the mirrors winking. She was radiant.

Earlier, loading my camera, I had watched her before my dresser mirror as her lips deepened to garnet. Zoomed to the eyes as she used wet violet liner to pull off a perfect imitation of Kavita's Cleopatra look and then, with surgical steadiness, toothpick, and cosmetic glue, applied tiny drugstore gems to the tips of the lashes. Snapped just the strands as she drew the scintillating choker in place, worked the hair-clip earrings from lobes to coruscating cornrows, adjusted the rakhis into armlets. She had looked like a doll too beautiful to make and too priceless to sell. And she had looked so beautiful I knew I had to stop feeling like less because she was more and just enjoy her for the wonder that she was. I stood behind her then, to get a fully Gwyn-faced frame, trying to get as close as possible without putting too much of myself in the mirror. And as she pressed the glitzy teardrop between her brows, Chica Tikka flashed, the last shot.

It had also been my last roll of black and white, I'd realized when I'd unloaded it to wind in some fast-speed color film.

We squeezed then slid through one slot, turnstiled together, hipbone humming against hip and metal cool through the cloth. But the moment we'd traversed the stone's throw from subway to club, my dreams of a quick entry into the open arms of the motherland vanished. The line of glitter-garbed dark-haired denizens of the night literally wrapped all the way around the block to the HotPot entrance. I wouldn't have even known where the entrance was if it weren't for the fact that the bouncer was about seven feet tall with a foot more of hair piled up under a rainbow knit hat. No one was moving an inch in this mile. I prepared to settle in for a long evening of watching my cuticles grow.

—Frock, look at all these people, I said. —By the time we get in, the whole thing'll be history.

Gwyn gave me an exasperated look.

—Do you remember who you're dealing with here? she said. —Carp and dee 'em. You know nothing ever falls into your hands unless you reach for it.

—Carpe diem, I corrected.

—Capiche, she said.

So Gwyn put her seize-the-day tactics to work and marched right up alongside the line, me a bit behind to allow her full vamping radius. I could see now—out of the corner of my eye, as I didn't like to look dead on at people when I was ripping them off (the opposite of Gwyn's approach)—that this line was ninety-nine percent Indian. The faces were all in a golden row against brick like a cheerful decked-out subcontinental criminal lineup —though the crime would be what? Eating with the left hand, smelling the flowers before offering them to the gods, touching someone else's food while on the rag? But upon a closer sidelong glance I realized this was a breed of Indian I had never seen before in my life: Though Gwyn would have to win the mix-and-match East-and-West award for the evening, these other girls weren't too far off, and were studded and salvar'd and pleathered and nose-ringed to the max themselves. Even the more conservatively dressed ones had snazzy platforms poking out from under their sari hems, or chappals and twisted silver toe rings on their feet, tattoos and body jewels littered across the soft stretches of exposed flesh. There was long hair, cropped hair, braided hair, highlighted hair, dreadlocked hair—even no hair. In fact, I felt quite outdated next to them all in my highly old-school outfit. (Despite my groans of protest, Gwyn had insisted I don the birthday khamees—minus the dupatta, which she'd snagged—and a pair of her too-high, too-narrow, size-too-big ruby pumps, claiming that everyone would be dressed likewise.)

The boys were a little less extravagant and fell mostly into one of two style categories: banker preppie in suits and polished shoes, or something sort of hip-hop but Indian—baggily low-hanging jeans and turned-around baseball caps and retro-looking T-shirts with numbers on them or names of teams I'd never heard of. In a flash I remembered the hip-hop boy I'd seen in Queens that day, the one I'd taken to be Dominican. I wondered if he'd been Indian all along.

These were definitely not the aunties.

Where had they been hiding all this time? These Indians who looked somewhat present in the twenty-first century? Why hadn't I seen them at Garbha and Diwali parties and the occasional wedding? Or had I—and they'd been as disguised in those contexts as I'd been? Or was their disguise one and the same, I was beginning to wonder, looking at a saried girl with blue-tipped porcupinal hair and a scintillating lip-ringed face; after all, a sari at a pooja looked traditional, but donned with a gelled-up hispid 'do at the leading melting pot music club of New York City (as this was, according to Kavita) it became something altogether different.

I could feel indignant hisses and livid eyes denting our profiles as we marched along, shamelessly cutting the queue.

—Think you're something special? cried out one enraged voice, I think belonging to the blue-tipped punk girl.

—Thank you! Gwyn cried cheerily, waving at her fans. Then she winked at a smiling boy with a tie insouciantly flipped back over his shoulder and a seashell cap, enraged the dark dryadic girl just behind him in line, charmed the bouncer, and walked into the first foyer.

But when I got to the entry it was a different story.

—Just where do you think you're going? the bouncer demanded.

—But I'm with her!

He didn't budge but turned to Gwyn, who was just inside the doorway, for confirmation.

—She's with us, Abraham, Gwyn kindly translated.

—All right. But I'll need to see some ID.

—You brought *it* right? said Gwyn, shooting me a meaningful look.

Wait a minute! Here I was three months closer to being legal than Gwyn, and probably even than some of these other folk, and I was the only one getting carded? Hello! My whole body screamed puberty and well beyond. Was there no justice in this world? I was five feet tall not five years old. Indignant, I handed him my card. He perused it, expression unchanging.

—It's nice to know you're literate, but this won't do.

In my quietly fuming haste I'd given him my Springfield public library card. I quickly grabbed it back and handed him the quack ID, courtesy of Dylan. Abe looked suspiciously down at it. Then suspiciously down at me. I tried to coax my posture up, vertebra by vertebra, but he was a tall man and there was no meeting eye-to-eye on this one; I wished I'd been taking my calcium. Oh flying frock, was it that obvious it was a dupe?

—But you don't even have a dimple, he said, finally. Then he gave me a smile, handing back the piece of plastic and bending down to look me in the iris.

—All right, in you go. And happy belated birthday.

He, however, as I now had the opportunity to see, had a dimple, deep in his left cheek. His whole face changed when he smiled, light clefting into it. And when he bent down, I saw the gold chain with *Abraham* in slanty caps glinting on his chest. So that's how she'd known.

★   ★   ★

Inside the first set of doors was a small foyer where people were paying and getting stamped on the wrist.

—Are you Dimple Lala? the girl in the ticket booth asked, checking out a Post-it on her desk.

Gwyn looked at me, stunned. I nodded, even more flabbergasted—was I known here?

—Yeah, you're listed plus one. Kavita Pradhan put you down as guests and said to tell you she'll be by in a couple hours to pick you up; she's caught up with work. But Sabz is here in any case.

As we were turning to go in, I thanked the girl.

—How did you know it was me, in this whole crowd of people? I asked her, happily amazed considering every female I'd seen here so far was pretty much the same coloring as me in terms of hair, skin, and eyes, and even around the same height.

—Her, said the girl, jerking her head in Gwyn's direction. —She said I wouldn't be able to miss her.

I tried not to let that get me down. After all, it made sense, right? Gwyn was the only blonde I'd seen on the sidewalk moat.

The second set of doors throbbed with music. I could feel it when I set my palm against the metal to push, even before they swung open and in we went.

We filtered into the room, which was fairly full, though not too many people were getting down on the parquet dance floor—just a couple slow dancing, and a guy who looked like he was definitely tripping, cutting out shapes in the air with soothsaying hands. A lazy R&B beat was playing, which probably accounted for the slow dancing, though I'm not sure what accounted for the shape cutting. From the looks of it, it seemed the party was either over or hadn't yet begun.

—Okay, location-scouting time, said Gwyn. We began to wind our way through the space, taking in the scene.

There wasn't much of one, though I had to admit the venue was far cooler than our gym could ever be, even if they lowered the ropes and let you swing and shoot baskets during dances.

From what I could see, the room was roughly shaped like a hand, splaying out from the palm that was the dance floor. I saw now that the couple there was actually two girls who appeared to be gazing down their own shirts as they danced with each other. The cookie cutter guy was sashaying around like the Pink Panther on glue, occasionally flinging his arms upward, as if invoking the rain god.

I followed his gaze to the high ceiling. It was covered in glow-in-the-dark stars arranged in various constellations. Hanging from the center of all this was what at a first glance appeared to be a sort of disco globe, and it swung low over the dance floor. Looking closer, though, it seemed to be a papier-mâché sculpture of a dozen or so leering black demon heads. These visages flashed with iridescent glitter, stricken in the lazy wave of the crisscrossing strobes.

The lights briefly washed over a couple of loungey areas, one beside us—past the foyer fish tank full of no fish and yes, perplexingly, drowned Barbie heads—and another kittycorner, at the shadow-dunked end where, from the incandescent signs, it seemed the back exit and bathrooms were. The area right by us consisted of low bamboo tables decked out with fat waxy candles and too many glasses. A few people, Indian again, lounged around eating crunchy things from wooden bowls and drinking drinks with little umbrellas in them like in the Chinese restaurant near Chimichanga's. They were going all slouchy from the low level of the furniture.

Flanking the dance floor on the left was a small stage with a couple of microphone stands and amps and techie-looking stuff hanging out on it; the floor snaked with wires. The exposed brick wall behind the stage winked indolently with what looked like garbled satellite messages—an image of Gandhi, and then an emaciated child, and then a roly-poly one. An elephant rooting out a plant and slapping the dust off against its ankles. A woman in flowing robes with a sweltering line of people in front of her, hugging them one by one. All the images were filtered in blues and reds. It was like CNN on acid.

And finally, directly across from the video wall, the bar, which was where we were heading, wading through the snowdrop patterns now sweeping the floor. The shelves behind the counter gleamed toothily. Amber and sapphire bottles stacked like smashed jewels to well above head level; ice clinked and glasses cut the light and sent it shooting, turning limpid the wooden ladder leading up, up to a high-walled runaround balcony area, which must have been storage space.

And when my eyes had runged back down, Sabina was before us, behind the bar. She was in a mirrored tank that flickered as she moved. When she reached up for a gold-capped bottle I was stunned to see tufts of hair under her arms, like grass pushing up through cracks in the pavement.

—Hey, you! I said as she uncapped the liquid into a swanky triangle glass on the bar. —What are you doing back there?

—Bungee jumping, said Sabina, winking and setting our bags behind the bar. —Whaddaya think I'm doing back here?

The straight swift bangs and the rest of her locks were tucked under a bandana that glowed ultraviolet in the nightclub light. She appeared much softer this way, her forehead rounding up and neck long and free.

—Did you have trouble getting in? she asked, raising her arms again to put the bottle back. There was something almost pubic about the hair there. —Kavita's coming by later to help when it gets crazy, but you know what a workaholic she is.

—No trouble at all, said Gwyn. She lowered her voice. —Um, Sabina, just FYI—I think you forgot to shave.

—I didn't forget to shave, Gwyn. I am fully aware of my underarm hair. I don't believe in shaving. It's not natural.

I wondered if she'd revise her thoughts if she'd been one of those girls who'd grown unfortunately into a hirsute upper lip, like Jimmy (Trilok) Singh's mother, who was a sort of Charlie Chaplin of Indian women. But then maybe Sikhs were used to lots of hair; I could only imagine the uncut quantity of it under those turbans. In any case I was pretty amazed at Sabina's reaction; sometimes I didn't shave either, but then I never went sleeveless. None of these concerns were applicable to Gwyn, who didn't seem to grow body hair.

—Not that many people, huh? I said, changing the subject and pulling up a stool. Gwyn thanked me and sat down on it. I pulled up another one.

—Are you kidding? said Sabina. —This is early, honey. You just stick around till it gets rolling and you won't be able to see your way out of here.

It was early? By this time any school dance would be long over, the parking lot full of parents honking like herds of leery geese. I'd thought we were arriving fashionably late.

—I didn't realize you meant bartending when you said you were working the event, I said.

—Well, turns out that means a few freebies for you two.

—What's that back there? I asked, indicating another fish tank, but this one flowing with nearly infrared liquid; a ladle bobbed in it like a lifeboat.

—Delhi Bellies, a special punch invented just for Desicreate.

—Delhi? Is that punch, like, an Indian specialty? asked Gwyn. She looked unsure now of her pink drink in its inverted-isosceles glass.

—All punch is an Indian specialty, said Sabina. —The word comes from *panch*, which means *five* in Hindi, because it used to have five ingredients.

She went on to explain how the English were introduced to it in colonial India and grew addicted. Good thing we hadn't asked her what the meaning of life was or we'd be here till the cows came home—which in Manhattan is no meager amount of time.

—Who can resist after an intro like that? I said. —I'll have one of those.

Sabina smiled approvingly and fished out the lifeboat.

—We've come a long way, baby—the colonized have *punched* out the colonizers! Independence reclaimed!

I didn't realize it was all that; I just liked the color, the same way I knew Gwyn liked the pink. But I knew when to hold my tongue.

She went off to take care of business at the other end of the bar. Gwyn air-clinked my glass so as not to spill.

—To a night to remember! she said.

—I'll drink to that, I said.

We looked out to the dance floor. Simmering strands were taking over the slow spill of the songs, and more and more people were beginning to gravitate there, to flow in from the street and into the beat-steeped room.

—God, Indian guys rock my world, sighed Gwyn, stirring her drink flurriedly, eyes whisking the place. —There are so many hot tamales here. Did you see that one?

In the vicinity of where she was gesturing now with her brows was a brown-skinned orange-teed guy with teapot ears and a nose that seemed like it had dropped on his face from a great height rather than grown organically from it, but I couldn't see behind him.

—The guy in the orange is blocking my view.

—That's the one I mean!

—Oh.

—What do you mean *Oh*? You can't be so blind. Can't you pick out even one dude you find shagadelic? I could hang here 24/7 and never stop feasting my eyes.

She seemed to be doing just that, looking around ravenously like a kid in a Krispy Kreme when the trays are just coming out of the oven. Or an adult in a Krispy Kreme when the trays are just coming out of the oven.

The dance floor now held a couple dozen Indians and the Pink Panther guy. Actually, this was a pretty good indication of the overall Indian/non ratio in the club so far. We were definitely in the minority. Gwyn seemed to notice this at about the same time.

—Maude, she whispered. —Looks like we're nearly the only white people in here!

—Yeah, I was just thinking that, I said. A split second later I wondered if I was the one on glue; it had come out of my mouth so naturally. Gwyn hadn't even seemed to notice: I was a minority, not a white person.

But the minority was the majority here. Which in fact meant that, here, Gwyn was in the minority. Maybe she was right and this was going to be my scene after all. Not one person had said hola to me. Not one person had said anything, actually, but that suited me just fine. It was a strange revelation, to be brown among the brown. Sure, it had happened in social situations with relatives and family friends, but on those occasions it still seemed we were a tiny ghee-burning coconut-breaking minority tucked away in someone's kitchen while the whole white world went on outside. And even in those instances I had never felt like my world was necessarily the one inside. And forget India—where I looked like I fit, acted like a tourist, and always wound up utterly lost (except when I'd been with Dadaji).

But here it could be different. This was New York City and the new century; these people were not my relatives and the chicas wore cool shoes. I couldn't believe I'd thought the place would be full of aunties. The girls here had their own brand of with-it. The boys—I wasn't sure about the boys. But they couldn't serve as an ideal for me to aspire to, so it didn't matter so much. And where was Karsh anyways?

The song playing was one I'd heard a million times on the radio, a number with a rappy outro by that utterly cool chunky deer-eyed woman whose head nearly comes off in the video and everyone looks caked in mud. But it seemed new again; there was something swirlier and ringier about it here—it was as if just before the heavy beats could sink into your skin they were bristled upwards by singing metallic fingers and sent to roam the air again. It reminded me of volleyball, but in slow motion and silver.

—Come on, Dimple. We're not gonna get anywhere just sitting here, said Gwyn. —Let's muster up some attention; you wanna go dance?

—How's never? I said. The music was pretty cool and seemed to be getting better by the beat; it wasn't that. It was just—me and dancing. That was something I did in my bedroom alone (rarely). And though the punch was indeed creating a hot spot in my belly, I hadn't had nearly enough of it to go there. I flagged down Sabina for another glass and looked out to the dance floor trying to imagine me on it. It was like when I tried to imagine me in the world in general; it was much easier to picture these things without me for some reason. Here, too, it was a tough match, unless I emptied the room and did away with the lights and pretended it was closing time.

I watched a few guys out there doing this nonstop shrugging motion with their shoulders and lifting their palms, hands twisting to the beat in a vaguely familiar move. The gesture used for indecisiveness and apathy had never looked so sure. How would I ever work my way into that, for example?

—I mean, check *that* out, Gwyn. That looks like it belongs at an Indian wedding, not a nightclub.

—Dimple, Gwyn scolded me. —You really have to open your mind. You're so judgmental sometimes. Think of it this way—you might even learn some *new* moves.

—I don't usually dance, you know that.

—You don't usually drink, either, and you seem to be adapting to that new hobby pretty well. Dimple, no one knows you here. You need to get out there and show 'em what you've got.

She looked at me mischievously.

—And then maybe you will be finding a nice Indian boy!

She did it in that mock Indian accent again. She was getting worrisomely good at it.

—Not like these dingbats you've been hanging with, she added. —Who don't deserve the time of day from you even if you're swimming in the Sea of Swatch, if I may say so. Bobby, Julian—watch out!

I had to smile. I loved when Gwyn dissed people who dissed me. Sometimes she also dissed those who really hadn't, true. But for the most part her nasty side was a good thing. They say if you don't have something nice to say about someone you shouldn't say anything at all and it was perfect, 'cause with Gwyn she said it all for me.

—Come on, this is your turf. Use it.

She even thought so! The second Delhi Belly had spread the fire from my stomach into my limbs. And we went out there. As I moved through the body-hot space I pictured it: my legs as two flames and my arms as two more. My body a melting candle, a wishstick, skin of sparklers.

The music had picked up still more and now innumerable arms were in the air shrugging like a wild bird herd with impeccable timing. A lot of guys were boogying, more than the girls it seemed. So far, the ratio factor was an entirely different one in this club: A much higher proportion of the male species seemed to be entering the place. And groups of them were dancing together, actually using their upper bodies. I had seen gaggles of girlfriends doing that—but guys? Never! I mean, I was definitely not drunk enough to use *my* upper body, and I was at least of the correct upper body gender. I don't know what it was about activating the arms but that was a whole other level of audacity in dance moves. And these boys had it. There was something simultaneously exciting and arrogant about how comfortable they seemed with their maleness. I hung my head low. Below me a sea of feet stamped and struck and rain-danced and rose to its toes and down. Sneakers and pumps and sandals and chappals and even a set of bare feet. My own peds among them; I began to shuffle them around in the ruby shoes to the choreographed pattern I did best.

But Gwyn. Gwyn went all out. A master assimilator, she warmed up by mimicking the boys around her, shrugging her shoulders and lifting her palms. Combined with her own jiggle hips and flirt-flit lids and sinuous waist whirl, that hair raying like an eclipsing, burning sun, it turned into something new altogether. It wasn't long before she had an entire crop of dance partners literally lining up to get busy with her.

To their credit they gave her a workout, limboing and lunging and revealing a flexibility that made me wonder whether they did sun salutations daily. It looked like a mating dance between two unlike species, a song of seduction and strutting feathers. I realized suddenly that not only was I not in this fast-forming inner circle, but I'd been pushed from the ring of her admirers entirely.

I knew this wasn't really couples music per se, but dancing with myself was starting to feel a little less like fiery and a little more like burned. I could see one of the boys peering past the flurry that was Gwyn at me and smiling. I didn't really want a dance partner, but at the same time I was relieved when I saw him walking over; it would be the lesser of two evils. He leaned into my ear and whispered something, and I was so set on hearing an invitation to conjoin shrugs that it took me a minute to realize what he'd really said.

—Beg your pardon, but are you doing the Electric Slide?

That did it. I signaled Gwyn, who took no notice, and then retreated back to the bar.

I climbed up onto my stool, soles throbbing. I reminded myself of a monkey I'd seen dancing to an accordion on Columbus Avenue and how he'd climbed back onto his perch to go simian again after his street performance. Except the monkey had made money off it.

—What's wrong with you?

It was Sabina, ladling me up with more Delhi Belly. She tracked my gaze to Gwyn.

—Oh, yeah, that would annoy me, too, she nodded. —I mean, come on, this isn't an aerobics class. It's bhangra, for Chrissakes. Look at these guys all licking their chops. But that's men for you. You can't live with them, you can't live with them.

I had to laugh at that one.

—But it shouldn't bug me, I said, tapping the glass to the whanging bass line. —I should be used to it by now. It's just that here I thought. I don't know.

—That you would find yourself.

—Yeah, I said, gazing in Sabina's sagacious face. —How did you know?

—Been there, done it, she said, to my bewilderment.

—But me, I feel as lost as ever.

More than ever. I was gesturing too much. My hands felt empty without Chica Tikka; purposeless.

—Crazy as it sounds, Dimple, sometimes you have to get lost to get found, said Sabina. —It's not such a bad thing, a little confusion. It makes you ask questions.

She saw me glancing over the bar to make sure my bag was okay.

—Uh, sorry if I'm a little paranoid, I said. —It's just that my camera's in it.

—Then why the hell aren't you using it?

—I would love to, Sabina—but I can't just go out there and start, like, taking *pictures*.

—What did you bring it for, then? You know, Kavita showed me some of those pictures you took for your grandfather. You've got the eyes. Now keep them on the prize.

I was extremely touched. But not convinced.

—I don't know where he is.

—Who?

—The prize.

—Not *he*. *This*.

She gestured to the wide span of the club.

—All this. You have to be ready for beauty, Dimple. That's when it comes, that's when you find it.

That did it. I took Chica Tikka out and gave Sabina my knapsack to stash back behind the bar. And it was true. The moment I had her in my hands I felt much better. Even without taking a picture. Just the weight of her in my palms, the sureness of the strap, the case weightless now, the way it should be, in my lap.

I looked my camera in the eye. I could see down there a tiny convex me. I watched the tiny me in the lens staring back with a piercing regard, one that seemed to arrow into my deepest part. The tiny me bobbled her head to the music, which was beginning to climb like a live animal up the legs of the barstool and into my own, massaging away the knots and lifting me on a wing out of my sadness.

A woman was singing, after all the man vocals, with a scorchingly sweet voice that sounded like India herself, mingling with the prodigy of the deer-eyed mud-caked rapper, all atop an ever-weaving tapestry of sitar and snare and cachunking key. Somehow the music felt exactly right. It was full of as many emotions as a bite of bhel puri; it crunched and it spilled and it lingered and was gone in a heartbeat. It trundled down the throat, eddied in the belly and dawdled; it satiated and made you want more. It was danceable and it was lonely and it was full of fields and fruit and skyscrapers, and it was the sound of a star forming in a black hole. Somehow it was just how I was feeling. It was funny, but it felt as if the DJ was playing just for me—which eased my agony at watching Gwyn, as usual, get all the attention. I was beginning to see what Sabina meant about having to get lost to get found—if I gave myself up to the moment I forgot myself, I forgot the fact I didn't know or understand the words, I became the tiny twiggling girl in the lens, drawing strands of light from a dark curtain.

And when I looked up to the dance floor again, startled to see all these people inhabiting a space where I'd just had such an ironically quiet moment, something happened that I couldn't believe.

Before my very eyes, Gwyn's position as dance-floor diva was usurped, gently but incontestably, by the most striking woman I'd ever seen.

She didn't even look human. This creature was an Indian goddess, like something I had seen only in museums or movies or the illustrations in the gorgeously spined books on Dadaji's shelves. Except even more fictitious and more vital, as if she'd come unclipped from the Hindi film images now brick playing, wandering multidimensionally out.

She was decked out in space-age Bollywood style in an argentine sari, and silver glitter dusted the apples of her cheeks. Her locks rang long, flawless as mannequin hair; her skin was like sunrise on sand dune. She had all the right moves and they seemed subaqueous, so flowing were they. Her face, too, danced to the beat, neck switching from side to side, seashell lids low, eyes skirting the faces before her from beneath them, like dark, slow darting fish.

She made everything around her disappear, the way the wish on the cake can make the cake, crowd, and kitchen vanish. But more than anything it was the energy around her that was remarkable. The way it felt you could cup it in your palm and keep a piece of it for later.

Without a word, a glance, a grin, she had moved me. And the entire place: The ring had widened when she'd stepped onto the dance floor; people who had been dancing stopped to stare, people who hadn't began, hands held to their hearts.

—Looks like your friend's been pegged for the hi-lo instructor she truly is, Sabina tittered into my reverie.

It was true: Beside the queenly one Gwyn—still flapping around like a cheerleader—suddenly looked a bit like a bhangra buffoon. It made me sad for a moment; much as I longed to be like Gwyn, when it came down to it, I didn't long for her to come off as foolish on the other side of the equation. But she hadn't seemed to notice, appeared just as intoxicated as the rest of the crew, in her bounding puppy-dog enthusiasm almost eager to please this enthralling new presence.

The woman was the image of all the grace and femininity I longed for—but with the silver lining of being, in a way, within reach. No, I would never be tall, blonde, and milky-skinned like Gwyn, but this petite, inky-haired, bronze-limbed being made that seem even conceivable as a good thing.

—Leave it to Zara, Sabina said, smiling to herself and shaking her head. —She puts the balls into Bollywood, that's for sure. Now *that's* what I call getting into character.

Before I could ask her what she meant she'd disappeared to the other end of the bar, which I now realized was packed. When had that happened?

I could have sat there staring forever. I doubted film could capture why, but I figured I'd give it a try and picked up my camera. But by the time I'd put my eye to the viewfinder Zara had vanished into the crowd.

This time I was prepared to jump to it. I hopped off the stool to the quavering ground and, Chica Tikka in hand, began to navigate the maze of the club, this time riding my tipsy shoes as if they were waves on the tidal floor, soon adapting.

Dadaji, you are going to love this.

The place had really filled while I'd been lost in Zara. The drums were getting manic, percussive beats shuddering feverishly through the skin. More and more boys and girls were unshackling, taking up the dance floor. They bobbed like life buoys, shrugged with one hand twisting up in a queen's wave to the pale plastic stars above, the other to the ear, as if straining to hear, oddly, the resounding beat. Many more girls had gathered since the last number with Zara, creating now a perhaps fifty-fifty mix, but, funnily enough, with the exception of Gwyn (who continued to hold on to her entourage), the men seemed to prefer dancing with each other.

No wallflowers in this crowd, and it felt as if at any moment the floor might cave in and roof drop down and they would just keep dancing as the pretend stars were replaced by real ones, clicking on one by one like tiny lights. Not that you could usually ever see stars in Manhattan; they were so often concealed under the dreamy purple gauze of the night sky, or turned around, the way women wore precious rings backwards on the subway.

But I had a feeling they were out wishingly tonight, and I slipped through the back doors, the ones with the embered Exit just above them.

★   ★   ★

The back of the building was fairly desolate, a few cars in the lot and a grille fence wrapped halfway around it, surrendering to the ground in parts, verdant knobs of grass choking through the wire diamonds. The sight of this gasp of green nourished me with tenderness.

Steam rose off the pavement, and I waded through all the accumulated heat of the day. Outside the air was balmy and soft and a child breeze brushed its fingers gently against my skin. I could smell the sea, the salt catching in my inhalation and filling me with an inexplicable sense of nostalgia. Plastic shovels and sand castles I hadn't built were as real to me as if I had, other people's memories seeming to flow into my body with the briny westward wind. The thought that the sea was close—that this was an island, and a moon-wound ocean was always within minutes of your touch, connecting you to every other imaginable place in the world—teased me open with a sense of possibility. I breathed deep, and in the sky an enormous star pierced my vision. First star I see tonight, unless you counted the plastic ones. I had to make a wish.

I didn't know how to put my wish into words. The image of a ladder trembling romantically up into a balcony, of princesses letting down their hair, of my mother's dance costume, of Zara's stunning grace—I had so wanted to keep her in my camera, beside the tiny me.

My star began to move, at first I thought in response to my crossed fingers and concentrating eyes. Then to blink red, white, red, a bit of blue. And then I realized it was an airplane, a celestial thread stitching a piece of sky. Could I wish on it nonetheless?

—It still counts, a smoky voice sashayed across the pavement towards me. I turned.

It was Zara. Just when I'd stopped looking I'd found her. And she wasn't alone, but was leaning with her back against the graffiti-kissed brick, the seashelled cell-phoned boy who had let us cut the line by her side, one of her hands in two of his. His jacket was off now, his striped shirt puckering slightly open.

—Go on, now, don't waste that film, she said, nodding to my camera. She had that hillocky English accent that my parents' friends who'd gone to nun-run schools in India had. —You've got a classic Kodak moment right before your eyes, yaar.

I couldn't believe it.

—Are you sure you don't mind? I asked.

—Mind? I would be offended if you didn't.

That was the last thing I wanted. So I aimed, pulling the two into my small framed view. Zara glowed against the hardened lava of the written wall. I saw now that she was barefoot and on tiptoes, a pair of the most unusual shoes I'd ever seen tumbled by her feet. I zoned in on them to take a look—they were silver, the heels vertiginously high and coated with glittering bits and pieces of who knew what to create a bedlamic mosaic. I pulled back and focused on the wider frame.

They both smiled for the camera, but it was no mere camera smile: Their happiness was as tangible as the grit in the bricks and the salt in the sky tonight.

—One . . . two . . . *teen!* I said.

—Jalfreezi! she cried.

I snapped.

—Now I want a copy of that, Photo Girl.

—Dimple Lala, I said.

—Zara Thrustra, she said. Then she indicated her companion. —Ye mere dilka sangeet hain.

—How should I get it to you?

—Oh, where there's a will, she said and turned back to face the many-named boy in a way so intimate it signified our conversation was over.

As I was leaving, heading to enter the club, I turned back for one last glimpse. And what met my eyes was the photograph I wanted but which required no film to imprint on my memory: The two were gazing, smiling at each other, the boy touching her cheek with his hand, her hand on his hand, foreheads together. Their view must have been a cyclopsian or even tryclopsian one; their eyes were so close their lashes could have brushed butterfly kisses. They imbued grace in the graffiti that slashed the wall apart behind them, brought everything together with the tenderness of their regard.

Tears blurred my vision as I passed through the doorway again.

My favorite part of *The Wizard of Oz* has always been when the film switches out of black and white, when Dorothy steps out of Kansas and into Oz and life goes Technicolor. And that's what reentering the room was like. But what was Technicolor about it was the music; it had hit high tide and a redolent wave of it surged and crashed upon me and I realized it was a song I knew by that singer with a voice so been-there and smoked-too-many it made it hard to believe she was a preacher's daughter but then it was all raw love she was singing about and you believed it, you believed her, you believed it could happen to you. But it was not quite the way I'd ever heard it on the radio or MTV: It was as if the song itself had taken drugs. Doying-doyinging through it were all kinds of swirly slink sounds, like Ravi Shankar and joint family were pogo-sticking through on their way to the opera. Except it wasn't invasive. It was really upping the ante of the song and a beat like a deep slapped lake buckled heavily in it as they went. And then the preacher's daughter, she skated somewhere else, pursuing her own dream, and the whole bottom part of the song rose up into the space she left behind and a man's voice was calling out *itchy itchy eye*, and then silence, and then everyone crying *oh ho!* and then *itchy itchy eye*, and silence, *hi hi!* the drums again, charging.

It reminded me of something and my head jumbled with half-thoughts and images, vivid and shorn from their original context. Like the memory of a memory of a dream. Rooftops and rungs and the stars just within reach once you got there. We were one and we were all and this DJ was playing my song.

I looked up at the plastic stars. The ten-headed demon had been smashed open and glitter-rain winked down upon the masses. It fell upon me, sticking. And it was literally raining men: stage diving and climbing up again and again, indefatigably, like children with new toys. Onstage dancers leapt this way and that, mingling with what seemed like millions of people flickering on brick. Then I realized the screen was playing the scene at hand, with its closest focus on the stage, so that each person and motion was exaggerated and amplified, echoing just behind itself in a doubled world.

The floor smack-crackled. Women in saris were bumping and grinding, hair windmilling off tawny faces. The corporate types were tearing off their ties and getting into the groove. The sea of hands had multiplied and fingers wiggled like antennae. Mad mind-bending energy pulsed through the venue. The entire space combusted, came undone, people flying through the air, on chairs, on table edges. I had never seen anything like it in my life.

Everyone was dancing.

I waded through the techno tulips, dripping languorously down the walls and pivoting pink and fuchsia on the floor. A circle had cleared just by the stage. Between every-which-way elbows and thumping hips I could make out what at first looked like a ruddy human vortex whirling down a drain on the floor but without getting smaller. A moment later I realized it was a couple of guys break dancing; from the turbans I guessed they were Sikhs.

When I pushed through the human barrier to examine the faces below me I couldn't believe it. A hawkish-nosed baby-bearded boy was down there, whizzing in and out of contortions as easily as if he were tying a shoe, his turban running color like paint. The thick silver kada bouncing light like a flash off his wrist and into his familiar high-IQ eyes clinched it for me: It was my own Jimmy (Trilok) Singh! He didn't look so shabby tonight, doing those on-the-back swirlie-whirlies. I stood at the forefront of the human amphitheater and poised my camera just above him, leaning in. Jimmy (Trilok) looked right up, but was so lost in his sweat grace he seemed not to see me. I snapped. Now why hadn't he mentioned *that* in his plan for world domination via fingerprint security systems? If he'd meant via the dance floor he wasn't far off.

The counter ran to zero. It had been my last shot.

And then Jimmy (AKA These-Are-the-Breakswallah, so it appeared now) Singh whizzed out of the circle like a turbaned bullet and a deus-ex-machinic Gwyn was in, egged on by her new fan club and matched with his former dance partner. He was a tough act to follow, admittedly, but in the end she caught everyone completely off guard by breaking out into cartwheels, flipping repeatedly back and forth across the expanding circle. No one had any choice but to move out of the way.

The circle was growing wider to accommodate her and I was sliding out of its radius. I found myself being swept as if on a tide, barwards. In the distance, a shifting, scintillating Milky Way grew closer and closer until it coalesced to become the mirrored tank top containing Sabina at the other end of the bar, arms floating on the trebled air and rounding around Kavita's waist in greeting, Kavita who was just climbing over the counter, surfing a long note, to join her. Their hair mingled when they hugged. It was an embrace that excluded everyone, and I came back to myself, and somehow I'd gone into the sad part of the punch. It was hard to believe I'd been able to see the limits of this room when I first walked in; now it seemed there were none. What a trip simply crossing it had been: from insecurity, to hope, to fear, to curious jubilation, and now to a strange strain of melancholy. These seemed to be the ingredients of the fish tank drink, not so much arrack and water, sugar and citrus, spice.

click

Around midnight the grooves shifted and weighed me to the stool, the stout beat resonant, a slowed stethoscope listen to a robot's secret heart, a sweet medicinal voice poured over it all but always floating above, never quite soothing the knots in the dark musical arrangement.

I was contemplating the foot of my barstool when a voice tunneled warm over ladder-rattle and into my ear, so close I could feel the breath the words were wrapped in.

—Is this seat taken?

I began to move out of the way, and when I looked up I was taken aback. It was Karsh, laying down a large cardboard box and pulling up the barstool beside me. I had a strange sense of relief when I saw him.

—Hi! I said a little too enthusiastically.

—Hi, you, he said, scooting onto the edge of the barstool. A bag crisscrossed his body, messenger style. It looked pretty heavy, but instead of taking it off, he ran his hands along the strap, shimmying it round till it rested against his back and the stool took up the weight. In the mottled light I could make out his red-sneakered feet resting one on each side of the box. They were the same sneaks he'd worn to our house.

—Yeah, I'm a little paranoid about my stuff, he confirmed.

—Guess that makes two of us, I smiled. Funny, I was sitting the same way with my knapsack, which I'd recovered from Sabina after my photographic wanderings.

—What's *your* secret treasure? he asked, nodding at the sack.

—Oh nothing, I said. —Just clothes and, well, my camera.

—That doesn't sound like nothing to me, he said.

I didn't say anything.

—I saw you trying to take that picture of Zara. In fact, I saw you track Zara all through the room and outside. It was impressive—when you focus, you focus! Drink?

He pointed to my empty punch glass, and the water glass beside it.

—Or maybe not, he said. —It's a good thing you've been hydrating all night or you'd be knocked out by now.

I nodded, speechless. Where had he been watching me from?

—It's amazing, you with your camera, he said. —You get so into it, this look of concentration—I can picture you as a little kid, chewing an eraser, solving a problem. You even start imitating your subjects, standing like them, moving like them, even *talking* to them. Or yourself, I guess. And your flash—I've never seen anything like it: Did you realize it was going off *to the beat?* Were you doing that on purpose?

—Uh, no. I don't know.

In the pause that followed he suddenly seemed embarrassed. But what did *he* have to be embarrassed about? I had no idea I imitated whatever I was shooting. Frock, I must have been doing the most cringeworthy things all that time.

—I, I talk to myself? I asked tentatively.

—Well, maybe not, he replied quickly. —Maybe it just looked that way.

—Oh, how blushable, I said. —I do talk in my head to my grandfather sometimes. But I didn't know I actually say things out loud.

—Oh, I don't know if you say things out loud. Maybe your lips just move, Karsh said by way of apology. —Why to your grandfather, if you don't mind my asking?

—See, he, well. He's the reason I even started taking pictures. I, we couldn't speak the same language and we sort of decided to talk this way, without words, for the most part. With, you know, images.

—That's amazing, said Karsh softly. —To show each other your worlds?

There was something so genuinely interested in his expression that I felt brave and went on.

—Yeah, but then, it's funny, the pictures began to describe emotions, too. Like, instead of saying *how are you, I'm fine,* we'd find images to do so.

And often they seemed more accurate. You know, you can be in a red mood but full of blue, or you can be having a sunny day but still feel overcast.

I heard myself and felt shy.

—Oh, I don't know. I guess you must think it sounds silly.

Karsh laughed.

—Dimple, don't ever quit your day job to be a mind reader. That's not at all what I was thinking. I was thinking that is beautiful, what you shared with your dada. You really miss him, don't you?

The way he said dada instead of grandfather warmed me and I began to feel safe. I nodded, still staring down. His feet had loosened their grip on the box.

—But it must be like he's there with you when you take those pictures, Karsh continued. —Looking back at you through the lens.

I started at his accuracy, and he mistook my trembling hand.

—Don't be embarrassed, Dimple. You are completely present when you take these photos. You become real in a whole other way. You know everyone has their hook—the chord that makes the song, that detail that tells the big picture. And I think that's yours. I was wondering at your house. And I could tell even then—the second the topic came up you got all shy and strange. Laid bare. I'd really like to see this side of you, if you'd let me. I mean, I'd really like to see your pictures sometime.

How did he know all this?

—How did you even—?

—Psychic, he said, laying a tip on the counter and handing me the glass. His balance was impressive; Sabina was filling them so far up the rim fizzed out. He had a beer in his own hand, and clinked me so gently with it not a dripple slid off the high surface of that risky lake.

As we drank, his eyes turned to the dance floor. In the club setting he looked the same but different—his skin had more gold tones in it, his eyes stoked two fires from the now slow-burning lights reflected in them.

His profile was actually quite majestic, leonine with the high forehead and long nose and the way he held his neck erect. His arm lay next to my own on the bar, not touching, but I could just feel the heat waver off his skin. I couldn't believe he'd been watching me. Somewhere inside, and not even so deep down to escape me, I liked that.

I followed his line of vision. It ended in the one-woman discotheque that was Gwyn. She'd taken over again and was now leading a group of salivating spellbound boys in a sort of bhangrified version of, believe it or not, our emblematic school cheer for the football team; I could nearly hear the *Gimme an L!* It wasn't quite matched up to the beat of the song playing—to her credit, it was no easy number to dance to, with all its chingly chunks and thudding footfalls and slightly dissonant drum machines—but the guys, who'd all seemed to be master dancers earlier in the evening, didn't seem to mind. Mainly they were just hanging around behind her, ogling her backside as she shook imaginary pom-poms and glided across the drink-sticky floor. We both watched her wordlessly for a moment; well, I suppose I was watching him watch her, to be more accurate. Karsh was studying her so keenly, and it was shameful, but I wished Zara were here to show her up.

—That your friend? he said gesturing towards her with his beer bottle.

—Sure is.

—She's something else, he said tipping the amber liquid back into his throat. I watched his Adam's apple bob gently as he swallowed. —Quite a fan club she's mustered up this evening. From the second she walked in.

—Yeah, well, that's a typical night out with Gwyn.

—Is it? said Karsh, turning back to me.

So that explained why he'd been watching me—he'd been watching *her*, and I just happened to be caught up in her epic climate, like a bit of yesterday's news blowing around the edge of today's tempest. I was surprised to find myself a little disappointed.

—Don't you want to dance?

Now I was on the spot. I certainly did not want to get jiggy out there with Gwyn. She had it going on. Me, my soles didn't even reach the floor. And it felt like a long drop if I began falling.

—My feet hurt, I said.

—They didn't seem to hurt when you had your camera out, he said, sounding slightly annoyed. —To tell the truth I was pretty surprised to see you here.

—Why is that?

—I don't know. I guess you just seemed so resistant the other day.

—Well, weren't you?

—Not really. The way I see it, what's the worst that can happen? At best you could end up with a new friend.

I thought of Julian and how I never heard from him after the whole hurlathon. And Bobby's belief that friendship was overrated.

—Don't you mean at *least* you could end up with a friend?

—No, I mean at best. But maybe that's just me. Maybe you don't need another friend.

—I'm sorry, I said. —My mind was in another place that day.

—Or maybe on another person?

—Maybe a little, I admitted. The image of Julian's shaggy face seemed discordant with this atmosphere, like a vestigial memory left over from a snapped synapse; contextless. —But not anymore.

—No? he said. —Look, I'm sorry. I should have thought to check in on your, your personal status first. It's just, when my mom brought it up she was so excited, and now that my dad's pretty much out of the picture it's become even more important to me to meet the people who knew them when they were happy. It feels like another lifetime—I barely remember it myself.

—Out of the picture? I said. —I thought he was just wrapping up business in India.

—*Losing* business in India, said Karsh. —It's all in the euphemisms. My mom kicked him out; he's a compulsive gambler, in short. It was the right thing to do, but I miss him. I miss him all the time.

His eyes shone too much and his mouth slung down.

—You know, it felt so wonderful hanging out with your dad the other day—I didn't want to ever leave! It was like all the good stuff without the pain.

Something came over me. I nearly reached out and touched his hand there on the edge of the bar, but caught myself and ended up laying mine just beside his.

—Your parents are really great, Dimple. They're really proud of you. They were?

—Well, your mother is really proud of you, too, I said. —Not to mention my parents.

He laughed, looking down into his glass.

—She's top, my mom. But I wonder sometimes if my dad would be proud. I mean, he could argue that we're gamblers, too, coming back to America without him and the things I'm choosing to put my time into.

—Honestly, Karsh, I think he'd be really proud of you, too, I said. —And if you want to borrow my dad in the meantime, feel free.

He smiled. His hand was nearly touching mine and I had a strange feeling. Electric, like a current was running from his skin to mine. The thin slit of distance between us was as tensely tangible as the moment between thunder and lightning. As music hidden in a piano bench.

—You know, I guess I just feel a lot of pressure sometimes to keep people happy, he said finally.

—Yeah, I know what you mean, I said. —I feel a lot of pressure sometimes, too, and I don't even know what about. Sometimes I just lie in bed and panic.

Why was I telling him this? But it didn't even feel that out of place; the entire undulating environment made untidy things possible. It was as if we were suspended in a reality where false lights allowed true things to be offered, loud music created an eye of a storm in which to be still, and part of me couldn't believe all the madness I was speaking. But I felt I could with him, like you could with a brother or total stranger, like I only had five minutes or a lifetime to tell him, we were on a train hurtling headlong into blackness and he would get it and it would be what life was all about, like when you read a book that transfuses your blood, or hear a song that not only matches your mood but shapes it. Like when you see a photograph that is so spot-on and say: *Now this. This is it.*

—Sometimes everything feels so huge.

—So nebulous, he said. —I know. But I've usually found making one decision can clear up all the clouds, the way one ray of sun can light a dark room. It's funny, but it's true.

We were leaning in close to hear, and it felt like we were in a cave and a storm was turreting just outside.

Then he told me a story and it was a beautiful story. He whispered tiny breezes into my ear, a current and an undertow. He told me about his last trip to India, staying in a very simple ashram in Pondicherry and rising at the moment before dawn to watch the fishermen going out to sea. And how it was all darkness and then darkness graded towards light, indiscernibly, nearly. How the fog and the sky and the waves were one and from the sky emerged a horizon and then from the horizon there were the slants of waves breaking and rising and then some of these ripples began to distinguish themselves and turn fleck by stroke into gaunt men on gaunter boats, pushing themselves out to the deep part with sticks longer than they were. And then how the sun bled into the water and began to rise, that burning ball of the world disco and the water was pink and the sky sangria and everything was on fire but not burning and how he felt like he was witnessing, in these few moments, the birth of the universe. And that you could do that everywhere, not just in the south of India alone in an ashram; you could pull a fisherman from the fog and blood from water and gold from stone and sound from silence. Anywhere.

And it made sense, this story. And after he told it, it was funny, but I felt we might have gone there together. He looked familiar now, but in a different way. The way my mother's melody had been familiar; the way the music had spoken to me, even the first time I'd ever heard it.

—You've got something special going on with your pictures, Dimple, he said as if in conclusion to all that.

I wanted to believe him.

—You haven't even seen them, I said.

—I've seen you taking them—right here, tonight. And, well, I've seen a couple of them already. But I guess those were . . . maybe from a different phase, from the looks of what you're going for now. I mean, *technically* they were right on—

—Huh?

What was he talking about? No one had been in my darkening room.

—You know, in your house. In the foyer.

My mind was drawing a blank. There weren't any photos in the foyer. There were just those . . . frames . . .

—Get out! I said, a shrouded corner of my mind instantly clearing. So he had just been trying to make me feel good! I explained to him what that had all been about, and we shared a laugh, which felt even better.

—So you see, you really *haven't* seen any of my photos.

—You haven't invited me, he said.

—I just don't know if they're . . . Well, they mean something to me, but I don't know if they're really . . . you know. Any good.

He paused, pensive.

—You can't let your fear stop you, he said then. —You have to let it move you and move beyond it. Sometimes the most natural things, the things that don't seem risky, are the most supernatural; they sneak up on you. You keep taking pictures and one day you might see something that surprises you.

He lay his unfurled palm there on the bar, and my fingers uncurled, too.

—That's what I love about clubs, he went on. —It's the same thing, but amplified. It's all about the dynamic—music plays the people and people play the music; you take a picture, it tells you a story. You're not alone. Your story, our families. It's yours, it's mine.

I was overwhelmed by it all. This network of connection, bringing together all these seemingly disparate things with an underlying logic that made sense even though I would be hard put to explain it: my mother's lullaby, my father's good-dream face, all the tears, the unbound laughter, the space between things, the undrunk tea; Dadaji on the lens's far side. And now the two of us, Manhattan, past midnight, and no question the most amazing conversation of my life.

—It even feels like our past is here tonight, I whispered. I felt I could really talk to him.

—Maybe the future, too, he whispered back. —You're an amazing woman, Dimple. I can really talk to you.

My breath caught in my throat. Woman? That was something. And the other part. It was as if we were reading each other's minds. Was it all written, as my mother always insisted?

—Karsh, I said. —Do you believe in destiny?

—I think it's all there, if that's what you mean, he said. —But that doesn't mean you can't revise, rewrite, bring the bass up. You've got to believe in both—fate works best in retrospect, right? Give it your best shot and only then what is meant to be will be.

—With your collaboration, you mean.

—You've got to believe that, or why even get out of bed in the morning? he said. His hand was so close to mine it hurt. —Nothing's static. Just look out there, at the dance floor. Even the lines in your palm—they don't stay the same.

And then he took my hand ever so gently, but the touch went deep. He turned it over, gazing into it. The mingled heat of our skins felt strangely comforting.

And then we weren't even speaking, just staring at each other, and it was still the most amazing conversation of my entire life. His eyes were swimmingly close. So close I could see myself in them.

—Your destiny's not some elusive thing, Dimple, he said finally. —It could be staring you right in the face.

—Hey there! a breathless voice called out.

We both jerked up, hands dropping apart before they'd truly touched, as if we'd been doing something wrong. Gwyn stood there, staring from the edge of the dance floor. The music heaved like a buried heart, and her boys were blurry in the distance. She'd fixed the dupatta over her hair, its ends trailing a veil unraveled as she moved towards us. And the way she moved towards us, flicking on and off in the strobing light, was like a mirage, an apparition—there in a blast of lightning, ever present in the darkness in its wake.

It was only a moment, the locked eyes between them, but it stung a little. We'd been having such an incredible conversation and it was all down the drain now, like an idea for a poem you catch in bed—you promise yourself you'll remember, sing yourself to sleep with it, and then wake to find you didn't clasp it close enough and it stayed in your dream and now you're not there anymore and you might never have the same dream again. Gwyn was a walking waking call, a harsh reality check. But that conversation with Karsh—I wouldn't forget it.

She sidled up next to me on the barstool, nearly knocking me and my bag off in the process (fortunately my elbow crooks are a highly developed part of my body and I caught it before it slipped to the floor). Funny how such a slight frame could take up so much space.

I reverted to looking down into my punch glass, which kept inexplicably refilling. I was lifting it to my lips when Gwyn dunked her head in and took a noisy slurp, as if at a trough.

—I'm parched—I haven't danced this much in at least a couple weeks!

she cried. —Claude, I love this place! I'm having the time of my life. Aren't you having the time of your life?

She gestured off into the dance floor distance.

—This DJ rocks! I swear I'm gonna have to hire him for a party one of these days.

—He's a she, said Karsh, smiling and gesturing directly up into the rafters, that veranda wrapping around the clubland sky. —DJ Tamasha. She's a friend of mine.

—I'm Gwyn, by the way, Gwyn said, extending her hand. Her eyes hadn't vacated his face for one moment. Had she given up blinking for Lent already? —Gwyn Sexton.

—And I'm Karsh, said Karsh, with that half-twist smile. —Karsh Kapoor.

A cloud blew through her eyes. Then she snapped her fingers and it cleared.

—Karsh? Karsh Kapoor? she cried. —Oh you're *Karsh* Karsh. Karsh*um*. Yeah, you're famous already. Dimple told me what a disaster that whole meeting was!

She said it cheerfully, as if this were the best of all possible greetings. Karsh looked at me. I wanted to drop through a crack in the floor. I remembered how casually I'd told her she could have him that night she'd slept over—as if he were even mine to give. She must have figured he was fair game.

—What was it you said again exactly? Gwyn said, almost to herself, my glass now in her hand as if it had never been in mine. She noddingly guffawed, remembering. —Yeah, yeah—that it was a total *Titanic*.

Taxi!

Karsh's half-twist slipped slightly. But if it was a hurt or offended look, it was gone in a matter of seconds and would have been hard to read anyways since his face was just a sliver away from all sorts of emotions all the time: Anger, pride, laughter, compassion all seemed to coexist in glowering glowing harmony there, like the music that was playing now, an ethereal she-angel voice gliding thrummily over moody beats and unsettling sitars, making you feel two things at once, more than two things.

The next three seconds felt like three years.

—I didn't say that exactly, I said, trying to give Gwyn a big-toe tap on the ankle.

—Oh, right, you didn't say that, she said, merrily twirling an ice cube with her pinky. Okay, better late than never; at least she'd caught the code.

—You said it was like *Titanic* without the *romance*. That's right. I knew I was forgetting something. Isn't that funny? And what was it? You had a great line—oh! You'd rather pick the eggs, no, the lint out of your toes . . .

This time I kicked her, which resulted in my knocking myself off the stool.

—. . . than continue this conversation, I said.

Karsh smiled to himself but he didn't look so happy; he spun his bottle slowly between his hands.

—Nothing personal, Gwyn said, finally catching on. —It's just an expression. And anyways, thank Maude it's over; now you're both free to do what you want to do, not what your parents say.

—Yeah, said Karsh. —Thank Maude it's over.

—Um, yeah, I said. —We're free. Look, I'm sorry I said that.

—It's all right, he said, still turning the bottle.

—I didn't mean it.

—You don't mean what you say?

—Oh, Dimple always says what she means, said Gwyn, rushing clumsily to my defense. —You can count on her. Anyways, I'm free, too. Though my kind of freedom was a harder one to come by than yours, I'm guessing.

—How so? asked Karsh.

—Well, this guy I was seeing, you know, he totally screwed me over for some chickadee who talks about herself like she's someone else. What's up with that? I mean, she calls herself by her own name and everything. *Anyways.* He told me we were just friends, and I thought, man, if you do what you did with me with all your friends, then I'm looking for an enemy next time around. This all fresh off the press, pretty much.

I stood like a small fool between them, the two on their barstool thrones above me. Gwyn settled comfortably into the seat, Indian style. She caught all the light and he was aglow in it already and the stools coalesced into darkness; it looked like the two of them were levitating, practitioners of some particularly advanced form of meditation, or drinking.

—Man, that's rough, Karsh was saying sympathetically.

—Oh, I don't want to get into it, said Gwyn, as if that prelude had been the epitome of discreet. She waved my empty glass towards the bar. —Sabina, honey, could you fill 'er up?

When the drink bobbed towards us, Gwyn straightened.

—To freedom, she declared, lifting the glass and mapping a little cosmopolitanation all over my right shoulder.

—To freedom, said Karsh, quietly raising his bottle.

But I didn't want it anymore. Freedom suddenly felt like a lonely thing, an empty house. In any case I didn't have anything to toast with so I suppose it didn't matter.

—Dimple! cried Gwyn, noting my empty hands just as she set down the empty glass. —Oh no, did you want it? Well, you weren't drinking it, right? You were just kind of looking at it . . .

—I'm fine.

—Cool, she said, turning promptly back to Karsh.

—You know, you sure don't look like *Titanic* without the romance to me! she giggled. —Sort of the other way around.

How was it that she could already have developed a thing for him? Rebound? Revenge? But for what? Nothing made sense, but her crush was clear as the glass. I was surprised to find myself both irritated and terrified by this; why should I care? I decided long before he wasn't for me, right? That I'd never be Indian enough for a boy like him?

And then, to my horror:

—You know, Karsh, it's funny we haven't met before, because it's actually already public information that you belong to me.

—And how is that? Karsh asked.

And she launched then and there into the Behind the Music about her run-in with Dylan and his 212 lovergirl.

—. . . and then to get back at him Dimple told him I was already with someone—and I became your girlfriend! she concluded. —So that's what Dickland and Julian think now, except I don't know if Dickland is buying it one hundred percent.

—Hmm, interesting, said Karsh. —And who's Julian?

—Dimple's boy.

—He is so not! I cried indignantly.

—What's your problem? Gwyn replied coolly. —Correct me if I'm wrong, but that's all you wanted a few days ago—and now you won't give him the time of day?

—Gwyn, it's not. *We're* not. I mean, what are you—?

—Speaking of the time of day, Karsh suddenly interjected, glancing at his watch. —It is just about that time of night that I think I've got to be making my move.

—You gonna turn into a pumpkin or something? said Gwyn.

—More like a coachman—can I offer you a lift? I'm heading back to Jersey if you are.

I didn't know whom that was aimed at, as he was bending down to pick up his box as he spoke. I was about to tell him we were staying with Kavita and Sabina—who were both heading in our direction, engaged in some kind of race to wipe down the bar as they approached—but Gwyn jumped in.

—I would love a ride, she said.

—But we're—

—Sorry, Dimple, I forgot, she said. —I've got to get home tonight. I thought I told you.

I don't know why, but I didn't want to let them go. What if he told her the Pondicherry story? Or called *her* a woman?

Kavita was scanning one face to another. Finally she spoke.

—Actually, yes, it's time you got home, too, Dimple, isn't it?

She was a genius.

—Thank you, Karsh, then I'm not having to drive them, she continued, pocketing an Oscar as far as I was concerned. —I'm a little tipsy, to be honest, and so is Sabz.

—I am? said Sabina. Kavita must have pinched her from behind the bar because she started. —*Whoa!* I mean, I *am.*

It was decided. If it were a choice between three being a crowd or two being company, I would have to vote for the former. The idea of leaving Karsh in Gwyn's hands was too distressing somehow.

—Thanks, Kavita, I whispered as we got up to go.

—Go get 'em, cowgirl, she said with a wink.

flash!

When we hit the sidewalk, I realized I'd better phone my parents to avoid having a squad team circling my house moments after my unheralded break-in.

—Can you guys hold on a sec? I said. —I've got to make a quick call.

—Checking in with Mommy and Daddy? said Gwyn sweetly, producing her mini-mobile and my umbilical cord in one go.

—Five—yeah, yeah, I know.

—No, you're one now, she said. —I did a little spring-cleaning—in with the new! Karsh, what's your number while we're at it?

She programmed it in, even asking him for his address, while I chippered up a little at the news of my numerical promotion and simultaneously tried to memorize Karsh's coordinates. When she handed me the phone and I called, my mother, though initially worried about why I wasn't staying with Kavita, took the express to thrillsville when I told her it was because Karsh would be driving me home.

—Oh, children are moving quickly these days—but thanking Prabhu it is in the right direction and not to the disreputable avenues! she giggled. —Shall I make chai? And I have some frozen samosas, but he will never know—did you know the other day they were frozen?

—They were frozen? my father piped up, revealing that, as usual, he'd been on the line all along. The two often embarked on their own conversations during these conference calls, chatting amicably from one room to the next.

Karsh and Gwyn had moved a little out of hearing radius and were now talking to a sedulous assembly of clubbers who'd just exited.

—No, no, no! I pleaded. Then, in a very un-Harish-Chandralike move, I turned to the art of the white lie in order to avoid having to turn purple with mortification later. —Look, we're not even going home straight away. We're—going to a diner. I'm going to be *really* late—in fact, you shouldn't even wait up for me.

—Oh, take your time, beta, these things take time. No curfew if I know you're in his hands!

A whole new rulebook had appeared, reprinted, and gone to paperback. I couldn't imagine this license to thrill if Julian, for example, were the boy in question. Or even Bobby O'Malley, who lived pretty much as close to our house as you could get and not be related or Gwyn.

—But wake me up in time for the wedding, she added mischievously.

We said our love-yous and I clicked off the phone and folded it in my fist. The party was winding down and the sweat-slick clubbers were heading out en masse now, and Karsh and Gwyn had moved even farther down the sidewalk. I was still by the door watching them, thronged as they were by people chattering animatedly or just swooping by and high-fiving Karsh, and sometimes even Gwyn, too, who raised her hand in the air whenever he did.

—Hey, Dimple.

Jimmy (Trilok) Singh had appeared next to me, perspiring profusely but with his turban impressively intact.

—Hey, Jimmy.

—Trilok, he said. —I'm back to Trilok. I'm pretty surprised to see you here.

Why was everyone so surprised to see me here?

—How come? I said a little defensively.

—I don't know. I didn't know you ever, you know, partied. Let down your hair.

—Well, I never knew you let down yours!

—I don't, he said grinning, and tapping the twisted fabric. —Maybe, I don't know, it's because you're Gujju and this is a pretty hard-core Punjabi scene.

Hard-core Punjabi? What did that mean?

—I'm half Marathi, I said.

—That explains it, he said.

—Explains what?

—Oh, you know. Marathas are known for being warriors and drunks. Which is pretty much what the dance floor is all about. Plus, they have star appeal.

I waited for the laugh track but there wasn't one. Had he been talking to my mother?

—You're a great dancer, Jim . . . Trilok. I got an amazing shot of you getting down—you were so into it you didn't even notice me right in your face.

—I never thought I'd see the day! You hardly talk to me in school and now you've turned into my own paparazzi machine?

—It's nothing personal, in school, I said, feeling bad. I'd always thought he'd been too wrapped up in his extra-credit homework and pakoras to notice. —I'm just always—

—Glued to Gwyn Sexton. I know.

He was the only person I knew who put the emphasis on the second syllable.

—Speaking of which, he continued, —I can't believe Gwyn Sexton is hanging with him! I thought she only dated . . .

—Cool guys?

—No! Dropouts, slackers. You know, total losers. Gulab Jammin' is the number one king of cool in my book.

—Um, his name's Karsh, I said. It seemed an odd nickname. Gulab jamun was an Indian dessert, fried milk balls in rosewater syrup. It was like jalebi but in a cake. For me, when it was served hot nothing beat it (except hot jalebi).

—But his DJ name's Gulab Jammin'. You know, sweet and sick, loaded and light, bad for you but so so good.

—What do you mean his DJ name? The DJ is Tamasha. Karsh told me himself.

—Obviously, yaar. The trip-hop be-bop stuff is Tamasha. But all that crazy energy bhangra meltdown magic between her and the opener? That's my man. He's the main act. Sole Mate's there to get the people warm and Tamasha's here to wind them down. But DJ GJ is the reason they all came in the first place.

He pronounced GJ *JiJi*, almost reverently. I followed his gaze and now watched in amazement as a trench-coated photographer—with a tripod and everything—cleared the circle of admirers and began to train his lens on Karsh. And on Gwyn, of course, who was going nowhere fast if any kind of film was around; she hovered behind Karsh, her hands on his shoulders and face nearly upon one as well. Karsh had his hands in his pockets and his lip twist looked not so much arrogant now as a mismatched mix between shy and just being used to it all.

So that had been him. The one who'd been playing only for me. That was Karsh.

—See what I mean? That photographer dude—he was shooting people at Sphinx the other night, and even at The Gloaming. Models and shit.

Trilok (Jimmy) Singh shook his head in disbelief.

—Man, Gwyn Sexton and my man. It's a little hard to take.

—They're not going out, I said too emphatically, dizzily watching as Karsh shook the hand of the photographer guy, smiling kindly and taking his card. Gwyn promptly reached out and nabbed a couple of cards as well, turning one over and scribbling on the back before handing it back and flashing a winsome grin.

—Yet, he said ominously. —Anyways, I've got to split. My girlfriend's already at Sphinx.

Girlfriend?

—Just don't tell my parents where you saw me. They think I'm spending all my time on business courses this summer.

He looked past me.

—Hey, Zara! Sphinx, heh? Can I catch a ride with you?

A taxi had pulled up right by Karsh and Gwyn and the flasher guy, who was snapping shut his tripod, one of those gypsy cabs where no one speaks English and that my parents told me never to get into under any circumstances (little did they know no one in the yellow cabs speaks English either, but I suppose there at least they had a shot with Hindi or pseudo-Urdu). Zara was hailing this gypsy, her boy lovingly in tow like a boat on a car heading waterside.

—Come on then, Tree! she replied huskily. —But get a move on, yaar, or I'll be late for Digweed, and if I'm late for Digweed, I'll be even later for my BNBB shift.

Did she live in a bed-and-breakfast? Was she just a visitor? From another planet? Turning to Karsh she blew him an almost visible kiss.

—Smashing as usual, darling. I'll see you at the talks!

—I'll be there, smiled Karsh.

—And ciao for now, Photo Girl! Zara said—to me! —Anytime you need a model, you know who to call.

She slipped leggily into the taxi, promoting it instantaneously to limo level, her long calf and the glittering mosaic slipper disappearing last into it. I felt shy for some reason and kept my eyes fixed on the taillights of Zara's gitano path, skidding tangerine streaks down the steam-gushing street, leaving a flock of low tinted clouds in their wake.

CHAPTER 20

and then there were three

Gwyn and I were soon sidewalked on the passenger side, waiting for Karsh to unlock us into his indigo Golf. She was giddily going on about the photographer they'd met—he was working for this arts magazine called *Flash!*, which was launching at the end of the summer. There was the slightest nip to the air, and I had goose bumps for some reason—I guess just proof that the club had been blistering if we could be standing around in a heat wave feeling frosty. Gwyn worked with it, stood mamboing like an impatient pony.

Then Karsh did something I've only seen my dad do: He came around to our side and opened the door. I stepped over to get out of his way and Gwyn smiled eye-battingly at him and stepped on in, in a perfect reproduction of Zara's gypsy limo entry—she didn't miss a thing, this one, picking up tips from 'zines and superhumans alike. Karsh shut the door for her and opened the one in back for me.

—You all right back there, Dimple? said Karsh, getting in and seeking me out in the rearview. —You're very quiet.

The strip of glass was all kindled eyes set in burnished skin, and I was enjoying having them framed solely on me when—smack!—Gwyn peeled the bindi off her forehead and stuck it on the mirror, making it appear as if it were on Karsh's face.

—Oh, I'm fine, I said. I'd decided to keep my mouth shut; Gwyn did a good enough job putting my foot in it without any help from me. —I'm just. You know.

—Snoozing, said Gwyn.

—Thinking? said Karsh.

I began to answer, but Gwyn flicked on the radio, scanning through the stations. Then she landed on this song—it was a big hit a whole loll of summers ago, with the Aussie girl's honey-husk vocals and the strum-strum ache and all the joy that can funnily enough be put into a sad song.

—Ooh, I love this song! said Gwyn, beginning to hummercroon along. —This was, like, the anthem of junior high. Come on, Dimple, sing it with me!

—I don't know the words, I muttered.

—No one knows the words! cried Gwyn, joyfully bopping around and rolling down her window. —That's not the point! Just do that line, you know, the *lying naked on the floor* part.

She belted it out now, with all the emotion of a young tenor auditioning.

—Oh . . . I'm *drunk!* And *hot!* I wish I really *was* lying naked on the floor.

—Hang in there, said Karsh. —We'll get there.

What was *that* supposed to mean?

—You know, Karsh, you should totally use this song when you DJ. It's so good—you'll have everyone singing along.

—Hmm. I'm not sure it works completely with the set I've been working on.

—Of course it does! You'd have a cross-continental hit if you did that. This song is the best ever. And you're the best DJ ever.

—Well, you're inspiration for a DJ, he said. —It takes two to bhangra.

Barf bag, please? This did not even seem to be true, first of all; it had looked to me like bhangra was something you could do all by yourself or with a million people, or all by yourself with a million people. Or maybe I was just being petty because I knew it was true, about her being an inspiration.

—So, bhangra, what is that anyways, if you don't mind my asking? Gwyn continued, her palm out the window now, pushing air.

—Well, it began as Punjabi folk music to celebrate the harvest—you know, bhang, it means hemp, explained Karsh. —Then it went West with immigrating South Asians, and in the UK people started fusing it with hip-hop and house and reggae and garage and disco—you name it. And it just kept right on moving till it got here.

—So what station is it on? said Gwyn, twiddling the knobs.

—I'm afraid there isn't really a major mainstream station for all that Hot-Pot music. Yet. I mean, it comes up occasionally on fusion theme shows and that kind of thing, but that's about it.

—Well, what are you waiting for? You've got to make it mainstream, Gwyn concluded.

—I'd love to pull in a more mixed crowd, if that's what you mean, Karsh said. —That would be killer.

—So when's the next bash then?

—Well, there's the Indian Independence Day meltdown in August—it'll be the same kind of scene as tonight. And then I've got nothing on my platter till school's on, unfortunately.

He glanced back at me again.

—Dimple, hey, you alive back there?

—Alive and kicking, I said. Kicking myself, that was, for being back here.

Their conversation hummed a summer lawn in my ear as they ran through an array of stations and played hit or miss with the music. We were crossing the George Washington Bridge and the cables fell supple and strong like white rain and the Golf tripped through it on the battered pavement. It was sadly, electrifyingly beautiful. It reminded me of a hanging oil lamp I'd seen at Hush-Hush Aunty's house, of a nude woman bronze bathing in an insinuated garden; the wires around her strung from lamp top to bottom and power on dripped a gold slow rain around her, one in which she remained mysteriously dry.

I turned back and watched New York City recede behind us, as if the whole island were floating away in the summer wind, this island like a birthday cake for an ancient giant with a mammoth appetite, a cake on fire with its blazing windows and broken promises, and kept ones, too, everyone's fifteen minutes and everyone's could-have-been, everyone's one-that-got-away and no one, lost children and grown-ups trying to get lost in its neck-cricking height, its rushing streets, its tunnel-deep icy-officed smoke of a thousand cigarettes clouding your eyes. All the light floating away from us as we headed into the night-cloak coast of the other side. Just the other end of the water, but another world and so far away. Like Karsh's house. Just across the pond, but just out of reach. And receding farther.

CHAPTER 21

photosynthesis

At Gwyn's, all three of us got out of the car, Karsh to stretch his legs.

—Thanks for the ride, Gwyn said, swaying coquettishly in the driveway. —You think maybe you could give me a DJ lesson sometime?

—Anytime, said Karsh.

—How about now? she said immediately. —That qualifies as anytime, doesn't it?

—Well . . . Karsh hesitated, dropping out of his stretch and glancing at his watch, then the car, then, for some reason, the double chimneys.

—No one's home. Just for five minutes—I'll make you coffee, a drink, whatever. You're only a skip and a jump from your house anyways, right?

All right, all right, you convinced me, he grinned. —I'm pretty awake now—I was getting worried at HotPot about driving dozy; I'm usually wiped after a set. No better time, I suppose, than two turntables and no one at home.

—Well, one turntable and a boom box, to be specific.

—That'll do for now.

Karsh got his record bag out of the trunk and clanked it shut, locking it even. This was a too familiar scene, me stuck in park and third-wheeling uselessly in Gwyn's driveway. But this time she wasn't begging me to stay.

—Well then, see ya, I guess, I said, embarking on a pedestrian three-point turn.

—Why are you going home? said Karsh. —Right, Gwyn? Why should Dimple go home?

—Well, she *is* old enough to decide what she wants to do, Gwyn said.

This was interesting.

—Is a DJ lesson a little too *Titanic* for you, too? Karsh challenged, looking me square in the face. I tried to go shadowy near the pines.

—No! I love DJs! I mean, I'd love to DJ! To learn how to DJ! It's just . . .

I felt awful, but he didn't look so wounded, actually. The boy sprang back fast. I had wanted to just casually vanish, but now my departure was turning into such a dramarama it was getting embarrassing. You know, like when you say something that's really funny at the time and then someone who didn't quite hear asks you to repeat it and by the time you finish explaining it all you just sound lame?

—Well, I'll drive you home then, said Karsh, reaching for his keys again.

—Don't worry, I said. —It's only around the corner.

—Exactly. It's only around the corner. So I'll take you. It can be a dangerous neighborhood—look at all these shady sorts lurking in driveways and all that.

He half-twisted.

—You need a strong man beside you.

—Are you a strong man, Karsh? said Gwyn, smiling coyly at him.

It was settled. There was no way I was leaving them alone together.

—Okay, I'll come in for a few minutes, I said. —That is, if I'm invited.

—Oh, don't be such a baby, said Gwyn. —Of course you're welcome.

—Then it's settled, said Karsh, and he slid off his sneaks on the porch. Gwyn giggled shyly, as if they'd been his Calvins.

—Why are you doing that? she said.

—A home is a sacred place, said Karsh. —Like a temple.

—Not mine, said Gwyn.

—Of course it is, said Karsh. —You live in it, don't you?

Her breath caught in her throat and she immediately flung off her shoes. I kept mine on. My feet were killing me by now, but I would still resist and make my point. Whatever it was.

By the time we got inside, Gwyn was melting like a chocolate kiss in direct sunlight. And the more she melted the more irresistible she became, a soft sweetness melding with all that swank slinkiness.

Mine was a different kind of dissolution, one that neither transformed me nor made me more delectable. To the contrary: I was vanishing before my eyes.

—Dimple, are you okay? said Karsh. Had I been staring at him? I nodded, looking down at my callused feet.

—She's fine! Gwyn assessed. —Better than fine!

She was digging around the sewing cabinet in the hallway and now produced three shot glasses and a bottle of Tia Maria.

—Nightcap?

Who were we to refuse? We clinked glasses. I didn't know whose aunt this was named after, but she must have been the life of the party. The drink was like spiked ice cream, and it snapped alligator-jawed down my throat, singeing my already overheated belly.

—Would you like the grand tour, Karsh? Gwyn offered, running her hand along the banister. —Dimple's seen it all a million times, haven't you, Dimps. Honey, if you want to go watch TV or whatever, you know it's your home.

Hello—did that even qualify as a hint, or more like a whack on the head with a two-by-four?

—Come on, what's a million and one? said Karsh.

—One too many, Gwyn replied, smiling brightly at him.

I plopped down on the second to last step with my shot glass.

—One too many, I said. —Go on. Enjoy yourselves. I'll just hang out here a minute.

Before the words were even out of my mouth Gwyn had set the bottle at the foot of the stairs and reached audaciously out to take Karsh's hand, and the next thing I knew she was marching him away, up along the wall lustrous with all those framed photographs of her childhood, most of them leading one to believe it never rained in Springfield, New Jersey.

These young golden images of Gwyn were plastered all throughout the house—even in her own bedroom. Gwyn beaming out from under a straw hat, a bunch of daisies in her hands and rake fallen by her feet. Gwyn stretched on star moss in a fairy-queen outfit, one wing crushed beneath her and a half-built playhouse in the foreground. Mrs. Sexton was always out of focus or cut off, decapitated or delimbed by the frame. (Perhaps on purpose, it occurred to me now, as Mr. Sexton had been the cameraman on all the shots.)

The sun blazed in these pictures, and it blazed unabashedly in Gwyn now. How did she get so ballsy? After all my agonizing at HotPot, with his hand just millimeters from mine unable to traverse that slim barrier of electrons and atoms and Formica, and she'd just reached out and taken it, carp and dee 'em, job done.

They were upstairs now; as their voices disappeared down what had seemed to me since childhood a mythical labyrinth of hallways, I leaned against the banister I'd slid down so many times and looked up at the photo of Gwyn beside me, the first one, framed on the bottom of the wall that followed the stairs up and away into what was fast becoming the heaven of her house.

I'd seen all of these pictures a million times. So many times I'd stopped seeing them at all, in fact. But a million and one was a new experience, especially when compounded by an evening that had sung bhangra and nearly held hands — not to mention a deranged liquid aunt now setting up shop in my body. And when I looked at the girl in the photo it was as if I didn't know her. Or as if I'd known her once a long time ago and forgotten her for all the years in between.

—It's like your own little Hearst castle, I heard Karsh say. The two had reappeared before me; they must have taken the second stairway down. Karsh climbed up to the step behind me; Gwyn followed suit, squirreling in next to him.

—It's incredible, all these photos of you everywhere, Gwyn, he said.

—Incredible? said Gwyn, a little indignantly. She was passing the Tia Maria around, fortifying our glasses.

—Obviously I can see why someone would *want* to take a load of pictures of you, that's not what I mean, said Karsh. —But I hope you don't mind my saying this, it's just a little strange — all these shots of you alone, as a kid growing up. And then suddenly — poof! No more, as if you disappeared at puberty, like at the first sign of underarm hair or something.

—Well, I did in a way. At least, that's when my photographer — my father — disappeared. I guess I wasn't pretty enough or entertaining enough to hold his attention when I grew up.

She downed the Tia.

—And I don't even have underarm hair, she added.

—Are you kidding, Gwyn? I said. —You got *more* beautiful if anything!

—Well, I worked at it, believe me. I thought about it, planned it all before I ever went out to Venice Beach to find him. But then that didn't turn out to be such a good idea—seems I got everyone to fall in love with me except him. His friends, that is. It irritated the hell out of him—he accused me of trying to steal them from him. Yeah right! I mean, I was what, twelve? As if I really went all the way across the country looking for him just so I could seduce his geezer pals.

She tipped her head back, emptied a fresh shot, and nodded for us to do the same.

—You went all the way across the country by yourself at twelve? said Karsh, in disbelief.

—Well, I was handling all my mother's accounts anyway, Gwyn shrugged, looking up at the photograph as if speaking to the girl she used to be. —You know, paying bills, balancing the checkbook. So I just balanced it a little in my favor and told her I was gonna bring him home and got on the train.

—Gwyn, you never told me that, I said. So that was what had been going on around the time she'd disappeared?

—There's nothing to tell. I got there and did my best but I still got sent back. In the end it was as if it never happened. I don't even know what got into me to talk about it now.

We were all so huddled together in this small space, such a tiny piece of such an expansive house, the way people always gravitate to the kitchen at a party, as if staving off a slowly encroaching unspeakable loneliness, all those empty rooms. I had a habit of keeping my feet off the foyer floor when I was on the stairs—so many years imagining it was a sea finned with danger, the edge of a battlefield blood blooming, a sheer drop to a distant pavement on hostile territory. Even now I sometimes caught glimpses of the house the way I'd viewed it in my childhood—rooms revealed a plethora of hiding places at a glance, ceiling lamps metamorphosed into gargantuan stained glass flowers with burning bulbs at their hearts, chandeliers to octagenarian birthday cakes with flipped-candle skeletons, nearly effortlessly, from all those stretched afternoons spent on our backs imagining we inhabited the world upside down. Back in the day when friends would lie on their backs side by side and do things like this. And outside, too, we would lie in the dandelion gauzy with wishes to blow and stare creatures and kingdoms and everyone we'd ever known or would know into the bobbing cumulus, the drifting cirrus, the rain swollen clouds, and I would always see what she would see, she could always see what I saw. We had time and telepathy on our side, and in those days we never ran for shelter when it rained. But now I realized it had always been a different landscape for Gwyn, that her beautiful house had always had a broken heart at its center, splintering further with every beat.

—Your mom wasn't worried? Karsh asked quietly.

—She wanted him back, too. And she knew she was no bait. I wouldn't have even gone, but he sent me this postcard—you know that one of Marilyn Monroe with the wind blowing up her dress? I had never seen anything like it.

Of course I knew the photo. It was the one Gwyn scotched up on the inside of my locker every year, but I'd never seen the other side, the sender's name. In fact, it had never occurred to me that there'd been a sender; I'd always thought it was just a pretty picture for a pretty person's locker wall.

—To me it looked like she was about to take off, fly away, Gwyn said.

—Yeah, I know what you mean, I said, closing my eyes and picturing it.
—Like from even a sewer on a street she could fashion a set of wings.

When I opened my eyes Karsh was staring at me. I wondered if I'd sounded foolish.

—Exacto, said Gwyn, plucking the rubber bands off the ends of her braids and beginning to unweave them. —Dimple, sometimes the things you say are so on, you know? Anyways, I read it as a sign that I should go out there and be a star—he always thought I looked like her when I was little. Lillian says great, he compares me to a dead person, what does he want, a bone? She says he was never emotionally available to begin with. But I get there, I wear my nicest dresses, I try to cook, to do the shopping. But I'm cramping his style, he tells me. He's finally finding himself then I have to go and come along—he married too young, he had me too young, and he doesn't want to die in a cage. He hopes I can forgive him like he's forgiven me.

—But you didn't do anything wrong! I said.

—Have you forgiven him? asked Karsh.

—I don't know, said Gwyn softly. She was undoing the last braid now, and her hair struck out in waves as if it had been dammed water. She was sitting just below her picture and she suddenly looked like a stretched-out version, a circus mirror reality of the same little girl who was gazing back at me through the bars of the very banister on which I was leaning.

In the photograph the carpeting was a deeper shade of rose, and Gwyn was all conch curls and sea wet eyes; her lips bore a valiant smile, upper protruding over lower and pressing into it, as if to stop the quivering. Her elfin fingers gripped the banister bars; these filled the frame, made it seem she was gazing into a cage with a frightening and fascinating creature inside. She was staring straight at me, and for a moment I wondered illogically if I'd made her cry.

—I hear shouting and I can't sleep so I come down the stairs, Gwyn said now. —They're fighting. They don't even notice me for a while. They fight a lot, but this time it's different. He's telling her she isn't gonna trick him into having another one; one kid's enough. And my mother says, *Do you really feel that way? So you really feel that way?* And she tips a bottle to her lips and then she's coughing and says, *Don't worry, you won't be tricked again.* A few days later she's in a hospital. I know something serious is happening and I know I am a trick somehow, which I don't completely understand, but I suppose it means I'm not real in a way, or that it's as opposed to being a treat. I guess I must be sobbing or something because they turn and see me. And my father tells me I look so beautiful like that, hold still, don't change a thing.

—And he took a picture? Karsh said, expressing my incredulity exactly.

—Yeah, said Gwyn. —And he took a picture. But maybe he was just trying to cheer me up; he knew I would always smile for the camera.

She smiled now as she said it.

—Well, enough about me, she said brightly. —You? What are your folks like?

—Oh man, I'm still reeling from all that, said Karsh.

—Please, said Gwyn softly, her smile wobbling slightly as if choosing between directions. And then I realized it was to gate back the tears.

—Well, me, said Karsh, seeming to catch on at that moment, too. —Let's see.

And then he went on to say how his mom was the bomb, a total self-made self-actualized person and that he had no end of respect for her. And how his dad, well, he was kind of the opposite of Gwyn's but the same: Whereas hers left her in this huge house surrounded by pretty things then disappeared, his was around, but a compulsive gambler, and he made all their pretty things disappear one by one, nearly to their very home. He wasn't a bad man, just weak. Too weak. His mother said their presence enabled him and he'd have to hit rock bottom to get up on his feet again. So they packed up and left and went west to America, not New Jersey yet, but way west, where Radha completed her residency training.

—Is he on his feet again? I asked.

—I think he's still on the rock bottom part, said Karsh. —He writes to me for money and I was sending him some for a while. Not a hell of a lot —I didn't have much to speak of—but, you know, I sold some of my stereo equipment and my twelve-speed and skateboard. But when it came to my records, it got tough.

DJing really meant the world to him.

—Because a lot of them had been his that I'd taken with me, he continued. —To keep him with me. The day I sold the first ones, my heart broke a little. I couldn't go on with it, and in any case, I realized it was just keeping him where he was. So I stopped.

No wonder he guarded those boxes, that bag so preciously; they were not only his own pride and joy, but were mellifluously marked with the fingerprints and scratches, the worn grooves and sweet center of his father.

—Do you think they'll get back together again? Gwyn asked.

—My head says no way in this lifetime, said Karsh. —But since we Hindus get a few lifetimes, my heart can't help but hope for a happy ending.

—I know what you mean, said Gwyn. Out of the corner of my eye I could see she was leaning on Karsh's shoulder now, seeking shelter, it seemed. —Believe me, I know. We're two of a kind, Karsh. Like you said—opposite but the same.

I thought of my dad on the sofa enjoying his outdated Beaujolais Nouveau and nodding his head side to side to Lata Mangeshkar and I had an overwhelming desire to run home and wake him up and touch him, just to make sure he was there.

I couldn't believe their stories. I mean, I knew all was not 101 percent well, but this was a whole other level of heartbreak, and I just wanted to take them both in my arms and say something comforting. But I also felt like I was watching all of it through a window, and a one-way window at that. I wondered if my parents knew Karsh's story.

And Gwyn's tale. Well, that hurt for two reasons. One, and foremost, because it was desperately sad and there was nothing I could do to undo it. And two, because Gwyn had never told me any of it. It had taken a million and one times in this house to make this story emerge. It had taken a one in a million person to make her feel like she could let it, I suppose. Watching Karsh now gently stroking her hair, his arm around her, I felt like a failure as a friend and I vowed to try to be better, to be kinder, to be the kind of person you could talk to. I had never realized until now that I wasn't.

I looked up at the girl with the liquid eyes and seashell curls and my heart ached for her.

—That's an irresponsible photographer, I said.

—Or a really good one, said Gwyn.

—Documenting the way you hurt someone? Finding that beautiful? I could never do that, not for anything. There are limits.

—You wouldn't understand, said Gwyn, a tiny edge to her voice. —Your family is perfect. It's easy to set limits when you have none.

—Perfect? I said, for some reason defensive.

—They are pretty damn cool, said Karsh. —It's nothing to be ashamed of.

—I'm not ashamed, but we're not perfect. Well at least I'm not perfect.

—Oh spare me, said Gwyn. —Honors classes, straight A's even post-breakup with Bobby, supercool cousins, ace at photography.

—Who's Bobby? asked Karsh.

—No one anymore, Gwyn replied for me while I cringed inwardly. —But at the time, you just couldn't get over him, could you, Dimple. He was the love of her *life*, Karsh. I never understood it. I mean, why don't you look for a guy like your father? You've got the world's greatest role models right in your living room and you still go slumming. Do you realize how lucky you are that your parents are together? They are so *solid*, so in love.

—What do you mean? They don't hold hands, I've never seen them kiss. In fact I'm not even sure how I got here, to tell the truth.

—What's kissing and holding hands? said Gwyn almost snobbishly. —That's a dime a dozen. They wake up together every morning, they sleep together every night; they managed to cross an ocean together and not fall apart. And they adore you. That's pretty perfect and you're complaining? What's wrong with you? You could use all that love to go out and conquer the world!

I wasn't complaining. I was just trying to find my place in this conversation, but it was looking more and more like a sold-out show. And I didn't even want to begin to try to explain to either of them how sometimes I felt my parents loved me so much that it was too much—they wanted everything perfect, they didn't want me to have a moment of discomfort in my life, and they cared so heavily that sometimes I worried that in comparison, no one else would ever seem like they did. But it was true: They were pretty perfect. I mean, of course they drove me a little crazy sometimes, especially recently. But they were supposed to—that was part of their job. And at least they were there to drive me crazy. Even I had to admit there was no way I'd trade them in for anything. But perversely, the whole time Gwyn and Karsh had been talking, I'd been feeling that maybe I hadn't been traumatized enough by them to make me a regular teenager.

—That's not fair, Gwyn, said Karsh. —You can use a lack of attention to go out and conquer the world, too. You can use anything. And I daresay you just might get it.

—You think? she said. She was contemplating her photograph again and Karsh gently turned her face towards him.

—Should we go play some music? he said. —Maybe we all just need to chill a minute.

So we went into Gwyn's mother's room, which is where the stereo was. There were two things that set this room apart from the rest of the house. One, it was the only room with no photographs of Gwyn—or anyone—in it. And two: It was white. *All* white—from the blizzardy carpeting stretching from one white wall to another to the king-size bed draped with snowy linens, the tasseled throw pillows and lampshades. A faux-fur-trimmed dressing gown hung silkily off the bedpost in the same Alaskan camouflage. Porcelain figurines of swans and sprites floated on the mirror-still surfaces of the glossy white vanity table and night table and dresser. And atop the entertainment cabinet: an all-white turntable, one speaker (the other was propped upon a wicker basket in the corner), and a cassette deck, like a sound system for Barbie's wedding.

The spooked sight of all this pristine perfection made me finally remove my shoes.

—Oh my god, said Karsh, shaking his head. —No offense, or maybe a little, but it's like a supremacist's dream pad.

—It's great, isn't it? Gwyn nodded, oddly. —It's like she's still trying to be a bride or something, have her white wedding.

—Oh, I didn't even think of that, said Karsh. —White is the color of mourning in India.

—My mother wore only white for fourteen days after my grandfather died, I said.

—My mother wore it for four after she kicked my father out, said Karsh, turning to me. Gwyn glanced from him to me then pushed her way between us, linking her arms through one each of ours.

—Whatever, she said. —Come in.

We were all nearly tiptoeing for some reason.

—It seems so unlived in, Karsh said.

—Yeah, at the moment, said Gwyn, bending to slide open the glass door of the entertainment cabinet. —But not after she gets a couple gins in her system and throws on one of *these* mothers. Dimple knows. She's been here.

Karsh dropped to a squat. For some reason I thought of Meera Maasi crouching on the concrete floor with the ayah, sifting stones from rice. It was an ancient memory, but it pieced now crystalline in my mind's eye.

—Holy shit, look at all this Grateful Dead. Was your mom a Deadhead?

—Even hitched across the country to see them play, with me in a backpack.

—Joni, Janis, and *Dark Side of the Moon*, more Doors albums than the Doors ever made!

—And retapes of all of them, said Gwyn, now creating a stacked city of cassettes on the carpet.

—Unbelievable. There has got to be a stoner in the house.

He turned when he said it, nodding at Gwyn. Gwyn gave him a funny look, one I'd never seen on her face before, which surprised me, because I'd seen a lot of her faces, in all of their jars by the door and on.

—Is there one in the house now? she asked slowly.

This was turning into a bizarro conversation.

—There may be one, said Karsh smiling.

—Or more than one, said Gwyn. —Shall I light your fire?

—What the hell, said Karsh. —I'm so far past sleep at this point. Come on, baby.

What were they talking about? Gwyn opened a dresser drawer and took out a small box. When she opened it I saw it was a sewing kit; inside was a set of needles, thimbles, thread spools in a brilliant array of hues. I was lost—it didn't seem like the moment to start hemming.

But then, very carefully, she lifted the spool tray and held out the box for all to see. Packed in a Ziploc bag under a thin stack of papers at the bottom was something that looked like a burnt hunk of backyard.

—Do you know what this is, Dimple?

—Looks like grass to me, I said.

—Exactly! Gwyn hooted, looking like a pleasantly surprised mama duck. —Sometimes you really surprise me with how with it you are.

I opted to perpetuate this myth by not asking her why there was a chunk of mowed lawn in her sewing kit.

—In a sewing kit? asked Karsh.

My thoughts exactly! So he was with me on this.

—Yeah, my mom says it rules 'cause, first of all, no one would ever think to look there, and second, if she's falling apart she can always sew herself together again.

—Plus, I'm sure sewing buttons was never so much fun, Karsh laughed.
—So let me get this straight: This is your *mother's* stash?

—So it is, straight from the Lillian, she said, burrowing now through the record collection. —Make yourselves comfortable. I won't be a minute.

We dropped down cross-legged on the floor and Gwyn pulled out —surprise!—an all-white album.

—The Beatles are perfect at times like this, she said, tapping a little lawn out onto the sleeve. It radiated against the blank background. A familiar sweetness rose into the air that I couldn't quite put my finger on.

—Do you want me to? Karsh offered.

—No, no—you're my guest, she said. She began nimbly to roll the grass into the paper.

—*That's* a joint! I cried, jumping as she held up the finished stick.

—Indeed it is! Karsh joined in enthusiastically. —You're a pro, Gwyn.

—Are you uncomfortable, Dimple? Gwyn asked, in a tone that fell halfway between concerned and challenging.

—No, of course not, I said. —Why should I be uncomfortable?

—Then sit down. I'm glad—I didn't know if you'd be wigging or dealing.

—Of course I can deal, I said indignantly. Lied indignantly, to be more precise.   I'm just surprised you can—you can make a joint.

—You certainly can, said Karsh. —That's some major Mary Jane.

I was wigging. I'd never tried drugs and had no idea Gwyn ever had. What if her mother caught us? Well, okay, in this case that didn't seem to be an issue—and let's not even get into how frocked up *that* was. But what if the police happened to come by? What if the stuff was spiked with . . . drugs? Yeah, I suppose that one was moot as well.

My head was buzzing. And Karsh. I'd always figured potheads were the grungy guys who hung out in the parking lot and wept during the Pledge and started looking confusedly around when the voice came through the intercom at bus call.

And in terms of Gwyn and Karsh—things were shaping up greatly in my disfavor. Now turned out they didn't have merely growing up in single-mothered families in common, but this, too. I was getting pushed further and further out of the loop, like I'd been on the dance floor tonight. I couldn't allow it to get any worse or I'd be out of orbit entirely.

I watched Karsh hold the flame to the end. Gwyn inhaled and then didn't exhale, her face flushing an extraordinary shade of pink. I thought she was choking and was about to slap her on the back when she squeezed her eyes shut and with a content *ahhh* let a strand of smoke slip through her lips. Then she held it out for Karsh, who took a searing swallow, and with his mouth clasped tight and the steadiest of hands he presented the little burning twig to me, raising his eyebrows and nodding slightly as if to say Go. I took it in my fingers and my fingers were shaking. To be honest, I'd barely even ever tried cigarettes. Gwyn had nicked them off her father once, and the two of us went out to the playhouse with a big mirror and sat in front of it and stared at ourselves, playing movie stars. We didn't even light the things for the first few minutes, just wove them glamorously around. And once we did Gwyn was inhaling in no time, blowing rings and exhaling from her nose and doing all sorts of tricks of the cigarette circus—which now made me wonder if she'd been secretly practicing all along. Me, the furthest I got was filling my mouth up with the indelectable stuff then parting my lips and watching it gently dollop out, clouding out my thrilled guilted face in the mirror.

Now I figured I'd just do the same thing but let it out like cirrus instead of cumulus and they'd never know I hadn't inhaled. I already felt out of it; I didn't want to create an even bigger rift by not being fun enough, crazy enough. Doors enough.

I tried to put on my best been-there-smoked-it look and if Gwyn was surprised she didn't show it. The tip of the twig was moist and my lips stuck to the rolling paper when I breathed in. I filled my mouth just a little, my hair hanging down so the smoke could hide in it and not in me.

—You're losing it all, Gwyn said softly. —You've got to hold it in longer. It's good stuff—Dylan had his plus points.

—Out of practice, I guess, I said. This was, technically, true. I took another lurch in the lungs and closed my eyes. The stuff didn't taste bad, actually, but lay a flame down my throat, unwetting the insides of my cheeks. This time I pretended I was underwater, at the bottom of Mirror Lake after a perfectly executed dive and had to make my breath last a long way up—a fear that was fantasy for me as well. I imagined myself swimming through sunken treasure, anemone and broken bottle and by the time I let it out it was a surprisingly small cloud. The rest must have escaped while my eyes were closed.

—Wow, said Karsh. —That was impressive. You could last a long time in a shipwreck.

—Yeah. Thanks. I guess.

—But I guess that would be me, the sunk ship.

—Huh?

My throat burned when I spoke and my words collided in a raspy cough.

But the rest of me didn't come out of the water. The now just pinchable glow-stick seemed to be making another circuit.

—You look like a chipmunk, said Gwyn, stifling a laugh. I could still see it rolling between her teeth like missed pinballs.

—What do you mean? I said. —You mean I look fat?

—Of course not. Why do you get so paranoid? I just mean you look so cute with your cheeks all rounded up like that.

What did she mean paranoid? Why did she choose *that* word, of all words? I mean, she could have said touchy, moody, wish-in-your-mouth, temperamental. And how come everyone was looking at me so funny? Was I speaking out loud? I put my finger to my frenulum to stop myself in case.

—Even without the pot, said Karsh, nodding and whispering, his fingers also by his lips now. What did he mean—that I looked like a chipmunk 24/7?

—Since when are you such a pro smoker? I said a little testily to Gwyn. Her face seemed to be floating a good inch off her head, the way the world starts to look if you stare too long through the diamonds in a wire fence, like from behind the catcher's spot on a softball field, the depth of field going tunnel deep and dizzy.

—I don't do it often, she said. —Just sometimes. It heightens some experiences, if you know what I mean. Or maybe you don't.

—I think I do, said Karsh. His face was still on his face. It was impressive, how well the two went together.

—Like what?

—Dimple, she said. —Duh! What do you think?

I didn't know what did I think. I thought, why didn't I think. Why didn't I know what she was treating as obvious knowledge?

—Why didn't you tell me you smoke marijuana?

—Oh, I figured you'd just freak out. I mean, listen to yourself—you even call it marijuana.

Was cannabis the proper term?

—Plus, I don't know, with all those doctors in your family, and the whole Indian thing. But tonight I just stopped caring.

About me? What was wrong with chipmunks?

—The whole Indian thing? snorted Karsh. —Are you kidding, Gwyn?

Some of the biggest stoners I know are Indian! Smoking dope was even part of some religious ceremonies in India—priests did it.

—Priests!

—Well, yours get drunk, ours get stoned, I said. I had no idea if any of this was true, but if it aligned me with Karsh I figured I'd go with it. Karsh was very aligned, in fact, while Gwyn was making me dizzy, snapping around like a kite.

—Yeah, said Karsh. —It's all the same.

Not what I meant!

—Everyone's trying to get high, he said. —To get to some higher level. But you know all rivers lead to the sea. It's a question of vocabulary—we've got different names for one thing.

—But what you call something changes it, too, I said. I watched my voice roll around, bending air where the words went.

—I mean, why am I Dimple? I went on. —I don't even have a dimple. I feel all this pressure to act happy all the time and it kind of backfires. Maybe if my name were, I don't know, Joan, I wouldn't feel that way.

—Then you'd wish you had an exotic name, said Gwyn. —And pressure to be happy? What are you complaining about? You have it all.

—Exactly, Gwyn, said Karsh. Did he mean *Exactly, Gwyn* as in, That's exactly the point? Or *Exactly, Gwyn* as in, What's the spoiled brat moaning about?

—I don't even have a dimple. I don't even smile much.

At least recently.

—You smile when you take pictures, said Karsh. —You smile when you forget not to.

That made me forget not to and all the bent air sprang back into place and Gwyn looked at him.

—I'm Dimple's model in most of her pictures! she interjected. —Aren't I, Dimple?

—And you make people smile, Karsh continued, still looking at me. —Maybe that's why you're Dimple.

—I wish.

—You do, he said. His voice enveloped me like an oven opening on warm bread in a cold room. He looked very serious when he said it, and I wished I could make him smile. More than anything I wanted that. I considered dirty limericks but I wasn't sure how any of them went anymore.

—There once was a boy who smoked pot . . . I think that he quite smoked a lot . . . He liked to play bhangra . . . And even to—

—I don't smoke much, he said in response, which was cool since I wasn't sure what rhymed with bhangra. Cangra, dangra, eyangra, fangra. A, B, C, D, E, F . . . J. Jangra. —But I'm pretty much willing to check out anything once. And it's not entirely escapist—I try to remember these feelings when I'm sober. Look at this thread, for example.

He was turning a spool in his fingers. He passed the end of it to me and Gwyn plucked out a part for herself.

—Look how beautiful this color is—bright as life, so much so it hurts. Now if I see it again in a couple days I'll try to conjure up this feeling. And the better you get the more you apply it to other things and the less time it takes to make the transfer. Do you know what I mean?

—Man, who's *your* dealer? said Gwyn.

—Washington Square Park. The guy with the missing thumb who asks if you want to buy a piece of sky.

There was a piece of sky coming out of my mouth now, like I was a cloud factory. I watched it loll out and piff up like whipped cream and I wondered, maybe there was a piece of heaven in me and I was letting it get away.

—It's kind of like DJing—every song sounds of every time it was played before and builds from there, said Karsh. —Speaking of which, what's say we get the needle on.

Oh frock, were they going to go class A? Gwyn was holding up a sewing needle with a quizzical look on her face.

—No, no, the needle on the record, Karsh cackled. —Though we all could use a little taking in, I suppose. Now come on—was this supposed to be a DJ lesson or what?

He stood and there was a hole where he had been, and I could feel the him that was still in it sparking, an invisible storm.

—Now you don't have two turntables so maybe if you run a cassette I can show you how to drop a beat in.

—Drop a beat? Gwyn said lazily from the floor.

He chose to demonstrate with something Apache something, which he pulled out from his record bag now and which, frankly, seemed like the wrong kind of Indian to me—but when he played it for us it did remind me of that night we went to this club in New York and space-age saris and pink drinks and Milky Way torsos.

—That's so cool! Here, let me try.

—I haven't done anything yet, Gwyn, he said. —I'm going to show you the basics of how to mix two tunes. Let's go with "Riders on the Storm"—it's slower tempo and might be a bit easier to beat-match.

—So it's really not just playing records? said Gwyn. —You know, like a DJ at a wedding? I mean, at a really *good* wedding, of course.

—It used to be just that, said Karsh. —But not anymore. It's about mixing sounds and vibing with a crowd and taking them to a higher place, making them love what you love as much as you do. And in turn they show you how to push yourself even harder. It's like losing yourself and being more than yourself all at the same time. I'm telling you, when I'm up there spinning it is a pure energy buzz: You never know what to expect—every night is your first and your last and it's all about the chemistry. You have to be prepared, of course. But there's this dynamic that changes you as much as you guide it.

We were both staring at him disciple-eyed. I couldn't believe he was talking about mixing records—he made it sound like Buddhism or something.

—And when you've got that one person who's been standing still all night finally moving—even if it's just nodding their head or tapping their foot, well *that*. That is something. It's like a direct infusion of Big Energy through the little machine and into their veins. Call me crazy, but I think that's what god is all about.

He was staring straight at me. I wondered if I had pot stuck in my teeth. See? I could call it pot. *Pot*. Potpotpot. Potty mouth.

—So, he said, turning to the deck. —In the best moments, as in anything where you are so immersed, you lose your sense of time—but ironically, it's always all about the timing. First off. The two songs you're going to mix—you've got to know them so well you can sing them in your sleep, even with a circus of noise going on around you.

Gwyn was welded to his side. He played the something Apache something a couple times, and she leaned in real close to him even though the speakers were spread out in the room and she was the one in his headphones. I couldn't hear the second song yet. He was going through a bunch of explanations—counting beats, cueing up, I don't know what else—and their voices mingled on *one and two and three and four* and I backed away to the bed, the spool bounding along with me, a tiny red thread pet.

The numbers hummed in the aft of my head, over and over to four they went, like a countup to a big event that never quite happened, Sisyphus rolling back just when he thought he'd topped the hill. I pulled the thread up to the edge of the bed and slid it down the other side. It looked funny now, thicker, deeper. It glistened, and I wondered if that transference someone had been talking about was going on.

I watched them from the side of the bed, rock climbing up with my glossy bit of rope. Gwyn messed up several times. The music sounded like someone was thwacking through it—scrambling against brick shatter, dishes over knocked, chains dropped on a china shop, a house cartoonishly coming down—keeping at bay two things that were supposed to come together. Each time the needle dropped like a small bomb on a spinning planet—with a resounding ear-piercing thud and a series of mini-splats through the microscopic debris on the record. I wondered if you were a person standing tinily on that record if that dust would be Himalayan, the grooves deep and dangerous valleys. I followed my spool into a crevasse between bed and night table and peeked out from that narrow shelter.

—I feel so stupid, said Gwyn. —I keep screwing up.

I could see her standing there, hands out over the deck like over a body at a sleepover séance. *Light as a feather, thick as a bone.* But they were shaking hard, and I don't think I'd ever seen her so nervous; tremors surfed up her arm, under her skin.

—Do you think I'm just a baby, Karsh? she suddenly asked.

—You're just perfect, Gwyn. Don't worry.

—My hands are shaking, said Gwyn, her voice blowing in from a faraway valley.

—Shh . . . it's okay, whispered Karsh on a gentle wind. And he went and stood behind her and reached his arms around her and lay his hands over hers. I saw it and it stung, felt like mine had been slapped and pushed away, though that made no sense, I was far from them, crawling out of the crevasse, using my thickly gliding brown rope to climb onto the snowcapped pillow peak. He held her hands till the quake subsided but then it was I who went seismic, as if it had rippled all that distance to me, and with his hands still on hers he led her through a cue-up and countup and this time when the needle released from their doubled fingers it bedded into the groove as if it had been made just for this moment and slipped right into the arms of the storm riders throatily riding the unpredictable weather like shimmer children in an echoing wasteland.

I saw all the motions in time lapse as they tried again, every nanometer of the needle's sliding rise and descent, like the clipped close motions in the eye of a tiny strobe. Thunder as the needle dropped. It seemed the world had the spins and I was watching—the opposite of the night of the nonstop nachos. And the record spun liquid and behind my eyes I could see the two of them reflected in it, the trembling doubled face of a drowned eclipse, gold upon copper in water. And a cloud floated from my lips and hung over that lake, dispersing dreamily.

Gwyn leaned gently into Karsh; he bore forward to take her weight and now the two rode the song, floating over the deep parts like wee boats, sinking and up again for air, oscillating. The song was replete in their joined body.

The turntable and equipment fell away like extra packaging and even a deaf person could have heard their song, in the way they were now gliding their large dawn in the small circumference of the two of them. The ring around their song grew clearer, expanding like the ring from a pebble tossed into a lake, and the space within the circle deepened, and it must have been only minutes and Gwyn threaded her fingers through his and my spool was out in a tangle in my hands and their mix was perfect, the only scratch on my heart.

I opened my mouth and cirrus whirled slippily between my teeth and out. I lay on my back and the clouds floated above me. Somebody was sending out a gypsy wail from a valley and someone was born into this world thrown, against a potter's wheel, and the words were so deep maybe that's why they'd scared me so much before when Lillian played them to soothe herself (how hurt she must be if this could soothe her). And the nonwords went even deeper and I was on my back on a hillside many summers ago and the clouds were horse-drawn chariots and the drone of lawn mowers and grandfather gods and turbans slowly unwinding and tea growing cold in a saucer a long time ago; anklets unclipping, bangles ringing down and off an arm in a collected clatter, sun salutations and gifts rife with castaway ribbons; a braid loosening. And my knees were mountains bright and my stomach a river stung shining with fish fins and rock smooth as the bellies of wind instruments.

And the gypsy man sang a cry of impending tempest and the other man's voice hid a boy, a moving shelter in its hollowy depth. I crawled along my thread into this dark and low-lying cave because now the clouds were raining and my face was dank, my eyes were night panes and the rain streaked down to shroud me. If I put my ear to the floor I could hear the sea. Salt on my lips and zarina aglow against a fabled wall. Wish on a moving sky.

India floated unhitched into this sea and went traveling around the world but the world was a puzzle and it was a broken map. It was a piece that seemed easy enough—an upside-down triangle like a stretched-out, raggedy pink-drink cup—but a bit that just didn't fit, especially anywhere near the coastal edge of where we were now on the planet, the thin gridded island where we had been. The severed part crashed and lodged in my heart, untidily poking its roadside temples and poached tusks there, making a sharp place to live. I thought about all the stories of there that were more true to me than history, and all the history of here where I had no story yet, and I didn't know which was mine to tell, or even listen to.

Here in my cave in the middle of nowhere I began to sense ground again. I felt strange but lucid; instead of numbness it seemed I was feeling too much—a pea in a mattress, every fiber of the rug imprinting against my skin.

Where was home? East or West or my body in between? If I rolled my head to the left, in the distance were four bare ankles clamped together; to the right, a darkness grading white by the marbled legs of the night table.

My parents knew why they came here so many years ago—but why were they still here? Even they seemed to be wondering lately, I got the feeling; the thought of them grounded me further, the small of my back plushed down. And now looking at Karsh and Gwyn's bedded heels I wondered: Why was *I* still here?

—I've got to go, I said. Nothing changed and I called out again from the low-ceilinged obsidian of my shadowless cave. —I've got to go!

—Dimple? Where are you? Stop shouting, stop—it's all right.

The feet disbanded and began to move around in a cut raw silence.

—Where are you—what? said the paler ones. —What are you doing there? Check it out, Karsh!

—Dimple? said the darker ones, moving closer. —Are you all right?

—Fine, why?

—Are you stuck?

—Why would I be stuck?

—Well, what are you doing under the bed?

Were they on drugs? Couldn't they see I was in a cave?

—Into the floor I'm thrown, I explained.

I could hear Gwyn's voice.

—My god, what have you done, Dimple? Come out of there right now!

I began to crawl out of my cave, blinkering into the room's painful light.

—Lillian's going to kill me! Look, Karsh! Dimple, if you don't like the Dead you don't like the Dead, but why the hell did you have to destroy her tape? Jesus!

I crouched rocking on the floor and followed her furious finger. I could see now the spool in a tangle across the bed and floor, wound around lamps, climbing the walls like deflowered clematis.

—Shhh, Gwyn, leave her alone. I'll tape it over for you if you want, or just get you another one.

In the silence of the room the whiteness was chemical, blinding.

Karsh squatted, his knees, lips, then the warm brew of his eyes following, and his face was before mine.

—Rani, he whispered. No one had ever called me that except my Dadaji. A riverbank broke within me.

—Dimple, are you sure you're all right?

His finger approached and skimmed my face. When it pulled away a raindrop glistened jewel-like on the tip. It reminded me of how my father collected my tears on his thumb, coaxing them off me with healing hands, without breaking them, as if even my sadness were a precious thing.

—That is so beautiful, I said. —I could cry.

—You're already crying, he said softly. —Are you sure you want to go home like that?

—I really want to go home, I said.

—Dimple, you are so stoned, said Gwyn her face suspended behind Karsh's shoulder now like a belladonna moon.

—I didn't even inhale.

—Are you crazy? You inhaled more than any of us—it blew my mind! Who taught you all that? Your cousins? That Kavita is a wild one—I can see it in her eyes.

Am I crazy? What did she mean by that? Why was she staring at me like some zoological phenomenon?

—I'm not crazy, I said.

—I'm not paranoid, I said.

—I'm not a chipmunk, I said.

—And I'm not paranoid, I concluded.

For some reason Gwyn fell over on the floor laughing.

—Of course you're not, said Karsh gently.

—I just don't feel so good.

—Are you going to throw up? said Gwyn, her giggles suddenly subsiding.

—No, not like that. Just. I don't know.

—I'll take you, said Karsh. I couldn't feel my legs but even the slight breeze of the shift to vertical seemed to stir a memory in my mind of how it all used to be. I remembered my mother's once cryptic advice to never make decisions when horizontal, even alone, and it seemed to make sense now, because your mind was much closer to extreme states in this position—depression, dreaming, insanity. Karsh reached over and helped me up. His face was a map I wanted to follow.

—Are you sure? I said. —No, never mind. It's all right. Besides, you're kind of out of it, aren't you?

—I have a feeling you'd be more dangerous standing still than me driving at this point, he laughed. —Look, let me at least walk you back. The air will do you good.

He turned to Gwyn.

—Close your eyes; I'll be back, he said gently, dimming the light.

—You promise? she said, sounding panicky for some reason. —You're not just going to disappear on me, are you?

—I'm not going to disappear on you, he said. —I promise.

joint family

Outside, air flooded my head and I could feel the fog clearing.

—Are you cold? Karsh asked. —Or just defensive?

—No, why? What do you mean defensive? Why is everyone on my case tonight?

—Okay, okay. It's just, your arms are crossed. Here, take my shirt.

He wrapped it around my shoulders. He was wearing a deep red tee beneath it and his arms were slim but strong and I could see the deeper brown circle of a cicatrice, like my father's smallpox shot scar, on the upper part of one. I wasn't cold but the feeling of the fabric was bittersweet, like a goodbye hug, and I clung to it. It felt like a goodbye to him.

—Dimple, you're just fine, don't worry.

—What are you, everyone's guru? I said. We were passing the Bad Luck House and I quickened my step.

—Hey, no! Wait up, that's not what I meant, he said, running to catch up with me. —Is that what I come off as? I guess I've just seen a lot of people get hurt and I don't want to create any more pain where it can be avoided. So yeah, right. I sound like a guru. Sorry—I guess I like everything to be in harmony. Maybe too much.

—I suppose that's why you're a DJ, right?

He didn't say anything. So he wanted to make sweet music with Gwyn without hurting me. Why should I be hurt? I should be happy for all parties involved, myself included.

—Gwyn's great, isn't she? I said. —She's smart, and beautiful, and worldly.

—Yes, she's special, said Karsh. —She's your best friend, right?

—Oh, the best, I said.

—Well that's a precious thing, he said thoughtfully. —And it should be handled with care.

I was sick of being treated with kid gloves.

—Don't worry about handling me with care, Karsh, I said, trying to sound cool. —Eliminating pain and all that. I just realized tonight I don't even have any. I just realized tonight nobody's perfect, except—ta-da!—me. But Gwyn—you better go back to her. She's alone and expecting you.

—Yeah, I better, he said. But he just stood there, at the end of my driveway. My house was dark and I wanted to fold myself into it.

—You can keep it if you're cold, he said when I gave him back his shirt.

—I'm home now, I said. —Thanks, I'm fine.

—Dimple, I'm sorry if I'm giving you the wrong idea about Gwyn. I'm a protective person, I guess. It doesn't mean I'm . . .

—Believe me, I know what it doesn't mean, I said. —I've been there before.

—Oh, what does it matter anyways? I'm a sunk ship, right?

—No, I said. —You're definitely not that and I'm sorry I ever said it. But you better go now.

I began to walk up the drive.

—Good night, Karsh, I said over my shoulder. —Thank you for walking me home.

—See you around? he called after me.

—See you around.

I went up the steps and got the key from the hippo planter and went in. I turned to drop the latch in place. Through the screen I could still make out his figure at the end of the drive. He waved. I put my hand to the screen and watched his finely green gridded shadow turn and go, bleeding into darkness.

★　★　★

I took a breath to steady myself before reaching for the light switch. But the light seemed to turn on before my finger landed. Had my finger landed? I stared at the switch for a clue and then, gaining none, at my finger. I had never noticed that my knuckle was like a pond after a stone thrown, that ring of concentric circles. After what seemed a long contemplative moment I lifted my eyes.

The table was laid out with a pot of tea and cups and saucers and stacks of samosas and chutneys and pakoras and, jarringly, an unopened bag of Mint Milano cookies. My stomach roared. Had I died and gone to heaven?

Or was I stoned?

Suddenly a flock of cappuccino peacocks flapped excitedly forth from around the corner. The Indian Marriage Mafia Welcome Wagon was up and at 'em.

—High! my parents yelped in unison.

I *was* stoned. Frock. First they catch me drunk, now this. I was doing the downward spiral a little too quickly. Was there a way out of it?

—No! I cried. —Let me explain.

I was about to tell them about the cave and the broken map and the puzzle and the snow cone peaks, but then I realized from their Cheshire Cat faces that they might have been just saying hello. My teeth unhinged, dropped onto my tongue like a paper cutter, just in time.

—Aaray, no need to explain, beta, smiled my mother. —But why didn't you invite him in?

Had they been smoking, too? They never invited *anyone* in.

—He's a gentleman, my father nodded approvingly.

—Of course he is a gentleman. Who is saying he is not a gentleman? scoffed my mother. —But then why is he hanging around in the driveway like some hooligan? I made chai and samosas.

I had noticed. I was starving. I pulled a chair up to the table, and my parents followed suit. I bit into a samosa; a moan slipped out my mouth. Since when were they so good? I would have to carry this feeling with me like Karsh had said and apply it to school lunches. The crust crackled away in my fingers, thinning out in my mouth and melting evenly at the end, and then there were gently spiced batata pincushions and tooth-sunk little peas rolling sweet in the hollows of my teeth.

—So now you are liking Indian food? my father winked.

—It must be love, beamed my mother. —Look, beta, your eyes are so red.

I tried to look but my eyeballs hurt when I rolled them around like that.

—Have you been crying? asked my father.

—No. Um. *Laughing*, I said.

—Don't worry, beta, said my mother. —Love is an *emotional* thing. And it is bringing up many . . . *feelings*. It is all right to laugh, to cry. It is all right to write poems that rhyme to express your amorous state.

I was on the chutney now, shoving a chunk of samosa into the mango tangoing jar.

—Dimple, it's easier if you put a spoonful on your plate and dip.

I spooned some jelly jam out on my plate and then shoved the samosa back into the jar. They were right—it fit better now. Why were they just staring at me?

—You must have danced a lot to work up that appetite, my father said slowly.

I nodded through a mouthful of minced scrumptious. Then I was on the pakoras, smacking through the spinach that—Krishna, Prabhu, and The Whole Posse—was too good to write a rhyming poem about and what rhymed with spinach anyways. And then the chai. The chai. Oh my, oh my. I poured the sugar onto the teaspoon, dunked it quickly in and out then crunched through the raw granules.

—So how was it? asked my father.

—Well, bhangra, you know how it is, I mumbled through crushed cane. —Ancient Punjabi . . . dhol . . . hemp . . . immigrants . . . the Immigration Act . . . jangra.

—Your throat sounds hoarse—are you catching a cold? my mother wanted to know.

—I had to scream to be heard in the club.

—Scream what?

I took a breath then belted it out.

—*Itchy itchy eye—oh ho! Itchy itchy eye—hi hi!*

—My goodness, that NYU has really taught you, my father smiled, thumping me gently on the back. —You sound veritably enlightened!

Lit more than enlightened.

—So do you feel you got to know him much better? my mother asked.

—Much better, I said, tipping the plate to get all the sauce on my finger.

—Dimple, Prabhu, you're acting like a pregnant woman! said my father.

—Oh, that will be a wonderful day, smiled my mother, tears welling in her eyes. —I was just in Gap Kids and you should have seen the fall selection.

Excuse me, but could they let me grow up first?

—Is there more? I asked, my plate cleaner than the day it was sold. And for the first time in the history of the house there wasn't. Out of the corner of my eye I re-spied the pack of Mint Milanos; holding my breath and creeping up on it very . . . very . . . slowly . . . I ambushed it—and won! I tore the bag to shreds. With the minutest coercion from the tips of my front teeth the cajoled cookie crushed to powder in my mouth, the chocolate swirling a lazy palette on my tongue, spiked green. How come I'd never realized what a perfect accompaniment they were for the spice-crackle-pop of samosas? Why weren't they served in Indian restaurants? The mint and sweet soothingly tingled through the zing of the spice, melting down to thin-quilt the belly. And the milk, which I'd leaped to pull from the fridge and back: Two percent had never tasted so straight off the udder.

—There's a glass, Dimple, you don't have to drink from the bottle. Shouldn't you think of the next person?

There would be no next person. I emptied the plastic container and stamped it down like a flamenco dancer before tossing it into the recycling bin.

—Mom, you're the greatest cook in the universe. How come I never told you that before? Those *cookies*. Those *samosas*.

—They were the frozen ones, she said proudly.

—Well, then, you're the world's greatest deforester!

The word hung in the air before me. We all seemed to be examining it, heads cocked.

—So where did it leave off? said my mother. —Did he say anything about next time? About meeting again?

—I heard! He did! He said *See you around*, said my dad. —So it is progressing nicely.

—When will he be seeing you around?

—Well, he wants to check out my pictures sometime, I said.

—We can arrange that, said my father mysteriously, now chewing on a toothpick and looking very mafioso.

—Why would he want to see your pictures when he has the real thing before him? my mother wanted to know.

—Not pictures *of* me. Pictures I take.

—Aha! So maybe it is not so bad we are helping you set up this darkening room, smiled my mother, victorious. —It is the fate.

She stood, and my father stood, like men did when women left the room in old films, and I stood, like drugged daughters did when sober parents did, in order to blend in as best as possible.

—So do you admit you were wrong about him? my mom asked.

I pictured the way he drew the joint to his puckered lips, all the little lines that grooved upon them as he inhaled. I nodded vehemently.

—Oh yes, I admit it, I said.

—You see? First impressions may not always be the accurate ones. Not everything is as it seems at a glance. Laugh at me all you like—but he is a suitable boy! I knew it. Like I know my own daughter.

Little did they realize how lawsuitable this boy actually was.

—You know me better than you know, I said.

—I know, she said. —And no pressure, beta—it is all in the hands of the gods now.

I wasn't sure why we'd had to arrange that whole meeting in the first place if it had been in the hands of the gods—unless the gods were playing catch with it and she was just giving me the play-by-play.

She took me in her arms.

—Mmm, you smell . . . strange, she said, pulling back and knitting her brow. —What is that, Daddy?

They sniffed at me like confounded airport puppies. I decided I better run before the real dogs were called in, and started down the hall.

—Clove? my father offered.

—Cinnamon, my mother argued.

—A touch of asafetida, my father attempted—which is what he always said whenever he couldn't pinpoint an ingredient.

I was sprinting at this point.

—Ah! I am knowing what it is, I heard my mother saying as I just narrowly made it into the bathroom and spritzed on some pine-scented air freshener. —It is bhang!

I lay in bed that night, feeling a funny feeling when I thought about Karsh. In other words, feeling a funny feeling all the time. Even though after tonight I was so sure he and Gwyn were meant to be. Glitter had dusted off him to me and now speckled my pillow. I could still smell him on me, too, the scent of his shirt, but his shirt had been long gone. How can a world change overnight like this? But it was one word that had done it. One word from the mouth of a person I was beginning to realize I had completely misjudged. That *Rani* had gone straight to my heart and made a hole there, a hole like the one he'd left behind when he stood in the room and went to Gwyn, full of his aura but leaving me emptier still.

CHAPTER 23

gur nalon ishq mitha

—I can't stop thinking about him, Gwyn whispered, picking at her diner salad. It was time for the lunchtime confessional. —I can't eat, I can't sleep. For Claude's sake, I can't even shop.

—You can't, I said dully. My triple-decker burger oozed grease, vying for space with a sweet pickle that I was saving for last and an explosion of fries. The fries were mostly on the burnt side, which I liked. I was picking the soggy ones out and making two little piles.

—I mean, he's amazing, Gwyn went on. —He just *gets* it, you know? He gets *me*. The whole thing about my dad . . . I've never been able to talk to someone like that before. Something about him makes me feel I can open up and he's not going to laugh and it's not going to hurt. That he would never hurt me.

There were sixteen fries in the burnt pile and six in the soggy.

—Not to mention how *beautiful* he is. His skin, that color, so smooth —it's like he has no pores.

This was true—I had noticed it first in the barlight of HotPot, where he'd gone from brown to bronze before my eyes.

—And brilliant—when he talks you can tell he's really thought about things. He's not just bullshitting to get in your pants.

I would have to agree there as well. Although I wasn't 200 percent sure he would mind eventually getting into Gwyn's.

—And talented. Did you even see what he did with the Lillian's lame old record player? He put magic into it. He put magic into *me*—I've never met anyone like him. Anyone. And do you want to know what he did?

I wasn't sure I wanted to know, but it didn't seem I had a choice.

—I was feeling so down after he left with you, she continued, sticking her finger in the dressing on the side and sucking it off. —I know, it's silly, it must have been only ten minutes. But it felt like an eternity and, I don't know, after all that talk about my dad, I just felt like he might—vanish into thin air or something. I know, it doesn't make any sense. But that's how I felt. And when he came back I told him how I dreamed of the days I would still hear my parents' footsteps in the house when I went to sleep, when I was little and everything seemed all right, and how every night no matter what, my father tucked me in, chin to toes—and you know what he did? Do you know what he did?

I didn't, but I had a feeling I was going to find out pronto and I was going to wish it had happened to me. She was eyeing my fries now, her eyes shifting between the two piles as if it were match point.

—He told me, she said, swooping up a good third of the burnt numbers. —That he would stay with me and walk around till I fell asleep if that would make me less scared. And he stayed, and he walked around, and I felt so relaxed I could have slept, but I didn't want to sleep, I didn't want to miss a moment. And . . . guess what he did to me!

I didn't say anything. I tried to think of what was the opposite of that thing you did on planes to unblock your ears so I could plug mine up against what I was about to hear.

—Nothing! He didn't try anything!

She crunched through the handful of fries and went for another one. So maybe they could be just friends? I breathed an internal sigh of relief, but it was cut short.

—I mean, what a major turn-on! I never thought I'd see the day! He just came in and pulled the covers up to my chin and down to my toes and kissed me. It was so gentle, so tender, I could have married him on the spot.

—So you guys sucked face? I said, the burger beginning to convulse in my grip.

—No, no, Dimple—have you been listening to a word I've been saying? We did not *suck face*, as you so Shakespearily put it. It was even better than that.

She waited for me to ask for more, but I didn't.

—He kissed me on the forehead! No guy has ever kissed me on the forehead—they always go straight for the mouth or more. It was incredible.

She leaned back, pushing her salad away.

—This could be it, Dimple. It's not like with other people; it's really special. I've never felt this way before. I know I've said that before. But this time it's different. I know I've said that before, too—but really. *Never.* He cares about me—I feel it. I'm so used to looking after everyone and he looked after me. He didn't treat me like a fool or a weakling or a bimbo. He just took care of me, like it was the most natural thing in the world. He even told me my house was sacred because I'm in it.

—I know. I was there.

—Oh, right. Well this one is special. And I'm saving him for something better—I'm going to play the game differently this time around. I don't want to mess this one up, Dimple. And I need your help.

—Help with what? You're doing just fine, I said. All the burnt fries were gone. I poked a soggy one in the side; my fingernail left a crescent there.

—It's just, he's so . . . Indian.

—You noticed?

—You know what I mean. It's obviously important to him, his heritage. After all, he agreed to go through with the whole arranged setup thing, right? I know he really likes me and all, but I'm just worried in the big picture that I'm, well, that maybe I'm just not Indian enough.

—Enough? Gwyn, I hate to break it to you, but you're not Indian at all!

—I knew it, she sighed, slamming a fist into the table. Then determination steeled her eyes. —But I'm not going to let a little thing like that get in my way. Be all that you can't be, right? That's what I'm made for.

She opened her fist, splaying her decaled fingertips on the table towards me.

—You're my best friend in the world, Boopster. You know that.

—You're mine, too, Rabbit, I had to admit.

—No contest, she said. —I'd do anything for you.

—I'd do anything for you, too.

—Great. Because I need your assistance: I'm recruiting you to help me get Indo—but genuinely so this time.

—But what do you want me to do about it?

I mean, I did okay in biology but I wasn't *that* good.

—Numero uno: Desicreate—you know, that NYU identity thing next weekend. I figure that's a great place to get the DL.

—You're going to that? I said.

—*We're* going, Gwyn replied firmly.

—Oh no . . . I mean, HotPot was one thing, but spending a sunny summer weekend cooped up in a college auditorium?

—Come on, supertwin! What better place to figure out how to be Indian than an identity conference? It'll be good for both of us. And besides, I'll look like an idiot without you.

This was a twist on the norm. But still, I had enough on my hands with my own identity crisis, thanks very much.

—Karsh will be there. Not only be there—he's doing a DJ workshop.

—You've got to be kidding, I said, but my interest perked and I poured too much brown sugar into my coffee. It nearly turned to gur, the jaggery palm-sap pabulum my mother said only love could beat for sweetness. I didn't know he'd be going. I mean, he was a DJ; I'd sort of assumed he'd have DJ things to do—gigs to play, clubs to check out, things to spin, 'zines to pose for.

—He says it's important to engage in a dialogue about these issues.

—Why do you have to go to a conference to have a dialogue? We're having a dialogue and we're not at a conference.

But even as I spoke, the idea of being cooped up in a college auditorium was starting to seem slightly cozier to me.

—I don't know. I didn't really get it. But I think you need more people to *engage* in one. Or something. In any case he lit up when he talked about it. It's really important to him—he wants more people to be exposed to all of these issues, to bhangra, to the music.

Well, then I wanted to be there.

—And it's really important to me.

Make that a double.

—Okay, okay, I said. —I'll go with you.

—And step two: I need to be transformed into a suitable girl by then.

The drugs were definitely still in her system.

—Try a self-tanner, I said.

—No, no, Dimple—being Indian isn't just skin deep. I'm serious. I can't change my color. But I can change everything else.

—Gwyn, I have a feeling he likes you just the way you are.

—But he'll like me even more just the way you are.

This was food for thought.

—Really, Dimple. The way he talks about you—it's almost too much.

—What do you mean? I said, my heart lifting in spite of my logy state, in spite of myself.

—Oh, I don't know. He says you have a great personality, that there's more to you than meets the eye.

Meaning I was ugly with the potential to say interesting things? Yay.

—And he says you're like family to him.

Like a sister. An ugly sister? An ugly sister.

—Oh. Okay. Well. So what exactly do you want me to do?

—Well, I'll need to borrow some more of your clothes for the conference. If that's okay. And your dad's records—you said they have all the same records, right? I'm actually getting pretty good at the beat-dropping thing, but I need to be better. Oh, and at some point, cooking lessons from your mom—hello. He mentioned how much he loves her stuff.

—In other words you need to borrow my whole family.

—I want to be the real thing, Dimple. You're the only one who can help me.

—Yeah, I can relate to that, I said. —I'm sorry—I guess I'm just kind of moody today.

It was true, much as it irked me. I could relate. Who was I to scoff, after all? I hardly knew how to be Indian myself and I even had race on my side. I remembered my vow to try to be a better friend to Gwyn. And after all, I couldn't like Karsh—I hardly knew him, right? He was The Boy, right? Besides, he'd already resoundingly hinted that he thought of me as a relative at best, so unless we both turned out to be on the Pakistani side of South Asian, where cousins could still intermarry, there was little hope that this could lead to anything of a romantic nature. So all this potential romancing between him and Gwyn—why should it bother me? So what if he'd turned out to be slightly cooler than I'd expected; then I should be even happier Gwyn was digging him. After all she'd been through with her family, and with Dylan and who knew who else. I should be overjoyed that she might be leaving the days of the nasty boys behind and riding off into the DJ booth with a bona fide bed-tucker-inner.

—And put in a good word for me, if you get a chance? she said now. What would have normally been a command ended in a tremulous question mark today, and made it abundantly clear if there'd ever been a doubt: This was no game; she was so earnest it seemed she hadn't blinked this whole time.

—There aren't any bad words for you, Gwyn, I said. Then I swallowed and said it, hard as it was, because to see Gwyn happy was well worth a moment's discomfort, was worth much more than that. —In fact, he already said you were special.

—Wow, she said, slamming back against the vinyl and smiling the big smile she reserved for when she had no reservations, revealing as it did a stunning number of cavities. —He told you that? No one's ever said that before.

She leaned forward again and squeezed my hands.

—You know, it seems it was only a few days ago I was telling you to find a prince for me, she said, looking excessively nostalgic considering it *had* been pretty much a few days ago. —Little did I know it would be the one for you! Gosh, Dimple, you really are my best friend; it's like you were there to bring us together. You can *definitely* give the speech at the wedding—hell, you can even give me away! I mean, I'm kind of shocked you guys didn't like each other. But believe me, I'm not complaining, not at all. Because this one's the one. I confess it. I can feel it. I've never met anyone like him.

—Yeah, I said. —I know what you mean.

—You think he's the one, too? Wow! You know, I've almost stopped trusting my own feelings, but if you agree, it's settled.

She took my face in her hands, squeezing my chipmunk cheeks towards each other and gazing into my eyes with blue-rimmed sky-wide pupils.

—I'm so glad you didn't like him! she laughed. —Can you imagine?

She abruptly let go and picked up my pickle and chomped on it. Half of it gone, and she put it back down. And I don't know why but I nearly started to cry.

—Gwyn! I said.

—What? What's the matter? It's just a pickle.

I bit back tears.

—Well you weren't eating it, right?

—I was saving it, I said. —Never mind.

exposure

—What are you so moody about? my mother asked when I got home. She hadn't even turned to look at me so I didn't know how she could tell; she was up on a stepladder in the corner of the family room, attempting to hang a mobile with a mess of metallic ornaments on the hook that had been there since we'd moved in.

—What makes you think I'm moody?

—I can hear it in your footsteps. Shuffle shuffle, mope mope, like those slacking people in the unemployment line.

—Yeah, whatever, I said. —Mom, what are you doing?

—I am channeling the energy flow.

—Say what?

—You see, these corners all symbolize different areas in life—like the lines in a palm—and it is best to put mobiles or fountains or chimes in them to deflect the bad vibes and keep them working at their optimum. There was a whole special on it just now. Feng shui, they are calling it—but, between you and me, this was invented in India. You know, like the back door theory.

My mother believed back door exits and entries stripped the wealth from houses. (Was this yet another ancient Indian proverb? I'd asked her once. Yes, and besides—what robber in their right mind is going to be entering by the *front* door? the ever-logical one had replied.)

—What area is that you're doing?

—The financial sector. First things first.

—Mom, what about love?

—What good is love without money? Did you know one out of every . . . certain number of couples divorce over money problems?

—Health?

—How to pay for the hospital? We can only get so many favors from our medical profession friends.

—I can't believe you! I cried.

—I told you you were moody. And now you are not believing your own mother who birthed you, to put the cherry on top of the kettle black. So, what is it?

—No, nothing, I said. —Well, okay, it's just Gwyn's insisting that we go to that NYU conference thing.

—Will Karsh be there?

—Of course.

—And the problem is?

That Karsh would be there, pretty much. But I figured I wouldn't share this.

—That Gwyn is—I don't know. She's *special*, said my mother fondly. That word again.

—What a supportive friend, she continued, untangling the threads of the mobile. The metal clanged as the pieces began to unravel. —You know, we misjudged her direly around that hanky-panky triple A time—she really is a good influence on you. I daresay we owe her a great deal for opening your heart.

My heart didn't feel very open. In fact, I think I'd stretched it a little beyond capacity, like an advanced yoga move on a novice, and now it was snapping ligaments and fracturing bones and getting generally grumpy.

—She wants to borrow our clothes and records and all to get prepared.

—Wonderful! I am just delighted by all this interest she's taking in Indian customs. She is a serious one. I never realized it from her grades, but that girl—when she puts her mind to something she always gets it. You could learn from her.

—I'm just realizing that.

—Dimple, don't be too selfish about sharing your culture with her. At least we *have* a culture to share. The poor girl—what does she have? Pokémon and McDonald's and *Survivor*.

—But that's what I have, too, Mom. And Pokémon's Japanese.

—It isn't only food that goes through the umbilical cord, beta, said my mother from her podium, dramatically rolling her cotton top up a smidge to reveal her belly button. She promptly snapped it back down as if two seconds was all the human eye could take, or deserved, of this mystical sight. —Memory and dreams and history—all the things of the third eye—these pass through, too, like spiritual food.

Her face was intent. I could nearly see her third eye dilate. It was the same look she'd had when she had Kavita and Sabina on the floor doing sun salutations.

—Mom, I don't know, I said, gazing where her navel had been and wondering if there was still a vacancy in the eleven-star suite behind it. —It's just that, I feel like I don't even have the culture myself. And now I'm actually being asked to give it away.

—Beta, you were born with it.

—Mom, I was born in the USA.

—But India is in your blood. It's not going anywhere without you.

She stepped off the ladder, the mobile now securely in place, and stood back to survey her work. The silver sailboats quivered in the current created by the air conditioner, splattering discs of sliding light all around the room. It was like a daytime disco.

I pictured the sun rising over these boats from an ashram window I had never seen. But I could see it as clearly as if I'd been there. Felt as if it had happened to me.

★   ★   ★

So if I couldn't fully open my heart, and I begrudgingly opened my cupboard, I would work on my mind. I'd give Gwyn the records, okay, the clothes—whatever she required. But once she was out of my hair I'd become the incontestable expert on South Asian identity.

Later that evening, I launched my plan of attack with my father, pouncing upon him moments after he'd stepped in the door and, car keys still in hand, flicked on the television.

—Dad, do we have any books on, you know, Indian stuff?

My father's eyes were flicking side to side and down, following the inscrutable ticker tape running on the screen.

—India stuff? he said with his Dow Frown. —Could you be less specific please?

—You know, like Gandhi and Nehru and the gods and all that.

My dad actually turned away from the numbers, which was pretty much the equivalent of my mother's turning away from a pot of nearly boiling milk.

—You did *not* just say Gandhi and Nehru and the gods and all that!

I nodded. Of course I had. Unless he could come up with a Jesus Christ and God Almighty/Cheese and Crackers Got All Muddy translation, I didn't see what else I could have said.

—Are you telling a joke? he cried, setting down the remote. He cupped my shoulders with both his hands and smiled down his bifocals past the perfectly ball-tipped nub of his nose and into my eyes. —Of course we do! Am I hearing correctly, Mummy?

—You are hearing most correctly, said my mother, proudly pausing in her watering of the palm plant. —Gwyn and Karsh are having a very positive influence on our daughter, Daddy.

—Well, it's just this NYU conference is coming up and I want to be a little prepared, I said. —That's all.

My father looked like he wanted to break out the Beaujolais. He threw his hands up delightedly.

—Prabhu, I feel like breaking a coconut! he cried. —Follow me.

★   ★   ★

In the study, not only crammed in no particular order on the bookshelves and blue trunks but also stacked over the unfilled-in warranties in the cardboard boxes that had once housed turntables and standing fans, microwaves and cassette decks, and even the Smith Corona typewriter: books. Books on Indian mythology, Gandhi and Nehru biographies, a personal history of Partition; travel guides; books on elephants, on Indian classical dance (which I realized now had to be my mother's), the British Raj, the overturn of the British Raj, the princely states; the poetry of Rabindrinath Tagore, the stories of Satyajit Ray; the *Mahabharata* and *Ramayana*; guides to Indian architecture, alimentation, and Ayurvedic treatments. How had I missed these?

I had my work cut out for me. I made myself comfortable on the corner beanbag and opened a mythology book, the one with the brightest of Ganeshas blooming on the cover, his curved trunk twining nearly the length of the page. My father smiled and tiptoed dramatically back out the study door.

—Any questions, you know where to go! he said, before closing it.

Well, I'm not sure where he was thinking, but it wasn't to him. The next morning while he was finishing his chai and my mother was beginning hers I blurrily joined them.

—Who was Krishna's wife? I asked, separating the dry flakes from the soggy in my cornflakes.

—Jashoda, said my father.

—No, no, said my mother. —Radha.

—Are you sure, Mummy? said my father.

—I'm sure, she said firmly. —It's not in the book?

—I don't know, I said. —I didn't see it in the book. It seemed to be written for people, you know, in the know.

—Let me call Hush-Hush Aunty, said my mother. —She organizes a lot of the temple activities—she'll know.

—And I'll check on-line, said my dad, sheepishly cowering behind the high-tech alibi.

—You don't *know*? I said, amazed. The number of soggy-side flakes was growing rapidly as I sat with my spoon in midair.

—It's not that we don't *know*, said my father.

—It has just been such a long *time*, explained my mother.

—We just need to confirm, added my father. —That they haven't, you know . . . changed it.

—What, Hinduism gets updated every year or something? I grinned.

—Dimple! That is enough! This is an exception, said my mom. My father had already disappeared down the corridor in search of the computer.

★　★　★

But a few days later when I was met with a blank upon posing a question regarding the avatars, I asked if we should go to the http something.

—I have an even better idea, said my father. —Maybe one of these days we can just go to the temple. It will give you a break for your eyes, and that way you can see the real deal—it's been a while since I went myself, and you must have been just a little girl that last time. You and me. Would you like that?

It had been ages since I'd done anything with him, just the two of us, other than count the seconds for my mother to get there and relieve the unspoken tension. Only thing was, I just didn't have enough time. The conference was fast approaching, and the books in my hands and the Web on the screen seemed a faster way to take in the most info possible.

—I'd like that a lot, Daddy, I said. —But would it be okay if we did it another time? Like as soon as the conference is over?

—Oh, don't worry, don't worry. I understand—you are very busy these days. Whenever you have time, beta.

He smiled, his lips stretching over too many teeth.

—At least we are talking now, isn't it?

It was true. In fact, I couldn't remember why it had ever been the case that the two of us had had so little to say to each other; since I'd started staying at home reading and joining him for his morning chai, it seemed we had plenty to share. Mainly, we had plenty of questions. But surprisingly many of these were the same.

★   ★   ★

And as the days went on, my mom grew to be more and more in touch with Hush-Hush Aunty and Radha, sometimes hitting redial to ask them more of my upcropping questions. And my dad, he was turning into an incontestable Webmaster, his list of favorites running to the screen bottom when scrolled open.

My neck cricked and when I took breaks from the books distant objects swam till my vision adjusted. It seemed I'd been holed up and reading for ages. Was college like this? But I had to admit, it was fascinating, some of it. There were really sad stories about Partition, when India was divided into India and Pakistan, and how the people you'd drunk tea with for years turned into your enemies overnight, sometimes betraying you in a heartbeat, sometimes risking everything they had to protect you. And Gandhi was a more complicated man than I'd imagined—there were stories that didn't match up between the British and Indian books. History wasn't that easy a thing to learn, seemed to be what I was learning. It wasn't a static story about dead people. It was a revolving door fraught with ghosts still straining to tell their version and turn your head, multifaceted and blinding as a cut diamond. In a book of folk tales I read a story of five blind men who were asked to describe an elephant. Each described the part he touched, crafting an entire creature from the tail alone, the trunk or ears, the belly. All of the versions true; none the entire truth. It was a bit like this.

And a funny thing happened then. The more I read, the more I forgot why I'd begun reading in the first place. And now at meals, we'd sit down together, my mother and father and me, and they would enthrall me with tales of freedom fighters in our own family! Hear No Evil Uncle—derailing trains at midnight to bring the cities to a halt. My grandmother spinning all the clothes to khadi. And I found even I was able to enthrall my parents; they would sit amazed as I recounted something to them they'd never learned or had simply forgotten, left to collect dust in an unused attic of the mind.

—Shampoo comes from the Sanskrit? my father asked incredulously one etymologically enlightening breakfast along the way.

—More specifically, from the Hindi word *champee*, meaning to massage, I told him.

If anyone was going to be an expert on Indian history—whether of fact or fable, war or word—it was going to be me.

CHAPTER 25

desicreate

The day of the conference I was ready. I knew that India had twenty-five states (and seven union territories), almost two dozen major languages (Hindi being the one primarily spoken by about a third of the population), and that Hinduism was the religion practiced by about four-fifths of the peeps (other religions included Islam, Christianity, Sikhism, Buddhism, and Jainism). I had Gandhi's birth date down (October 2, 1869) and that of his assassination (January 30, 1948). I had the names of the four principal castes (Brahmins, Kshatriyas, Vaishyas, and Shudras). And a bindi.

Gwyn had a messenger bag (newly purchased) of records (my father's) and a level of determination in her eyes that frightened me. And a bindi. We were taking the train in, staying at Kavita and Sabina's the night, and then my parents were going to join us for brunch in the city—after giving me and Karsh some quality time together (with an auditorium full of people, they'd neglected to notice).

—Do I really look all right? Gwyn asked me for the—what comes after gazillionth?—time.

She didn't look all right. She looked, in SAT-speak, *pulchritudinous*, and I had to remind myself that looks weren't everything at universities. I thought. In the fresh painted day she was a sun goddess, a street she-Surya, her beauty rendered still more blinding by my birthday outfit. My mother had agreed to lending it to her, chappals to dupatta, figuring I shouldn't be caught two times in it. But I suppose it *was* a pretty memorable getup: Even in New York City, home of the fashion fringe, heads were turning like tops as Gwyn sauntered by.

I was in a paisley shirt and jeans—but now that I knew paisley was linked to India (based on the mango pattern from Indian shawls) I'd convinced my mom it was traditional enough and gotten away with it. In truth, there was really nothing Indian about it (as the Made in Taiwan tag attested to) but I had the facts now. I could have been in a calico, cashmere, or seersucker tube top, a chintz bustier; cummerbund, dungarees, jodhpurs, khakis (yes, like Karsh and Radha that fateful day), or even pajamas—all these words of South Asian origin—and had backup for it. At least I was comfortable on the outside.

I had to not be intimidated by Gwyn. After all, we were technically entering my territory, right? So the club had turned out not to be; my mistake. But I'd always been smarter in school than in social situations, and this was not only a school we were treading towards through the Village streets, but a renowned university. Even she'd said she needed me to be legit there. But to tell the truth I was nervous.

As soon as we slipped through the arch and were crossing Washington Square Park, I began to look for him. Subconsciously at first, I suppose. I felt like I could feel him around already. And it was a thrill being in his land—this is where he went to school and thought all those thoughts and spun and ate and dreamt. And did drugs, I realized, as we passed a grove of shadowy, whispery men clearly selling. But my folks wouldn't believe this level of unsuitability of him even if they saw the most suitable bong before them, and his lips attached (superglue mishap, of course).

A definite buzz was in the air as soon as we slipped into the foyer of the Modern Culture and Media building, where the conference was being held, hosted jointly by the South Asian Studies and Women's Studies departments (as the banner declared). Kavita met us at the auditorium doors and promptly chided me for being MIA and on IST, was I an ABCD about my ETA or what, much to Gwyn's perplexity; she tried to work in an EFC to no avail (she didn't speak NRI—nonresident Indian).

When, program in stamped hand, we broke on through to the other side, I nearly gasped. We stood at the higher altitude of an auditorium that sloped to the podiums. There stood a woman who looked like she was from India but spoke with the Jersey accent I'd thankfully been spared due probably to my parents' slight Indian lilt.

There were at least a few hundred seats. And they were full.

We made our way to our reserved trio and sat. I began to seek out Karsh, but was soon lost in the maze of people. I glanced at my program to make sure he was listed on it. Sabina's name was under a section called "Appropriate Behavior: The Disenfranchisement of Identities Via Media Subterfuge"; Karsh's, way below, just after DJ Tamasha's (who I now discovered was really named Shailly) under "DJ—Shaman or Sham: The Perks and Pitfalls of Nonverbal Communication." All the titles on the program had colons and a second title. And there seemed to be a lot of women on the panels, and in the audience, too.

South Asian Identity. Were all these people that confused, too? I wondered, gazing now at the row upon rows of rapt and far from daft faces. The auditorium was packed with Indians, mainly ABCDs (if the sari-clad woman with the Jersey accent was any indication), some neo-hippies, and even preppies. I was again struck with the question, as I'd been at the club: From where had they all Athena-like sprung? Well, I suppose from the club. My heart began to pound at the thought of speaking in front of them. It wasn't at all what I'd imagined—I'd been picturing classroom size, like at Lenne Lenape, maybe twenty little Indians. And then there were two hundred.

I was lost already, and according to my program, we were still on the introduction. When the panels began it got even worse. They were all in English, but with these really specific multisyllabic words that meant nothing to me in this context, or any. I had no idea what they were talking about but I was pretty sure they did, which amazed me. Maybe I wasn't even monolingual after all; it was like this whole other language was being spoken—one I'd gotten a whiff of through Sabina and Kavita, and even Julian and Dylan: Diaspora and Discourse and Dialogue. Representation and Appropriation. Grassroots, Hegemony. Colonialized, Collective Unconscious, Community. Sociocritical, Semantic, Semiotic. There was a lot of "activist consciousness" being tossed around, too.

And "people of color"—that was fired out there a ton as well. At first I thought they meant black people but then the sari-clad woman said *We as people of color* and I realized she meant we, as in us. I'd never thought of myself as a people of color. It made me picture the Muppets or Teletubbies or those commercials where the green and red M&Ms talk to each other.

Gwyn was wearing her best behavior face, but I could see her eyes skatting wildly over the aisles in search of Karsh. Kavita was making little grunts of accord or disaccord under her breath and looked as captivated as if she were at the Cirque du Soleil. Other people in the audience emitted a lot of knowing *mmms*.

And everyone, I mean *everyone*, said South Asian. South Asia was, by the way, Bangladesh, Bhutan, India, the Maldives, Nepal, Pakistan, and Sri Lanka. The term itself was even the topic of a debate about whether it was a positive (unifying identity that acknowledged differences) or negative (effacing term that omitted significant political, historical, economic, and religious discrepancies) one.

The power of a shared term, an endearment. That I could relate to. *Rani*. And even if it effaced our perhaps even insurmountable differences, it had softened me, like butter left on the counter; unintentionally.

Now Sabina took the podium and went into a revved-up thing about the appropriation of South Asia by the popular media and that most coffeehouse chai doesn't even really have tea in it but chai means tea and what was *that* all about (which made Gwyn sigh disillusionedly). But now it was going in one ear and sticking there. Because when Sabina stood, I saw him. He'd been in her blind spot but he was in plain view now, and Gwyn gave a little gasp and tugged my wrist. I smiled back at her, too; I couldn't help it.

He was slouched back in his seat, elbows on both armrests and eyes peering out over steepled fingers. Beside him, straight out of a comic book, was a pixie girl wearing what looked like a pair of swim goggles on her head and a zip-up vinyl jumpsuit. Her face was a mesh of angles, like a Picasso but pretty; it had to be Tamasha.

The DJ duo vanished out of view again as Sabina began to pace, gesturing wildly at an equally enraged and opinionated familiar-looking woman named Upma Abichandi who, according to the program, ran the South Asian Women's Shakti Collective for Gender Conception Reform (whatever that meant) and who definitely got her hair cut by a hairdresser with issues; it spiked up, blue-tipped, serrating the very air as she violently shook her head. They both seemed really mad and I didn't know why, like people on the subway in the morning before they have their coffee. But we weren't on the subway and it was late afternoon already.

Kavita was beaming with pride at Sabina, who was onto something about mehendi not being tantamount to temporary tattoo, and how it's been appropriated by Western capitalist culture. But the mehendi originated in Africa, and so India appropriated it from a people of color as well, according to Upma, and thus we shouldn't wear jeans or listen to Queen, then. But Freddie Mercury was Indian, Sabina pointed out, Parsi, and plus, half of these things are made in India anyways if you check the tags. Somehow eventually arriving at: Whatever it was, why did a white girl have to wear it before it was regarded as cool?

—Oh god, do you see Karsh? whispered Gwyn. —He looks so impressed.

—. . . the most obvious example, Upma was adding. —Being Madonna in her South Asian phase.

—This is my moment, Gwyn whispered. —Do I look okay?

—You are looking fine, Gwyn, said Kavita. —It's an identity conference, not the spring collection, isn't it?

—But clothes are a huge part of my identity, said Gwyn. Then, to my stundom, her hand shot up, body following a moment after.

—Excuse me?

A hush descended upon the audience as they stared amazed and prêt à pouncer at the salvar'd blonde before them. Oh no, now they would definitely maim us.

—I just wanna say: Why are you guys still talking about Madonna's South Asian phase anyways? Gwyn began. —Hello—that's already ancient history. Madonna's just done what we all should do. Get into the groove. You have to subvert. Be all that you can't be.

Upma didn't look so pleased.

—So what are you saying? she snapped, steeling her gaze right at Gwyn. —How am I supposed to subvert my South Asianness? Tell someone, *Hey! I do Bharat Natyam, I go to temple—fuck you*?

—Sure, said Gwyn. —Oh, and by the way, regarding the whole South Asian thing: I don't think you should worry so much about using the same term. Of course we can't become the same. You'll never be a size zero, and I'll never be a twelve—you're about a twelve, right? We can dress the same and still maintain our differences.

She just stood there a moment, every head doing a 180 to check her out.

—What would you know about people of color? Upma sputtered finally. —Do you have any black friends?

—Do you have any white? Gwyn retorted. She gestured at me and then Kavita. —I have South Asian friends.

She pointed Karshwards.

—And him.

Karsh lifted a half-steeple in a tiny wave. A stunned silence ensued, punctured by a quick but thick round of applause, before Upma could huffily continue her spiel.

Gwyn nearly curtsied on her way down. An ear-to-ear grin was glued to her face from that moment on. And me, I was utterly depressed. I thought that at least here I might be one step ahead of my popular pal, but looked like I was, as always, more than two behind.

As the conference continued it occurred to me finally that it wasn't really about Indian history as it was written, but really about rewriting it by taking a fresh look at race, ethnicity, gender, and a mix of sociocultural questions—as the opening paragraph of the program laid out in bold text; I had been so busy trying to locate Karsh I had failed to notice this.

I just couldn't believe how far along the desi scene was, not just socially but intellectually, how many people were out there thinking about it. This whole event had so far rocked my world, muddled me still more, and delivered a series of tiny epiphanies, all at the same time. To be honest, I was quite intimidated by the dialogue going on, as well as by the passion and conviction of these people on so many subjects which I, frankly, had never really even thought about.

The litany of dates and place names in my head suddenly seemed a futile thing. Here were topics I'd never seen in any history book, whether American or Indian or British. A history of a people in transit—what could that be card catalogued under? And the history of the ABCD. Everyone seemed to know about this ABCD thing—that didn't seem very confused to me! And it was a relatively new phenomenon; it had never occurred to me that things going on now could have a history already. The moments that made up my life in the present tense seemed so fleetingly urgent and self-contained to me: I'd always felt my life had very little to do with my parents' and especially their parents' histories (save for the shared place Dadaji and I had created for ourselves)—and that it would have very little effect on anything to come.

But the way these people were talking—about desis in Hollywood; South Asian Studies departments; the relatively new Asian Indian slot on the census—was hummingly sculpting the air, as if they were making history as they spoke. Making it, messily but surely, even simply by speaking. I was feeling it, too—a sense of history in the making. But where did I fit in to any of it?

And how come no one had told me? How come I had to gatecrash, ride on the salvar-tails of my Bombay-born cousin to even be let in on any of this?

Shailly/Tamasha was speaking now, an ironical amount, on transcending borders through the unspoken word. She talked about Outcaste and the Asian underground and some brilliant barbed-haired London DJ who Madonna had personally called up (and who, frankly, she really seemed to be crushing on).

I watched Karsh as he waited his turn to speak, and wondered now where he fit into it all himself—raised partly in India, partly in the States, and done a little UK time. He was definitely on the local, making all stops. Technically he wasn't AB but he was E and HIJ now. And he left me pretty C, that was certain.

When it was finally his turn to speak, he strode center stage.

—And this is Karsh Kapoor, also known as DJ Gulab Jammin', the sari-swathed woman announced. —He assembles together individually distinct media to create a nonverbal postmodern discourse that eradicates the signifier/signified boundary.

Oh no. Even he was going to be incomprehensible.

—AKA I play cool records, said Karsh, not using the mike. I smiled, relieved. —And I'm going to let the music speak for itself. I'll be holding a basic DJing workshop in Rich Hall in ten. I hope you'll join us.

I felt for a moment that he was looking right at me.

—He's looking at me! cried Gwyn. Mona Lisa, the boy was. —I've got to check my makeup and get a prime seat, Dimps. Meet me in the bathroom.

And she was gone. I stayed a few minutes through the closing comments and claps and then told Kavita I'd meet them later back at the apartment—she was splitting to study, and gave me an extra key. I ended up at the tail end of the fidgety line of enlightened women waiting to enter the bathroom. And by the time I got in, the space had pretty much emptied out except for Gwyn and—thrillingly!—Zara, who were side by side at the mirror touching up their makeup.

To be more specific, Zara was involved in the delicate act of applying teardrop beads of paint over the sweep of her brows, and tiny rhinestone bindis between them, and Gwyn was watching mesmerized, her own lipstick immobile mid-mirror before her.

Even in this highly unideal lighting (fluorescent), Zara's luminosity glowed from the inside out, like candles gone deep in the middle. She wore a spangly chaniya choli, gold and satsuma, the dupatta in a twist round her neck, and the gold chains and black beads of a mangal sutra resting upon it. On each of her hands was a pocha, medallion resting in the center and from it, five chains trinkling up and finishing in a ring for each finger, a bracelet connecting the entire thing to the wrist. She worked surprisingly well with all this jewelry on.

—That is so freakin' cool, Gwyn said finally, unable to contain herself any longer. —Hey, Dimps, isn't that so freakin' cool? What are you doing, if you don't mind my asking?

—This is bridal makeup, said Zara calmly, speaking in a way where only her mouth moved, leaving her forehead a smooth palette.

—Are you getting married or something?

—He hasn't asked yet, she said, a slight smile tugging her eyes. —But I figured I might as well start preparing now—it can take me a while to get ready.

—Can I try some? asked Gwyn. —He hasn't asked either.

—Yet, said Zara. —Shall I apply it? You don't mind if we use another applicator—I'm a bit of a stickler for cleanliness.

Gwyn hopped up on the counter and slid back between sinks and presented her face to Zara, eyes closed like a sleeping baby or a girl about to kiss. And Zara set to work. Her generosity was touching—she was sharing her gift with a stranger, completely unthreatened by the competition. Well, not that there could be any between them. She was in a category by herself —the way a ravishing animation character cannot be compared to a ravishing person. As she transformed Gwyn's face drop by drop, Gwyn assaulted her with a barrage of questions, imitating the nonmoving forehead technique when she spoke, to which Zara replied sweetly and expertly.

—And how'd you get your henna so dark? she asked finally.

I noted the jungled up pattern on Zara's palms, the letter P swirling in the center of one hand, a K in the other. It was true: Her mehendi was the darkest I'd ever seen.

—Well, you know what they say: The greater the love between a couple, the darker the mehendi, said Zara. —But a tip for even the loveless: Just before sleeping, lay your hands over a tava with eliachi on it, and you can't go wrong.

I moved forward, captivated.

—Frock, that looks fantastic, I said.

—Would you like me to do you? Zara asked me, indicating her Gwyndi'd masterpiece.

—Oh, no, thank you. I'm sure it wouldn't work on me.

—And why the fuck not?

She even made *fuck* sound classy. She was now squiggling a lightning bolt out from Gwyn's bindi's diamond heart.

—Come on, Dimple, get in the spirit! said Gwyn. —But just don't make them exactly the same. I mean, you already look Indian enough—me, I need all the help I can get.

—Girlfriend, you're trying to look Indian? said Zara. —Well, as you said yourself, be all that you can't be. I hear you.

She capped her makeup pencil with a satisfied smile.

—There you go. Don't say I didn't dress you for it.

—Thank you so much, said Gwyn. —You know, I don't even know your name.

—Zara, she said. —Zara Thrustra.

—What an interesting name! Me, I'm Gwyn. Gwyn Sexton.

—That's not so bad either.

—I'm . . .

—Dimple, said Zara. —I know.

I couldn't believe she remembered; my hand froze a moment on the stall door.

—Well, I've got to go nab my man, Gwyn said. —Catch up with you there, Dimps. Zara, it was a pleasure.

—It still is, said Zara smiling.

When I came out, Zara was entering the stall beside me. I washed my hands, glancing under her door. Those studded slippers that tilted the feet to nearly vertical. The deluge continued as I admired the heels—now that I was up close, I saw they were embedded with coins in different currencies, bits of scrap metal and plastic, pricked ballon and beer bottle glass. Like she'd stepped into life and it stuck. I hadn't seen all the detail before. But then I'd never before looked under a women's room stall to have the heels facing me either.

And then I had a strange thought. I remembered what Sabina had said: *She puts the balls into Bollywood.* It made sense now, and I wished it didn't. I suddenly longed for a world where things were as they appeared. Now, my own seemed to be turning upside down and around. Like Gwyn's house when we were kids, but then it had been of my will, and now it had ambushed me, and I couldn't make it go back so easily. But maybe that's how things really were—upside down and around, a carousel with the earth for a sky and heaven at its feet.

This new world no longer seemed to fit in the tiny defined space of my viewfinder. I didn't know whether I wanted to laugh or cry, and I held Chica Tikka close. That's why I'd liked black-and-white photographs; things were clear, made manageable in them. I wished I could feel more like that inside.

The flush went off, sending me running.

★ ★ ★

By the time I entered Rich Hall, the room was packed and Karsh was just wrapping up his intro.

—So now you have the basics, he said. He was standing before two decks, rubbing his hands together as if about to make fire. —Does anyone dare come up and try a little beat-matching?

The question was barely out of his mouth before Gwyn shot to the front of the room and opened her brand-new messenger bag. She began lifting out her (my dad's) records and holding them up for all to see like a game-show hostess, or a kindergarten teacher with a picture book.

—Well, Karsh, I thought I'd give it a go with my own Lata Mangeshkar and Asha Bonsai favorites. Dil something and another. Which I happen to have right here.

—*Bhonsle*, corrected Karsh, smiling. —You don't pronounce the N.

Gwyn smiled back, unfazed. She stepped up beside him and, dropping discs to platter, set to work. She cued up, counted out loud with the headphones hanging off one ear. The needle sank into the groove and, sitars sparkling and voices twined, the songs settled together as if there had never been a frontier to cross. The crowd cheered her on; even the sulky girl who'd raised her hand first looked at me and shrugged with a *well, if she's got it, she's got it* look.

Karsh gave her what he claimed were increasingly tougher tracks to mix. And Gwyn rose to the challenge, even seemed to have copies of many of them in her bag.

Watching them there—she, teardrops arching gracefully over tearless eyes, dressed like a bride DJing her own wedding, and he beside her, mouth proud, stepping back to let her have her space, be a star, dancing a little dance to the beats that fell from her fists like gems to the platter—I could see no border between them. Joined by music and a night of conversation, the seam was invisible, invincible.

But I could feel a frontier rising up between us nonetheless, leaving them harmonious on one side and trapping me with my useless information on the other. Even here. Again. The other side of the lens.

It was too much to take and I left. Out the door, out of air.

the spice grrls

That evening, Gwyn and I met up at Waverly and Waverly as planned; Kavita and Sabina had split to pick up some slumber party victuals for us. Gwyn was still blathering on about her DJ experience. She'd hung out with Karsh till well after the workshop—he'd had to cut out for some work stuff, or she could have played with him forever.

—That's great, Gwyn, I said dully.

—You know, you could take a little more interest in something that's this important to him, and to me. He even asked why you walked out on the conference. That's just plain rude, Dimple.

—Sorry, Gwyn, I said. —I guess it just got too hot so I went outside for some air.

—You headed on into a heat wave for air?

I didn't feel like arguing—and I didn't feel like getting into the Zara topic just yet, not without Sabina and Kavita here to back me. And, frankly, I just didn't even want to deal. I could already hear Gwyn ridiculing me for my feverish imagination; I could already feel a headache coming on.

We gave ourselves a tour of the apartment as we talked. And this tour soon enough distracted us from our conversation. The first thing that struck me was the number of books. Uncountable! They were stacked from floor to ceiling, wall to wall. Many of them were what I assumed was Sabina's Women's Studies stuff—*The Second Sex,* and lots of spines with *Feminist* and *Recreating* and *Alternative* and citrus fruits in the titles. And there were at least as many India volumes as we had in our house, some in the original Sanskrit.

—Man, said Gwyn. —All these books sound straight off the conference program. Don't they have any fun stuff? I mean, Sabina is supposedly doing Women's Studies, right? Then how come there isn't a single *Elle* or *Cosmo* in here?

There were two rooms in addition to the bathroom: an all-red bedroom that barely fit a queen-size, with a door that kept swinging open even when I tried to shut it behind me, and this living room, complete with couch and inflatable furniture, which ran right into the kitchenette. It was quaint, but minuscule, and I wondered how one person could live in it let alone two. No wonder New Yorkers were always out.

—This wouldn't even serve as a decent closet, said Gwyn. —Though still, it would be a closet in Manhattan, so that's something, I suppose. Where does Kavita sleep? On the sofa? That can't be very good for you.

—Well, Kavita was in the apartment first, I think. So it's probably Sabina out here.

—Yeah, but knowing the Sabz personality, it's probably Kavita out here.

—True, I conceded.

—So where do we sleep?

—I don't know. The floor I guess.

—The floor? said Gwyn, wrinkling her nose. She seemed to immediately think better of it and unscrunched it. —Okay, I can deal, I can deal. It'll be like roughing it—if only Dylan could see me now!

Just then the door opened and Sabina and Kavita entered, bearing a stack of big flat boxes.

—Two extra large pizzas coming right up! cried Kavita. She was wearing a turned-around baseball cap; it rose a comical couple of inches off her head with all that hair piled under it.

—One straight-up cheese, for the vegetarians, announced Sabina. —The other too bloody disgusting to discuss.

—Hamburger, pepperoni, sausage—the works! grinned Kavita, now noisily pulling out plates and glasses and the spice dubba. —I talked her into it.

—She's such a bad girl, clucked Sabina. —If you saw the Meatpacking District at the wee hours when they're unloading all the carcasses and shit your world would be blown. I'm telling you you should go—you'd never eat meat again.

—Then why would I go, silly goose? said Kavita. She looked at Sabina with a surprisingly challenging expression on her face. —And tell the truth, yaar: You've gone to the Meatpacking District in the wee hours and seen this, isn't it?

—Well, no. But I read about it in *The Times* or somewhere.

—You know, you don't even have any magazines here, Gwyn informed her now. —What's up with that? It's not normal. I was just telling Dimple . . .

—Okay, okay. Upma read about it, said Sabina, brandishing a knife. —But that doesn't make it any less valid.

She plunged it into the pizza and began cutting. Moments later, after changing into our slumberwear, we were all picnicking on the floor.

Sabina cracked open a bottle of wine, the cork gulping out. I was happy to drink again; the mood was an oddly intense one in the room: Gwyn and Sabina seemed to be overexcited—they just couldn't shut up about the conference, recounting everything to us as if we hadn't been there ourselves. I was trying to maintain observer status but to be honest was completely disturbed by all the goings-on of today. Kavita was fairly quiet, too, silently sprinkling cayenne on slice after slice.

—She is one brilliant woman, that Upma, said Sabina, downing her wine in a go. —That dialogue I had with her today was one of the most stimulating I've ever had in my life!

—Uh, thanking you very much, said Kavita through a mouthful of pepperoni.

—Come on, Kavity, you know what I mean.

—What dialogue? That seemed to be more along the lines of a monologue, as far as I could see, said Gwyn.

—That is so untrue! What do you mean?

—No—what does *she* mean, this Upma? Gwyn demanded. —It sounded to me like you both were actually just saying the same thing over and over.

—Likewise, said Kavita. —Did you even conclude anything after all that?

—That's not the point! cried Sabina. —Shame on you, Kavita. But if you must know, we did in fact continue our discussion well after the debate, and we did indeed come up with a conclusion. But since you all are obviously so unreceptive this evening, I suppose I just won't bother sharing it with you.

No one begged for more.

—Is that why you were so late meeting me? Kavita asked finally. She was looking very pouty and there was a pepperoni stain on her nightgown already.

—I lost track of time, Sabina sighed. —It's just, when Upma gets talking, she's so *passionate*. And she's read everything under the sun. I mean *everything*. She really knows her shit. It was the first time I ever felt challenged like that—it was a buzz, pushing my limits, pushing the envelope. That's all.

—Oh, *now* I am feeling much better, said Kavita, but she didn't really look like she was.

—What's the big deal? Gwyn piped up. She was sitting like a frog, legs splayed out behind her. I could see Sabina was pretty irritated with her from the way her features thinned still further, pursing in on themselves. —Personally, and no offense, but that part of the debate was cake. It wasn't pushing *my* envelope. I mean, duh, everyone knows that fashion is a shared thing. Indian, American. In today, out tomorrow. You've got to go a little ahead of the flow, that's all.

—Come on, Kavs. It's just an intellectual high, a mental connection, said Sabina, ignoring Gwyn completely. I could tell Gwyn was getting annoyed now.

—But that's everything, isn't it, Kavita replied. She was looking bleary-eyed, sitting there with her knees up, nightgown pulled tight down around them, arms holding it all together like a small mountain. I wondered if she was stressed from all that studying.

—Don't be so territorial, said Sabina, tweaking her nose affectionately. —My mind is expanding. You shouldn't be afraid of that.

She nudged her mischievously.

—Would a little henna help?

—I'd love some! cried Gwyn, all slights forgiven.

Sabina looked surprised for a moment to see us sitting there.

—You know what: You're right, she finally said, clapping her hands as if to wake herself. —What's say I henna us all up so we are so stylin'ly family-I-got-all-my-sistahs-with-me for the wrap tomorrow?

—Oh my scrod, I've never been hennaed before! Gwyn exclaimed. —I mean, I've seen the kits and stencils and all, just lately I haven't had the time to go through with it—the drying takes so long. But tonight would be perfect!

—Kits? Stencils? said Sabz indignantly. —This is no shopping mall temporary tattoo kit we're talking about, missy. Weren't you listening to a word we were saying today?

—It's not temporary? Gwyn said hopefully, and me despairingly, in stereo.

—Of course it's *temporary*—though it should last you a couple of weeks. What I mean is this is freehand, freestyle. The real thing, my dear. Straight from . . .

—Edison, New Jersey, said Kavita, falling back and laughing as if cheered by the thought. —And via Africa, as *Upma* pointed out.

—Two weeks! cried Gwyn. —Is that all?

—Okay, Miss Thing. These two, I'll do right now, said Sabina, kicking Kavita gently in the hip. —But *you* I will deal with later.

—Is that a promise? whispered Kavita impishly.

This was turning into a very odd dialogue. And it was definitely a dialogue: The two spoke to each other as if they were the only two in the room, the only two anywhere, in fact. And the way Kavita was looking at Sabina, up from under her lazy lids, it was sort of like the way Gwyn looked at Karsh. Or Dylan. Or most boys: flirtatious. I couldn't imagine ever having this kind of exchange with Gwyn.

I was getting a jittery, slithery feeling in my gut, or rather, was starting to pay attention to an instinct I guess I'd had for a while now; why did it always take me so long to do that? And I must have been staring because Kavita turned to me. For a second she looked startled to be out of the world of two, but then, watching me intently, her face filled with affection, almost as if it had taken a moment for her to recognize me and it was a relief when she did. She nodded slightly, that Indian side-to-side move that could have been a yes, a no, a maybe, a dunno, or a little of all, depending where you were watching from.

—And shouldn't that be *Ms.* Thing? Gwyn had just asked. But Sabina was already heading into the bathroom.

She came back, clearly excited, and immediately broke out her materials. She set to work on Gwyn first, rubbing eucalyptus oil on her skin for the color to come out richer. The room began to smell like a sauna as she started squiggling Om symbols in the center of her palms and then a vinefest of leaf and thorn from foot top to mid-calf. (Gwyn didn't want to bother with the soles, since she had a great pair of Candies to wear the next day; legs were cool since that would show up faboo with her sequined mini.) Sabina worked efficiently, and with surprising steadiness of hand for someone who waved them around so much to speak.

Kavita watched for a minute, but seemed to have her mind on other things.

—Dimple, could you give me a hand? she asked, suddenly standing and beginning to clear the remains of our picnic. I joined her in the kitchenette where she was tying up a mostly empty bag of garbage.

—Come with me, she said, unchaining the door. —I'm just going to go leave this on the sidewalk.

I wasn't sure what she wanted help with since she refused to let me carry the single sack. We stepped out into the hallway and then the stairwell, door clacking metallically shut behind us.

—Man, I'm stuffed, I said as we descended, just to say something. —I must have eaten half that pizza.

My voice echoed in the stairwell, sounding for some reason unnecessarily dramatic. Kavita spun around to me, stopping abruptly on the landing.

—Don't, she said softly, her voice tremoring as if she were about to cry. She was staring at me so openly I dropped dead in my tracks, speechless. But for all the intensity of her gaze, the rest of her was fidgeting like a little kid, and the bag slipped with a hushed thud to the floor.

I took both her hands in mine to still them.

—Dimple, listen. I know you've probably already figured this out by now, but Sabz and I. We're. You know. Together.

Her speech seemed to steady as she spoke, as if simply hearing her own words in her own voice, resoundingly confirmed here in the echoing stairwell, made her more sure of them.

—Yeah, I said. —That's cool. Don't worry, I knew.

This wasn't exactly true. I felt far from cool, and of course I hadn't figured it out. But I wasn't completely shocked, either—it was as if all the pieces had been accumulating in my mind and heart and now they fell together to create the full picture. Still, it was a whole other thing to be hearing it straight from her mouth.

—So . . . you're not completely shocked or anything, is it?

—You know, I told her slowly, truthfully. —I think I'm most shocked by how brave you are. Does anyone . . . ?

—You're the first in our family to know, she said.

—Wow, I said. —I'm. Well, I'm honored, Kavita. So you two are really—?

—This is it.

I didn't know what to say, how to even begin to understand it all, so I began to babble instead.

—I mean, wow. That's great. It must be, like, totally cool to be with your best friend. Right? Like, if I were with Gwyn but in a guy. I guess. Being with a girl must be so much . . . easier.

—Easy is hardly how I'd describe Sabz, said Kavita. She rolled her eyes, but fondness shone in them, too.

—Okay, that's true, I smiled. —But you're in love. That's great.

—Thank you, Dimple, she said quietly. And then, as she settled her arms around me, she let out an exhale so prolonged I wondered how she'd been breathing all along. I could feel the buried shudder as she set loose a small sob on my shoulder. When she pulled back, her face was shining.

—There now, she said. —That wasn't so hard, was it?

I didn't know if she was speaking to me or herself.

I felt we'd been gone a year. But when we exited that epic stairwell, I wondered whether we had even had that whole exchange. And when we got back to the room, semi-normalcy resumed with the comforting sight of Gwyn lounging across the couch, legs dangling off the armrest to dry; she looked like a starlet relaxing between takes.

—Where were you two? asked Sabina.

—Just throwing out the trash, smiled Kavita, winking at me.

It was my turn, and in the palms of my hands Sabina created a jungle of twisted text. It tickled a little as it went on. I couldn't look her in the eye right away; for some reason I was the one feeling self-conscious, and I was glad to have something else to focus on. The henna dripped on mahogany, a thin stream cool to the touch and stiffening, growing cooler still.

But not enough to stop the surge of emotions and questions stewing inside me. I dropped cross-legged on the floor, palms up to dry—you could say in a yogic pose, but it felt more to me like the hands-thrown-up-in-despair asana. This day had delivered me more than I could process.

Did Maasi and Kaka have any idea? Perhaps they knew in the back of their mind but not the front, like the gnawing peripheral feeling I'd had. It occurred to me that maybe that was the reason for all the sudden pressure on Sangita. Had Dadaji known? Had Kavita even known in those days? She had always been so much a part of my life I'd stopped thinking about her, stopped questioning the outdatedness or inaccuracy of my perception. And now she was close enough to ask. But though nothing had really changed in these last moments—except that Kavita did look visibly more relaxed, and kept smiling at me—and she clearly wasn't even trying to hide anything, I still felt she'd just slipped on out of the tidy mostly untended room I'd set aside for her in my mind, leaving the door ajar.

Sabina was darkening the lotus on the nape of Kavita's neck, which I now realized was what I'd seen the night she'd slept over. Kavita was sitting Indian—South Asian?—style, one hand on her knee. With the other she held her baseball cap in place, neck stretching taut to keep the flower intact, which left her navel-gazing. We looked a bit like we were at a séance, and Gwyn was the vision we had conjured up, levitating there between us. Only Sabina was free to move around at the end of it all—every now and then administering a mixture of sugar and lemon water onto our hennaed sections to further deepen the hue—and I had a feeling she probably liked it that way. I didn't want to imagine what that translated into with Kavita. So don't imagine, I told myself. Merely observe. Take a lesson from Chica Tikka.

The hush while Sabina and the wine worked slowly through us had chilled everyone out a bit. Now when Kavita spoke it was poutlessly, thoughtfully.

—I'm sorry I was so touchy before, she said. —I suppose it was just a bit odd for me, all this talk of India. Sometimes it feels like it's not even my country you are discussing, isn't it? I am of course happy that it is stimulating such concern and interest. But much as it thrills me, somehow it makes me feel far from home.

My thoughts exactly. In a way it did for me, too. It was as if with every step I took towards the place I got pushed back two.

—Strange, said Sabina. —I've never felt *such* a sense of belonging as I do now.

—Yeah, it's funny, Gwyn agreed. —For me—I know you'll say I'm crazy, but I feel like I'm really finding myself in this crowd.

—Have you considered you might just be appropriating it? said Sabina, striding around the room now, cleaning up.

—What do you mean? I don't get all this appropriate/inappropriate stuff you were all obsessed with, by the way. Is there some kind of etiquette hand-book to being Indian?

—Appropriate: making it yours, Sabina translated. —Have you considered you might be doing just that?

—Yes, exactly, said Gwyn, smiling at the ceiling, oblivious to Sabina's irked look. —Yes, I feel I'm making it mine. And you're letting me.

—You *are* the one who hennaed her, Sabz, Kavita commented to her lap.

—See then? said Sabina. —I suppose my mind really is expanding, then. And anyways, the guest is goddess in a South Asian household.

I was examining my hands, staring at the new lines in my palm.

—You know, I said slowly. —This pattern reminds me of Zara's.

—Of course it does, smiled Sabina. —I did her myself. Even though hers always seems to come out even better than everyone else's.

—Why do you call her a her? I asked now. The wine had loosened my tongue. —You know, you were right—the balls in Bollywood and all that. She's a he.

—No way! cried Gwyn. —Impossible! We were with her in the ladies' room today.

—Come on, Gwyn, haven't you seen the size of her Adam's apple? Sabina scoffed.

—Of course not. Anyways, she's always covered in chokers and scarves and stuff.

—Yeah, it's never in view, I said.

—Exactly, said Kavita.

—Dimple, this can't be true, Gwyn insisted, lifting her torso and legs and holding a V shape there. —I mean, take that guy she's with. I saw them looking all lovey-dovey after the workshop today.

—And he was with her at the club, too, I joined in. —I mean, he must know by now, no? I think they might even be sort of unofficially married. She's got a mangal sutra and all.

—You can't hide your Thing forever if you're in a relationship, said Gwyn solemnly.

—Of course he knows, laughed Kavita. —That's why he's with her.

—But he's always in a suit, said Gwyn. —Like a banker.

—And she's in a sari, said Kavita, now inching closer to Sabina. —You never know what's going on under all those layers, isn't it?

—But a *sari*. I mean, she's *Indian*, I said. Recalling the evening's stairwellian confession, I immediately felt foolish.

—Well, I do admit, if I were a drag queen I'd want to be an Indian one, said Gwyn thoughtfully. —Such great jewelry, and the clothes and the makeup. It would be drag paradise. But yeah, it is a bit of a mindbender.

—Come on, yaar, Sabina cried. —India is one of the most blatant places in the world when it comes to transvestism. Drag packs walk down the street in broad daylight. In fact, the drag queen was probably invented in India —haven't you ever seen a hijra?

The drag queen invented in India? I'd always thought India was the only place they *weren't*. And then I realized she was right: I *had* seen hijras. A horde of what I'd taken at the time to be heinous men in lipstick and solar spectrum fabrics had wiggled up to our window when we were stuck in Bombay traffic once and demanded money. They were scary up close, and even tried to reach into the Ambassador when it started moving away. I was relieved when we left them behind in the dust. But it had never occurred to me to make a connection between hijras and drag queens. I don't know why. Maybe because men in India sometimes wore a lungi, a sort of skirt. Maybe because there were so many colors and sounds and smells there already, so many forms of human—from stick-and-tire children whose hair had gone vitaminlessly red, to cloudy-eyed old people, bones like lace under the thin film of skin. The toothless, the turmeric-covered bride. The extra-thumbed, the under-limbed. It jolted me that I had seen something as a child that, placed in a new context years down the line, was capable of throwing me off kilter. It was funny how much you knew without knowing.

* ★ ★

Gwyn used the bathroom first to wash off the hardened henna. She returned with her calves and palms blushed a deep red, and rubbed lemon on the pattern to help it hold, as Sabina had instructed.

—I'm pretty wiped, she said, yawning. —You don't know how late I've been staying up learning all those songs.

I was still drying so Gwyn went to work on the sofa, tossing the cushions to the floor. When she got the frame unfolded, we could see that the mattress was still shrink-wrapped, a warranty stuck just under the plastic membrane. It had never been opened.

—Cool, said Gwyn, bouncing on the mattress. —Firm but supple. Why'd they leave the plastic on?

—Maybe it's new.

—But didn't you say they've been living here a year already?

—Something like that, I said.

—Well, where the hello's our cousin been sleeping all this time?

She seemed to have answered her own question because she abruptly desisted bouncing.

—Kavs and Sabz, said Gwyn, dropping her voice several decibels. —They know so much about drag queens. And all these women's books and no women's magazines. I don't mean to be rude, but are they . . . you know . . . together?

—More together than I'll ever be, I said.

—You know what I mean. *Together* together.

—Yeah, yeah, I know. Yes. Yes, they are.

Gwyn was so overwhelmed she forgot to chastise me for not having 411'ed her a half-second before I knew myself.

—Dear Claude, she whispered excitedly. —I can't believe I just met a real live drag queen and two real live lesbians in the same day. It's just too much. This would never happen in Jersey—it's too fucking cool!

My hands were numb with cold. I left her and walked to the bathroom, quietly so as not to wake anyone. As I passed the bedroom door, I could see soft light swirling out from behind it.

I heard a hushed giggle.

Kavita's voice: That feels . . . nice.

Sabina's: Wait till I take it off.

I don't know why I did this, but I approached, breath in the back of my mouth, until I could see through the slit between door and frame and into the room.

Inside, a genie lamp whirred slowly, casting magic carpet shadows into glowing rotation on the walls and ceiling, deepening the already scarlet space. Kavita was lying on her back on the bed. Gone was the filmy night-gown and in its place something that looked skintight and intricately patterned. Sabina knelt over her, shirtless now, small-chested, with a look of great concentration; one leg on either side of her hips, she held the tube in her hand, dripping a rivulet of dark liquid in a whorling pattern upon Kavita's chest. She sat back, capping the tube, and stared down at Kavita. Who I realized then was naked, the breasts turned to flowers with aureole centers, a circus of petals hewn from henna and panning out from her nipples. Stems ran a thorned path down to her navel, intertwining all along the length from breasts to belly button, disappearing below in a soily mass. The burnished garden of her body lay breathing, the flowers seeming to exhale open.

—You are too beautiful to put into words, whispered Sabina.

—Then don't say anything.

I pretended it was just a picture, a beautiful image, the way their skin flushed to one, the roses trapped between their undulating bodies, the scent of sweat and honey and mud and mushroom and baking cake stemming into open air. But when I closed my eyes I still couldn't lid off the vision of the two of them, the view from an unhinged door.

In the bathroom, I turned on the faucet and furiously washed my hands. The henna splintered off as I rubbed under the stream of flowing water, crumbling in tiny twiglike pieces into the white basin. Pattern emerged vividly in its wake, a vermillion stain intertwining with the lines of my palm to create a new design on old skin, to write a new fate on the written one.

The world was shifting in my very hands. I could feel it, and I closed them into fists to hold on to it. But even then I had the sensation it was slipping through my fingers piece by piece, grain by grain, a coastline eroding before my very eyes.

CHAPTER 27

subcontinental breakfast

In the morning, I wasn't so shocked but I don't know if it was due so much to an opening of my mind as a numbing of it. Like the broken door—you can only push it so far before it goes loose, stops blocking the thieves, the uninvited guests and ideas.

Gwyn, however, couldn't contain her excitement when Sabina and Kavita emerged dressed and ready to go.

—I just want to tell you guys. Women. That I think it is so *cool* you are together. I mean, wow, it's just so efficient. Your best friend and your lover all in one package—I wish I could do that! It's so . . . *rad.* You are my first lesbian friends, and I'm really proud of it.

—Uh, thanks, Gwyn, said Sabina.

—Do we really need to label it? asked Kavita.

—Isn't that what this whole conference has been about? cried Gwyn, slapping them on the back. —Now come on—out of the closet and into the day! It's gonna be a good one.

—Gwyn, I said when we had a moment. —You might want to kinda not talk about this with my parents. I don't get the feeling it's as out there as you might think.

—Oh, yeah, no prob. And Dimps—while we're on the topic. I don't think you should say anything to them about me and Karsh either. Until we've got something really solid going on. I don't want them to think I stole him from you for, like, a fling. I mean, I know I didn't *steal* him—but parents are funny that way.

—Gotcha, I said.

The Subcontinental Breakfast, which also turned out to be subedible, was being held in the lounge of the Modern Culture and Media department, a room that reeked of cigarettes even at this hour. After a round of passive inhalation the four of us were waiting for my parents outside, and they arrived only mildly IST, in a jubilant mood having scored a parking spot smack in front of the building (my mother had stood in it, bounding wildly from side to side like a goalie till my father got back from circling the block).

And when I saw who they had in tow I realized that unmetered parking wasn't the only source of their triumphant gigglishness.

—Karsh! we all cried in unison, an orchestra of elated, plaintive, cool, and amorous voices.

—We ran into him on his way here, my mother beamed. —It is the fate.

—Gwyn invited me along, Karsh grinned. —I hope you don't mind.

—Oh, Gwyn, beta, said my father, turning to behold the golden one. —What a good friend you are.

—So you made it, Karsh said to me. —I thought you might have walked out by now. That being your specialty.

He turned to Gwyn.

—And how's my favorite spin sister? he said, ruffling her hair. I found myself running my hand through my own as he did. Gwyn didn't even rearrange her bobby pins, just hung out there, all googly-eyed. Everyone seemed to rewrite the rules when it came to Karsh.

—Much better now, she said.

—Come on then, chalo yaar, said my mother. —Let's get us some real home cooking.

—Oh, so we're heading back to Jersey then? said Gwyn. —Cool—I'm on at Starbucks later, so that'll give me more time with you.

—Jersey? snorted my mother. —I meant Sixth Street. And let's give Radha a ring, too—she's only working Shakti a half-day, isn't it? What's the office number?

—They don't give it out, said Karsh. —But she has my mobile today.

Gwyn had already pulled out her own cell and was dialing. Or pushing, to be more precise. One button. I tried not to look but it was too late; I'd seen it.

One.

We decided to walk to the restaurant; my mother didn't want to lose the parking spot she'd so athletically acquired, and Karsh pointed out that by the time we parked again we'd already be there. My parents had tried to flag down a series of occupied taxis (they never checked the light on top before embarking on their cab-hail jumping jacks), and that failing, claimed their boots were paid for walking.

As we made our way through that island with the sculpture where the streets cross, my mother played her favorite outdoor sport, Spot the Indian. Not as in bindi application, but as in:

—Look! An Indian! she said, gesturing excitedly across the street to where a spindly turbaned fellow hunched, paranoiacally withdrawing money from an ATM.

—Mom, there's no need to whisper, I think he knows already.

—Aaray, and there is another one! my father joined in.

Sometimes they spoke in Marathi or Gujarati to cover their tracks. But for some reason they always seemed to do this when the person under surveillance was potentially either Marathi or Gujarati.

—Jo—Gujarati chhe!

—Bagha—Marathi aahe!

I suppose after years of using these languages to talk code in public, or even around me, they'd never fully realized it wouldn't work with speakers of the same native tongue. I don't know why it bothered me so much when they did this. Maybe I felt like they'd just stepped out of baggage claim or something, like those people who thought the king was still in when Washington became president.

Gwyn, of course, didn't like being left out.

—Look! An Indian, she said, poking her finger right into Karsh's ribs and smiling.

Interestingly, by the time we got to Second Avenue and the Indian restaurant row they seemed to have stopped noticing. Or maybe it simply would have been too tiring to call it out every two seconds.

We went to this place called East Is Feast. It was the only one on the strip, my mother claimed, that was not run by Bangladeshis, who to her palate destroyed the cuisine no question (it was they who had invented chicken tikka masala, which she deemed a diabolical Tex-Mex type perversion of true

Indian cooking). I personally don't see how she could tell the difference. The same Christmas lights twinkled in the windows, but I wasn't sure what we were celebrating.

I was forced to join my parents to wash our hands before the meal, something they'd been making me do since I started riding the New York subway, even though I pointed out that we had walked to the restaurant and been in contact with nothing but air and pockets and each other the entire way. By the time I got back to the table everyone was just about seated, having left the king and queen seats open for my folks.

Sabina planted herself with a resounding flump on Kavita's left. On my right was Gwyn, who promptly turned away from me and towards Karsh, on her other side. This was the strategic position she was to assume nearly the whole meal long.

My mother was peevishly studying the menu.

—No, no, she said, clucking her tongue. —Who is translating these things? Saag paneer—*cottage cheese chunks floating in spinach.* That hardly gives the correct impression of paneer. It is sounding even . . . ruminatory.

She slammed down the menu and a gust of cool air blew into my face.

—Shall I just order for the table? she asked, guising what was inarguably a dictatorial command as democracy. —Radha won't mind, correct, Karsh? She's running late anyways, and I think I still know what she likes.

She didn't wait for a reply but turned and began to issue instructions to the haggled waiter to ensure that the turka (spice mix) would be fried to her liking by the chef.

—Why don't you just go in the kitchen and show him? said Sanjit (nametag), exasperated.

—Why thank you, young man! she said, standing. And she vanished into the recesses of the restaurant.

A moment of silence ensued, which my father filled like a dad with a tableful of kids he doesn't understand.

—So Sabina, he said. —It is wonderful to finally get a chance to talk to you. Kavita has told us what a special part of her life you are.

—She has? said Sabina, arching an eyebrow; her mole arched up with it.

—Of course—we know you are her roommate. You have changed the college experience for her! my father proclaimed. —Now, what are you studying again?

—Women's Studies, said Sabina loudly, even menacingly, it seemed.

—Women's Studies? he said, chewing on a toothpick. —Like cooking, sewing? Are there instruments involved? Personally I have always found the veena a very feminine and romantic instrument.

Sabina didn't even dignify the comment. I thought it was pretty funny.

—That's a good one, Dad! I said, winking big so he could catch the drift.

—Good one? Ah, yes—a good one!

—And South Asian Studies, Sabina continued. —It's a combined major.

—Meaning, how to be South Asian?

My father looked puzzled.

—Believe me, since yesterday it's not as simple as you'd think, I said.

—That must have been some conference, he now said helplessly, flagging down another waiter and ordering a round of mango lassis. He did it as if he were ordering a whiskey straight up, and he drank his that way as well. I could sense his relief upon the arrival of the steaming dishes and my mother, who had clearly beaten the cooking staff into submission.

—We were just saying, uh, what a wonderful conference that was, said Gwyn. —I learned so much about South Asian identity.

—And spinning records, said Karsh. —This girl is really something—in a matter of days she learned things that took me months! I'm really proud.

—Dimple, too, is learning things in days that take months, said my mother.

—I'm right here, Ma.

—Aren't you, Dimple?

—Let's just eat, Mom, I said. —Bon appétit, everyone.

—See? For example, Dimple speaks French, don't you, Dimple?

My mother thinks I speak languages even when what I'm saying is the same in English—like *the hors d'oeuvres are really quite luscious* or *sauté in butter*. And forget learning things in days that take months; this was going to require learning in a matter of minutes what I hadn't learned in years if it got going. That piano panic was filling my stomach faster than the spongy appam.

—C'est pas vrai! said Karsh.

—Likewise, I said.

—And her mother tongue is Marathi.

—Mom, I don't speak Marathi!

—Well, it is my first language, and therefore it is your mother tongue. Am I not your mother?

She leaned towards the fused corner of Gwyn and Karsh.

—Gwyn? Do *you* speak Marathi?

She said it sweetly but I knew something was up.

—You see, she said, sitting back satisfied. She gave Karsh a pointed look. But Karsh was already busy demonstrating to Gwyn how to dip the idlee in the sambar and then coconut chutney it up before taking a bite. Well, c'est la vie.

But la vie was getting out of hand: Karsh had lifted his hand and Gwyn opened her mouth and I was just cringing at the idea of having to be subjected to watching them feed each other when there was a blustery noise and we were joined by the tornado of energy that was Radha. She pulled up a seat now and plunked down, squeezing in right between Gwyn and Karsh. Forget the fact she obviously hadn't noticed we had a seat saved for her on the other side—this woman was scoring tenure in my book.

—Bloody bollocks! she cried. —Pass me a plate! What a day I've had.

—What happened? my mother asked.

—Well, I can't talk about it.

—Shakti?

—Shakti.

—Do you know an Upma Abichandi? Sabina asked. —She works there sometimes.

—Upma? Yes, I know Upma. Who doesn't know Upma? Could you miss her opinions from a mile away? But we're not usually on the same shift.

Radha plunged an appamful of tamarind rice in her mouth and spoke starchily through it.

—Friend of yours?

—She's amazing, isn't she? Sabina nodded. Kavita gave her a dirty look.

—You know, Kavita, if you keep it up, your face is going to just stay that way, snipped Sabina.

—Whoa! said Karsh. —Come on, Sabz, what are you so angry about?

—What wouldn't I be angry about?

—No, as a matter of fact, what *are* you so angry about? Kavita demanded. My mother was quietly observing the scuffle and though her expression remained the same, her pupils had visibly widened.

—I'm Radha, by the way, said Radha loudly breaking in. —His mother. But there's more to me than that.

—Of course there is, Sabina retorted bitterly; she made agreeing sound like disagreeing.

—So you're Radha! said Gwyn. She had been sitting completely still watching all the goings-on from the moment Radha had entered. —Wow. It's, it's a total honor to meet you. Karsh has said you're, um, like the bomb.

Probably only I could see this, but Gwyn was twisting her napkin to near shreds in her lap now. Her eyes flooded with the canine zest I'd seen in them when she'd danced with Zara that first night.

—How odd, said Radha. —You mean because I have the potential to destroy his life?

—Oh my god, no! Gwyn cried, horrified. —I so didn't mean that, Mrs. . . . Aunty. No, not Aunty. Um . . .

—Radha.

—Mrs. Radha. It's just, like, an expression. It means you're totally down with it. Actually, I've never ever heard anyone talk about their mom that way.

—You haven't? said my mother, shooting me a betrayed look.

—Except Dimple, quick-saved Karsh.

—Don't try to ghee me up, said my mother, alternately glowering at me and shooting a honeysuckle smile at Karsh.

—So where are your brothers, Gwyn? Radha asked now, shoveling some dosa into her mouth while the rest of us sifted through kheer and carrot halva.

—What brothers?

Radha nodded towards her wrist.

—Oh, the rakhis. Well, no, I don't have a brother. I just.

—They matched her outfit is how it all began, I said sulkily.

—You don't have a brother?

Gwyn shook her head sheepishly.

—Well, my dear, I didn't always give rakhis to merely brothers, said Radha mysteriously.

—You didn't?

. —No. Believe it or not I once had a particularly sticky suitor, the son of family friends and whom I wanted to rid myself of plainly and painlessly. And a very wise woman I knew had the solution for how to achieve this without creating any bad blood between families. She gave me an envelope to deliver to the boy the next time I saw him. I carried it with me day after day; it was the monsoon and I came upon him one wet morning at the train station—I remember the entire bottom of my sari was soaking, sticking all around my ankles. I handed him the envelope. And inside it was a rakhi.

—Oh, Mrs. Radha, I would have been even *more* into you if you gave me a rakhi! cried Gwyn. She looked at Sabina and Kavita and threw a palm up, quickly adding. —I mean, if I were a guy.

—No, no, you're missing the point, yaar. What this did was make wordlessly clear that I thought of him as a brother, that I would be like a sister to him.

—I guess it makes sense, Gwyn said. —I mean, Dimple gave them to me, and she's the closest thing to a sister I've got.

—How sweet, said Radha approvingly. Just then Sanjit came up to see if we wanted coffeeteacoffeetea. My parents suggested Karsh and I drop Gwyn off at home so she could get her things for work, and that the five of us reconvene for tea at our house, after they'd made a paan stop for old time's sake.

On the way out I scooped up a fistful of mukhvas, the mix of nut and seed and leaf in the thali bowls by the exit, sifting out everything but the pink and white sugar crystals. I held them so tightly in my hand they'd melted by the time we got to the car.

a brief history of
love and laddoos

When we'd rolled around from Gwyn's dead end to my part of Lancaster Road, the Marriage Mafia four-wheeler was already there. We kicked off our shoes, adding them to the other pairs on the porch, and stepped barefootedly on in.

—So! Nice ride? big-winked Radha. She was poised regally in the smoking section of the family room (which had never existed prior to her entry), exhaling flagrantly out the cracked window by the financial sector; the sailboats whiffed about goldly overhead. Funnily enough she didn't look guilty at all—but my parents did, glancing up from the sofa at us when we entered, cheeks stuffed hamster-like with paan.

—Mother! said Karsh indignantly.

—I know, I know, yaar—she's not that kind of girl.

—I'm not that kind of boy!

There was something so loud about it all I wasn't ashamed.

—Don't worry, we kept a foot off each side, I smiled.

—Aaray beta, you see? Radha proclaimed. —East, West—it is always about the feet! Just like when Rohitbhai was fighting off the girls in India.

—What do you mean? I said, sitting on the floor by the coffee table. Karsh joined me and I handed him a cup of the chai brewing there.

—Dimple, didn't you know your father was quite the sought-after bachelor back in India? I bet you never imagined that about your bapu!

—*My* dad?

The man in question was waving off the encomium, but I could see he was pleased; his cheeks puffed with pride as well as paan now.

—Oh, yes, a veritable heartbreaker—which is not to say your mother was not a catch. In fact it was a match made in Bollywood, this couple. I nearly expected palm trees and dance troupes to spring up and moonwalk wherever they went.

—Bus bus, Radha, said my father, making a lame attempt to stop her now that he'd successfully swallowed. But Radha was on a roll.

—You never told her? Dimple, this man was our Elvis! On that little motorbike with his hair combed back like an American star.

—Motorbike?

Were we talking about the same person? I couldn't believe all the astonishing bits and pieces of information that emerged every time Radha entered our home.

Now my mother caught the fever and bounced in her seat like a little kid, clapping delightedly.

—Oh, Ram, I remember that bike! He would scoot me up and I'd ride sideways with him, like in Westerns, on horses! We were the talk of the town!

—Oh yes, it was all well and good, said Radha. —Until . . .

She regarded me ominously.

—Sita arrived on the scene, she whispered loudly.

—Sita? Like Ram and Sita?

—Oh, your father had a Sita of his own.

Now I wasn't sure I wanted to hear this. But at the same time I was on the edge of my seat (even though I was on the floor). I mean, my parents had never dated anyone before each other. The story of their love was one, well, frankly, that I didn't know, I guess because I hadn't asked. You know, sometimes you don't want to know about these kinds of things. But today I kind of did.

—Don't look so horrified, Dimple! Radha yelped gleefully. —It's much more innocent than you think. Let me tell you the story.

My mother wasn't turning green with envy or getting ready to bat my father over the head or anything, so I figured it couldn't be anything too sordid. She even looked eager to hear, or rehear, the tale.

—Sita was a girl from your bapu's village, who had been in love with him since they were of an age to walk and talk, Radha began. —Your father, of course, had no idea. Girls weren't on his mind then at all. Years passed and many later, when we were all in medical school in Bombay, Rohit fell head over heels in love with, of all things, a *city* girl.

I flinched.

—Your mother, she added when she saw my alarm.

As if on cue, my mom looked down into her lap with a diffident smile on her face, as if this news was only just now coming to her knowledge.

—One day your parents were sitting on the bench by the bus stop just next to the girls' hostel, gazing into each other's eyes as those wholly in love are wont to do. Your mother's mother always made these wonderful tiffins of laddoos for your father—I pilfered one or two myself every time.

—Or six or seven, my mother grinned.

—Okay, okay, or eight or nine, Radha conceded. —The two of them would sit for *hours*, Dimple, feeding each other these delectable concoctions.

The ashes grew long while Radha talked, but didn't fall.

There was something strange in my parents' eyes as she sat there, dreamily exhaling their story. I know they were just sitting on our Columbus Day Sale divan, with those hibiscus patterns on one side, diamonds and triangles on the other. My father was leaning back looking as usual not quite comfortable in this chilled-out position, and my mother perched on the cushion edge, staving off osteoporosis with her Encyclopedia Britannica S edition–on–the–head posture. They were listening like children at their grandmother's feet, as if it were a story they did not know, even though it was their own.

And once, when Radha slunk way back into the financial sector to blow a locomotive breath out the window, I saw my parents glance at each other. Now this might not sound like a big deal, but that was something they never did in polite company, or even impolite, usually using me as the intermediary for all interactions; it was much more common to find my mom talking with her back to my dad, always productively utilizing her time: purveying the oil till the mustard seeds popped, keeping watch on the cauldron of kheer that had to boil and be broken.

But today they looked at each other without a word between them, and it was something I don't think I'd ever seen, or maybe I'd just never paid attention, but they seemed nearly shy; my mother even lowered her eyes and something approximating a blush crept up her neck and flushed through her jawbone (which can be a tough thing to make out on us brown folk). And for a minute it looked as if they were back on that bench again, cardamom crushed with bus dust, hands sticky, mouths melting, wanting to kiss but not daring. Or maybe daring; personally I'd never seen them kiss except on the cheek and the occasional peck that seemed executed to humor me more than anything. But now I was the one blushing.

For some reason I couldn't look at Karsh while this story was going on. I kept staring at his mouth when I did: It was so defined, the lips so full, I didn't know why I hadn't really noticed before. And a funny thing happened as I heard the tale; my parents turned into us and back without changing, like in dreams. And I had this bizarre urge to put something in Karsh's mouth, too. But paan didn't quite have that romantic ring to it.

—Well, when word got back to Varad that Rohitbhai was seeing not only another girl, but a city girl, and not only a city girl, but a *Bombay* girl, Sita grew so fearful that she actually came to our school to see him and declare her love. Which may not sound like such a big deal to you, but at that time, and being the kind of girl Sita was from the kind of village she was from, the idea that she took a train by herself and traveled all that way was already well beyond what anyone would expect. It would be like . . . like . . .

—Like someone from above Fourteenth Street going to see someone from below Fourteenth Street, said Karsh, which made Radha laugh, but I didn't really get it.

—Or better—from East Eighty-Sixth to West Eighty-Sixth, she said, and they laughed even harder.

—So then what happened? I asked impatiently.

—When your bapu broke it to her that he was already committed to another, Sita maintained her dignity and in an act of utter poetic perfection asked if she could at least have the shoes on his feet to take home with her.

—She wanted his shoes? I asked. How about train fare, pronto?

—Of course.

—Well, maybe if they were Nike high-tops, yeah, but chappals?

Karsh was grinning. I suddenly remembered he'd been in Nikes and felt shy.

—Oh, bacchoodi, it's because you don't understand what this means in Indian culture, said my father gently. —The shoes and feet are . . . well, you know that in India children touch the feet of their elders to show *respect*.

—You were that much older than her?

—No, no, I'm not saying that. It's just that you have to understand what a moving request it was.

—Sounds more like a stalker request to me.

—This girl was not dangerous. She was simply deeply in love, he said with complete seriousness. But before I could tease him he went on. —Not even necessarily because it was me. It was just the way it was in those times. She grew up in our little village and never left and it was too small a space for all of those emotions. And when you grow up reading the great Indian epics—the *Ramayana*, the *Mahabharata*—you cannot help but read a little of them into your life. In fact, they *pervade* your life, perhaps as the Bible does here.

—Oh, yes, Ram's padukas, Karsh nodded. So even he got it? I must have appeared baffled, because he continued as if clued in to invisible cue cards:

—When Ram, heir to the kingdom of Dasaratha, was unjustly banished to the forest by his stepmother—in order to clear the title for her own son, Bharata—this son kept Ram's padukas, his wooden clogs, on the throne as a sign of his love and respect and devotion for his elder brother, who he himself felt was the rightful heir. Bharata sat beside the throne, beside these shoes, looking after the kingdom and guarding Ram's place until his return—fourteen years later.

This was an incredible story; Karsh looked truly moved when he told it, as did Radha and my parents. It was like some kind of cult that everyone was in on but me. But there was one thing I still had to know. I turned back to my father.

—So did you give them to her?

—Of course not, he said. —It was touching, it was poetic, yes. It was resonant of a great epic. But let's not get carried away.

★   ★   ★

After they left it was nice to see the small mess in the kitchen, the teacups ringed with tea stains, a sugar spill on the tabletop. Crowded with life, all that laughter still ringing off the walls clear as the ring of cup to saucer.

CHAPTER 29

sole mate

That night, I just couldn't get to sleep. This glimpse of my parents in love had been as much of a shock and stimulant to my system as all that chai. Four teaspoons of sugar per cup—overload in the beginning, but I have to admit by cup five it was starting to taste pretty good. And as much as the tale of my parents' courtship startled me, it was also a delicious one, perfumed my mouth like a bit of clove caught between the teeth.

My parents in love. Did they get butterflies when they looked at each other then? Did they now? It was funny imagining my mother shy and sari-swathed, iridescent threads illuminating briefly the dust motes stirred by passing rickshaws and Fiats, Ambassador taxis. There, on a Bombay bus bench, easing laddoos into my father's mouth with a little smile playing on her own, all thoughts of good versus bad cholesterol gone with the wind, or not even there yet. For the first time in a while I had an overwhelming desire to see this land that sent such an ache deep through me, a river pushing up through stone, if only for a glimpse of that bench. Lying here in my Springfield bedroom I could smell the dung fires as you stepped off the plane, the way you thought you'd choke on them but didn't, pungent as if they were burning in our backyard; I could see all those children, children carrying children as if the house were indeed as full as my parents had meant it to be. I recalled that my mother had told me the first time I ever went there I gave away everything I had till I was standing by the fishmonger's *in just your chudees!*, naked as they'd been.

It was strange reconsidering things and conceiving of my parents as normal teenagers. Translate the laddoos into fries, the bhangra to pop, the street bench to the school bus, and the caste problem to the country/culture one and, it occurred to me, we were talking pretty much the same issues, whether it was over there or here, back then or this night.

Now summer was pressing its face to my window screen, coming through the sieve of it in concentrate, seeping into me. Fresh-cut grass, chlorine clean in a pool of night swimmers, whose occasional laughter and splashter trickled this way. It was the laughter of skinny-dippers, I was quite sure. The wistful remains of a barbecue, that mouthwatering scent of wood and grease and hot stone. Silence began to distinguish itself into the cacophony of cricket, the nightbird's wing wisp. And if you listened closely and separated out the bees and the birds, still more sounds played, below them, in the blade brush of the wind. Keening your ears still more: a bassline buzz of water suctioning up through root, of burrowed soil, the stars rotating like diamonds on a girl's craning neck.

Maybe that was what DJing was like. Layering sound upon sound and creating a complete summer night, where if you listened close enough or danced lost enough you could even hear the bugs and stars in the mix.

Some photographs are like that. In some photographs you can almost hear the held-back phrase as the smile catches it for the camera, or feel the sun on that shoulder and all the laughter in this room. Sometimes someone's happiness is so enormous it pushes right out of the four-by-six glossy to touch you. Or their loneliness. Or destiny. An entire life coming at you through one perfectly caught detail. A photograph of the uncle I never knew, Sharad, my mother's brother, is like that. In it he is crossfired in black-and-white sunshine on a cricket field, puffing up his chest in all his youthful pride for the lens. But his eyes are somewhere beyond the camera and afraid, a shadow over their light. He died only days later.

I was in the hallway now, trying to listen down to the room tone. In the kitchen, the start-stop drone of the refrigerator and a delicate tap drip like rain falling off a petal edge, a tear off the tip of a nose. Away, up the stairs, behind a door, my father's splitzy snore — and my mother's wistful sigh, the bedspring creak of her toss and turn.

It was all nearly beat-matched. So much music everywhere, I nearly felt an urge to dance.

I moved quietly through the house, catching the screen door before the clack, and out to the steps. On the second from the top I sat, the stair above not quite touching the small of my back, and hugged my knees to my chest. Summer storm air pinned and needled along my arms and neck, bare in the tank top. The sky was loaded with too many stars to wish on. It was hard to think some of them were dead, not even there anymore. I hoped these weren't the ones I'd wished on before. That would explain things. Or perhaps it still counted, just took longer for the wish to travel down and be realized.

I liked to think Dadaji was an inside-out star; you couldn't see him but he was there, and you could wish on him. When I used to pray I would picture Dadaji on a fat cumulus throne, his ear hair grown out like twisted antennae wired to the sky, in my father's plaid shirt and a lungi, blowing his tea cool in a saucer. Maybe the sun was just not hitting him at the right angle.

Dadaji would always tell me we weren't so far apart; he drew holes that led directly through the grass and dirt and bedrock and magma, connecting him to me. He sketched us watching the same moon from different sides of the planet. We made moon dates with each other. Our choices were somewhat limited by the ten-hour time difference, but occasionally he was up early and I late and it felt good going through the sky hole together like this.

He could still be looking at the same moon, just from another side of that aperture. Perhaps it was all connected, constellated, I thought, gazing down the stone-pebbled path poured with painstaking care by my father to the drive and then the street stretching away into darkness as if off the edge of the world when the world was flat. I ached suddenly for company, for my laddoo partner on my porch bench. But I felt hopeful somehow. Maybe things didn't have to fit together perfectly to be connected. Maybe this path linked my driveway to street and then highway through perhaps lake and sea, all the way to that exit and route and road and then driveway to the house where my soul mate was right now at this very moment thinking the same thought, high on too-sweet tea. Maybe we were on a moon date without even knowing it. It was the most confident thought I'd had in a while. (When taken in certain proportions, night and caffeine could do that to me.)

I felt reassured. I mean, he had to be out there somewhere, right? The sheer number of streets and exits proved the probability of this theorem being true, didn't it? And every day new roads were being built. Every day, extra lanes were squiggling their white-dotted yellow-striped way onto them. Was he in France? Zanzibar? Antarctica? Retracing my steps, I tried to picture him traversing that long vallied path, following the street to the drive to the stone path to the bottom step to walk right up before me now.

My eyes fell on something, a shape like a curled-up cat on the bottom step of the porch. I leaned down. It was a pair of sneakers.

My heart plunged into itself and out. For a moment I had the completely illogical thought that he was standing right there before me, gone inside-out-starred from the shoes up. Then I remembered his penchant for being barefoot. He must have forgotten them when they left.

They were still pointed leading into the house and I felt calm. I leaned in closer. The red was fading; they must have been a fiery number when he first bought them.

I picked one of the shoes up. He could definitely use a new pair of laces; one end was chewed ragged as if a zealous pup had gone to town on it. And then the other. He had biggish feet, I realized now that I was holding them in my hands. They hadn't seemed so big on our family room floor though I had noticed he had a lot of space between his toes. Not like my feet; my renegade big toes hung out on their own, then the others cliqued together, the little ones shoving their heads all the way behind the second-to-lasts, as if too shy to be seen. Sometimes when I looked at them I felt something like compassion for myself.

Karsh had brave feet. Toes that could strike out on their own without caving in together for confidence. His laces were all still tied and the back top lip of the shoe was dented down. So he clearly pulled them on and off without opening them. A lazy streak!

I stuck my feet in them now and felt a little Richter of naughtiness.

They smelled slightly of cedar closet and mown grass, cinders and overripe things. They were warm inside, and I had plenty of wiggling room. A little sand or something grainy dusted the bottom.

His heels were evenly scuffed (mine usually wore down on the inside). And a pale pink pebble wedged firmly in the sole of his left sneak.

Mud was caked onto one side of it but not the other.

I wondered what he'd been doing, walking with one foot in the rain and one out. And where had he picked up that pebble? It was so clean, so perfectly round.

It felt funny being in his shoes. Cozy and creepy and intrepid and protected all at once. It blew away being in somebody's football jacket, not that I ever had been, but it seemed a lot less territorial. And funnily it also felt a little like an honor, too, as if I were touching the Lladros in the mall's locked glass cases or a beautiful drowsing endangered species.

And then I understood how mundane things could be sacred. People were embodied in everything they wore or touched; traces were everywhere, clues to entire lives. And shoes—well, they held the person up, and even empty insinuated the whole. That was why Rama's brother kept his padukas on the throne beside him. That was why my father's own Sita asked only for his worn chappals; it didn't seem so strange now she'd wanted to keep a trace of him with her if she couldn't have the rest. It was the next best thing.

I pushed the tongues up to make them easier to get into. The Nikes looked funny like that, as if they were chatting or lapping up breath, perking their ears like dogs out windows of moving cars, picking up signals. I brought them up so they were on the porch proper—you never knew with summer showers. Set them down still leading into the house. Feeling strangely comforted, I went back inside. And with comfort came a wave of fatigue.

And with the wave of fatigue came an unhindered thought at the border of sleep, just as I rolled into fetal position, my heels coming up into my palms, head nesting down.

I was falling in love with Karsh.

chimera

My mother says if you think really hard about something before you fall asleep your mind works on it in slumberland and you may even find the problem solved by morning. Well, if that thought about Karsh I'd had was a problem—and it was—I don't know what had gone on during the REM portion of the evening: If I'd been falling for him before, when I woke I'd fallen. Splat, to the pavement. A feeling that had been a safe one to doze to became a scary one awake, my Dimple demolition team calling to alert and calling me crazy. I had a new organ in my body, or had become aware of an old, unused one; a new heavenly body in my solar system. But what to do with it? It could never work. He could never feel the same about me. And then there was Gwyn.

I longed to sustain the sleepy feeling, to womb away in a dark timeless space unhindered by other people's realities. To be safe the way in dream you can be safe in strangeness.

There was only one place I could do that. And it seemed as good a day as any, better even, to pay a visit to the darkening room. As soon as I was inside with the door shut firmly behind me I felt better. And as I reviewed the pictures hanging on the line I even began to feel hopeful, though about what I wasn't sure. I'd been improving but still had a long way to go; I had been overheating, overcooling, and the last time I was in here, spilled fixer on my shirt and burned a fast hole through the fabric (of course, it could have been worse, considering how much higher temperatures were for color processing). In any case, might as well burn myself before I got burned.

But the mere sight of color in all the bleakness was revelatory; the slice of vivid however imperfect life thrilled. This room was like the inside of a dreaming eye, the way there was a sense of it all being projected Technicolor in a nearly cosmic blackness, cast on shadowbrick in a room pulsing with invisible bodies.

I surveyed now the Queens photos. Despite the fact that one was too green, others too magenta, cyan, yellow, some still seemed accurate depictions of that day, of the memory of it. A patch of sidewalk scarlet with spat paan, two hobbity toe-haired toes flexing up-chappal in mid-wade. Birds rooting off railings, the American flag vigorous now, captured in a proud unfurl. Fantastic frontierless shots of sari fabrics. Men squeezing into the frame, not realizing the focus was on the women hanging back, staring shyly, it now seemed. Longingly.

I considered developing the rest of the Queens shots. But now I was aching to review the HotPot night; I couldn't believe I hadn't gotten around to these rolls yet.

I figured I should get the first one out of the way, and rubber-gloved, levering off the end of the cassette with a bottle opener. Cut off the tongue, straight between the perforations, and wound the film onto the reel, slotting it into the flanges. For some reason I always found this moment immensely satisfying—the way the two grooved together.

I continued on, sank into darkness. To be honest, I completely lost track of time—I had no idea whether I'd been down there minutes or hours and I'd just finished up a set of test strips when I heard a distant flurry of chimes and tinkerbells amid a deeper toll, and my mother's voice filtered into my reverie.

—Beta! You have a visitor!

And then, to someone else, in an equally voluminous voice (for my benefit):

—Go on down, Karsh—yes, it is fine, beta, I am sure. She is in the darkening room.

Karsh! I nearly dropped the developer. Frock—I had no makeup on or anything. Thank goodness I'd brushed—but I hadn't flossed. And I was in a tank and pajama bottoms, braless. I considered making a run for the hatchway but realized that perhaps the safest place to be in my current condition was indeed this tenebrous vicinity versus an upstairs unsparing summer day.

By the time I'd arrived at this conclusion, an escape was out of the question: Tentative steps were descending and approaching. A slight rat-a-tat-tat.

—Dimple?

—Uh, yeah.

I slipped the door open a crack and went out, closing it behind my back. The basement was fairly dark, the only light cookie-cuttering in through the scant rectangular windows against the ceiling, these mostly blocked by unmown grass.

Karsh was so close I could smell that shirt smell on him. I didn't look him in the eye for a minute, focused on the chappals and his big toes looping out instead so that he couldn't see what I'd been thinking. You know, last night.

—Hi, you, he said softly.

I loved the way he said that. Like it could only be me. I wondered if he said that to Gwyn, or Trilok (Jimmy) Singh, or his computer science professor. I looked up at him. And now that I was in love with him there was no mistaking his beauty. It normally hurt my eyes, these rapid shifts of light. But the backlit view of him was a welcome one. The concrete cooled my feet. Here in the shadows I felt we might be in the club again, but there was only a somewhere sound of lawnmowers and the neighborhood malamute's daytime moon call and, upstairs, the continuing hustle-bustle—turned up now it seemed (which was proof she was most likely eavesdropping at the doorway)—of my mother's kitchen choreography.

—Hey, I didn't want to disturb you. I just came by because I—foolishly—forgot my shoes here in all the fun we were having yesterday.

Foolishly.

—Oh yeah, I said, trying to sound casual. But nothing sounded casual in this dim dazed setting. I crossed my arms in front of my chest, realizing if the concrete was cooling my feet into a toe curl, it was possible that certain upper protrusions were popping out to say good day as well. —Yeah, I saw them yesterday. I was going to tell you. They're in the—

—I know. Aunty showed me.

Aunty. Meaning, I was like his cousin. His cousin-sister.

—Really—I can see you're busy, he said. —I just. She told me to come down and see you. I just wanted to say thanks.

—Thanks for giving back your shoes?

—Uh. Yeah. I guess I'm such a footloose and fancy-free kind of guy I just didn't notice.

— Well, you're welcome.

—Okay. Then. I guess I'll be seeing you.

But he didn't go anywhere.

—So you're working on your photos? he asked.

—Uh, no. Well, yeah.

—Oh that's right, I think you mentioned something yesterday. I really must be bothering you.

—No, you're not.

—Well, if I'm not, I'd love to see you at work. Only if you don't mind. I promise I won't disturb you.

I felt shy, but a little excited, too. Laid bare, like he'd said. I was really aware of my skin.

As soon as we slipped back into the darkroom and I closed the door behind us, I even almost liked the feeling. Night nakedness was different. He was keeping me in that red-toned dreamspace we'd created in the club, the Pondicherry dawn. The state I'd been in last night.

Karsh's pupils were dilated, iris all but gone. It was strange thinking they were literally apertures into him, like a human Chica Tikka. I fluttered up inside, belly cocooning. I tried to be very matter of fact as I set up the processing trays.

—So I was just—

He put a finger to his lips.

—No, don't worry. Don't explain. Just go on like I'm not even here. Really. I don't want to disturb you; I just want to see.

There was no way to pretend he wasn't there. But actually as I continued, pouring in the developer, stop bath, fixer, I found his presence wasn't something that made me uncomfortable. Somehow he contributed to anchoring me, while still allowing me float space. His extra presence warmed the room.

When I took the tongs, he came and stood close behind me, watching over my shoulder. I immersed a sheet of the exposed paper in the first tray, his breath against my neck now. That thin space between us felt simultaneously like miles and nothing at all. We were so close, and it felt like we were in a cave and a storm was rushing just outside.

I could just nearly feel him against me as I rocked the dish back and forth. His breath smelled like cinnamon and clove and when I moved, our bodies brushed against each other, and even with this butterfly kiss of a touch I could nearly feel my cells changing as they collided with his, a chemical reaction just like the one on the sheet of printing paper before us.

The image began to take form. I could see general shapes, shadowed light; one piece of the page, on the upper left, didn't seem to be bringing forth anything, but above the center stretches of simmering fabric the features of a face floated surreally up from under the liquid, like a person emerging upwards after diving to a bottom so deep they'd disappeared. A perfectly defined mouth, upturned nose, and not one but three jeweled eyes—the third eye blindingly scintillating—gazed back up at us. Gwyn's eyes.

My heart sank: Even here I couldn't get away from her! It was the picture from the night we went to the club: Gwyn in the mirror, looking unbearably beautiful (and even more epic in black and white), and me taking the photo from behind, my own face partly obscured by the flash going off in the glass. Even burning in might not be able to bring me back to life here. It would be best to crop me out to save the rest of the image.

I tried to concentrate, transferred the print to the stop bath, the fixer. I was hesitant to turn the light back on, but there was no reason not to. Illuminated now, my stomach wringing emptily, I washed the print and hung it to dry. It was strange to imagine she'd only been staring at herself, the fairest of them all in my mirror. Because now, from the clothesline, I could feel her eyes on us. On him.

I worried he would come back to his senses and leave me now. But he didn't say a word, didn't go, and my hopes struggled up again. Was it possible that he—? The wattedness of the room seemed not to disturb our secret space so much after all, turned it into something shared, cathedral, the now visible borders confirming that we were securely within it. Nervous at my now wildly geysering sense of hope I threw myself into the film, moving on to color. And when the time came to turn off the light, I even dared to imagine the unkiss that hung there between us, tangible as the reel I was loading in my hand.

We remained there, developing photographs for hours it seemed. The dreamy silence of the room just served to emphasize the feeling that he was a live wire beside me, a cut cable in deep water.

When I'd clipped Zara and her future husband up to dry, my stomach grumbled. In this stillness it was avalanchal, and we both laughed a little. It was the first sound we'd made in here. And we finally turned and looked at each other again, so minglingly close I felt strange. I could see myself in his pupils like in Chica Tikka's third and only eye. I envied the tiny me, swimming there in the open passages to his heart, his belly, his memories. His future memories. I wished I could dive in, follow her through.

—Dimple, he whispered. —I don't know what to say. *Wow*. It is so beautiful to see you like this.

My breath trapped in the back of my throat.

—That was so much like music, he went on. —Funny, since it was all silent. But the way you shook that tank, counting the seconds along to the tick of the timer—it was like you were layering snare on synths on cymbals. Your timing was impeccable. And then that thing you do—moving your hands around, and the light. Swap it for a song, and you looked pretty much like a DJ to me.

He took my ungloved hand and turned it over.

—Yeah, it says right here, he whispered, tracing his finger along a tributary in my pulsing palm. —You're plugged in. You've got the Big Energy.

Now I was definitely not breathing, trying to memorize the certain weight of his hands on mine.

—And these images—

He gestured to the array of them.

—They're amazing, he said. —Can I ask a favor?

—Anything, I said quietly.

—Would you make me a copy of one? I'd love to have it for myself.

My heart stuttered up at the compliment.

—Of course! Which would you like?

I followed his finger, and my heart sank again. The first one, the one of Gwyn. What made me think I could ever stand a chance?

I nodded and he went on.

—I'd love to see more—the ones you love the most, the ones that mean the most to you.

I nodded again, dumbly. He'd already asked for the one that meant the most to him. And I had no idea what meant the most to me anymore. Or rather I did, but I had no idea how to develop it, this image in my mind that would never resolve itself, of the two of us together.

I walked him upstairs. Just before we came out into the room I heard skittering footsteps and then the anthem of the Feng Shui Springfield Orchestra—my mother had set everything in motion and now chimes tinkered and water trickled and mobiles slam-danced together. She had definitely been eavesdropping.

—Won't you stay for a bite to eat, beta? she asked. —I made samosas.

—Thank you, ji, but I've really got to go, he said.

—Baapray, after all the slaving over the dough . . .

Defrosting was more like it.

—Maybe next time? said Karsh. —I'm really sorry, it's just that I have to get back to New York. I have a meeting to see an apartment.

My mother scuttled off into the kitchen and returned with a Tupperware box. She handed it to him.

—Well, I insist you at least take these with you, then, she said. —Now that I have heard how you are fed at this NYU.

—Thank you, Aunty, he smiled, stepping out to the porch. He turned back to me. —Don't forget that photo, okay?

—I won't easily forget, I said. It was time I woke up and smelled the bleach.

—It would mean a lot to me.

—I know what it would mean to you.

—Good, then, we're on the same page.

He waved from the bottom of the drive now. I turned to go back inside and nearly knocked over my mother, who had been hovering just behind the door. She latched her arms around me and called mischievously through the screen.

—Don't forget to bring back the Tupperware, Karsh!

She smiled, nudging me.

—You are looking very flushed. What is happening in this darkening room?

—Nothing, I mumbled.

—Wonderful! Nothing always means something when it comes from the mouth of a teenage girl!

She was staring at me now.

—And your eyes are red again.

—Must be the chemistry, I said, trying not to spill. —I mean, the chemicals.

CHAPTER 31

walk like an indian

—You are not going to believe who dropped in during my shift after lunch that day! said Gwyn. She'd called me over for a quick 411 before work, and I was standing in her kitchen now, watching her pack up her low-cal saladic lunch.

—Who? I said.

—Flashman! You know, that photographer guy. Whose name is Serge Larmonsky, if you can believe it. He was actually in Jersey for a shoot and came by to say hi.

She was checking the oven and stove and all the settings to make sure everything was off.

—Thank Todd I showed up in time, she said. —And thank Claude I was looking so fabulous—you know, all hennaed and bindi'd and rakhi'd and all. Of course I ripped off that ralphable green smock the second I saw him.

—So, what, he came by to ask you out or something? I said hopefully.

—Of course not, Gwyn sighed. —He's a *professional*, Dimple. Anyways, he asked me if I had really been serious about wanting to be on the other side of the camera—that's what I told him, you know, at HotPot: I wanna be in pictures, and the whole kaboodle and cat.

She had certainly been efficient those few moments on the sidewalk.

—Anyways, he tells me—get this: that he would *love* to work with me. That he would be *delighted* to get my input on the magazine. He says I'm their *target audience*.

I was stunned. As she double-locked the double doors and we headed out, she went on to give me the d's on a Central Park shoot she'd been asked to participate in at the end of the summer. Things were really picking up for her, and I wished I could get involved. But I guess they hardly needed another photographer.

—Wow, I said. —That's great, Gwyn. Maybe I can come along and watch when you do the shoot?

—You betcha! She nodded, making the jackpot gesture. —This could be our ticket to real jobs, Dimps. There could be a *future* in this. You know how many people will be reading the magazine? Well, I don't either but. But a *lot*. A lot of people read magazines. I could get discovered. And Karsh—imagine once Karsh sees my photo in it?

I didn't want to tell her he already had seen (and loved) one of her photos, but being the kind of person who feels guilty about this sort of thing, it was already coming out of my mouth, which at these moments morphed into an independent state with its own currency, public transportation system, and village well.

—Oh my god! Why you didn't *tell* me, Dimple?

—I just did. It, it was sort of a surprise.

For me, I didn't add.

—Well, this is inspiring—my quest to be a suitable girl seems to be working after all! she declared. —Now I need to move on to the next step: the nosh. So I was thinking—you know the Lillian is leaving for a romantic weekend in the Hamptons with, you know, that little chap of horrors she's been hanging with? Of course, that's the night she was actually supposed to stick around for this mythical mother/daughter rain date, but who's counting? You know, even when I'm famous I won't forget her. So anyways, I was thinking of throwing a big bang at my house—like a sort of beat-the-heat housecooling party. Get it? Housecooling instead of warming. So here's the plan: I whip up an irresistible Indian feast to woo Mr. DJ—and to wow the other guests while I'm at it, you know, like our caf table posse and the Starbucks crew and all, but Shoshannah can't make it because it's her grandmother's eightieth . . .

She'd already invited them?

—Thanks for mentioning it to me.

—Of course! said Gwyn, gallantly slinging an arm around me. —I wouldn't not invite you! And Sabz and Kavs are bringing their henna kit.

—You invited Sabina and Kavita!

—I thought you'd be happy.

—Well, I'm happy, yeah, I'm just—

—Besides, they're my only lesbian friends and I'm really proud to know them.

—They're not toys, Gwyn.

—Exactly. And I want to show that to the world. It's gonna be a great night, Dimple. There's just one minor problem. I'll need to borrow your—

—Entire wardrobe?

—Well, it's a little more serious this time, said Gwyn. She squared me in the eye. —Your mother.

—My mother?

—I don't know a thing about cooking. Actually, I'm meeting her today after work. Do you want to come, too?

—Where?

—To your house. You're totally welcome. She's gonna show me how to do a few dishes—I took total mental notes on what Karsh was digging that day at East Is Feast. Well, actually, I told her *you* wanted to learn these dishes for Karsh . . . so I guess you'll have to come with me.

Now I was being invited into my own kitchen? And my mother, with all her sixth sensory perception, hadn't even been an itty bitty idlee suspicious about this request?

—Gwyn, I can't believe how you just take over everything!

—Aww, Dimps, don't be jealous about the modeling career, she said. —I'll never forget my roots.

She pinched my cheek like my relatives do sometimes when they're noting how I've grown.

—Proof? I got us both officially on the guest list for the big Flashball launch party in August—it's for the Disorientation issue, "subverting notions of place" or something like that, and all the media bigwigs will be there. Once they figure out somewhere subversive to have it, that is.

Now I knew a way to get involved.

—Well, that's a no-brainer, I said eagerly. —They should have it at Hot-Pot—that's a pretty subversive place, isn't it?

We were at the end of her street, where it forked off towards my house on the right, stationward on the left. Gwyn had been about to take the train way, but turned back to me now instead.

—I mean, it's all about subcultures, right? I went on. —And you can just tell that place is about to explode; it's an undiscovered gem. Well, not undiscovered by Indians, but undiscovered by pretty much everyone else.

Gwyn gave a little gasp of delight and hopped up and down in place.

—You are so on! she cried. Her enthusiasm, and my own, multiplied as I spoke. My mind was suddenly percolating with ideas.

—They could even, like, project pages from the issue on that wall where they do the movie clips and videos of the crowd and all. And they could name the drinks after stuff in the magazine. You know, the way they did the Delhi Bellies. Like Wicked Mix of the East and Wicked Mix of the West and all that.

I was nearly hopping now, too.

—And of course, the cherry on top? I said giddily.

—What, what?

—Karsh should DJ it! I grinned. —It'll pull in that mixed crowd he was talking about. He'll get so much exposure he won't know what to do with it.

I was thrilled at the idea of him reaping such a big gig.

—You are such the Phi Beta babe, Dimps! cried Gwyn. —That is a fantastic idea—can you imagine the smile on his face when he hears about it?

I was already imagining it as we said our goodbyes. I couldn't wait to tell him. I couldn't wait to see him smiling like that. At me.

★　　★　　★

When Gwyn arrived after her shift, my mother was to be found alarmingly attired in an apron that she must have purchased especially for the occasion; I'd never seen it around before. It was covered with clawing lobsters and a bisque recipe and hung stiffly past her knees.

—So I am not being invisible in the kitchen anymore, heh! she beamed, victoriously ushering us in as if into Betty Crocker's inner sanctum. —Suddenly everyone is wanting my expertise, is it!

—It is, indeed, Aunty, smiled Gwyn.

Aunty? As they went to it I have to say I felt more than a little betrayed, lollygagging on the kitchen outskirts while they mixed and measured.

My mother usually cooked with her body, feeling her way through the proportions by how much weighed well in the palm of her hand or clenched between two fingers, guarding a discerning artist's eye on the changing shades of the frying spices, an ear on the maracas of the mustard seeds. She rarely tasted to test, her other senses were so well attuned. But today she actually cooked with measuring spoons and cups; odd, as on the blue moon when I'd ask her how to make something she usually replied with the mystical near-adage *You look and you see*. I supposed she was just making things easier for Gwyn and the upcoming shindig, which hurt a little. I tried to act like I was into it at first, but neither of them seemed to be taking stock. So I gave up and sat dejectedly down at the table.

My mother had tossed the East Is Feast menu out the South window and gone with a robust gust of Northern inspiration: In the course of an hour, a chicken was curried, a bhaji butter-fried, and basmati rice plumped with raisins and cashews into pulao. My stomach was growling like a vexed pup and it was torture standing by as my mother Tupperwared the vast majority of it for Gwyn to take home. She even created a sort of dubba for her—a spice box with the former pepper jars (instead of thali bowls) arranged in a dusky array that rivaled only her own, all the labels in all caps. She never printed; I'd seen her doodling script in *TV Guide* and book margins and calendars and birthday cards. And making up a spice tin seemed to me a strictly mother-daughter pass-the-message-through-the-generations genre of activity. She'd never made *me* one. Granted, we lived in the same house and I'd never shown any interest in cooking other than occasionally watching the Food Channel, but still. Who was she trying to set up with Karsh, anyways?

Gwyn exited, carrying the dubba like it was a piece of Atlantis, or Versace.

—Aunty, thank you so much for letting me sit in, she called fervently from the porch. —And Dimple, thanks a mill for cooking up the idea in the first place! Get it? *Cooking—*

—Got it, I said.

We watched her descend the driveway, and as soon as she was out of earshot I whipped around.

—Mom! I can't believe you did that!

—Did what? said my mother, all innocent-eyed as she latched the door in place.

—Made Gwyn a *dubba*.

—What do you care? You are not keen, so why should you mind that I show somebody who is?

—It's just. It's like now you're—I don't know. It's like you're setting *her* up with Karsh. I mean, giving away your killer curry recipe—that's serious business!

—So! Are someone's eyes turning green, my dear? said my mother, smiling amusedly at me.

I was embarrassed and looked down, in case they really were.

And then she leaned into my ear.

—Do not forget I am Kshatriya, she said. —We are warriors.

I didn't know what that had to do with it, but I nodded, still tile-eyed. She'd already turned away to finish loading the dishwasher. And as she set the dials, she said one more thing, and in an unsettlingly ominous voice.

—And one bit of advice for this housecooling schmousecooling, she whispered, even though there was no one here but us. —Do not be tasting the chicken, beta.

I didn't dare ask. The machine whirred into action.

★ ★ ★ CHAPTER 32 ★ ★ ★

hot like spicy

The night before the party Gwyn called me up from the bathtub where she was in the middle of a beauty ritual prescribed in one of her old women's mags: soaking in a color therapy bath and lighting candles and the whole she-bang.

—Dimple, she said, and I could hear the water hitting her shoulder; she'd always liked sitting in the tub with the faucet running over one side, a liquid sari. —You've got to do me a favor. I told Karsh to go by and get you first because you need help carrying the pots—so you've got to fill a pot with something and, well, carry it. And make sure neither of you come over before eight o'clock, either.

—Why not?

—Just. Just do it. I don't want him to catch me in the kitchen in the middle of things. But promise me you won't be later than half past, either. I don't want everything to get cold.

—Promise, I said.

★   ★   ★

The night of the party, on the dot, he did ring my bell (but then, he'd been ringing my bell for a while now). I'd had monarchs cruising my belly for hours before and had changed every quarter stroke of the grandfather clock, but then figured it was all a little foolish since he'd already obviously succumbed to Gwyn's charms, and I reverted to jeans. Now, I just managed to grab a mega pot and go out to greet him.

★ ★ 296 ★ ★

—Hey, you, he said smiling from the porch. —Gwyn mentioned you might need some help.

He took the cauldron from my hands. But I'd forgotten to fill it with anything and now it felt a little silly, him holding a very manageable piece of nostick and me nothing. So, in order to maintain Gwyn's cover, I reached for whatever was nearest—and found myself gripping a bag of charcoal for the barbecue we didn't yet own (my father had bought the briquettes under the false impression that we already had one, somewhere in that study that seemed to spawn more and more gadgets and appliances as the years went on).

—So this is a cookout? he asked, now taking the charcoal from me as well and thereby totally undoing the entire purpose of my grabbing it in the first place.

—Well, I guess you never know, I said.

My mother came to the door now and tried to inveigle Karsh into a feeding, as if he were a recalcitrant pony. He declined politely, saying he had promised to save his appetite for the fête.

—Just do not be eating too much, er, curry, she advised with a near remorseful look in her eyes.

—Curry? Karsh asked. —I thought it was a barbecue.

—I do not *know*, my mother said very quickly. —I just have a—*feeling*. A—six sense.

She threw up her hands.

—I have nothing to do with this, she added.

My mother was acting very strange indeed.

Kavita and Sabina still hadn't shown up, but since I'd promised Gwyn to be there on time, we headed off.

★   ★   ★

When we got to her dead end and were looping up the double drive, I saw that her house was unremittingly dark. At first I thought there was a blackout—but the neighbors' lighting systems all the way through to the Bad Luck House seemed to be intact. I wondered if she'd run out on an errand.

I rang the bell anyways and Karsh kicked out of his chappals. I heard the chimes go off down the hallway, and then the door wedged a snitch open—still no light nor Gwyn in sight, but the space kept crevicing wider. So we stepped tentative into the eerily silent house.

—*Surprise!*

The lights flashed on. And it took my eyes a moment to adjust to the crowded vision that greeted us: Bright balloons intermingled with familiar faces, arms laced in streamers as they waved. It was as if my life were passing before my eyes: cafeteria posse peeps, friends from the hood, coffeehouse crew, HotPotters. And in the forefront, Gwyn—grinning ear to ear, hair coiled in glittered-up braids on her head and decked out in one of my tiny sari tops and the airy ankle-clinched pants from a salvar khamees combo. Thus attired I'd look like a midget Aladdin with a gender complex. But she was all genie.

She reached right past me and took Karsh's arm.

—I don't know all your friends yet, and I figured you already celebrated with them, so I invited mine, she smiled. —Happy birthday! Are you surprised?

We both nodded, dumbfounded.

—It's your birthday? I said to Karsh.

—Well, yeah. It was yesterday, actually. Great memory, Gwyn.

He looked deeply moved. Now I felt awful. I hadn't done a thing, or brought a thing, other than my empty alibi pot and bag of briquettes. And as we entered the house and I began to make out all the gifts and flowers and bottles blooming upon the hearth as if spilled from an early Santa sack, I felt even worse.

—Gwyn, why didn't you tell me? I whispered, leaning in to her ear.

—I wanted it to be a surprise, she smiled, not into my ear and still focused on Karsh. And then we were in the living room.

I said my heys, stumbling upon Trilok (Jimmy) Singh farther back in the room, and Tamasha, too, whose feline green eyes were spiraling over the stack of records in the corner.

—Hey—Tree, Shy! My peeps, cried Karsh, catching up to me. —Dimple, you've met Shailly, right? Gwyn, you are just too much. How can I ever thank you?

—You'll find a way, she smiled. She placed a beer in his hand, holding it longer than necessary I thought.

I was walking in a daze. The house didn't look like the one I knew and had known for so many years. Furniture had been muscled out of the way; mirrored throw pillows decorated the floor, and candles, candles created a seriously romantic fire hazard everywhere you turned.

A buffet was set up at the end of the room, covered in deep dishes. At the far side of the pushed-together tables was a cooler and the sewing cabinet, opened to reveal the minibar inside—which everyone had clearly already been raiding. I took a beer to have something to hold on to, but to tell the truth, I was a little scared to drink. I'd already seen the sad side of the cup before and I no longer trusted myself to maintain a grip under pressure. When I turned, Trilok (Jimmy) Singh was right behind me, and clinked me in a wordless toast.

And then I noticed the most impressively altered part of the room. Gone was the TV area: Gwyn had transferred the entire stereo system from her mother's all-white bedroom here. And was I already seeing double? Not one but two decks lay side by side on the cabinet, and Gwyn was behind them now, headphones hanging off her ears.

—This one's for you, Mr. DJ, she called out.

She dropped the needle on the record, and Marilyn Monroe set out on a twisted version of "Happy Birthday, Mr. President," breathily looping through the room on top of a squirmishing punk-dunked beat.

The music cranked up, fast mingling with something sitarishly familiar. Gwyn stood spinning, all her moves exaggerated: rolling her hands in the air, pursing her lips, swaggering her hips.

Karsh was watching her the whole while with eyes so soft they made mine close so I wouldn't have to see them. The song got most of the way through and then Gwyn gave it over to Shailly, who started spinning some spy-movie-soundtrack-sounding sounds. And then Karsh went over to Gwyn and gave her a bear hug that left me cold all over. He was thanking her, and I stood choking the neck of my beer bottle, trying to breathe calm.

I wished Kavita would get here already; I hadn't heard from her the past few days. Her presence was a reassuring one: She was the only person in the wide world who was somewhat on to my feelings, and she put pressure on me neither to run away nor towards them, rather, treated me as if my disrupted sentimental state were the most natural in the world.

—And you say they're not together? Trilok (Jimmy) Singh remarked, watching the record-breaking embracers come out of their hug; Gwyn's hands rested just above Karsh's hips. —Certainly looks like it to me, yaar. You know, I'm starting to think Gwyn Sexton may actually be cooler than I thought—a guy like Karsh wouldn't go out with just anyone. He's on everyone's most wanted list already at NYU. Hell, it was hard enough for me to get my own woman to stop checking him out.

—Where is your girlfriend, anyways? I asked, swallowing hard on my Sam Adams.

—Well, we're having probs at the mo, he said.

—What kind of problems?

—We broke up, actually.

—That can be a problem, I agreed.

—Religious differences, he nodded.

—What religion is she?

—Same, he said. —But she thinks I'm not religious enough, that I am too much of a party animal. She says I am Sikh in the head only.

—Sick in the head? I thought she was all into Sphinx and all.

—Now she claims she was humoring me.

I felt I related even though in my case the breakup was preceding the relationship.

—Well, I'm sorry to hear that, Jim— I said. —Tree.

—It's all right, he shrugged, something he was prodigiously skilled at, as I recalled from HotPot. —It made me understand what I want and don't want in a relationship. It made me realize what is truly important to me, the quality the woman I'm with must indisputably possess.

—Which is?

—She's gotta be able to throw it down, yaar. Dance till the light of day. He nodded towards my hands.

—Were you at a wedding or something? he said. The pattern was fading to pumpkin and I self-consciously closed them into fists, shaking my head.

Gwyn now stood beckoning everyone over to the buffet.

—Great tattoos, by the way! Maria Theresa Montana exclaimed, nodding at Gwyn's come-hither fingers. —Did you go clubbing or something?

But Gwyn wasn't listening, was hithering away at Karsh to come join her.

We were now nearing the front of the food line. Karsh saw me coming and handed me a plate, I guess to pass down the line; I bestowed it upon Trilok, who slipped it to Maria Theresa Montana.

—So, did you help cook this up? Karsh whispered. I enjoyed the conspiratorial feeling we were briefly sharing. —That looks like your mom's kind of style to me.

I was about to outlandishly take some credit when I saw the vast vat of chicken leering balefully from the other end of the table. I remembered my mother's proclamation of warriorhood and wondered at it; it all looked too toothsome, unfortunately.

—Well . . . I said. Could I try it before confirming? Would just one little bite hurt? I was tempted, but having been warned by a bona fide Kshatriya, opted for a spatula serving of rice instead. But Gwyn, being that most suitable of girls, leapt between us, ladling Karsh's plate full of the curried bird. He dished up a forkful and was lifting it to lip level when I had a vision of my mother's penitent eyes and something came over me.

—Don't eat that yet! I cried.

He froze, then glanced at me and nodded.

—You're right, he said. —That was nearly very rude of me. Let's have our mostest hostess take the first bite.

—Well, Karsh, Gwyn said slowly. —This *is* an authentic Indian meal. And in India the authentic way to eat is with your hands.

She started sleekening towards him.

—Wanna give me a taste? she asked now. Karsh looked a little embarrassed, but he reached into his plate and scooped up a fingerpinch. Gwyn leaned in.

Since when had eating with your hands turned so sexy? When I was little my mother would rush to place cutlery in my father's dahl-soaked fingers if we were caught off guard by an unannounced visitor, including even the Girl Scout selling cookies.

My cry came too late. What had begun as Gwyn's saucy attempt to lick up Karsh's fingers fast degenerated into a coughing fit, a face-turning-fuchsia fit, and then a hand-fluttering-before-mouth all-out Munchian scream session.

—Water! Gwyn rasped, stumbling through her own private Kalahari to the cooler, out of which Franklyn Thomas Porter the Fourth's glorious bottom was now protruding like a honey-stuck Pooh.

—What's wrong? he yawped, emerging. —It looks like you're on fire!

—I am on fire! This chicken is on fire! I—I must have screwed something up.

My mother. I should have known she'd be on my side—but I hadn't realized how far *over* on it! I was ready to bet she'd switched around the spice proportions. Though I couldn't really put money down with anyone here.

—Water won't do it, said Karsh. —Sugar is what kills the fire. Do you have anything sweet out here?

—Oh no . . . Gwyn gasped, setting down the Evian and letting out a prenatal series of quick short exhalations. —I've gone and ruined everything now . . . and I wanted it to be just perfect for your birthday.

She looked about to cry. Or combust. That was the question.

—Forget the chicken, sweetie, said Karsh, wrapping an arm around her. I could see her miracle recovery; now I felt the fire. —This is a housecooling, remember? Isn't that right, everybody?

A chorus of accord.

—Actually, she said. —I *do* have something sweet—I was saving it for later, but carp and dee 'em.

She headed for the kitchen now, and Maria Theresa Montana was covering and then crossing the cauldron of killer chicken when the lights went out. Skitting flames floated into the room at chest level, on a just visible waxy sea, Gwyn's face luminous above them, rendered even more beautiful by the flaxen light.

—Happy birthday to you . . . she began. And then everyone was crooning, myself included. Who could resist singing happy birthday, after all? As she came closer I could see that it was a huge ice cream cake she was carrying, and no ordinary one at that: It was in the shape of an LP, ridges cut into the fudge to look like true grooves, and *Hey Mr. DJ* frost-gunned in the center circle where the names of the songs would go.

She was standing just before Karsh now, their two faces illuminated in the cake halo.

—Make a wish, Karsh, she whispered in the sudden silence after the song. But I was already making mine; I didn't know if it counted on someone else's candles, but it was worth a try, and I wished that I would be part of his wish, long shot that that was. I must have been staring really hard, because he looked up at me a second and half-smiled just before he blew them out.

Applause, then someone flicked the lights back on. Gwyn plucked the candles from the cake, one by one, then cut the first slice.

Once everyone was ice creamed up she set her own plate down.

—People, may I have your attention please! she cried (a little unnecessarily, considering she'd had it for just short of forever by now). —I have a very special birthday present for a very special birthday boy. And it is one that will benefit all of us. Are you ready for this?

Nods through full melting mouths.

—So, I think all of you know by now that I was discovered recently by Sergio Larmonsky of *Flash!* magazine, she began. —Anyways, what you don't know is that I was invited in to the *Flash!* offices to meet the editor-in-chief, Elizabeth Lupine. And as it turned out, everyone was in the middle of trying to figure out where the hello to throw the end-of-summer launch party. Somewhere cutting edge. Somewhere attention getting. Somewhere *subversive*.

I was getting excited in spite of myself: So she *had* put in a good word for me.

—So I turned to them all and I said, *Well, I know just the place for you, people*, Gwyn continued in a voice meant to raise suspense. —This place, well, talk about subversive—it's all about subcultures. It's like an undiscovered gem. Well—the Indians have discovered it, but other than that. It is *the* next big thing.

This was sounding unnervingly familiar.

—Where am I talking about? New York City's leading melting pot music spot: HotPot!

Wha—?

—And who else to DJ it but—as Serge himself agrees—the most up-and-coming cutting-edge spinster in Manhattan, the hotter than HotPot one himself?

She turned spoonily to Karsh.

—So, Karsh, what would you say if I were to tell you you'd nabbed the gig of the year?

—What? said Karsh, looking stunned. Gwyn trained her eyes on him.

—It'll score tons of PR for you, honey, by attracting a not-just-Indian crowd—and plus, we're gonna have *Time Out* editors and *Village Voice* peeps and all types of industry folk there. You'll get so much exposure you won't know what to do with it!

Karsh was clearly overwhelmed. As was I. But, I had a feeling, for different reasons. Was it too late to copyright my vocal cords?

—Everyone was so impressed they actually put me in charge, she went on. —Zeb said she couldn't believe my ability to spot and snag a new trend.

New trend! Bhangra had been around for years!

—But that's what *I* said, I said.

—Then we all agree? Gwyn beamed. —Perfect.

Now everyone was clustering around Karsh, licking up the last of their ice cream and humdingering with excitement.

—How'd you become a DJ, if you don't mind my asking? Betsy Glick inquired in a flustered voice that made it sound like she'd just run across town to get here.

—I started out doing parties, Karsh explained. —Mostly in New York.

—So you're a New Yorker?

—Well, from India, technically, though I did live in London a little. I'd like to spend some more time there one day. That's where it's really happening—the Asian underground is so full-on it's above ground, from what I hear.

Betsy Glick and now Maria Theresa Montana were so rapt it was embarrassing.

—It's a really exciting place, Karsh continued. He almost *had* to, the way they were just standing there gawking. —So many types of music are cultivated there, and if you go to a so-called Indian event, you won't even necessarily find South Asians in the majority. There's often such a mix the minority/majority distinction drops away—which is ideal, and the main reason I'm so grateful you've set up this gig for me, Gwynoo.

—Don't mention it, she said. —I've always wanted to live in London, too.

—Yeah, it's a real melting pot. Interracial relationships and friendships all over the place. At least from the glance I got.

—So . . . you're into interracial relationships? said Gwyn.

—It's all about the love, he grinned.

Love? Now he loved her?

—I can't believe you said that, she whispered.

—Well, that's what the best moments in anything are about, right? he said, folding his napkin into ever-decreasing fractions. —DJing, for example—there is a moment when two becomes one: You are playing the music and then suddenly it's playing you. Everyone's moving more, and you're grooving more, the sweat is on their skin and it's on yours, their mouths are open singing and it could be your voice, and it builds . . . and it builds . . . and when it happens for you it happens for them—the roof comes down, the floor dissolves, you find the wings you forgot you had. The room is flying with nightclub angels and you can't tell whether the music is outside or in.

He was beginning a tune on one of the decks. And this is going to sound crazy, but while he was talking I felt the bass between my legs, within my trebled chest, and I wanted to listen to what was playing inside him.

—It's almost like when you and someone. Well, match in other ways, said Karsh, ducking into the headphones. —And you can make a big room out of a small moment.

Gwyn actually let out an audible moan of delight. Then he seemed to feel shy and looked away.

—You must be really good at that, too, she said, giving him her arrow-to-the-deer eyes nonetheless. —You know. *Matching* in that way.

—Like I said, it's all about the chemistry, he said, suddenly beguiled by his record bag. —It takes two to be one.

I thought about my darkening room, all those different strands of color coming together and fusing to create one image. Even the mistakes were beautiful.

—Show 'em how you do it, Karsh, Gwyn said now.

And a moment later, as if on cue, everyone was chanting in unison:

—Karsh is in the house!

He hit the decks. Of course it mattered not he'd brought nothing along; by now Gwyn's collection was a total dupe of his, so he could really make himself at the home, as my dad would say.

A mere moment after he started spinning his irresistible rhythms, the sweat was indeed flying, even in this small space. People I never thought I'd see dance were dancing: Tony Mahoney began to jump straight up and down, right on out the room, and Franklyn Thomas Porter the Fourth was doing some kind of Twist type thing; even the now double-bottled Maria Theresa Montana rose to her toes and did a surprisingly splendid pas-de-bourrée. But it wasn't long before the latter two were twirling a kind of three-way mating ballet around the one-man fast-speed planetary orbit that was Tree. They were soon involved in a triangular tango all their own and it was fairly unclear to me what that dynamic was all about. I wound up caught in their little vortex, momentarily turning it to a parallelogram before half-heartedly shrugging out of it and into the hallway.

The music was so voluminous at this point I barely heard the bell ring; at first I thought it was all just in the mix. But the chime eventually tolled off beat and made itself known, and I went to the door, following close on Gwyn's tracks. Maybe it was Kavita; I certainly hoped so.

But it was far from the fact. A familiar now flocculent face was out on the porch.

—Trick or treat?

—Always a treat to see you, said Gwyn. —Come on in, Jules. What impeccable timing.

She winked at me. Impeccable timing? What was she doing? Why had she invited him?

—I would never want to be late putting the Joy into Joysey, he smiled, stepping in. I took two steps back as he did.

—Hey, he said to me.

—Hey, I mumbled.

—You two *certainly* remember each other, said Gwyn loud and clear for all to hear as we reentered the living room. —Everyone, this is Julian.

—Julian, said Karsh. He turned to me and raised his eyebrows. —*Julian* Julian? Well, this is a pleasure.

He didn't say it like it really was.

—Man, Gwyn—you've got a DJ and everything, cried the newly goateed one. —That is too cool.

—That's right. That's my Karsh, you know, the one I told you about, said Gwyn proudly. —As you can see, I've moved up to NYU honors. But I guess you've got to start at zero sometimes—speaking of which, who's Dylan I mean how's Dylan doing these days?

—He's . . . he's cool. I think he'd like to see you again sometime.

—Well, you tell him if he wants to see me he should keep an eye on *Flash!* magazine, which hits stands later this summer.

—You're kidding!

—My modeling career has kick-started, Mr. Rothschild, she said, mock-fluffing her coiled-up hair. —And my DJ career, as well. And now I hope you don't mind, but I've got to get with the jams.

Julian's mouth dropped open as she joined Karsh behind the decks. Karsh glanced up momentarily, his eyes flicking from me to Julian and back, but his face remained expressionless.

—Now she's a *DJ?* Julian whispered incredulous into my ear. His goatee tickled my lobe.

—You name it, I said. Karsh looked away. Gwyn looked at him. And Julian began to look around.

—Is there anything to nosh on here? he asked. —I haven't eaten in at least a couple of hours.

Now when they leaned their heads in together to share the headphones it hurt like my head had hit a wall.

—You should definitely try the chicken, I said.

★ ★ ★

After a while, Shailly took over the tables, the beats swigging lushly down to her loungey electronica. Karsh and Gwyn stepped off the decks to the dance floor. The beat sank still further, to a scuba breath. And then they were slow dancing, Gwyn bringing her hands to the nape of his neck.

Seamless—like something that has never been broken. Like two bodies must be when it's the superglue of superlove. There was something to put on the market, I thought, watching the two move: superglue of love for all cracks, crevices, and fractures to the human heart.

One of Gwyn's braids began to slip out of its mollusk loop, a dyed platinum snail uncurling lazily then swinging merrily off the side of her head, revealing a gold root. How interracially her blonde braids mingled with his raven waves. They could definitely get a grant for that. They'd be perfect in London; she would pick up the accent in no time. I couldn't believe that he was moving, and how well the two were grooving, and that it mattered so much.

I missed them both already.

★　★　★

I stayed as long as I could. But tonight this crowded living room was the loneliest place in the world. I figured I'd sneak out the back and avoid an epic farewell. But just as I got there, Julian exited the bathroom and placed a (hopefully well scrubbed) hand on my arm.

—Hey, Dimple, he said. —Hold up. Can I talk to you a sec, alone?

Was I ever going to be able to leave this place? I pointed to my ears and waited.

—Listen, I've been rethinking things, he said. —And I just want to say I'm sorry about my behavior. You know, the way I acted that night.

The timing was off, but I suppose the intention was on.

—I don't know what gets into me sometimes when I'm around Dylan, he went on. —In any case, I'm not around him much these days. We've sort of decided not to work together anymore. And I think it's for the better. But I just wanted to say, well. If you're free sometime, I'd like to make it up to you. We could hit Chimi's and, you know, hang out.

Here it was. The moment I had been waiting for. How was it possible that only a few weeks ago, I'd been so ready to let my head (and public opinion) convince me of what my heart, I realized now, hadn't been feeling at all? And tonight my heart was like a skinned fruit, out there and open and so ripe that if no one tasted it soon it would go rotten. But there was only one person it was meant for.

And here they were. His chestnut eyes millimeters from mine. How was it conceivable that up until so recently I'd been ready to just forget the humiliation and run back towards them? If his eyes had been millimeters from mine then, it would have been so easy to keep on closing my own, drift into his arms.

But it wasn't so easy now. My eyes were wide open.

And I could see Karsh watching me. He was standing in the corridor. Maybe he just wanted to use the bathroom. Or maybe he wanted me to say goodbye or something. And I was about to when I saw a rakhi'd arm bo-peep around his waist, pulling him back to the other side of that doorway, to what might as well have been the other side of the sea.

—Apology accepted, Julian, I said, coming to. —But to tell you the truth, I'm not really interested in—

But there was no need to repay an eye for an eye and make the whole world unkind.

—It's just, my mind's on something else these days, I said gently.

—Got you, he said, trying a smile.

—Goodbye, then, I said, unlatching the door. —I hope you find what you're looking for.

★   ★   ★

I exited by the back door, but there was no chance of my stripping the wealth of that house. Its treasure was securely inside, discovering the other one who lived there.

I waded through the uncut grass. The moon was out, and the windows of the playhouse let off a little glimmer. I moved closer; it had been so long since we'd been here, and I felt for a moment I might stumble upon ourselves inside, two little girls having a tea party in the world before boys arrived and men left.

I wiped a patch clear off one pane and was startled to see a face looking back at me—a sad smile and huge eyes, gazing opaquely as if through a block of ice. Through the layer of dust on the inside I could just make out another face, and then another. I would have been afraid, but then realized in a heartbeat what they were: the Nativity statues from all those Christmases ago, from the first time I'd ever met Gwyn.

CHAPTER 33

homely girl seeking

When I got home I nearly stumbled on something tumbled by the bushes near the bottom step. I bent down to have a look: Karsh's shoes. So he'd never picked them up that day, just gone along his chappaled way. I considered weeding them out of the bleeding hearts and dropping them off, but heading back to Gwyn's seemed like a backwards step in more ways than one. I figured if he really wanted them, he'd come looking.

Inside, my parents were in the family room, my father slumped morosely below the Boatmobile, my mother, phone clenched in hand, pacing and waving her arms around and muttering in Marathi.

—Hey, guys, I said. —Did Kavita call? She never showed up at the party.

—Yes, she called, my mom answered. —In tears, weeping so hard I am hardly able to understand a word coming out of her mouth.

—Weeping? What happened?

My mother turned to me and shook both her hands over her head like an angry restaurateur at the guy who dropped the pizza.

—The bitch dumped her.

—Uh . . . who?

—Sabina Patel Schmatel. For that Upma Loompa character.

So that's why Kavita had been out of touch.

—That Sabina, my mother now proclaimed to the dangling sailboats and my astoundment. —I never did completely trust that girl. There is something . . . pointy . . . about her face. She is reminding me of a fox. And she never let Kavita get a full sentence in. As if what *she* is having to say is so important that no one should be allowed to interrupt the flow of her *genius* mind. Hello—

She pronounced it *Halo*, and her Indian accent was coming on full force.

—The badmash saali couldn't even do a proper surya namaskar! And henna? Heh! I was only being polite—any nonarthritic monkey can paint like she paints, and with these temporary tattoo kits I am seeing everywhere, it has never been so easy.

—And the sitar? added my father. —Who is giving a hoot? It only takes three chords to play all the Beatles songs anyways.

—And she is never looking me in the eye.

I felt my mouth unhinge in amazement.

—How dare a Vaishya like her mess with a Kshatriya like us, my mother declared, puffing her chest. She seemed to be including my Vaishya Gujarati sire in this honorary title—and me, a mutted mix. I suppose the dowry deal was she took on his name and he got to take on a little of her caste through marriage.

And my mother's warrior lineage had never been more apparent. Before my eyes our family room prepared for battle: The peacocks on her dress turned to a formidable army capable of transforming itself in an incantory breath into a god or two to be reckoned with, her gesturing hands stringing up an invisible but potent bow and arrow.

—You knew . . . about Kavita and Sabina?

—Halo, as you say, Dimple! Even the blind could see this. Our chhokri wears her heart on her sleeve and always has. Plus, that Sabina was having one of those wallet chains that day—this contraption hooking to the belt? And her nails were very short—but not *bitten*.

My mother, supersleuth.

—Besides, the story of love between women in India is nothing new, she added, shrugging. —It is an age-old saga. But love between women in New Jersey? This is taking a little getting used to.

—Please be sparing me the details. The simple fact of it is enough, said my father.

—Dad, you knew, too?

—Your mother told me though I did not believe her for a long time.

—Would I be lying to you? sighed my mother, exasperatedly tossing the telephone down on the coffee table. —I am a child of Harish Chandra.

—And what do you think of it all? I asked carefully.

My father stood and paced now, shaking his head despondently.

—I told her exactly what I think, he said. —She is needing a saras chhokri, a *nice* Indian girl.

—Yes, said my mother. —None of these hanky-panky Western Heston girls. And what is wrong with our dikree? Heh? Who is this Sabz Blabz bitch-eswallah thinking she is? Kavita needs someone like herself—a person with heart, soul, pep!

—Sabina has pep, I said. —Maybe a little too much, I guess.

—Not pep! PEP! P-E-P—Potential Earning Power.

Her accent was on to the max now, like a sprinkler turned all the way up. The T's clacked, tongue rollicking farther back to tap the roof of the mouth, the R's took up their own space (urr-en-ing for earning) and went a poquitito Spanish, the W's mysteriously lower-lipped into V's, V's to W's.

I couldn't believe it. My parents were dealing with this like pros. They were so radically open-minded they were blowing my own blown mind.

—The way I am seeing it, I suppose it could have been worse, at least as far as Meeratai is concerned, my father mused. —For example, she could have chosen a black boy, a kala boy.

—Dad, that's totally racist!

—It is not racist, said my father, looking wounded.

—No! cried my mother indignantly. —It is not racist! It is *sexist*. She could have been with—even worse—a kala girl!

—We're already halfway to black ourselves, in case you—or, I guess, Meera Maasi—haven't noticed.

But they were ignoring me, were somehow onto the improbable scenario of Kavita's narrow escape from a starcrossed romance with a black Jewish Muslim boy. They stopped a moment to consider the sheer horror of this. I could understand now how a case of Sabina was looking rather like a mild malady to them.

—You see, there is a bright side coming to everyone who waits to call the kettle black, concluded my mother.

—Is she awake still, Kavita? I asked, coming out of my stupor and realizing there was a broken heart buried somewhere under all this mess. —Can I call her?

My mother gestured to the telephone on the tabletop, then picked it up and put it to her ear.

—She is right here. Kavita? Beta? Your cousin is requesting to speak with you.

—She's on the line? I cried.

—Of course she's on the line.

—Why didn't you just put her on speakerphone? I said, grabbing the handset.

—Dimple! This is a private moment for her!

The receiver burned and I could smell my mother's cloved breath. All-out sobbing filled the line, invisible tears spouting through the tiny holes.

—Hey, Kavity, I said softly.

—Hi—hi, Dimple, Kavita managed. —I'm sorry about tonight.

—Their loss, I said. —How are you doing?

—I've been better, cowgirl, she said. —The apartment seems so empty. Everything is too . . . *big*. I cannot believe it ever seemed like a crowded house. I cannot believe we ever complained. Any noise makes my heart pound—at first I think it's her, and then there is only fear. I have never spent a night alone in this city. I'm sorry. Would you mind staying on the phone with me a little longer?

—I'll stay on with you till you fall asleep, if you want, I said. —I'll stay on with you *while* you sleep—I can leave the phone next to me, so if you wake up or get scared I'll be right there.

My father was already in his coat, keys in hand.

—Where are you going, Daddy?

—I am going to New York City, he said. —And bringing our dikree home.

—I'll drive, I said.

This time, nobody argued.

We drove quietly through our small town. The orchards stood like shadowy high-bosomed sentinels over dream dark fields and the cider mill. Streetlamps washed on, encouraging harbors of light along our night way, and the neighborhood malamute howled his ancient message to the dangled moon, floating egglike in a cloud nest. The radio sang a decades-old song soft of last summers, suddenly, a woman's quavering voice hearkening me back to an era I'd never even experienced. Funny, music, how it can do that. I could barely remember my own last summer, this one had so fully usurped it. But I didn't mind remembering hers. My father turned and smiled at me, his bifocals glinting in the dashboard light.

—Are we road tripping? he asked.

—I think this qualifies, I said, smiling back and swervelessly squeezing his hand.

When we got to the highway, it was funny, but this time I wasn't so afraid to merge. It seemed like the natural state of things, to try to fit in and at the same time keep your space, your speed, your radio station from staticking out. It was maybe even like beat-matching, slipping your song into an existing groove and turning it into something seamlessly new. We drove through the oil lamp rain of the George Washington Bridge, and in the song-silent tunnel just after, among the converging cars, night vented in vertiginous with exhaust, and the caramel smell of burnt rubber. Going down the river now, the lowered skyline of where we'd just been followed us alongside, never touching, never losing sight.

Kavita was standing on the corner of Waverly and Waverly, a small suitcase set beside her on the sidewalk. Her hair brambled almost all the way down her back now, summer longing it rapunzelian. She was swathed in a raincoat, though it wasn't raining. Before I'd switched to park, she'd opened the back door and climbed in, lain across the backseat without a word, using her bag for a pillow. My father reached around behind his seat and held onto her foot, and she slept, finally, her breathing like a second steady motor purring behind us as we headed back to the ranch.

At home, my parents left us in the kitchen where, happily, we found two half-pints of the over-the-top ice creams that make me proud to be American.

We went into full-on Ben and Jerry's mode, and finally, half a pint down, Kavita emerged from her tress shield and spoke.

—I suppose I should have seen it coming, isn't it? she sighed, licking the curved back of the spoon. —I am feeling a bit foolish.

—It's easy to say now, I said. —But don't feel like that. I can't believe it myself—almost as much as I couldn't believe you were with her!

Kavita smiled and reached out and took my hands.

—She was my beloved ABCD, she said. —But she left me with the C and ran off with the rest.

—I don't understand how anyone could leave you, Kavity, I said, shaking my head. —Like I said before, you are a dream woman.

—She told me that I was a little too Indian, said Kavita. —That I wasn't gay enough.

—What do you mean not gay enough?

She went on; it was as if that half-pint had opened a valve.

—Because I did not wear my sexuality for all to see, because I was taking too long to walk with her openly, because because. But I tried to explain to her that everyone comes to terms with things in their own time, isn't it, and that perhaps I had a different set of things to come to terms with. And that I was not comfortable wearing anything like a banner. That maybe I wasn't ready to proclaim that I am a woman who loves women. That it was enough for me to be a woman who loves Sabina. And that did not mean she was going to lose me to a man, or to anyone. I was in love with Sabina whether she was in the body of a man, a woman, or an elephant. Okay, maybe I'd just be friends with the elephant. But that wasn't enough for her, no—I was not advanced enough to wear my name with pride.

—Maybe you're too advanced, I said.

—She says I am too Indian.

—Versus South Asian?

Kavita smiled.

—I suppose.

She was in her diaphanous nightdress and I could see through it that the henna had paled, the flowers fading from the surface of her skin. Fat tears dripped into her ice cream, salt melting sweet. Her words moved me, and I could really relate. I couldn't believe it was such an issue becoming who you are. I gazed into my upside-down reflection in the spoon. But it seemed to be for everyone these days.

—Well, Kavs, I said. —If it makes you feel any better, I've been spending my summer finding out I'm not Indian enough, nor American enough, it would appear.

—How's that?

—I don't know. I guess I'm just not Indian enough for the Indians or American enough for the Americans, depending on who's looking.

—What if *you* are looking?

—What do you mean?

—I mean, you are saying that you don't feel like you measure up, isn't it? Depending on who is looking at you, heh? But what if you still all the voices and stares, all the things you think you're supposed to think or you think everyone else is thinking, and go to somewhere in yourself like when you are underwater, for example, or in an asana, that truly conscious silence—and *you* look at you?

—Hmm, I said, thoughtfully. —I guess I've been so busy feeling I don't fit so well into either place that I never really thought of it that way.

—But Dimple. Maybe that is because you are too big for one place; you have too much heart and home and information to be contained in one tidy little box.

—You mean I'm all over the place.

—You are . . . interdisciplinary, if you will. But you have to realize, there is no such thing as this tidy little box you think you have to fold up and fit into; it simply does not exist. That's what I'm learning, learning as we speak.

She was right. After all, if she herself had wondered whether she was Indian enough—she, who had always been to me a sort of epitome of Indian—then who could be? Who could claim the sole right of way to an identity?

—And you have to realize that you don't need that box, she added slowly, speaking as much to herself as to me. With every word the veil of tears burned off her face like sunned dew. —That there is something that connects it all, even in wide and open and uncontained space. The way a constellation makes a shape.

I tried to picture it, and found to my surprise that I could. It was beginning to make sense.

—The way a silent room has a sound, I said.

She nodded, smiling.

—You, she said.

—You know what, Kavs? I said, winding my arm conspiratorially through hers. —If we have your people talk to my people, I think we may be on to something here.

★ ★ ★

In our room that night, just before I turned off the light, Kavita turned to me.

—So how was the party after all? she asked.

—No party without you, I said.

CHAPTER 34

snap shot

Gwyn was now with Karsh all the time, planning the big gig, and I was, in a highly unGandhian way, passively (and rankledly) resisting to my heart's discontent. That could have been me, was all I could obsess over—I still couldn't believe how brazenly she'd taken my idea. Maybe I would have been less upset if she'd included me every now and again in her busy schedule. But I'd been dropped like a hot tandoor.

It was an all too familiar pattern, this jilting the friend for the more-than-a-friend. The part that *wasn't* familiar—my feelings for the boy at hand—only made it worse.

And simple fact was, I missed her. I'd recklessly dared to get used to having her back in my life in the period A.D. (After Dylan), and to be honest I was suffering a little withdrawal. But sitting around waiting for a friendship fix wasn't going to get me anywhere, as was becoming painfully apparent. So, child of Chandra that I was, I decided to call Gwyn and tell her the truth. (Not the part about the tandoor or Karsh. I wasn't actually a *blood* relative of Uncle Harish, after all.)

I caught her on her cell in the city, moments before, as she breathlessly informed me pre-hello, a "real live" editorial meeting at the *Flash!* offices. She'd been attending these recently now that she was their freelance fiesta femme.

—Oh, never mind, I said. —I guess you must be too busy to talk right now.

—I always have time for you, Dimps. Shoot.

—Well. I guess I just called. I don't know, to say hello, I said. I could hear

New York City bleating and yammering and whizzing around her, and I felt foolish now for taking up her time. I wished I had something more defined to say, like *Do you have Maria Theresa Montana's e-mail address?* or *I need to borrow your bathrobe.* —Well, I haven't, you know, seen you in a while. I guess I was just missing you.

—Miss you, too, Dimps! she called out gaily. I could picture her looking both ways before theatrically crossing.

—No, I'm serious. You're just so MIA these days.

—What do you mean?

—I don't know. You're so *busy* all of a sudden. I just wish we could hang out like we used to.

I could hear her mumbling *Excuse me* to someone, and now pictured her slecking through a packed people patch.

—Dimple, honey, I just had an idea, she said when she'd finished navigating. —I'm coming home straight after this meeting. Why don't you come over and we'll have a good old-fashioned powwow? The girls. You know, we could go to the mall or something. Do some party shopping.

I pictured us trying on Style Child outfits and rating passer-boys from benches.

—Just like we used to? I said, relieved.

—Just, she said.

I was really bleepingly happy. Maybe I'd misjudged her. Underneath that busy bee was still my old honey-hearted Gwyn.

—Listen, I'm about to lose you, she said, and I could hear her descending what had to be the subway stairs. —See you—

Her words broke up into a million little particles then cut, but I filled them in. So I'd see her, finally, happily, wonderfully—tonight.

★　★　★

When I walked over to the double-drived house at the appointed hour, Karsh's bindi'd indigo Golf was poised halfway up one arc, parked at a polite distance. Bindigo.

So who exactly was powwowing with whom?

The sight of his Birks on her porch, with her own strappy sandals tumbled wantonly against them, felt like nothing less than a betrayal. I'd just barely vowed to keep my own feet sheathed when they stepped out the front doors.

—Hey, you, Karsh smiled warmly, setting down his bags and bending to shoe up. Hey you, my foot!

Gwyn double-locked the doors, slung her slipping shades on top of her head, and turned to me.

—Hey there, Dimps, she said. She was dressed to the T, in fact, all the way to Z. It clearly looked like they were heading somewhere.

—I thought we, you know, were going to the mall, I said, confused.

—We are. I just invited Karsh along—he's gonna give us a lift. I hope you don't mind.

Karsh was already busily organizing the contents of his trunk. I was speechless, and she casually patted my cheek as she passed to catch up with him.

—I didn't think so, she said.

She swished regally into the front seat, this time reaching over to Karsh's side to open it a whit as he wrapped up out back. Like a real girlfriend. I was watching all this from the sidelines since for some reason my own door wasn't opening and no one had reached back to unlock it. Like a girlfriend.

Once he was in the car, Karsh angled over to pull the lock up manually.

—It's been having trouble lately, he explained. It seemed a portent.

I wasn't really sure why I'd been invited along. But despite the fact that I would once again be the third wheel (or seventh, considering the Golf was already rolling), I couldn't stay away from him, and so I settled in on the hump; it had my name written all over it. But at least I could watch his beautiful brown eyes a little more discreetly from here. I just wished that bindi weren't there, shifting over his face in the mirror as he moved; I knew it was mine, but I hadn't stuck it up, and it troubled me.

—So how was your day? Karsh asked, eyes squinting and going sun gold as he switched lanes. Hadn't they already covered that at Gwyn's?

—Fantastic! she exclaimed anyways. —As you know, my sweet silly goose. Oh, but I forgot to tell you—I talked to Zeb; I'll need a sample tape from you pronto—she wants to, you know, feel in the know by the time the party rolls around. And anyway, that next one you do, that Indian Independence Day meltdown thing—she's coming to check you out for sure. You know, she's telling everyone you're the next big thing—there's already a waiting line to get in!

—Wow, thanks so much, said Karsh. —You really got me the gig of gigs. I seriously owe you, Gwyn.

I tried to focus on the stuck lock for distraction. But it wasn't going anywhere.

—How about dinner at Chimi's on me? Gwyn was saying excitedly. —I can charge it to *Flash!* after today's meeting—I feel so official! And Dimple just *loves* Chimi's, don't you, Dimps.

She checked me out mischievously.

—The last time she was there was how all the trouble began with Julian, she now explained to Karsh. (I'd have to remember to thank her later for that one.)

—I've got to go with my mom to get her car from the shop first, remember, Karsh said. —But when I come back to get you, we can all go do the Chimi.

—Actually, maybe I better not charge it all, Gwyn said pensively now. —If they question me I don't know how I'll justify three meals.

—I'm not really hungry anyways, I maundered.

—You could always say Dimple's doing the visuals for the party, Karsh suggested. He sought me out in the rearview. I did a little bhangra and shrugged. —That's your thing, after all, isn't it?

Gwyn was quiet a moment, her eyes clouding as we passed under a bridge.

—Yeah, actually, that's a good cover-up, she finally nodded. —Brilliant! That's my Karsh.

—It's not really a cover-up, said her Karsh.

—True—she's taken some great photos of me. I should add those to my portfolio sometime, Dimple, if you could get me some copies.

—Portfolio? I said.

—Yeah, well, I figure with my big modeling debut coming up, I should run with it. We are in New York, after all—if not here, then where? Once I have a few shots together I can get an agent, and once I get an agent, I can skip college altogether.

—Hmm. We'll have to talk about that a little more, hon, said Karsh.

Hon? Hun was more like it. I decided I had to tune them out for the sake of my own sanity. I began to count the number of times I saw red out my window.

—Dimple, you're awfully quiet, Karsh said as a banana-yellow truck passed. —Are you okay?

—I guess I'm just a little tired, I said. —It's nothing.

—No such thing as nothing.

Gwyn's shades were down and I couldn't read her face. She was monopolizing the scanner button, creating more static than song on the radio. But Karsh's eyes were so intensely on me I had to turn away, to the trees and the water and the buildings pulled all ablur like someone had stuck their hand out the window with a huge brush in it, a forty-five-mile-an-hour painting.

★　　★　　★

At the mall, Karsh dropped us off by the Macy's entrance.

—I'll just go run my mother over to the dealer's and then be back for you two, he said. —It should only take a few. Maybe you can scope out whatever you're interested in, and then we can start charging when I get back, okay?

—Sounds good, honey, said Gwyn. —Meetcha by the video arcade. Promise you won't be gone long?

—Promise, he said.

—I just get a little antsy here, she said in a baby voice so authentic it made me wonder if she'd just been dubbed. —Last time I was here and at Chimi's was, well, with Dickland.

—Don't worry—we'll undo all those nasty associations. Isn't that right, Dimple?

—Uh, right, I said. —I mean *riiight.*

—And dinner's on me when I get back, he said. He rolled his window partway up and she blew him a kiss as he pulled away. He blew one back, which she pocketed, and one to me, too, to be polite, I guess, but Gwyn intercepted that one as well and made like she was sticking it in her lunchbox purse. I couldn't believe it; now she was even stealing air kisses! This was irksome to the max. Karsh's presence had alleviated some of the tension, but now, as the Golf disappeared into the distance, it all came back twofold.

We were both feeling the lack of him. The two of us stood there a moment on the sidewalk, silent, as if we had nothing left to say to each other.

—Well, I'm going to go to the camera store, I guess, I said.

—No! Wait, I'll go with you. Karsh won't be back for a good half-hour.

Of course. She had a little time on her hands.

The two of us walked through the suffocating perfume fumes, the blinding boxed jewelry, the pumped-up stereo section to the south part of the mall, where the photography store was.

It was really strange being here. I hadn't been back since the night of the double date from Hades. And before that, for the birthday shopping ritual. The mall used to seem like a safe however stressful (when it came to trying on clothes) place. Now all the blank nippleless mannequins and bossy bright signs urging you to *Buy! Buy! Buy!* just depressed me. The floor was too grey and the light too artificial. Old couples were here to walk in the controlled climate; younger folk came to go broke. Everything seemed like such a rip-off today.

Except here at the camera store, of course, the only place that was about making the world a more beautiful place, not just yourself.

I was heading straight for the fisheyes when Gwyn took my arm.

—Come on, Dimple—for old time's sake!

She was gesturing towards the photo booth in the corner, the one where she'd, unbeknownst to me, taken my fake ID picture late last spring. Old times? It did feel old, that day. And it was old news, too, that she could never resist having her picture taken, even now.

—Oh, I don't know, Gwyn, I said.

But she was already yanking away the curtain, dragging me in.

—It'll be fun, she said. —Just one round.

We squeezed into the booth. A piece of advice: If you are already feeling so nervy around someone that the wide walking promenades of the county's biggest shopping mall don't alleviate the claustrophobia, the last place you want to go with them is the interior of a photo booth. Now the tension was almost unbearable—but it was the opposite of the way the distance between Karsh and me had been tense. There it had been an ache that made me long to bridge the distance. Here, it was a closeness that made me long to run away, widen the gap, dilute the pain with every fleeing step. All the held-back things—what I wasn't saying, what we hadn't talked about—seemed to inhabit the small space as well, like riotous, neglected, overweight people, and I had the sense I was being crammed up against all their sweaty skins, even though it was just me and Gwyn on the brief seat.

The last time we'd been here she'd pulled me into her lap. This time, we avoided that, maintaining the façade that we were each mighty comfortable with a mere half butt on solid seating (well, *her* entire one probably fit).

I was already uncomfortable both on the inside and out, and once she dropped in the change and the machine hummed to life, I couldn't take it. The blinking began, and Gwyn eagered up, pushed her way farther into the indicated frame, thereby knocking me off the sludge of seat I'd been balanced on. I went with the momentum and shot out the booth. She stayed inside, her feet calmly kitten-heeled on the floor below the now ruffled curtain.

—What did you do that for? she asked when she came out.

—I don't know. I just got . . . too hot.

Under the collar.

But she wasn't paying attention. She was reaching for the strip of pictures, and curiosity drew me in to look over her shoulder.

The first shot was of the two of us. Well, of about one-quarter of my face and three-quarters of Gwyn's, caught in mid-blink. The second one was of my right earlobe—I must have been falling already—and Gwyn looking exactly like she did in the first one. The third was a fully lobed vaguely stunned Gwyn glancing after me, the lighting gone all funky from what my tumble must have done to the curtain. And the fourth was an overexposed solo snap of her doing her sexy looking-up-from-lowered-lids look, which I was pretty sure she'd poached off Kavita.

—You're hardly even in them, she said. —Well, whatever. I can give these to Karsh. I wanted him to have a wallet-size of me—so now he can have four!

She smiled brightly and carefully tucked the strip into her lunchbox purse. I gritted my teeth. I could feel the words clogged up behind them like old gum; if I opened my mouth even a bit, they'd escape and trap us in a sticky mess, which I wasn't sure was preferable to just shutting up, swallowing, and letting that proverbial rubber tree take root in my belly instead. But I was choking on all the unsaid things.

We left the camera store. I was walking really quickly, but still couldn't get up to speed enough to outrun the situation.

By the boho store with its windowful of feathers and florid lights, kinky bulbs and hanging beads and rasta tie-dyes, Gwyn paused to use the reflection to reapply her lipstick.

—I just had a flash, she said smacking her lips together and winding her Smoosh Bouche back into its silver tube. —You know how they have all those Christmas lights up at East Is Feast? Well, I was thinking *that* would be a great idea to steal for those palm plants at HotPot.

—Well, I guess that's your specialty, isn't it, I blurted out before I could stop myself.

—What's that?

—Stealing.

She turned away from her reflection to face me.

—What's that supposed to mean?

—Nothing.

Now I wished I hadn't started, but I certainly couldn't stop there. That was the trouble with holding back; there was going to be a landslide now. I could already feel my feet twitching.

—Well, okay, I said. —It's just, I can't believe you stole my idea like that.

—What idea?

—What do you mean what idea? The whole idea about the party!

—I stole it? Gwyn laughed icily. —I was the one with the connection.

Well, I'd been the one with the connection *to* her connection.

—And anyways, Dimple. Ideas are just—

Now she gestured towards the potted plants, the stalls selling Roman candles and teddy bears and reindeer ornaments and automatic menorahs already.

—*Out* there, she said. —And besides, you weren't going to use it.

—Well, couldn't we at least have shared it? I thought we shared everything.

—Shared everything? Well, you didn't share Kavita or the HotPot party—I had to find out by accident! You didn't share Zara, or that book about your grandfather; Sabz told me. You didn't share your *feelings*.

I was dumbfounded.

—Whatever, Dimple, said Gwyn, looking off towards the teddy bears. They looked more like fuzzy brown punching bags right now. —It's done with now. And anyways, don't you want Karsh to be happy? In the end it was all for him, right?

—Of course I want Karsh to be happy, I said.

—Then what does it matter? He's happy.

—*I* wanted to make him happy.

I felt embarrassed as soon as I said it. She snapped back towards me, neck cricking, and she looked like a stranger.

—This isn't about the party at all, is it, Dimple? she said coolly. —This isn't about stealing any stupid idea. Go on—just say it.

—Say what?

—For once, say what you mean, for god's sake.

—What do you want me to say? I mumbled.

—This is about stealing Karsh! Admit it—isn't that why you're so upset? Isn't that what you're getting so worked up about?

—I'm not upset! I nearly shouted.

—You always want what I want, Gwyn continued, and a vein I'd never before noticed poked an abrupt blue path in her forehead. —Ever since we were little—the Special Dolls, the donuts for breakfast. And even now. Even now.

—I could say the same for you, I said.

—Oh, come off it, Dimple. I can't understand why you can't just be happy for me.

Because her happiness, for the first time, was truly getting in the way of my own. Because she always had to have her way, and this time it was getting in mine.

—Do you have to have everyone? I asked her instead of saying all that. —You could have had any boy in the world. And you had to pick this one.

—I don't want any boy in the world. I want *this* boy. I'm in love with *this* boy. And that was *my* idea: I spoke up first; I confided in you. Face it, Dimple: You forfeited the right—you told me you didn't like him.

I bit my tongue. This was true—but I couldn't help it if it took me a little longer to realize things than her, could I? To figure out who I was, who I liked, what I wanted? I wasn't a born pro at any of this, and I didn't know how to speed up my RPM. Self-actualization wasn't like the 600-yard dash where you could work out and do laps and get better and speedier and stronger—was it? And regardless of anything, how was I to now just turn off my feelings?

—I liked him first, she concluded.

—Well, I was Indian first, and that didn't stop you from trying to take that, too, I said. —It's not just about stealing Karsh, Gwyn. It's much bigger than that—it's. It's about stealing identities. *My* identity.

—What—you have a copyright on being Indian? Well, then, I have one on Madonna and your e-mail account, so the moment you're ready to give those up, I'll give you back your—your rakhis and recipes. Weren't you listening to a word at the NYU conference? Don't you get anything? That was the whole point of Desicreate.

Had we attended the same conference? (And didn't she know Hotmail was created by a South Asian?)

—Weren't *you* listening? I cried. —Do you know how hard it can be from this side of the pond?

—We're on the same side of the pond, Dimple.

—Not Mirror Lake. This side . . . of *things. Of life.* Gwyn, I can't tell whether I'm Indian or American half the time. I don't know how I'm supposed to act, who I'm supposed to relate to, where I fit in. I don't know how to bring anything together. To be myself. And I finally thought maybe I was getting it, maybe I had met someone who would help show me the way out of this—this cultural conflict.

—What cultural conflict? Gwyn snapped, flinging out her arms. She looked like she might shake me, but just held them there. —Not knowing how to act, relate, fit in? Dimple, that's called being a teenager! That's called being a *person*—growing up. Which you should try out one of these days; it might do you good. It's not *your* personal drama. In fact, you didn't even know you had a quote cultural conflict till you read about it in books and heard about it in lectures.

She stepped back, dropping her arms to her sides and then crossing them.

—You just have fancier words to give it, names that make it sound *so* unique and *so* complicated, she said. —What, you think I'm not struggling with all the same stuff?

I didn't know what to say. I had never thought of it this way before, and I didn't know if I agreed one hundred percent, but when Gwyn got in the mood to argue, mercy on anyone who attempted to talk back.

—And you think I'm, I'm thwarting your quest to find yourself or something?

She was rubbing her arms now, hard. And there was a chill creeping up on us, and I was beginning to feel a little sick sad feeling in my belly.

—What about supertwins? she said now, and her voice fractured a nidge. —And Queens, and the suitable boy thing? I was trying to help you, support you. *Give* you that identity.

—I don't know, Gwyn, I said quietly, but I was shaking, whether it was from my unscreamed scream or unsobbed sob I couldn't tell. —It's just. Lately I feel you've been taking things away more than anything.

Her mouth stuttered open but she didn't say anything; the gum had turned her tongue purple, and her eyes were going very very blue.

I could see she was feeling that same unscreamed unsobbed tension; it was in the way her shoulders hunched slightly. And I could see that she recognized it in me, too. Somewhere inside neither of us wanted to be doing this to each other. And I didn't understand why we weren't reaching for each other, why we didn't just say *come on, come off it* and laugh it off, put it in perspective, count the years in our favor.

But now, with a heavy heart, they were a weight, these years. A burden, these memories, keeping us in clothes that no longer fit, repeating patterns that no longer applied. It was getting too hard to hold them without breaking them in all their strangely ponderous fragility, too hard to carry a childhood friendship into an adult world. It seemed it might just be easier, however unwise, to loosen the grip and let it all go.

Still, that *shutupshutupshutup* was looping in my head, and it was directed at both of us: Don't ruin a precious thing. This moment could serve as a moment of grace and each of us, warily watching the other, knew it; a moment in which we could save each other from ourselves, when we could change the heart-wrenching direction this was all taking with a word, if someone would just say it.

But I said nothing, thinking all this. And when she spoke, it wasn't that word either.

—Well, then, if you feel like that, I don't know what we're even doing talking to each other, she said finally. It was a voice I didn't recognize, was like hers but not, like hearing yourself on somebody's answering machine. —Maybe we need to make a break from each other. Maybe the next thing I need to take away from you—is me.

She was back in her shades now, but I could still see her glare, as if an unsparing sun were on the other side of them.

—No, you know what? she said. —*You* go. *I'm* meeting Karsh. And you just stay out of our way. I don't think I want to talk to you for a while.

★ ★ ★

I was too upset to do anything *but* go. I was shaking. My blood seemed to be running a new course; organs wobbled around like furniture in an earthquake. I walked and I walked, and before I knew it I had actually walked all the way back home, back to Gwyn's house, as if it were in fact out of my control to stay away from her. But of course she wasn't there.

I went out to Mirror Lake, to the three-holed bridge, and sat, dangling my feet off the edge.

How had this whole mess started? When had it become such a complicated thing to just be who you were?

My birthday. It had all started around my birthday. I reached into my wallet now and pulled it out, the perilous piece of plastic. The identity she gave me. I stared at the girl in the palm of my hand, this girl with the headlit eyes, surrounded by a web of lies as to who she was, and when, and how. How could I have ever hoped to be her?

I turned my hand over, knuckles rising. The plastic flipped over a few times before landing. Water caught, it hurdled through the middle hole of the bridge and was gone.

CHAPTER 35

jugalbandi

Gwyn's words still burned inside me. We had never had a moment like this one. It felt like a breakup, but worse, because I had never been friends with any boy the way I'd been with Gwyn; she had been in my life for as far back as my life went, nearly. There was no me before her, no me without her, it even felt. If she walked my childhood walked out the door with her. It actually hurt too much to think about; there had been something so final in her tone.

It was only afternoon and the day was heavy, sagging at the middle. Clouds scuttled overhead, their bellies gorged and grey. I was at the fork in the road that went off towards her home, by the Bad Luck House, sitting on the curb before the Sold sign. Even from here I could see her shade drawn and window firmly shut. Earlier, when I'd come out to the driveway to see my parents off to a hospital function, I'd seen her take off, too, looping unlicensedly up the street without so much as a backwards glance.

—Wasn't that Gwyn? asked my mother, who never missed a thing.

—What? I said looking away in the direction of our dead end.

—The car that burned rubber up this street about twelve seconds ago.

—Oh that. No. No, I think that was Mrs. Sexton.

—Baapray, I cannot believe how alike they are looking these days, my father had clucked.

—They are not looking at all, said my mother, watching me carefully. —That is the part I cannot believe.

Now I could hear a car coming down Lancaster Road again, just rounding the bend. Could it be Gwyn had forgotten something? I would look a fool if I started running back to my yard now. Actually, I would look a fool if I were caught sitting here at the fork like some forsaken lover, too. So I did the most unfoolish thing possible and stayed right where I was, squeezing my eyes shut. Maybe if I couldn't see her . . .

—Hey, you, I heard as the tires paved closely slow. —Need a lift?

I knew that voice.

I opened my eyes and Karsh filled them, leaning out of Bindigo's rolled down window. He looked at once ethereal and real, in his car on my street, as if he'd traveled a great distance to get to this neither-here-nor-there spot at the fork. He stepped out of the car and squatted down to face me.

—Forgot your way home? he smiled.

—Hey! I said. —I mean . . . hey. Um, you just missed her.

—Hmm?

—Gwyn.

—Oh, yes, Gwyn.

He leaned back into the car and dug around in his glove compartment, then produced a cassette.

—So I have this tape, he said, handing it to me.

—Tape?

—A potential mix for the party.

He looked at me a moment without speaking, and seemed to be thinking hard about something.

His eyes were too intently beautiful to look at, all coal and campfire, and I turned away. Just as I did a humming like a trapped bee went off and he pulled out his cell.

—Oh, hey there, sweetie, he said, voice hushing down. —No, no . . . You are? Okay. Okay, I'm heading over right now.

He clicked off.

—Oh well, I better be off. Gwyn's caught the club manager by chance and is holding on to him till I get there.

I guess I must have looked like I'd bit a lemon.

—Dimple? What is it—you look worried. Is everything okay?

I could barely talk.

—It's Gwyn, isn't it, he said softly.

I was embarrassed to have my heart so ragingly sleeveless, but I nodded.

—Don't worry, he said. —She'll be fine. She won't be hurt again. I'm going to prove to her all guys aren't jerks.

So he was really serious about her—and reassuring me of that! Not only did I seem to have lost my best friend, but the boy was definitely off limits now, too.

—You and Gwyn have a great friendship. Nothing should come in the way of that. Nothing great, nothing small and petty.

Now I wondered if she'd complained to him about me and the stolen idea issue.

—I know, I managed to say.

—You're a really good friend.

His sister, his friend. Could he be any clearer?

—Uh, yeah, thanks, bro, I said. I could think of Karsh as a brother. Frock, he'd make a great brother. I could do this. For Gwyn. For myself. I could let him go. But the more I thought of him this way, like family, the harder my heart ached. It made no sense: I'd lived seventeen years without him—why did I feel his absence so acutely now, even from all the years before I'd even known him?

He gave a half-laugh that matched his half-smile except he wasn't smiling. He slid back into the car and started the engine.

—Do you want to join us, Dimple?

—Um, no. I think I'm better off— It's best if— I just have a lot to get through tonight. You know how it can be when you're . . . you know . . .

—On summer vacation? Right, he nodded. But he lingered a moment as if he'd forgotten something.

—So you coming to the next gig? he asked finally. The car purred gently, the only other sound on the afternoon street. —You know, the Independence Day one? I'm going to sort of treat it as a warm-up for the Disorientation party. Try out some new ideas and all.

—Oh, I'm not sure, I said. —But . . . well. Good luck.

—Try to come if you can, he said. —It would mean a lot to us.

They were already in the plural? I toothed down my lip.

—Oh no, Dimple. Sorry I've been me-me-me, he said now, eyes contrite. —How's Julian? Are you still—?

—No, no, not at all. Hardly ever were.

Karsh watched me as if he were gauging something. Then he reached back out of the car and took my hand and I tried not to wish he would never let it go as he turned it over, nodding to himself.

—Mmm hmm. Just as I thought, he said, pointing to a network of creases below my pinky. —You should be—and will be—with someone who knows that when he's with you there's nowhere else he'd rather be.

The buzz went off in his pocket now and he let go of my hand to check his cell again.

—Oh, man, he said glancing down at the little screen. —I've got to go.

When you meet someone like that, beep me, I thought.

After he'd gone, I noticed he'd forgotten to take back the cassette, still lying tumbled in my lap. I examined it now. It seemed he'd made the cover himself, a sketch of the sea and sand and some two-stroke boats.

I couldn't resist. I went home and dug up my Walkman.

The music slunk in slowly, a shimmering strum, and then tentative drumbeats, a hesitant knock on a submerged door playing off from left ear to right. And as it went on recognition struck a match in me.

I watched now as the first drops struck the pane. I pictured them as the shivery percussions, watched the storm shudder from my ears and out to all the inhabitants of the big girdling world disco as if what was inside my body could affect the outside like that, as if music really did make the people come together. But I suppose it did—that had been the point, right?

It was raining ropily now, the colors from the pines and porch steps and beaten grass all streaked and running. And one by one, the other instruments fell away until it was only these deep-end drums rising up in all their submarine clarity, like my own overfull heart, into my own ears.

Dhage na Dhin, Dhage na Dha, Dhage na Dhin, Dhage na Dha, Dhage na Dha tiri kita Dhage Ti na Gi na . . .

There had been a day when these drumbeats might have been a hello. But in a heartbeat that had all changed. And now they sang only of goodbye.

I hit stop.

CHAPTER 36

shree disco paradiso

In the next weeks, there wasn't much to do but mope. *Flash!* had apparently gone to press and as the HotPot events veered closer—the impending Indian Independence Day meltdown and the final fiesta—my spirits sank. I was going to be steering clear of any scene where I'd have to face Gwyn and Karsh, particularly Gwyn *with* Karsh. Kavita was still staying with us, and that was a great help; granted, she was gone a lot of the time, carrying on with her studies in New York. But it felt good having her there for late dinners and pillow talk, having her in the room with me; we were kindred spirits more than ever these days.

Me, I was spending more and more time at home. Mainly hidden away in the darkroom, not even developing pictures. But one morning when I was down there I was surprised to hear a knock on the door; normally no one descended the stairs to the darkening lair. When I came out, my father was standing there, backlit by the rectangles of sun slicing in through the grass-level windows.

—Dimple, I know you are not developing, he said. —You cannot fool me—your camera has not moved an inch for days, and you do not have that . . . that darkening *glow* about you. Maybe you need a dose of light—you know that people truly suffer without sufficient light? We are like the plants. Or photos, I suppose. So I was thinking—if you are free—how about that temple date we talked about?

He was right. I needed to get out. So later that day, while my mother was lunching with Radha, in fact, I drove us to Signs Central.

The Shree Ganesha Temple's almost librarial exterior completely belied the raucous ruckus—on every level, assaulting every sense—going on full speed inside the square brick structure. Little did I suspect any of this, however, as we stepped out of the car (impeccable parallel parking job on my part; I was definitely improving), the double clack of the doors and the soft tarred thud of my sneaks and my father's loafers the only sound in the world. Even the blare of highway traffic wasn't making much headway through the thick barrier of oak and elm, shimmying with jewel green leaves in the summer breeze.

The foyer doors were marked, unsurprisingly, with a sign imploring all who entered to refrain from various inappropriate activities, and then a short list of friendly recommendations for appropriate behavior, the first of these commandments being "please remove footwear thank you" (punctuated authentically vis à vis India, where commas were often dropped before niceties). My father kept smiling at me and ruffling my hair. He looked so chirpy. It occurred to me that I'd never considered hanging out with him of my own free will on a post-pubescent free day, and it was a lot less painful than I'd imagined.

The foyer was stacked with cubicled shelves in which you could stash your shoes thank you before entering. Karsh would definitely appreciate this, with his penchant for barefootedness.

When we entered the room, I was stunned to receive several surprised, censuring and grinning stares—all from men. Because that's all there seemed to be seated on the carpeted floor. A beat, then I realized the women were on the other side of the room.

—Uh, you'll have to go over there, said my father. —Is that okay? We can stay close to the barrier so we're still somewhat near each other.

He squeezed my shoulder and sat down on his side of the barrier (a small table where for a smaller donation you were handed plastic bags of home-fried nibbles, like duck-feeding packets, or movie food). I moved tentatively to the women's side, swept up on the droning tide; a harmonium was blasting from the speakers and a drove of warbling dissonant voices was chanting something over and over in Sanskrit (I guessed; it was incomprehensible to me save for the Ganesha part).

I felt shy as I sought out a sitting space on the floor: Everyone was in a sari, or at least a salvar, the older women in gym socks and cardigans, too, with sometimes jarringly trendy hair accessories glitter-pinning their buns or securing their braids in vivid plastic-sunflowered place. Even many of the young girls were in saris, but some of them had painted toenails, which gave me hope. I don't know why but I felt even more of a misfit here, like I could distinctly see the disappointment of the older women at my literal unsuitability (blue jeans and tee); the slightly smiling younger girls appeared merely to be laughing at me. Seemed my tee screamed out Failed Indian Girl rather than My Parents Went to Cancun and All I Got Was This Lousy T-Shirt. Was that what an ABCD was? Or was that just me, I thought, recalling the with-it crowd at the Desicreate events. I felt I didn't belong, but as if that wasn't enough, was experiencing serious pressure to connect nevertheless; after all, these peeps could be (and maybe even were) my own relatives. Under the silks and salvars, they looked enough like me.

Even though there were actually plenty of people getting up and walking around, I felt too self-conscious to do so myself, especially while some, or all, were praying. I plunked down almost immediately, almost afraid to look up and meet the surely vituperative regards of my new neighbors. But then one elderly lady with skin soft as the pages of a much-loved book turned to me and smiled so kindly it brought tears of gratitude to my prodigal-daughter eyes.

I decided to revert to observing. Trying to participate was too risky, achy-breaky.

Everyone was seated facing front, which had led me to believe the main event was taking place there—but in fact there was no main event happening anywhere. To some extent people seemed to be doing their own thing, while the speakers blared popped-corn-crackle out in surround sound. On the other side, a man would occasionally fling forward and prostrate himself, touching his forehead repeatedly to the beige carpeting. This surprised me, as I thought only Muslims touched their foreheads to beige carpeting. None of the women seemed to be doing that. But I guess catapulting yourself was a little more difficult when you were sari-bound. Maybe saris had been invented to keep women from escaping from temples and marriages in the first place—after all, how fast can you run when you're in one? The chicas were barely shifting position, save to clap, and I felt a wave of sympathy just thinking about the severe cases of pins and needles they'd be experiencing soon enough.

I tore my eyes away from the templegoers to take in the temple itself. Christmas lights were tacked all around the room (well, perhaps, it occurred to me now, they weren't really Christmas lights, just festive ones) and some kinky bulbs like in the boho store blinked seedily along the ceiling's perimeter. Three of the four walls were decorated with large square paintings depicting Krishna and sundry gopies, and Hanuman, and scenes from the *Ramayana* and *Mahabharata*. The front wall was made up of a few sort of boxy mixed media assemblages, like you find particularly in post-Thanksgiving department store windows. Enshrined in the glass case before me: an adorable rotund gold Ganesha. One of those silver-magnet two-piece sculptures—this one of dolphins on either end of a thin metal arc—bobbed and balanced itself before him. Strewn by the elephant god's feet was an eden of fresh flowers and apples and pears. Upon closer examination I could see tiny white blotches on the fruit. The price tags!

I sat back and made like an aperture. I took it all in. The hues, the croons, the unbelievable mix of sacred and everyday. The scent of incense and hair oil and sleep and fried food. The sounds: At first the chant had seemed and, well, *was* repetitive, but it began to feel strangely intoxicating, to grow more powerful as it repeated, the way choruses to great songs only gain momentum as the song goes on. These people were completely lost in the music, in the lights, in their worship. The atmosphere was drunken, heady with blinking lights and blasting beats, and it reminded me of something.

HotPot.

I wondered why nobody just got up and started dancing. I imagined these women undoing their braids and springing into whirling dervishes. The place had all the elements of a discotheque—right down and up and panning to the speaker system! I wondered who the DJ was, stringing along the harmonium. I felt my cheeks condense and realized I was smiling; I was swept with such a sense of peace at having found a way to connect to it all, even if most of the folk around me might beg to differ with the disco analogy. And it now occured to me that maybe the whole point was, in fact, to lose yourself. But not in the sense of confusion—in the sense of connection to something bigger than yourself. HotPot certainly had felt that way: getting lost to be found.

When I came out of my musings I noted my father gesturing to me, and we rose to meet in the nongendered foyer.

—Sorry, beta, he said as we slipped our shoes back on. —I can't sit like that too long—my legs fall asleep.

When we got to the car, we slid in and snapped on the belts, but my dad didn't shut his door. He paused, smiling at the front window, as if particularly pleased with the windshield wipers, then turned to me.

—Isn't this so nice, beta? he said. —Like our Millburn Diner dates when you were little, when you used to leap out of bed at the crack of dawn every day . . .

I was sure this was heading towards a reproach regarding my laziness, but then I saw he was somewhere else, his face soft as a dreamer's.

—Remember, beta? And we'd leave the coffee on for your mother and sneak out, just the two of us.

Of course I remembered.

—Two corn muffins split with butter one egg fried extra pepper please and a junior hot fudge sundae with extra fudge and chocolate sprinkles, but only after, I said.

—And could you replace the vanilla with one scoop cookies and cream one pistachio and two spoons, thanking you very much? my father finished.

He winked at the memory of our innocent outings. Our last one would have to have been about seven years ago. I remembered never being able to stifle my giggles as the two of us would tiptoe exaggeratedly through the house, stage-shushing each other, index fingers so firmly against our noses they snubbed upwards, so as not to wake my mother, who slept deeply in those days despite all that Maxwell House. Now I realized she must have known what was up all along, maybe even orchestrated it—she was big on father-daughter time, even though, to tell the truth, I'd never ever felt he hadn't been there for me, no matter what his call schedule had been. But back then I thought we were really pulling the synthetic comforter over her eyes.

We used to have this Smith Corona typewriter in the house, a relic my father bought before I was born, when my parents first came to America. He used it to make things look official: complaints to the telephone company, invoices, thank-you notes. I'd adored the *ting!* it would make at line's end, which never failed to get my mom double-checking the microwave or drying her hands anxiously on her slacks, glancing doorwards for unannounced visitors. After I started writing and reading, my father would boost me up on a stack of the yellow pages so I could reach, guide my fingers over the keys. A switch allowed you to go from black to red ink, and we both always opted for vermillion, decorating the sheet with scores of shift key symbols: ruby asterisks and apple ampersands, bleeding pound signs, chokecherry copyrights and percents.

The Smith Corona played a vital role in how we would organize our corn muffin escapades, my father and I. I would be casually strolling through the dining room, and there it would be, lifted out of its hard black suitcase and positioned carefully before the head chair, a piece of paper rolled neatly in its mouth, still crisp. I would bounce to my knees on the seat, my heart a hummingbird in my wrists. The paper would usually read something like this:

@$% My Dearest Miss Bacchoodi %&#
I was thinking that it has been a Very Long Time since we had a Corn Muffin Date. What do you think? I have an Idea: If you do not have anything else on your Schedule, and you might be available this Sunday at 8, The Two of Us could sneak out for Breakfast (and maybe a Hot Fudge Sundae with Extra Fudge)? Do let me know. (We can replace the Vanillas.)
I Love You Very Much.
%@%Your Bapuji%&%

He wrote like the offspring of Pooh and a cursing cartoon character. And, one finger at a time, my rose red response: *Let me check my Schedule: Of course! And Chocolate Sprinkles!* I could never sleep the night before, dreaming dreams of our favorite waitress Ilene's crinkling smile and surreally spotless apron, the butter melting in all the nooks and crannies of the muffin tops, the way the whipped cream stayed cool and the fudge hot, the little puddle of it at the bottom of the dish that I would find when all the ice cream was gone, that Ilene always poured in first, so I could "end on a chocolate note."

—How I cherished those mornings, said my father, shaking his head and smiling sadly to himself

—You did? I said. It sounded immediately silly: Of course he had. As had I. And even my mother, who greeted us with open arms and feigned surprise when we got back sticky grinned, probably enjoyed it all immensely as well. I had just forgotten, that's all. Forgotten how fabulous it could be to be with my dad. And how it used to be enough to be with my dad and a hot fudge sundae on the horizon, with my father, the first man I ever wanted to marry.

—It's just then you got so busy, with school, your friends, your life, he continued now. It sounded like the way I felt sometimes about Gwyn. —And now you are all grown up. I know it took years, but I still can't help feeling it happened in the blink of an eye. Sometimes an expression will come to your face that I was knowing when you were only months old, when you saw a puppy for the first time, or when your diaper was ready to go. But now it is not for puppies and diapers. I suppose that's what happens; it is only natural, especially in America. But it's funny—if someone had told me before we left India that I might lose my daughter even more quickly in the process, I would not have budged one inch.

He grinned suddenly, and frantically rubbed his thigh, the itch that wasn't there that popped up at moments like these, embarrassed by his sudden display of emotion. He didn't usually talk like this.

—And been a farmer in Varad today . . . not!

He was trying to make a joke of it, but I knew it was no joke. I don't know why but I wanted to cry. I looked at my father and I saw for the first time, it seemed, the silver spreading at his temples, a wave breaking on a black sea of hair, and that just discernible bald spot creeping up reeflike underneath it all. The wiry strand curling out from his ear. There was a jaggery-colored cluster of spots on his forearm I didn't remember being there before. I saw that familiar smile stretching too tight against too many teeth and for the first time in what seemed a long time it didn't irritate me. For the first time I saw that it was a beautiful smile, one that was trying to enjoy something so that somebody else could, to not say the wrong thing, to not spoil the moment, a smile stretched tight to not let that wish escape. Or maybe it already had escaped, that wish, and it was to not let one in again, to not let one grow again, like a dandelion gone gauzy to be blown bare by a passing wind.

It was strange. It was the same face in all of those photo albums and shoe boxes and frames: the fading black-and-white childhood shots in Varad, the wedding days album, my mother garlanded like a Hawaiian hula dancer beside him, the one of him standing proudly before his first car, a used Plymouth Valiant, the coconut for his thank-you to Ganesha still uncracked in his hands.

And then I realized. It was the same face . . . but it was not. These other smiles were full either of expectation or disappointment. The corn muffin smile was a smile that showed a soul happy to be exactly where he was.

And a smile unabashedly happy with me.

—Daddy, I said, and I rested my head on the wheel so he couldn't see my face.

—Yes, beta?

—Remember you used to tell me a guy would be crazy to not want to marry me?

—Yes.

—Do you still think it's true?

—Of course it's still true! More than ever now, bacchoodi.

I was terrified to go there, but I had to ask.

—Then why are you doing so much wishing for a husband for me? I blurted.

—What are you talking about?

—You know, all that extra time praying in the morning. To the Saraswati.

—A husband? said my father, genuinely surprised. —I haven't been praying for a husband for you, beta. Though I suppose that could be one interpretation of jeevansaathi.

—Jeevan sutthy?

—Jeevansaathi, he corrected my pronunciation. —That means life companion. Soul mate. Jeevan, life; saathi, companion. Someone to share the world with, this life with. That's what I've been praying for, for you. That's all.

My breath caught in my chest. Was I so warped in my interpretation of things? What else had I been wrong about? All this while I'd been pegging my father as a control freak obsessed with barbaric medieval rituals and all this while he'd been asking for something so wonderful and at the same time so humble and beyond judgment. A life companion. Not even the gender was specified; Kavita would appreciate this. And then it came together the way things do sometimes: It wasn't so odd she was opting for the chicas after all, that you could love with your body what you could love with your heart and mind. A life companion could be someone like Gwyn, except with kisses. Or someone like Karsh. Except with kisses. At the same time a great understanding filled me, I felt a profound emptiness, that very understanding swiveling me around to face unexplored rooms in a house I thought I knew by heart.

I was very happy and very sad and my father's face was too kind and concerned and comprehending to behold. I suddenly realized he'd had all this time that most unimaginable of things: a clue.

I was sobbing, and he pressed a hand down on my shuddering shoulder, steadying me; I collapsed on the horn, which let out a sympathetic toot. The hands that had drawn the fever from me when I was sick, warm even in winter and nutmeg smelling, like gingerbread cookie dough spreading into happy people in the oven, the same ones I'd ironically thought about to still the pounding in my head after the date with Julian. I felt him catch a tear off my cheek.

—Beta, I hope I didn't upset you, he said, alarmed. —I always seem to say the wrong thing these days. I suppose I am no replacement for your mother, isn't it. Do you want to go home?

—No, I said. —I don't.

I made an attempt to swashbuckle up, pushed my hair back behind my ear and turned the key. The motor wheezed to life. I exited the parking lot and turned down the street. Then I had a better idea, and executed a three-point when all was clear.

—Where are we going? asked my father looking from the road back to me.

—I'm having a certain craving, I said.

He looked surprised for a moment, then grinned, loose and uninhibited. It was the corn muffin grin.

★　★　★

Late that night, well after ending on a chocolate note, I crept into the study. There, on the floor of the slatted closet, I found it. The hard suitcase, now mottled grey in a coating of house dust. I ran my finger along the surface and watched the ebony rise, a black river on barren land. The latch creaked open, and I carried the old machine to the dining room table, wound the page in. Clicked the color switch. The chair height was just right now and, softly, I lay my fingers on the keys, taking a breath as if I were about to launch into that long-awaited rendition of "Für Elise." But this was for someone else.

Dear Bapuji
Thank you for A Lovely Day. I didn't realize before how much I miss Replacing the Vanillas with You. If your Schedule permits, maybe We could do this again sometime? Soon?
I Love You.
Your Bacchoodi

CHAPTER 37

durga slays the demon

I was cleaning out my room when I came across some childhood photographs of Rabbit and me, at the bottom of my crate of all things Gwyn (from notes passed in class and self-penned horoscopes to valentines and secret-crush journals). Class pictures in which we'd leapt flagrantly out of alphabetical order to be beside each other. Birthday shots with both of us tiara'd so you couldn't tell whose day it actually was. Moving back in time, the passage of it marked by piggybacks and pajama parties, forgotten dolls, and in nearly every photograph nearly audible giggles over who knew what anymore.

A snap of us that Halloween we'd put aside Cinderella, Sleeping Beauty, and Snow White (me) and Jasmine, Pocahontas, and Mowgli-ette (her) to celebrate our supertwin status. We'd gotten an extra-large hot pink sweatshirt, widening the neckhole to allow both our heads through (which we then loosely conjoined with one of my mother's dupattas) and belting in both our waists over the fabric to turn it to a minidress. Matching striped tights on both sets of legs, but the middle two—one of hers and one of mine—we'd swathed together with black fabric, so the joint limb could blend into the night and vanish. My arm out one sleeve, hers out the other; jute bag in my hand and shopping bag in hers, and our inner arms wound securely around each other's waists to allow us to stand as close as possible. We were both grinning with toothy optimism.

But posing for a photo as Siamese twins in my bedroom proved to be much easier than actually trick-or-treating with our new conjoined status. Fortunately we were closer to being the same height then, and though dangerous curves lay ahead, this was pre-pubescence, too, or we wouldn't have even made it out my front door. The first few houses, we bumped into each other the whole way, accidentally ramming one another into curbs, potholes, trippingly over sewer gratings, one of us always striding too quickly or too slow. We held on too tightly, were, in fact, banded together too tightly, and moved stumblingly, the weight of the extra person difficult to carry. The candy was slow coming, as it took us much longer than usual to navigate Lancaster Road alone.

But as the night went on, the fabric binding our inner legs together stretched just a smidge, the belt around our doubled waist loosened a notch, and my mother's scarf gently unknotted. We learned to listen to each other's breath and footfalls to gauge whether the speed was all right, to look out for two instead of one when scanning the street for bumps and slopes. Our inner arms unlocked from around the doubled waists to lie tensionless on our nascent hips. And when we let go some, we went a lot farther. When we learned to walk beside each other without holding on, we found we were less tired, our baskets crackling with sweets in no time at all.

It seemed fitting, and in any case, I had no choice now but to let Gwyn go, at least a little. It was holding on so tightly that was hurting my heart. Who knew a picture taken so many years ago could show me a way to live my life today?

I wondered if looking at a photograph of Karsh might elucidate me, too, teach me how to deal with his absence. And then I realized: I had no pictures of Karsh. Yes, I had a shot of the ladder leading up and disappearing into the darkness of the HotPot balcony, as if into a lightless heaven. Yes, I had taken the magical place on the porch where his shoes had been the night of my heart's revelation, and even a zoom-in of the sheet music. But no Karsh. Still, it was funny how these spaces where he was not took on his shape nonetheless.

★   ★   ★

This made me want to look at other pictures again. What was missing, and what was not? Would they appear different now, tell a new story? I began digging through the shoe boxes in the study cabinets, poring over the images of my family. And indeed the photographs looked different now. I had always viewed their subjects as simply youthful versions of the parents I now shared a home with; today I began to see them as visions of young people who'd never imagined getting old, nor what their lives might one day become.

People like me.

A couple of months ago I would never have seen the connection, but today it was tangible as the photographs themselves. A small but certain weight: the weight of a moment. But a moment contained the whole, perhaps not a stolen but offered soul. My parents' wedding photos now seemed inextricably linked to everything that had come before to bring them there, together—my mother's posed studio shot with her brother Sharad at the age of five or six, in which she appears both terrified and mesmerized by the camera and clings to his, I now noticed, rakhi'd wrist, and my father's baby picture, his eyes lavishly lined with kajal, as was the tradition, looking like infant Krishna on the peepul leaf—all retrospectively but irrefutably part of the whole design. And in the same way it was linked even then—that day the two took the seven steps round the spousal fire—to me, here, beholding them. The images looked different now that I felt connected to them, now that I was looking at them differently. But that changed them. Maybe there was no such thing as simply observing after all. In the same way I could see the tiny convex me in Chica Tikka's third eye, I was perhaps inextricably in the photographs she took.

In one of the shoe boxes I came across an old black and white of my saried mother, the corners curled as fallen petals. She must have been a teenager in it, and she was looking out and up from under her lids in much the same way Kavita did. A secret smile danced on her mouth; she seemed at once shy and thrilled by what she saw. It appeared she was looking right at me, right into this room, and I smiled at the idea of the young Shilpa Kulkarni having this kind of prophetic vision, perhaps that day experienced simply as a slight tingle up the spine, or momentary warming of her skin. And then I realized she held a camera in her hands, a clunkily beautiful contraption, lens aiming out from just above her belly. Upon closer scrutiny I saw the make of the machine, the white print across the front of it legible only to inverted eyes. It was a mirror image, my young unmother taking a self-portrait. Sitting here and contemplating the image today, it seemed to me that she was looking in that mirror to lay eyes on me. And my gazing at her reversed image was also like looking in a mirror from the other side. And I had a strange sensation of time, not so much as standing still, but the eternity capsulated in a single moment.

I wondered what that day had been like for her, tried to fill in the moments around the actual click of the camera. The delight she was clearly experiencing from what she saw—herself—made me happy-sad. Happy that she had felt it; sad that I wasn't sure whether she did anymore.

Had she danced that day?

Most of the images of my parents in these boxes at least overlapped somewhat with stories I had heard, information I vaguely recalled about their histories together and apart. But there was one glaring omission from my mother's tale. I wasn't sure if I should ask, but now I knew I had to; I'd been pussyfooting around it all summer.

I found her in front of Oprah, doodling the names of deities and celebrity guests in the *TV Guide*.

—Mom, I said tentatively. I took a breath. —Why are there no photos of you as a dancer anywhere?

Gwyneth Krishna Prabhu Madonna . . .

—What do you mean? she finally replied. I could see she was trying to act casual, but she was doodling harder. —Why should there be photos of me as a dancer?

—Because . . . you were a dancer.

—That Radha, filling your head with stories.

—It's not true? But even Bapuji said.

—I suppose it *was* true, she said, now starring sitcoms. —But it was a long time ago.

The hushed fret of pen to paper.

—And there is no point in discussing it now, she added, a little loudly.

I was doing that thing again, *shutupshutupshutup*, but my mouth voted independent.

—Yes, but that still doesn't explain why there isn't a single picture of . . .

The pen stilled.

—I burned them.

I was stunned.

—You *what?*

She was silent a moment, and the pen rolled soundlessly into the fold of the magazine.

—It hurt too much to see them, she said softly.

I dropped down beside her and wrapped my arms around her.

—Why do you never talk about it then? I asked gently. —Wouldn't it help?

—Who was there to talk to, Dimple? she said, trying to shrug. But it caught on the uptake, turned to a hunching of her shoulders. She averted her eyes. —Your father was working night and day to make a living for us. My parents—I was not able to speak to them for six years after coming here, until my first visit back to India, since they had no telephone. When I think back to that I can hardly imagine it—if I had to spend six years without talking to you I would simply . . . well . . . I would never allow it.

—But before, in India, why did you stop? Radha said—

—They didn't let me. Well, they didn't actually hold a dagger to my heart to stop me—but they said it wasn't practical, what if I didn't get married, how would I make a living like that, what was I doing with my life. I had to be a good example to my sister, I had to. Be rational.

—Even Dadaji?

She was staring straight ahead now, as if she could see it all before her on the flickering television screen.

—He was different as a father than as a grandfather, Dimple. Though he always wanted what was best for us, and for you.

I couldn't believe it. That what he could have thought was best for my mother could be so off, and that what he thought was good for me was so *on*. Maybe age really did bring on wisdom. I considered Mrs. Sexton. Well, in some cases.

—That is so strange when I think of how much he supported my dream to be a photographer, I said. —Created it, in fact.

Now she turned to me.

—What do you mean, created it?

At first I thought she was joking. And then I realized she really didn't know. And of course she didn't know: I'd always foolishly assumed she wouldn't understand, that she didn't have an artistic bone in her body. And so I'd never told her. Gesturing for her to wait, I went into my bedroom. I tugged the photo album Kavita had made me from between the mattresses and brought it out.

She looked at me quizzically, taking it into her hands. Wordlessly she turned the pages. And then the tremored silence of her crying.

—Oh no, Mom, I didn't mean to make you cry, I whispered, touching her cheek. —I didn't mean to make you sad.

—They are such beautiful photographs, she said through her tears. —Why didn't you ever show me?

—I don't know. I guess I thought—

—That I wouldn't understand.

I nodded, wishing I didn't have to.

—Dimple, I am so sorry. My beta, my daughter. I don't know what I have been doing to make you feel this way, but it is true, you have seemed so stressed, especially lately. I suppose I have been repeating history —although looking at these pictures I'm not even sure I know what that is anymore.

She ran her finger along the border of a page, as if to work off the dust that wasn't there yet.

—It is peculiar seeing our house, our friends, you, me. It is like a completely different story than the one I thought was going on, she said. —It is like a rewritten history.

She lingered over the pages, smiling sadly over Dadaji's smooth script.

—So this is why you love so much your darkening room, she said.

—Yes. Yes, it is. When I'm in there, when I'm taking pictures, I feel like there's nothing else I'd rather be doing, nowhere in the world I'd rather be.

—I suppose that is how I felt dancing, my mother said quietly. —Perhaps we're not so different, Dimple, you and me. Even in romance—I fell in love with someone out of caste. You have dated boys out of . . . well . . . outlaws. And I suppose without even realizing it I have been quashing your dream, just like my parents tried to talk me out of mine.

She closed the book gently.

—What a funny summer this has been, she said, now taking my hand in both of hers. —You know, I have to admit, it was hard for me to see Radha after so long—she reminds me of all the roads not overtaken, all the things I stopped doing when I got married. All those things it is too late to do now.

—Mom, it's not too late. You just said so yourself. That even now you can rewrite history.

—Easier said, Dimple, she sighed.

But then I had an idea.

—Will you do me a favor? I asked, knowing her unequivocal answer before she even nodded. —Come with me.

I don't think she realized what I was up to when I loaded Chica Tikka. Even when we got to the study. But when I opened the trunk and she heard the jingling, the ghosted child steps as I plunged my hands into the silken sea, understanding dusked her face.

—Oh no . . . I couldn't possibly . . .

But I was already handing her the pieces.

—The choli, it will never . . .

—Then don't hook it all the way; just hang the sari part over it.

—The pallu, and this . . . they will never . . .

But she couldn't fool me here, and I called her on it.

—Mom, these always fit—they're just pieces of fabric, there's no size!

She had run out of excuses. And the moment she did, pleasure bared her face; she touched the silk so lovingly, like she had that evening, the sadness stripped down now. She held it up to herself, rustling it open to the floor.

—Okay, I will do it, for *you*, she sighed dramatically. Still, I could sense the eagerness in her fidgeting hands. —But only because you are so stubborn.

—Like a certain other Kshatriya I know, I said. —And I'm only half Kshatriya!

She had to smile at that.

And I waited.

When she returned she was a vision.

A sunset over a night sea as slow burning as any I'd ever seen, the choli stretching at the hooks but still flamingly on, deep purple sari stitched gold as summer waves cresting, creased fabric fanning between her knees, and the final piece of cloth knotted round her waist, hanging over her backside. Upon her clavicles the jutting necklace lay, the chunky pendants not quite flat, and the chain hanging still lower around it. Earrings swung to nearly her shoulders, thin links trickling up from them to clip into her hair; the ponderous waist chain sloped angling down a hip. Anklets, which I now realized that density of bells on black-brown fabric were, shimmered gigglingly thick halos above her bare feet; bangles swum her arms glidingly gold. The tiara flashed in her now fade-to-black hair, sun and moon clipped on either side of the parting. She had even put a touch of lipstick on.

She bowed down now to touch the ground—an apology to the gods in advance for treading on it. And when she ascended—weight in front black-legginged leg, back one strongly extended, an imaginary spear spanning from hand to ringed and mudra'd hand (Durga killing the demon, she explained, the power of all the gods in her grip)—must gone, all roses, she was the dancing girl come to life.

—One . . . two . . . *teen!*

Click. And it was definitely not too late.

★ ★ ★ CHAPTER 38 ★ ★ ★

using my religion

In just a few days, my parents had gone from being a couple who I thought could never understand me to two individuals together who got it beyond former imagination. And it had come about, I realized, from my taking a moment to try to understand *them*. Why had I never done that before? Now I could not believe the hitherto unappreciated beauty of that single light left on for me, and the way it could give your life shape in, even with, all the darkness.

But there was one person who needed to make her move now from this house of eternal Diwali, and much as it saddened me to open our arms and let her go, it was the right thing to do.

After several days living with us, Kavita decided it was time she face her Manhattan apartment again and deal head-on with the new state of things. I offered to go along to help her make the transition.

In India, whenever you come upon a new beginning you invoke the god Ganesha, remover of obstacles, and have a pooja, which was, in this case, a sort of Hindu housewarming. So the plan was this: Kavita and I would poojaficate her "new" home, and then have a girls' day out. Neither of us was too keen to hit the club that night for the Indian Independence Day meltdown/ Flashball warm-up—and deal with seeing our beloveds melting down and warming up in the arms of another (Karsh with Gwyn; Sabina with Upma).

So fairly early that morning my parents drove us to the station. My mother had supplied us with a packet of tea rose incense and a sandalwood peacock incense holder (the sticks slotted in like feathers). She'd also equipped us with, well, Ganesha, since Kavita had lost him in the split.

When we got downtown, we bought flowers from a deli by Waverly and Waverly before entering the apartment. It looked strange with its other half gone, and so tidily so: one set of bookshelves bare, the next packed; one kitchen cabinet full, the next, ringed with dust-cutting circles where glasses had been. It was amazing to see how evenly they'd shared everything, but how separate they'd kept their spaces.

I had never actually held a pooja before, nor paid attention to the few I'd attended (been dragged to) by my family; it had all been Kavita's idea. But I was really excited for some reason. At first I thought it was simply my joy at seeing my cousin her old-now-new self again. But then I realized I was excited for myself as well: It seemed a great idea, in no small part to celebrate all the positive things that had been happening with me and my parents lately. And as far as the new duo of Karsh and Gwyn was concerned, who couldn't use a new beginning now and then? Maybe it would help me cut the cord.

—So, I said, looking to Kavita. —How do we begin a pooja?
—Well, first we are having to wash our hands, isn't it?
So we did, in the kitchen, drying them on paper towels.
—You did not smell the flowers, heh? Okay, no. Good.
We kicked off our shoes and kneeled at Ganesha's feet, there on the hearth of the nonworking fireplace where we'd placed him. We lay before him the carnations with a dish of sugar cubes and cashews and a Bounty bar (coconut was always used in Indian ceremonies and we didn't have one lying around). We lit the incense in the peacock holder. The scent of tea rose mixed with sandalwood, plumes of smoke rising and dispersing through the apartment.

—Now what? I said.
—Um, what do you mean?
—Don't you have to say something? The priest always says something.
—Yes, but I don't know what he is saying.
—Kavita! And Sabina thinks you're too *Indian*?
—Well, nobody is even paying attention during these ceremonies, isn't it? The aunties are always discussing whose son is achieving higher grades and their husbands' promotions and the children are shooting marbles and the uncles sleep with their eyes open—and even closed! Sometimes I ask myself if the pundit is speaking gibberish just to see if he gets caught.

All this was true.

—Shouldn't we at least throw rice in the fire or something?

That always seemed to happen at Indian weddings.

Kavita agreed, but she didn't have any rice on hand (that had been on a Sabina shelf) so we threw penne instead, till all the hearth needed was a little parmesan and the dons could have dinner. And finally, as she couldn't find any tikka powder, she stripped off her own bindi and placed it in the center of Ganesha's forehead; it appeared enormous, the third eye even bigger than the two he used for the visible world. But Ganesha didn't look like he minded, nor considered this cross-dressing; he simply grinned back at us from the midst of his tea rose halo.

Kavita took my hand.

—To new beginnings, she said.

—To new beginnings, I said.

And fairy tale endings, I added silently.

Kavita fed me a cashew. I fed her a sugar cube. Then she tore open the Bounty bar and we carried our ashing peacock through the apartment, burning out the old smells with a fresh perfume.

★　★　★

I liked the way this little ceremony marked what otherwise might have eventually disappeared as an ordinary moment. It was sheer genius, actually, to treat transitions with care like this, as times to be celebrated rather than feared. And it certainly seemed my life had entered a new phase—even from the simple fact that I was participating in a pooja; I would never have done that at the beginning of the summer. In fact, I wouldn't have done much of anything then; I hadn't yet realized how much my life was in my own hands, had felt merely a victim of forces out of my control. And there were some, of course. But you certainly couldn't go around acting like that, could you?

Tradition—what an innovative idea! It was like catching up with an old friend.

Once we'd wrapped up our second generation pooja, Kavita and I launched into our new beginning. (I seemed to be having a lot of those these days.) We headed out, and over the course of the next few hours managed to: eat ice cream for breakfast (a second breakfast, since my mother had insisted on making us her red hot chili pepper and boursin omelets before we'd left); get our caricatures sketched near the Plaza; paint each of our nails a different color in Sheep's Meadow. We then promptly mangled these manicures in our haste to ride the Central Park merry-go-round.

When we got back downtown late afternoon we finished off the day with a surprise, grace of Kavita. She led me into a slypey gallery near NYU where an exposition entitled East/West was running.

—I noticed it the other day on my way to the library, she smiled, pushing the frosted door.

The exposition was mainly photographs—of the Ganges, the Ajanta and Elora caves. Margaret Bourke White's images of Gandhi and Partition. But there were also shots of Indians in America doing pretty Indian things: the rearview of a cabbie's car, decorated with a swinging glitterball Laxmi, the driver's dark disembodied eyes pitched over a dashboard of fresh flowers. Or American things: a blue-jeaned bustiered brunette who looked a little like Shailly lighting a cigar on a candle. Or doing neither Indian nor American things (or both): a girl-child benched outside a store with a two-for-one sign propped in the window, a goldfish in a plastic bag by her feet; the light caught the water and turned it glassy, to a chunk of ice in which the goldfish's image refracted into two. Light ran up the girl's kneesocks and dappled her brown knees, the fish burning sun orange, a small caught universe.

We moved on to stand before a photograph of a sculpture of an Indian classical dancer. It reminded me of the statue in our house, and it was stillingly beautiful, the way the light was skidding in to touch her, her skin silvered pistachio, a pale wash as if she'd just jingled up from the sea. She twisted at her tiny waist, muskmelon breasts wisting forward, nearly one atop the other, the massive apple of her bottom as well. Her thighs were definitely the kind that stuck together and her belly rounded out voluptuous over the carved necklace draped round her rolling hips. There would be no clean view to the toes for this woman—and it didn't matter. She breathed grace, her almond eyes capacious, open but irisless, which gave the impression she was wakefully dreaming. Her ringletted hair chiseled up into a sort of crown and her lips played a smile as enigmatically knowing as that of pregnant women, of people in love, of children with visions. As if she were really on to something.

I felt so complete just looking at her, even with her missing arms, cut off at the armlets by invading Islamic armies aiming to desecrate her and thus the temple she had once been a part of. But she seemed even more sacred somehow, more imminent, despite the twice-removedness of being a sculpture within a photograph within a room in which we were now standing utterly close. As with Zara, I got lost in her beauty, and only after a moment realized with a start that I was not feeling too short, chubby, geeky, clumsy, clueless. I didn't feel like I had to say something brilliant; I didn't feel any pressure at all. Funny what paying attention to something outside of yourself can do for your self-image.

—It's amazing, I whispered.

—Well, it's nice you think so, isn't it? said Kavita. Her voice wound a cool river through the hushed room. —Because she looks just like you.

This was news to me; I was actually so stunned that I forgot to say something self-deprecating. Kavita came and stood behind me. She put both hands on my shoulders and her chin on the right one.

—The nose, she said, tracing my own with her index finger then pointing to the dancing girl's. I half-expected a marbly virescent version of Kavita to spring out from behind the statue's shoulder, pointing back at me. —The eyes. The definition of the lids, of the upper lip. The proportions of the body. Even the hair. Well, minus this tiara business.

She looked like me? Geekmeister me, always the last picked for teams, the only one in the school that had to walk off the last lap of the 600-yard dash for the President's Fitness Exam? I tensed up a little waiting for the laugh track, the ha portion of the evening to begin, but nothing happened.

—Yes, you, Kavita laughed, as if reading my mind from the back of my head. But it wasn't a mean laugh; it was one that spilled champagne down my bones, bubbled and unlaced all my doubts. She gave my shoulders a squeeze. —Except you've got better posture. Now come on, I am starving.

I turned to look at my cousin twinkling before me. And I knew what we were going to eat.

Later that afternoon, two bottles of wine and resoundingly carnivorous pizzas later (pepperoni, sausage, hamburger, bacon, hold *all* veggies, easy on the cheese) we lay back on the dislocated cushions of the sofa bed, bellies plunging skyward, digesting.

Kavita breathed in deep.

—Sandalwood, she sighed. —Much nicer than Sabinawood.

—Kavita, I said. —Don't be offended, but I can't believe you were with a woman at all. I mean, you wear kajal, you have long hair. And you're always in salvars and chaniya cholis. You're so feminine. You're so *Indian*.

I was gazing at the ceiling. If you looked long enough, white wasn't merely white, but you could pull the pink from it, the greyblack in the shadowed areas, even yellow and blue.

—Being with a woman doesn't make me less Indian! she laughed.

—But it just seems like, like such a loss to, I don't know—to *men* to have you going for the girls.

—But then it would be a loss to women if I went for the boys, isn't it?

I had to admit that was true.

—And more important, I would be even more lost if I were not true to myself—no matter how I may appear to others, even to my own family.

—So that's what you meant about pressure being on Sangita? I asked.

Kavita nodded.

—But does Maasi know?

—Oh, I don't know if she *knows* she knows. But she is certainly aware I have always been a little off-center. *Her* center. And that I will probably continue to be. Just not with Sabina. But who needs Sabina? She was always interrupting me, never letting me speak.

—Yeah, I hate when people do that, I said. —Gwyn was always doing that, or stealing my ideas. Or quoting me at exactly the wrong moment.

—And Sabina was so bossy about what I ate. I mean, please be giving me a break!

—Well, Gwyn never *let* me eat—half the proteins on my plate were being broken down in her stomach before I even put my napkin on my lap.

—And Sabina always had to be the star, the center of attention—like that whole debate situation.

—Yeah, I know someone like that, too.

The fridge hummed as we mulled this over.

—But there was something, I don't know. *Exciting* being around her,

Kavita said finally. —Like she was always just about to discover something. Like *you* were about to discover something, not only about her but yourself.

—Yes, I said. —A familiar mystery. A mystery you know by heart.

—A buzz, a pulse, she nodded. —And then she could be so tender— whenever I would be studying late, she would try to stay awake with me so I wouldn't feel too alone in the middle of the night. Half of the time she was dozing behind a propped-up textbook. But still. And whenever I would come out of the shower she'd be waiting with a towel to wrap me in so I wouldn't catch cold—she knew how easily I catch cold.

I thought of Karsh draping his shirt around me on our walk home that needling night, the way he worried about Julian, said a person with me should want to be nowhere else. And Gwyn's EFCs, her insistence on making my birthdays special, the long-stemmeds she sent me to infuriate Bobby last year.

—I always felt I could tell her anything, said Kavita. —Or say nothing at all.

She made an angel in the rug and then stopped, curling into herself, knees to stomach.

—I miss her, she said.

—Yeah, I said. —I miss her, too.

—And him, she said, staring unerringly into my eyes. But it wasn't really a question.

—And him, I admitted. —Though I never really had him at all.

I was amazed at the parallels between how Kavita felt about Sabina and how I was feeling—not only about Karsh, but about Gwyn as well. I suppose love was love, ultimately, whether it was straight, curving, or crooked. Kavita and I had even more in common than I'd once imagined; in fact when I thought back to those days when I felt otherwise it was as if it was an entirely different person I was talking about. It was as if I'd been a different person, too.

—But have you ever really tried? Dimple, you must be honest with Karsh and with Gwyn, Kavita was saying. —You must take authority for your feelings.

—But I'll look like a fool.

—There is nothing to lose. There is nothing to be ashamed of. This is how you feel, and if you tell it like it is at the very least it is true. And if it changes later? At least it was true once. But now you must express yourself so that everyone is playing with a full deck of cards, heh? And if it does not work out when all is said and done, you must come to terms with the fact that if you cannot have him, you cannot have him. That does not mean you can't be his friend; who can't use an extra one of those from time to time, isn't it?

—Isn't it, I agreed. I certainly didn't want to lose him, either of them, as a friend. They both meant more to me than even I'd realized till talking about it. But somehow I felt better, too, just talking about it. Like asking the question was part of finding the answer.

—And in the meantime and always, she counseled me. —Focus on your strength.

—Which is?

—Taking pictures, yaar! You are very lucky to have a passion like this, and to be so good at it. Now use it. You know what you want to do. Now do it. Acts of love will lead you to more love. Turn your pain and confusion into beauty and power, like I am trying to do with this breakup. I did learn a lot from her.

—You know, it's funny, but Sabina told me almost the same thing once, I said.

—Case in point, said Kavita. Then she turned a sideways face to me, half her grin cut off by carpet.

—You see? she added proudly. —You can even learn something good from a no-good hanky-panky bitcheswallah!

I was laughing, too, then. But I'd never felt more serious.

CHAPTER 39

thus dished zara thrustra

When Kavita hit the books, I hit the streets, gear in hand, on back, and in arms.

I have seen photographs of Paris and the snow-lit steps of Montmartre leading up to the Sacré Coeur. I have seen the craggy belly of El Capitan shuddering feverish light off the dawn of a postcard. I have witnessed perfect summer days without a care in the world. I have viewed lunar eclipses and (through special glasses) solar eclipses and once, even, a fatly lusting moon over the water in Baja so huge it had seemed an abruptly emerging planet that had all the time before been hidden by an accident of astronomical alignment.

But there is nothing like Tribeca light at sundown.

If my bedroom could be lit with this, if offices could order Tribeca bulbs and apartments Tribeca track lights, life would always have a night-before-Christmas feeling, a charged but peaceful expectancy, and for wondrous things at that.

When I left Kavita's the sun was runging down and I followed it only to lose it, then come upon it again on Spring Street, a block from the river. Buildings flushed like blood just before it breaks through skin; the cobblestones distinguished themselves, thinly iced cupcake flowers tinkering together with an almost audible echo. In the near distance the water went steely pink with the great fire nesting over it, the burning ball of flame that always seemed so much nearer when it fell in New York's choppy sky than from the uncharted heights of New Jersey, as if there really wasn't that much distance between us and it, as if there really wasn't that far to fall.

There was nothing much happening on this street, but one pub, the Wife of Bath, was crowded with life, people spilling out with mugs, panning gold from the day; they plonked on the curb, on streetside school chairs with folded-down desks and dilapidated couches. The pub beckoned like the rickety kitchen of a house of a big family, and I gravitated towards it.

And when I got there I did something I had never done in my life. I ordered a ginger ale and sat down by myself on a lovably ornery stool and I didn't pretend to be reading a book or checking my watch for an extraordinarily late person. I was right on time, and I sat back and watched the sun go down. We all seemed on some level to be there for that miracle, and no matter what was going on the moment before—whoever was hitting on or splitting with whom, or quitting their job or getting fired or breaking their lease, seeking asylum, or trying drugs, or coming off them—as that fireball gained speed going down, conversations dulled to a hush, cigarettes stemmed to confounding lengths of ash that mysteriously did not fall, and we were tiny creatures in a great universe and it never felt so good.

To the blues, the violet blues and slowly, quickly: darkness. So many colors only moments from being something else; day and night not two ends of the spectrum but two moments in a life. Nothing was merely black and white—not even a black-and-white photograph. It was all about the in-between, the grading shades. And maybe I'd just been—as everyone was, I was beginning to think—inhabiting not the outside, nor the edge, nor the nowhere, but the in-between in all its vast variety all along. And if a group of strangers could hush to a sunset together, there was a chance we could all meet there.

I stacked my tip into a silver turret and left. Walking, listening to my breath. I could hardly feel my feet below me. Through the desolate parking lot parts of Ninth Avenue, dotted occasionally with delis selling dirt-cheap and beautiful flowers under plastic rainshield awnings, angling out abruptly into the overactivity of Times Square. There: a colossal soda bottle in the sky emptying through a straw, world headlines running an electric current around the periphery of a building, larger than life women in smaller than life underwear spanning the rooftop lengths, carnivalesque.

I followed the tall buildings with illuminated clocks all the way to the park, and studied the huge shadowy sweep of it, vanishing out of my view into a complex darkness. The sight of it made me long for light again—all that unlidded life had been addictive. And I descended onto the train.

An almost pleasurable sense of loneliness drew me from stop to stop. And because I felt like that, it didn't make sense to get out at the HotPot pause and relive any of this anymore. To torture myself watching the two of them come together under the swaggering lights, missing them both right before my eyes; I'd rather miss them from afar. And so I let it come and go and then go. I had to find my own path.

I exited with the next gusting halt of the train. I wasn't sure where I was exactly; I think I'd traveled full circle and then some, but this time everything was different. Coming up from the subway I thought: *This is how vampires are born*. From a swift tunnel of cut blackness and counterfeit light through a yellowy pool of candle wax turnstiled, metal still muggy to the touch from that rush of hungering hands and up the stairs and out the narrow door into that greater darkness but this one enormously ongoing and violently adorned.

Steam fumed rollingly upwards out of manholes in the uneven street, as if genies were trapped just below the surface. Coming out into it all, my heart began to beat wildly; I was sure it would poke a hole through the fabric. It was a city where anything could happen. And a city where maybe nothing would happen at all; a light on in every viewable window, but no one at home.

I had already gone through a serious stash of film; my Kavita supply was happily dwindling. I walked and I clicked and I clacked, feet easy in sneaks. Onto Bleecker. Bedford, Hudson. Morton, Barrow, Weehawkan. West Tenth and its mathematically baffling intersection with West Fourth; Charles and Perry. West Eleventh. Filling the frames with the jumble of signs so I'd know where I'd been: Greenwich Street. Bank, West Twelfth, Jane. Gansevoort. Little West Twelfth.

I was heading farther west with each step, and the area was becoming more desolate, gnarls of cobblestone streets echoing tinnily against the broad expanses of empty warehouses. Even the streetlamps grew few and far between; lighthouselike, I used them to guide my path.

A metallic smell of flesh hit me like a knife slid from sinew as I turned the corner. Coming around the bend I could see sizeable trucks parked by the back of a line of buildings, reflectors flashing and hubcaps, too, unloading their cargo through thrown-open cooler doors. I could hear the blood before I saw it, the way you can hear snow or unspilled tears, and when I looked down, the street was running with it, a nearly black river percolating down from the loading platforms and into the crevices wound round each step-smoothened stone. I caught a small glimpse of their cargo—a pang of matted brawn and bone—and realized where I was: the Meatpacking District. I stared in fascination; I felt I was observing an ancient sacrifice. At first my nostrils sealed against the smell and then, breath by breath, they budded open. And strangely, it didn't kill my appetite, as Sabina had said it would. In fact, it kindled my desire. To take a step towards it and in so doing, understand it. To photograph it. In blocks of light sliced and fallen from the insides of these secret sacrificial kitchens, I loaded Chica Tikka and went to it.

I began to snap the cobblestones, leading away from the trail of blood and around the bend where they resumed their river-bottom pebble-smooth state.

Before me lay another uncluttered stretch of darkness. But in the distance I could see a beacon burning, warm flooded panes. The draw of a well-lit window cannot be underestimated, and I found myself walking mesmerized towards it. The sign upon it grew clearer and gladdened my heart: 24/7 Café Bar Chill Lounge & Home Away From Home. Below that, scrolling in long-tailed curlicue letters across the front window: Boudin Noir, Boudin Blanc.

It seemed a perfect finish: a cup of coffee and a nighttime kitchen. But little did I know the night had only just begun.

I took a seat in one of the deep purple booths, cushioning my things between myself and the wall. The place was packed with folk, even at this hour. Where had they all come from? Or had they simply always been here? Other than the silent shadowy men unloading their sanguineous cargo, there had certainly been no trace of life in the streets radiating from this cozy center. I couldn't tell if these were people who were just ending their evening or beginning their day or taking a break in between.

At the other end of the room was a cluster of rowdy women engaged in tooth-filling-flashing uproarious laughter. They were a mix from pale as light ale to black as blue, and were dressed as if they'd just stepped off the cabaret circuit: ultrashiny minis in all the colors of a peacock's hallucination, sweeping silken peignoirs, Victorian gowns, garter belts in plain view stretching longingly towards zip-down buckle-up snap-snazzy boots. Their faces were dramatically made up, everything lined and filled in and blushed and based. They reminded me of Kathakali dancers, those elaborately painted and posturing men I'd seen perform once in India. And from their exaggerated gestures and husky voices I knew what I would view when I let my gaze drop from face to throat: a bobbing crop of Adam's apples. One of the waiters, a skinny little red-and-purplehead, was leaning in to them, gesturing madly with his right hand, fingers flowing individually as he spoke, and switching his head from side to side to punctuate his story; for all that movement it was noteworthy not a drop seemed to spill from the tray of ice cream sodas in his other hand, the chocolate and vanilla and strawberry scoops snapped bulbous onto the sides of the glasses, just beginning to soften.

It was he who had them in stitches. I didn't know what it was about him, this boy, but from what I could see he was very young and very beautiful. His slight frame swam in overalls and a muscle tank, gold toned arms raying from it, skin aglow as if torchlit from the inside. His deep red-purple hair scuffed out in chunks as if he'd been sleeping on it wrong and his eyes wisped fishily over his audience from under low-lying lids.

A round of applause cluttered the table as he finished his tale. He blew them a kiss, set down the sodas at a tableful of black-clad rockers, and sewed his sinuous way to the window that fed into the kitchen to pick up the next order, an extra-large plate of fries that looked like it had to be mine and a French press of coffee (it had sounded so glam I had to order it); glancing around I saw my own waiter seemed to have disappeared. But I didn't care about the food anymore. There was something about my new waiter that struck me, the way he walked, gracefully navigating the sated space: a dancer's walk. The way he lit up the room, slight as he was. The way I felt that if I cupped my hands, I could hold his energy there and change the picture. It was that tangible. I'd been hanging on to a piece of that magic for a while now, in fact, ever since I'd met him. I couldn't take my eyes off him. But then, I never could.

It was Zara. No costume, no cosmetics—but definitely Zara.

He picked up the order and made his way towards me, and if there had been any doubt, a full-on view of him quashed it. He set the tray on my table and cocked his head down into my smiling face.

—Now that's a nice way to wrap up my shift, he smiled back. —Last order of the day, and a friendly Photo Girl to eat it.

—Hi, Zara, I said, happy he remembered me.

—Hi indeed. How are you?

I must have been looking confusedly at the coffee contraption in front of me. Zara gestured to the knob on top.

—You've got to push it.

I lay my hand down on the lid and weighed down, watching the water filter slowly up, the coffee crushed beneath. I liked the feeling, the resistance in the small container, then the relenting.

—So did your friend woo away her man after all?

—She may be doing it as we speak, I said sadly.

Zara slid into the seat facing me. He looked younger, more vulnerable, but no less magical. Up close I could see freckles dusting the tip of his nose.

I gestured to the coffee before sipping. He shook his head.

—I'm too awake as it is. Now listen. Photo Girl is not sounding like a happy camper.

I sipped, staring into my cup, which gave me the beginning of a headache.

—So you and Karsh, he continued. —Hmm. You two could be a very tasty combination.

—I don't think he finds me so appetizing, I said. The fries were burnt just the way I liked them, a brazenly flamed one crowning the pile. I decided to save it for last.

—How do you know?

—He likes my friend.

—Your friend has balls, pardon my Portuguese. And you should, too. Better to be bright than dim, that's my philosophy. You have to show yourself, speak up for what you want. For example, that fry.

He pointed to the queen cruncher on top of the platter.

—What about it? I don't want it, I said. —Go ahead.

—You do too want it. You were eyeing it just now. But you are being, if I may say so, absurdly polite—instead of simply asking me if I want it and making a go for it. And somewhere inside you will be disappointed if I take it.

I felt a tad blushy.

—Okay, I get your point. You know, I wish I could be more like you.

—Believe it or not, Dimple—and I *would* believe it—I am just a regular person who has decided to be who I am in life. That's all. That's how you make your life magical—you take yourself into your own hands and rub a little. You activate your identity. And that's the only way to make, as they say, the world a better place; after all, what good are you to anyone without yourself?

He was blowing my mind and I was refilling my cup. It spilled over, I'd been so intently watching him.

—You're a genius, I said. —I feel so clueless so much of the time. Did you know I didn't even know you were a drag queen, Zara?

—When you're good, you're good, he grinned.

—It must be exciting being a drag queen, I went on. —You get to, I don't know, change who you are. You know who you want to be, right down to the nail polish. Sometimes I feel like I was just born confused.

—You are born knowing all you need to know, said Zara, pressing his index finger between my brows. —Besides, you seem to me like you're having a pretty good night in spite of it all.

—I am, I admitted. —But sometimes I wish I could become someone else.

—It's not only about that, yaar. It's about becoming yourself. My particular way of doing it is just more noticeable because I have such impeccable style sense.

He smiled.

—The world is my catwalk! he declared. —And New York City is my world!

—So, did you grow up here then, Zara?

I hungered to know everything about him. It was funny, but for someone so superhuman he was really human. There was a raw heart in everything he was saying.

—Of course not! I had to learn a lot about creating my home inside myself. You know, ever since I was very young I knew I was different. But where

I come from that is not welcomed and celebrated, it is feared and despised. I have been threatened, I have been stoned; my family menaced for the simple link of blood to me—as if what I am is some kind of disease, contagious or genetic. I knew that much as I love my country if I didn't leave I would be not only a threat to myself, but to my brothers and sisters and anyone who dared get close to me. So I had to seek political asylum here. It took years. But it was the only way. And when I finally arrived I found so many others like me—I'd never known a kindred drag spirit before. And all this, just to be me.

He contemplated the pepper shaker.

—People have been persecuted throughout history for this, he said. —We Parsis not the least of them, nor, of course, Persian drag queens. And I may not be able to stop history from having happened, but I can at least stop persecuting myself. Stop it in me.

I swallowed hard.

—You were threatened? You were . . . hurt like that?

—Indeed I was. And sometimes most by the ones I've been closest to—even here in New York, even at HotPot, I have met and been with men who've told me in nearly the same breath that they loved me and would kill me if I were to breathe a word to their wives, their friends, their coworkers. Do you know what that feels like? What that does to a person? I hope you never know. I have had men tell me that only *I* can do things to them and they will not touch me, or the other way around, who have divided up our bodies into zones. And I went along with it for years. To please. To enjoy my freedom. But I finally realized, there is no freedom without love. And there is no love with this kind of division and denial.

—How did you realize that? I whispered.

He leaned in so close the tips of our noses were nearly touching.

—When I finally found love, he smiled. —That is why I am so grateful to have met my Bengali blessing, PK.

He looked genuinely moved when he said the two letters.

—He is my SOS, my 911, my 411, my infinity.

—He's pretty cute, too, I grinned.

—Are you joking? he cried, flushing and springing up. —He is an absolute god!

He radiated, a strongly open window; there was a tenacity to his fragility, a commitment to remain porous that was clear to me now. He had never appeared so beautiful. And I was three cups of coffee down and nearly bouncing off the walls with an idea. It was a question I'd normally have been too nervous to ask—to even think—but the fluffy cloud of caffeinated exhaustion I was riding got me checking my inhibitions at the door.

—Zara, I said. —Could I maybe take some pictures of you getting ready? Turning from man to woman? I promise I'll make you copies, and I promise I won't show anyone, and—

—Girlfriend! Horse holding moment, please! he exclaimed, raising his hand. —No promises needed. I am very proud to be who I am—and I worked a long time at it. Show them to the world! I've been hiding long enough.

I was nearly springing off the seat.

—Do you have everything you need right here? I said.

—Of course—you never know when a Photo Girl is going to turn up at BNBB and go paparazzi on you.

Chica Tikka was already out and loaded.

—Can I, can I take a picture of you now, Zara?

—Now? You're joking.

I shook my head.

—All right then, he said. He ran a hand through his hair, which only seemed to scruff it up more. —Go ahead.

I aimed.

—One . . . two . . . *teen!*

And just as I clicked I was surprised, then alarmed, to see a tear well up in the duct of his eye.

—I'm sorry! Zara, did I upset you?

—No, he said, and it fell, splattering on the tabletop. —I just can't believe you want a photograph of me like this—no makeup, no fancy clothes.

—Are you joking? I said. —You're even more beautiful like this.

—This is true, he said, smiling. —But I didn't know anyone else could see that. Great balls of fire, I even forgot to say jalfreezi.

Once Zara had wrapped up business and returned with a couple doggie bags, the two of us headed into the café bathroom. It was surprisingly clean with soft lighting and lots of space to maneuver in. Perfect for my purposes.

He was a professional, this one, and immediately sat on a small stool before the mirror and set to work.

First, a true artist, he lay out his various brushes and mixing palettes, and a medicine cabinet's worth of tiny jars of dun-hued liquids, flasks of shimmer dust, vials of gloss, bindi sheets. Soon enough the bathroom counter had been transformed into the poshest of vanity tables.

He sharpened his pencils. Dabbed a cotton swab in astringent. Cleaned his face. And began.

I took roll upon roll of this beautiful boy turning into that most beautiful woman, moment by moment, step by step. It was a thrill being around such a confident creature, and pure photographic pleasure, too.

And I had a flash as well as Chica Tikka this time. Watching Zara engaged in this quintessential act of desicreation it occurred to me: Those nine lives we'd talked about, Kavita and me, perhaps they were being lived all the time, at the same time. Life viewed from nine different camera angles; life played at nine tempos. Mixed, montaged; multiple. In the course of one lifetime. Maybe that's what reincarnation was all about.

Reinvention.

It was like looking back on my parents' photos now, and finally clicking that those were part of the continuum that included them today. There was no such thing as a fragment, I knew that now; a moment was a chapter of a life. In fact, a person at any given moment was a chapter of their own life, of the lives of everyone they knowingly or unknowingly touched—the way a confluence of two doors opening had sent music flooding from club to street level to the underworld of the subway.

Black was only a few steps from white, negative to photo. A song was only a notch off silence. A black hole was an inside-out star. Suitability—two letters away from unsuitability. End a mere three letters from friend.

And Zara, now red-and-gold saried Zara—filling her part with crimson powder and laying the tikka in it, the piece of bridal jewelry hanging down to where the bindi would be—was ready.

I finished the roll with a picture of the self created creation posing against the sliver of wall that separated the men's room from the women's.

And just as I snapped Zara pulled a hunk of boudin out of one of the paper bags and slid it into her mouth, Adam's apple ripely in view, and winked gemmily big for the camera.

She closed her eyes while she chewed. Then she opened them, slowly, like women in mascara commercials, women who wash the grey right out of their hair and meet their husbands in elevators, in Levi's. Their inky black poured over me. She stretched out her solidly bangled arm, the dupatta skittering down and gathering auroral in the crook, and that hand—that gold-bangled, ringed-and-thinged hand unfurled towards me, revealing patterns of fate and smatterings of henna and then my own nail-bitten fingers inter-linked in hers.

We went outside.

As the weighty door of BNBB closed upon our heels, I was stunned to be met with birdsong and the thinning fleece of daybreak. I hadn't even seen it coming; it had seemed the night would go on forever. But the neighborhood was still enchanting at this hour, a something tangible following you out of your dream into your waking day.

We wandered. And I tracked her with my viewfinder, chimeric in the moorish morning streets leading riverside, dragging her gold light along brick and stone, from her laughing profile down to her jaunty shoes.

And by the time we were upon the river, with its bordering stretch of park grass, the sun was up and it was the beginning of a new day. And the sight of water did something to Zara. Before I knew it, she had kicked off one shoe, and then the other, and was loping waterwards, her dupatta and sari, the long false braid unraveling behind her, trailing off as she ran to reveal the head of cropped hair, the body far less curvaceous than it had appeared in the pinned and tufted layers of fabric.

I was following, photographing her manically as she dissembled into the hazy distance. Then I zoomed in close and closer to where I was till I landed upon the first fallen shoe several feet away, glittering a hidden treasure, a crushed corner of the city in the raveled grass.

—Jalfreezi! she called from the distance.

—Jalfreezi, I waved back, capping my lens and running to catch up with her. We stood and watched as the sun burned the film off the water and the boated day hummed open.

—How can I ever thank you? I said.

—How can *I?* she said. —Do you know Nietzsche's theory of eternal recurrence, Dimple?

I shook my head.

—Well, I hardly understand it myself, to be honest. But I have pulled an easily applicable day-to-day rule from it that always gets me out of a jam: You must live every moment of your life in such a way that if you had to live it over and over again till infinity, this would be a good thing.

I couldn't quite wrap around that yet.

—I know, she empathized. —It's a tall order. But it's not a shabby thing to aspire to. And I just wanted you to know that thanks to you, my night has been just like this.

I was moved.

—Thank you, Zara, I said. —Man, this Nietzsche guy must be a National Merit Scholar to have come up with that.

—Oh, he was just dumped like the rest of us, she shrugged.

—Really?

—His main flame had the hots for a poet friend of his.

Before we parted ways in the commuterized morning, I noted her telephone number, and she handed me the second paper bag. I opened it after she turned the corner.

French fries, on the burnt side, to the top.

CHAPTER 40

the big picture

The magic of the evening did not fade with morning. I'd hardly noticed day go to night and then to day again. Like that Pondicherry dawn, grading into becoming, no beginning and no end.

I couldn't wait to get home and get to work. Kavita was still sleeping when I returned to the apartment, so I left her a note to tell her what a tale I had to tell and put the coffee on the timer so she wouldn't miss her class. Birds gathered at her window grating, chattering boisterously, and there was a chill to the sun—just a touch, but it was enough to remind you the days would start to crouch now, squeeze into smaller spaces.

The entire train ride home I kept my sack full of rolls gathered to my chest like a sleeping child. I didn't even have to close my eyes to see it all before me. It was as if a little bit of Zara had infiltrated me and the world was a more glitter-filled place because of it. If I had to relive last night again till eternity, I was happily surprised to realize, I would do so with pleasure. It was good to feel that way about my life.

At home, it was early enough that I could still hear my father in the shower. He hadn't even had his pre-rounds tea yet; the World's Greatest Dad mug was still by the stove, alongside the silver spoon, cane sugar, and sachet of Earl Grey my mother always left out for him the night before. The sight of this tendered me. I put the water to boil, fixed up two steaming cups, and went out to wait on the back porch steps.

He was stunned to say the least when he saw me through the screen door.

—Good morning, Bapuji, I said, handing him his cup.

—Aaray baapray, beta! he cried. —But—is this possible? Why are you not at Kavita's?

I assured him that all was fine with my cousin-sister and told him I'd just wanted to come home.

—But why are you not asleep at this hour?

—Because, if it makes any sense, I said. —I finally woke up.

He had tears in his eyes when he sat beside me on the red-painted porch step. I could see now why this was such a precious moment to him. The birds had just begun their day; the ground sparkled dropped diamonds and an expectant hush hung over everything, like a bridal dress rustling on a rack. Mist cloaked the trees, made them seem farther away; it accentuated the sun's rays, turning them into shining playground slides from heaven.

He clinked my cup before sipping.

—Well, to waking up then, he said.

I drank to that.

Once my father had pulled out of the drive I beelined for the basement, slipped on my magician gloves, and set to work. While the film dried on the line I joined my sleepily surprised mother upstairs for a second cup of tea, this time steeping the sachet in hot chocolate, a favorite variation for her.

—Are you on the IST? she asked me. She'd clearly been talking to Kavita, with this new lingo.

—Ma, Indian Standard Time means late, I said.

—Not in America! she said. —You are ten hours ahead of usual.

—I guess I'm not in the L.A. anymore, I smiled.

When I returned to the darkening room, the first glimpse of the first negative strip through the enlarger took my breath away. I dialed in the filters. Safelight on, then my first test strip; the wait was agonizingly delicious, counting out the five-second increments, like a countup to a new year.

I was pleased by how comfortable I felt with it all. Just a few weeks ago—which seemed much further away, considering what this summer had shaped up to be—it had been another story.

I shook the stop bath, thirty Mississippis to the percussive beat of the stopwatch. Karsh had been right—it *was* all about the timing, but in the end it was all about having it so down you could lose your sense of time. The way wondrous dancers make tough moves look easy. Being so prepared for beauty that beauty comes naturally—I suppose you could call that a state of grace.

It was indeed all about the chemistry as well—and I went to town with it: balancing, imbalancing, the red bias, the green. Adding magenta, removing yellow, adding yellow and magenta, removing yellow and magenta, like the bass, the treble, the strands of different songs coming and going in fused sound.

Lights strobed from safe to full-on, depending on whether I was loading or unloading. Dodging and burning, my hands spinning like Karsh's over his magical records, I realized: It was a dance of sorts, my own little subterranean disco. I stood with the final sheet and cupped my palms to shift the exposed area for this last shot—an old-sole fabulist shoe, grassed in a toss, a slowly dismantling figure ghosting away in the distance. I hung it up to dry on the line and surveyed my work.

Today, in my little darkening room, it was amazing to see all these color prints where once had only been black and white; one by one they'd slipped in, nearly replaced them. Not that I disliked black and white, but now, oddly enough, I was learning from color how to stop seeing black and white in, well, black and white, how to begin seeing all the nuances of shadow and light.

A tear tracking down a face shot so close the pores breathed through. A hot dog o' boudin riding into a mouth glisteningly crimson as inner fruit, Adam's apple bulging and jeweled wink.

They looked like what it had felt like, all of them. Which, considering it had been the evening of a day I'd redo till eternity, was a pretty good thing. Larger than life prints (I'd used a bigger processing dish) for larger than life subjects. All the stages of the city's slide into night and then day, and Zara's own seamless transformation. The making of a woman; the creating of a person. And, I dared imagine now, the making of a photographer.

I realized now how much these images summed up so much of the summer to me. The sadness and beauty of this metropolis of lost and found souls. The making and breaking of identity—what was in your hands and what was not. A stranger becoming familiar despite her strangeness, because of it, over a hot cup of coffee and a night touched by the season's first chill. Lips flowering to a flame. Wings sprouting from a sewer; starbursts from skidmarks—

the way there was no such thing as a false star: You could wish on anything as long as you meant it.

There would be rain and there would be sun, I knew now, and the big picture was much bigger than all that: It was the minutest detail—a callus on a foot in a stylish shoe, a tear in the duct of a smiling eye. And then it clicked. Better late than never: I knew now what to give Karsh for his birthday. These photos were the closest to my soul, were the first tangible way I was beginning to understand this summer, and, through this summer, life. In a way, they'd been a way for me to understand him, allowing me my own form of DJing. Maybe I couldn't have him the way I'd hoped, but sun and rain, I could share with him what I was proudest of; these images were perhaps the best way for me to explain myself to him, better than all my fumbling words and awkward silences and moody moments, at least. I would leave them in a book on his doorstep, with the one of Gwyn he'd asked for, so long ago it seemed.

For whatever it was worth. Just to express myself, as Kavita said. To take authority for my vision.

To take a chance.

zoom

The day I got my bona fide certified driver's license my parents nervously rewarded me with a day of unlimited access to the car. My instinct, of course, was to immediately swing by Gwyn's and pick her up for a crazy day out. But then I remembered I couldn't. It would have all been so much sweeter if I could have shared this with her, or the Zara adventure. But perhaps that adventure was one that needed to be undertaken alone.

I hadn't seen her for a long time, Gwyn. Miles had sprung up overnight between my house and hers, a distance that had seemed a mere half-step before. I hadn't even rounded her dead-end circle since our whole falling out. It hurt too much, and I didn't know what I would say if she caught me just hanging around like that. I doubted she was home much at all these days, anyways. As the Disorientation party drew closer, I imagined she and Karsh were drawing closer, too, for more than organizational reasons.

Still, it was hard, knowing that we were to stay away from each other. We still knew so much about each other: I could picture what she would be wearing on a day like this, where it might rain or not (hair in braids to beat frizz, vinyl tee, waterproof pleather pants, no bottom-lash eye makeup). I knew how she would eat an Oreo, were she to eat an Oreo (the entire thing in a go), how she would stop to scratch behind the ears of a golden retriever were she to see a golden retriever (in the middle of oncoming traffic if necessary), the way she would turn a snort to a sneeze if she lost control at a really funny joke in public. The way her mouth would look like her eyes were crying if she heard a sad story. Her dentist appointments, mother/daughter non-appointments, and entire personal calendar took up hard drive space in my head perhaps as much as in her own.

I drove along, very slowly as the sky grew fumy around me. I'd decided to go downtown to take some more photographs. I'd considered Manhattan but today I was afraid of the city again. Afraid of how alone in it you could be—how obscure, indistinct, lost, even in the midst of all the usual shiny speedy plethora of Things. How alone I would feel knowing Gwyn was somewhere in it today. The day, as my hard drive reminded me, of her modeling debut: the *Flash!* shoot.

I parked and got out, walking around as if in a dream, as if behind a curtain in my own hometown. I zoomed in and out, but for the most part just held Chica Tikka close and went on. Before I knew what I was doing, I found myself in the plaza, the farmers still holding their hazy summer market, just across the street from Gwyn's Starbucks.

Well, not just across the street. It only looked that way as I spied on the world through Chica Tikka's zoom, but in reality I was quite a ways back, just one in this smoggy crowd of cheese-shoppers and bread bakers, the tart queens and the flower kings.

My eyes ached with knowing she wasn't there. But I suppose that was why I'd felt safe enough to come myself. I could picture her uptown ethereal, posing wraithlike in Central Park as mist rambled over the rocks jagging into the water, phantom swans in the foreground, and I crossed all my fingers and then even my thumbs that it would all work out for her.

But then I didn't need to picture her at all. Because she'd just come out of the Starbucks and slumped down on the paint-chipped bench, on the end away from the panhandler there on the sidewalk.

My heart lifted, struggled at the sight of her. I lowered Chica Tikka and began to duck behind a stall, but then realized I was too far for her to see me, and even if I were closer, it would be tough on a day as veiled as this. Maybe she had already finished the shoot? No—doubtful she would have even accepted a shift with something like that going on. Doubtful she would be wearing her green fog-cutting smock if she had any modeling to do. I wondered what had happened.

I zoomed in closer. She was sitting cushioned between her knapsack and the little lunchbox purse, a coffee clutched between two hands, holding on to it, not drinking, as if to ward off a wintry chill. And she looked different.

Her unbraided hair spiraled ravingly out, all the gold parts gone in the gauzy day. The smock covered most of her clothing, but I could see there was no vinyl or pleather involved underneath; looked more like jeans and a T-shirt that claimed to love nowhere. Makeup: minimal, and her face was a child-face—one that looked like it hadn't tasted an Oreo or heard a really good joke in a long time. The eye-crying mouth looking more like she'd just heard a really sad story.

It was the face of a little girl in a banistered cage. And I wondered how we'd put up this barrier, bar by bar, boy by boy, between us.

Gwyn stood now, slinging on her backpack. I was watching her and she was swimming in my eyes, rippling like a reflection and receding. She seemed to notice her unseen companion patchworking out from under the bench just then, and leaned down and placed the unsipped sippy-cup-lidded cup just by the panhandler's hands.

I brought my camera to my belly to get myself together. But I could still see her on the insides of my eyelids, and I suddenly felt like touching her face, telling her it would be all right. It occurred to me that maybe Gwyn didn't have it so easy. That maybe she was just as confused as everyone else. And it occurred to me a moment later that maybe I was being selfish by not reaching out to her, by not letting her know I'd be there for her, no matter what mess we might be in. I'd been so worried about Karsh could be I'd been giving her the cold shoulder when what she needed most was a set of open arms.

When I opened my eyes to take my first step towards her, she was gone. An uncertain ghost. As if she'd never been there.

★　★　★

The sky had cleared by the time I got home, and my father greeted me at the door with giggling eyes.

—Somebody stopped by to see you, he said, handing me an opaque plastic box. —To return your mother's Tupperware! What a good boy he is.

—That hardly qualifies as coming by to see me, I said.

I took the still rain-damp box in my hands, wondering why my father looked so delighted. And then I realized: It wasn't empty. I could hear a shuddery shivery sound inside, like sand or sugar or maracas, and I peeled off the lid. Inside, a piece of paper lay folded on a bed of what looked like innumerable matte pink and glossy white beads.

I ran a finger through the tinily pinging pieces. But upon a closer look, they weren't beads at all. I brought a fingerful to my lips to test my theory and crunched, the sugar crystals melting away on my tongue. The sweet part of the mukhvas.

I unfolded the paper.

Rani. I don't know how to thank you. That was the most marvelous gift I have ever received.

He had liked the photos. Clearly, a lot. When I examined my gut, I realized questions knotted my belly more than answers. Could it be that—? But he couldn't. (Could he?)

I could feel my father's breath in my ear as he read over my shoulder.

—What a grateful letter! he beamed. —Imagine if we had given him stainless steel!

CHAPTER 42

shutter

I was utterly confused. I wondered if there was still time to slip onto that bench beside the lost-looking Gwyn. And I knew one thing: that that was what I needed to do first and foremost—be beside Gwyn. So now, one day down to Flashball, and I'd e-mailed and texted and even snail-mailed her a note calling for a 2 Mega Ultra Chica Historical summit. She'd said not to talk to her—but this wasn't technically *talking*, right? I had no idea whether she would show, but I was pretty sure she came home these days (eventually); after all, Karsh was a Jersey boy, too.

A 2MUCH was the most urgent of calls to meet. The last time we'd had one of those was when I'd gotten my period for the first time in sixth grade. These meetings were held in one place only, the ovary office of our little girl government: the playhouse. So that night I tied a sweatshirt around my waist in case I was in for a long wait and headed over, crunching through the dried twigs and acorn shells to our home of old.

I pushed the slatted door and entered, must clogging my throat and spiderwebs trapping me in their invisible netting. Motes quivered in lazy suspense in the shafts of setting sun. Mary, Joseph, angel and wise men, and of course baby Jesus crammed together into corners, lay toppled on their sides, all coated the same grey shade now. They were much smaller than I'd remembered; I would never have imagined then that they'd all fit in here.

But then, the playhouse was much smaller than I'd remembered, too. I suppose from the outside it had always seemed about the same, but in our spriggiest youth the inside stretched its ceilings Taj Mahal high when we played princesses, the floor sprang sweet-smelling miles of meadows for us to cowgirl-and-Indian in, and the world outside our windows rocked rowdy waves and we were pirates on a horizonless sea. Now the four walls seemed nearly to cave in on one another, and I had to duck my head to avoid sweeping against the crumbling ceiling.

In the once-far now-near corner was a tiny dining room set, which I remembered with a pang. One chair was shaped like the Calico Cat and the other like a haberdasher dog and the table had once been decorated with a nursery rhyme in bright shades of red and blue. A pile of seashells was strewn across the fading paint, and a toy teapot and saucers lay there, the thin-handled cups appearing even more delicate in the grit. The table was still set for two.

I couldn't remember the last time we'd been here. I couldn't remember what we'd been playing.

You certainly couldn't step in the same river twice. My mother was right as usual, her adages seeming more perspicacious as time went on. I wondered now whether it had been foolish of me to imagine that Gwyn would ever come back here to meet me. Perhaps she wouldn't even remember the code, 2MUCH, what my message had meant; could be I was already so far expelled from her head that even memory couldn't draw me back in, playing a momentary magnet.

I was sitting on the Calico Cat, my knees nearly up to chin level on either side of it and my bottom sliding off the scant seat when I saw a movement outside. Through the cleared bit of pane: a pair of blue eyes, woesy as Mary's, staring back at me.

She'd come.

I leapt up, banging my head on the ceiling in the process, to unhook the door and let her in (an old habit, locking it behind me).

She stood on the outside a moment, the door frame cutting her forehead from view, and I wondered whether she might just stay there.

—Hi, I said.

And then the golden roots ducked down and in she came.

Neither of us said anything, and tension crackled electric in the wooded space.

—It, it feels strange in here, doesn't it? I said, gesturing around a little helplessly. —Like it's all too small, like we don't fit anymore.

—Frankly, Dimple, I think it would feel like that just about anywhere with you right now, she said.

That stung.

She was trying to maintain her space, arms crossed on her chest, but it was a tough thing to do in here: There was no room to keep any kind of physical distance and so we both sort of automatically ended up sitting at the table.

—So what do you want, Dimple? Why did you call me here? I don't have all day.

We used to have all the time in the world, I thought, watching her work her fingernail into the ridges of a particularly big pink seashell. But she didn't look like she was going anywhere soon: She was in sweatpants and a T-shirt, her hair swooped up in a ponytail. She had no makeup on.

I figured I'd break the ice by telling her how I'd spotted her the other day, by letting her know how much I'd longed to speak to her even then.

—Well, I just thought you should know. Remember that, um, day of your shoot?

She nodded.

—Well, I saw you. Outside the café.

—And your point is?

—You. You looked. I don't know. Like a little girl. And I just really wanted to run over and—

—Dimple, if you've come here to humiliate me, you can save your breath, she said icily. I was stunned.

—Humiliate you? What are you talking about?

—You know what I'm talking about. I can just hear you thinking it: Oh, there's that airhead, Gwyn Sexton, who actually thought she was being asked to model, and—surprise!—was only being asked to lug around equipment. I admit it. I got it all wrong.

—That's not at all what I meant, I said. So that's why she'd been in town that day.

She picked up the pink-striped seashell then set it down again.

—Well? So? What . . . What are you leading up to—Serge's asking me to assist? Are you going to be jealous of that, too?

—What do you mean? I said, fumbling. I hadn't expected this to get confrontational so quickly, but I figured I might as well step up now that it was. I took a breath. —I'm not jealous, Gwyn. Okay, I have been jealous, but not about that—not about Serge, or any old magazine thing.

I exhaled.

—So . . . how's Karsh? I asked.

—Why don't *you* tell *me*?

—What do you mean?

—Don't play dumb with me, Dimple, she said. —He hasn't said anything to you?

—Well, no, I said. —He did give me a . . . well, a sort of present. Mukhvas. A sort of candy that made me . . . wonder.

—Wonder, she said. —Well, I'm wondering about something, too. Wondering why you couldn't just back off. Why you couldn't just—stay with Julian, stay out of my way.

—That's why you wanted me with Julian?

—Well, that wasn't the original plan, obviously. I was with someone, so I wanted you to be with someone, too. And Julian was the next best thing to Dylan.

—But even if your own boyfriend was running around on you like that, you wanted me to be with his closest clone?

—Yeah, I guess I did, she shrugged, looking down. —Maybe I felt it couldn't be so bad if you were doing it, too. You, the one who never makes mistakes.

She suddenly seemed irritated. And I couldn't figure out why, since she was basically admitting she'd wanted to bring me down with her. But I suppose, then, she'd also always wanted to bring me up when she was going up, too, and I held my tongue.

—Besides, what are you complaining about? she said now. —You told me yourself how upset you were after the whole double date fiasco, how disappointed that you'd lost him.

This was true. But not the whole truth.

—I don't know if I was ever into Julian so much as the idea of Julian, you know? I said. —And after I found out my parents had set up this suitable boy thing I wanted to do something to rebel, to make it clear to them and to Karsh that I wasn't interested and would never be interested in him.

—And are you never interested in him now? she asked, staring down at the shell again.

—No, I said looking down, too. —I suppose I was falling for him all along.

—Well, then. Why didn't you ever tell me how you were feeling about him? Letting me go on and on like such a fool, even buying that second turntable. What am I going to do with that turntable?

—Gwyn, it was all happening in such a strange way, I said finally. —It was almost like I didn't even realize it—because he didn't match up to anything I'd ever dreamed of, because I was trying so hard to go against my parents, to be what I thought was cool. To fit in with you. I didn't see he was getting under my skin until it was too late. Until the two of you were already falling for each other.

—We weren't falling for each other, sighed Gwyn.

—What do you mean? Of course you were—I saw it right in front of my eyes.

—Well, yes, of course I liked Karsh. But he never *liked* me liked me. He thinks of me as a sister—he finally said it himself. Not only that, but he even told me I should be myself more—like *you* are—because what I am is just fine.

She softened a moment, visibly.

—And the thing is, the way he didn't like me was still so much better, kinder, more loving than the ways all these other guys have—even my own father. I couldn't so easily give it up.

She pulled her hands off the table and into her lap, and her face shuttered down.

I was speechless. After spending all this time convinced the two of them had been getting it on I still found it hard to believe, even with the mukhvas and everything. And the idea that Karsh thought I was a self-actualized person was the biggest whammy of all, as I'd all along been of the humble opinion that I hadn't figured out in the slightest how to be me.

—Anyways, it's ruined for everyone now, she said. —Now he's all worried he has to back off because he's wrecked our friendship. But I think we did that ourselves if you ask me.

—We did? I said softly, hoping I had misheard what I knew I had not.

—Of course we did. You were dishonest with me, Dimple. Much as you said you thought of him as a brother, that you weren't into him and all, I could see what was going on. I mean, I'm blonde but I'm not blind. I could see how he would look at you. The way the two of you would use this, this vocabulary I could never be a part of, like the one you have with Kavita. And I tried so hard to be what he wanted—to be a suitable girl. To be you.

To be me?

—Why didn't you just come out and tell me what was going on, Gwyn? I finally managed.

—And play the fool twice? No thank you.

—Not even just about that, not just about Karsh, I said. —But there were so many things you never told me. Like about your father, about Dylan.

—These things are hard to talk about.

—But you managed to talk about them to Karsh and to Kavita. Even to Sabina.

She paused a moment, turning to the window. The light angled in steeper.

—Well, sometimes it's easier to tell a stranger, she said then. —Like at confession. And with Karsh, well, it seemed he could relate with his dad being gone and all. But I don't know how you could ever relate—I mean, your life's so perfect.

—You keep saying that, I said. —You make me feel like I have to apologize for that, and how can I? Just because my family's intact doesn't mean I don't feel for you when you tell me what's troubling you, even if I don't understand firsthand. It doesn't mean I don't have any feelings; it doesn't make me impervious.

—And just because mine *isn't* intact doesn't mean I am, she replied. —I'm not some independent powerhouse, Dimple. I mean, I have to be for a lot of people. But I need to feel I can lean on someone sometimes, and I always counted on you for that. Like you could count on me. At least, I used to.

—It didn't seem like that lately, I said. —For my clothes or my mom's recipes, yeah. To borrow my cousin, to get a mehendi. But it's not even really about that, Gwyn. I mean, you always just come and go. It's like you get so wrapped up in your romances, but as soon as the boy's out of the picture you're back in my life, wanting to sleep over, to be supertwins. How do you think that makes me feel?

—But that's what friends are for, right? To be there for each other no matter what.

—But you were always getting beeped and celled. You were always too busy for me. If I'm so important to you, how come you let a boy get in the way?

—And if I'm so important to you, how come you let that matter enough to get in the way?

That had me thinking, but to be honest I wasn't really sure who was right, where the truth lay.

—Well, getting in the way or not, I think you understand why I was always doing the family thing, I said. —I don't know why you're always so condescending about it. Maybe it's not as glamorous as having a boyfriend with an apartment in the Village, but that's part of my life.

—Condescending? said Gwyn, seeming genuinely stunned. —I never meant to be condescending. I just wanted to be included. Or, if I couldn't be, to have you with me.

Now I was stunned.

—To be included?

—Dimple, *you* are my family, she said softly. —You know, you're not just an accessory. You're the something I rely on to keep a little sanity in my world. You're the only history I'm not ashamed of, the only thing that makes me feel the future might be bright. And if I think you're going to be disappointed in me for doing the things I do, or turning out the way I have, then . . . Well, then I'm lost.

—I'm hardly ashamed of you, I cried. I couldn't believe it. —In fact, the opposite! I had no idea I was making you feel—

—Believe it or not, Dimple, but your opinion really matters to me. And it put me in a bad spot from a ways back—to know how you were judging me for sleeping with Dylan, or maybe not even figuring it out, I had to stop telling you things. I was . . . embarrassed. I mean, you treat me like this invincible love goddess and he was humiliating me, and what was even worse was I couldn't stop letting him. I so needed to talk to you—but how could I? When I think of how much I want you to approve. And I was scared you would just write me off for being fool enough to keep going back to him—I mean, you've already said a million times how I deserve so much better and all. I was afraid of your—your unspoken sentence.

This was news to me: that even in my passivity I was being judgmental; without realizing it I was playing more of a role in our falling-out than I'd ever imagined. I'd always thought I was just a wallflower, a camera-carrying observer. I'd always thought I was the victim—but maybe I'd created that stance myself.

I wanted to touch her but, despite all the words that were being spoken, she still seemed miles away.

—Gwyn, I said. —I never realized. I guess I was too busy worrying that I wasn't cool enough to be hanging around with you.

—And me, I felt like I always had to play cool with you. When what I wanted most was to be the real thing. Like you.

—You are the real thing, I said. —You don't have to keep trying on other people's identities—frock, see for yourself, we hardly know which way's up, half the time. Just be yourself.

—So it's that easy?

—No, actually, I suppose it's not.

I looked at the tabletop set for two, the fading poetry around the rim. How simple it had been to be princesses and pirates when we were little. How it had never seemed like we were not being us, but more like we were slipping on exciting extensions of ourselves. Why was it so complicated now, all the things we did so easily when we were children? I saw Gwyn was looking, too, rubbing a verse clear with her forefinger.

—What do you suppose we were playing at? she said quietly.

—I have no idea, I said. —But it looks like it must have been fun.

I ran my thumb along the teacup handle.

—God, Gwyn, remember when we used to come here? Before we kissed boys, before we even thought about them. Part of me wishes we'd just stayed here, the two of us, and kept right on drinking our sugar water. Safe and sound behind our password—what was it again?

She just shook her head. And there was a finality to it.

—Why can't it be like before? I whispered. The teacups were full of dust now, I saw.

—I don't know, she said finally. —I have to think about it, Dimple. It's not so easy. Too much has happened; I don't know if we can ever really trust each other again.

—Nothing has happened with Karsh, if that's what you mean, I said. —If you want me to stay away from him, I . . . I will.

I was praying she would say no, though. And she did shake her head, but before my sigh of relief was fully out, she made me choke on it.

—But I just need some space. I need to be alone for a while. And time. I need time.

—Space? Time? So, aren't you going to the club tomorrow night?

—I . . . I'm not sure, Dimple. I think maybe I'd like you both to stay away from me for a while.

She was standing now, her head crooked against the ceiling.

—Oh, no! I cried. —I can't stay away from you. A world without you would be—

How could I put it, the way these last few weeks had been? No matter what the positive moments, they were only a fraction of what they could have been had I been able to share them in some way with my best friend. And the negative moments were accentuated even more by the gaping hole her absence had left in my life. Gwynless. I had been there before, briefly, as a child, and it was an awful place to be. It was like sunless.

—*Please*, she said. And I knew she meant it.

And then I knew, too, what the password had to be now, though whether it would make a door swing open was doubtful on a day such as this.

—I'm sorry, Gwyn, I said. —I'm really, really sorry.

She looked at me now, from the other side of the doorway. Sans any high-maintenance getup and not a trace of makeup on her, she was softer, more beautiful than ever, as if I were watching her through a lens with a bit of stocking pulled over it. The blues of her eyes smudged bluer, the shape of her upper lip seraphic as it began to bud forward over the bottom one. Vulnerable. In the end, I suppose she'd just been looking for love like everyone else. And I hadn't given it to her, not the way she needed it. Now I thought of the glitter, the bindi, the sipping through the teeth. The sunglasses always within reach. And it struck me: Maybe she was just afraid of being ordinary if she showed herself. Like I had been. Of not being that something special. Even though she was.

Her face was naked and when she spoke her words were, too, and I knew they came straight from her hurt heart.

—I'm sorry, too, she said.

On the outside it sounded like the beginning of a reconciliation. But on the inside it felt more like something truly precious was ending.

the disorientation of dimple rohitbhai lala the first

The night of Flashball I actually felt like I fit in my clothing for the first time. Not because I had lost weight or anything. Simply, I suppose, because I *was* wearing my own clothes, of my choice. I'd bought a new pair of jeans and they were the closest thing I could get to vintage without actually waiting a few years and going through a few tussles to rip 'em up myself. These were faded blue bell-bottoms with velvet roses embroidered all along the edges; it was the first time in a long time I'd found a pair of pants that fit so perfectly. On top I was in a black tank, the dupatta from my birthday outfit wrapped around my shoulders. Down below: red and neon orange trainers (mine) on my doubly ankletted feet (however mismatched; I'd double-wrapped a necklace around one).

But on the inside I was a hotpot, a melting pot, of emotions. Still, these emotions seemed to go together, despite how wildly varied they were. The sad part of the hotpot was, of course, all about Gwyn; I still wasn't sure whether she would make it tonight. But my fingers were crossed that maybe she'd have a change of heart, and it was my hope for this, as well as my hope that a certain other someone's heart had *not* changed that had brought about my decision, ultimately, to go. I couldn't just sit and watch this one out.

And my heart. Beating. Trying to beat-match. It was a lone tabla, longing for its other half. Karsh was already at the club setting up, as Radha had informed me. So I hadn't seen him. At all, in fact, since the delivery of the tempestuous tape. And I was nervous. Make that a very. Would he be angry at me for my distance? What if he had changed his mind? What if he'd never made up his mind, and Gwyn had misunderstood the whole thing? What if he didn't, couldn't, wouldn't be with me?

What if he wasn't angry. Hadn't changed his mind. Had made it up.

Did. Could. Would.

This was the moment, tonight. It could go either way. It could go no way at all. But no matter what happened, it had come a long way already from June, from July, from much of August, even. From that first turned-around birthday.

It was hard to imagine that had been him, that khakied pleated piano-benched foyer-photo boy in our living room that day. Startling to imagine that had been me. Returning to that afternoon now in my mind, with this accumulated level of emotion and information, everything seemed different. It made me wonder if all the signs had been there even then, but I had been so out of touch, so turned against myself I'd missed them. Or if it had transmuted into this awe-inspiring affair of the heart in retrospect—when it became part of a context, a story: communicable.

I was moments away from seeing Karsh. I placed his sneakers now, tenderly, as if they were a living thing, into my bag, zipping them into safety.

When I came out of my room, my mother and Radha were in the living room, primping then preening like flared peacocks. The two were dressed in matching maharajah robes they'd bought on a shopping excursion together, my mother in forest green and Radha in burgundy. They were giggling like girls as they styled each other's hair; the semipermanent was entirely out of my mother's by now, and she'd returned gracefully strand by strand to silver-lined blackness. My father, of course, was in his suitable-boy-meeting outfit. They were to be joining us for the first part of the evening—to my initial horror Karsh had insisted for some reason, at least according to Radha, who seemed to be operating as our go-between lately—then they were going to head out for dinner just the three of them. I'd probably be holding off on the punch till that exit!

—Don't worry, you will not even know we are there, my mother had assured me.

But I could hardly imagine that would be the case: Already the two emperial ones were engaged in some kind of moonwalking Macarena dance sequence, all the while shrugging with bhangric fervor.

—Bollocks, yaar, let's get some Gujju moves in there as well, cried Radha, as if over very loud music, one hand then the other going to her hips in time with my mother. —Got any Garbha up your sleeve, Rohitbhai?

My father shyly joined in and then very unshyly demonstrated a harvest-happy upsweep and toe-touch.

—Come and join us, beta, my mother shrugged at me. She missed not a single unheard beat as she spoke. —We are just warming up our moves.

I stepped in. I was feeling more together than usual, but still, the idea of my parents . . . dancing in public?

After a couple minutes of all of us hopping in sync (and me secretly enjoying it), Radha suddenly finger-whistled.

—Bus bus, yaar, I think we've got it. Now to the car, we don't want to be late.

But my mother still had one thing she wanted to do.

—You all go on out, she commanded, herding them towards the front door. —We will be right with you.

Once Radha and my father were safely shoed in the drive, my mom drew me to the Krishna temple in the kitchen, where a low flame was burning off one of those waxy rounds that float through punchbowls at holiday parties. The temple with its Sai Baba pendant and lottery ticket and jar of hand-sewn silk roses, a gift from Hush-Hush Aunty. The incense holder, and of course, the magnificent ivory-encrusted Krishna. And in the corner the tiny silver pot of tikka that my mother's own mother had pressed between her brows the day she left for America, so many years ago.

My mother opened it now and before I knew what she was doing dabbed a bit between my brows; the pulverized dust crimson clouded my eyes a moment and was gone, and she was before me with an expression of such tenderness I felt my bones go loose.

—I thought you were saving it, Mom, I whispered.

—There is no point in saving things, said my mother. —I realize that now.

—But I'm not leaving for another country or anything.

—You are beginning a journey, she said, blowing out the candle now and picking up her purse.

The moment we crossed the bridge I felt the pulse. And when we pulled up to the club and parked in the already dimming day, a simmering sense of anticipation filled me. The night was ours. I could feel it, rearing up in my hand, a bucking diamond. It was one of those moments of pure possibility, like when you wake from a nap and the sun is still shining, or you find it snowed all night and no one in the wee-hours world has realized it yet but you. But here, now, the night was young and so was I and I had a dazzling flash where I felt it: My whole life lay ahead of me, and it was all going to take place tonight.

It was HotPot all right, but that was about all there was in common with my last and first time there. Take entering, for example: no ID required tonight—which was fortunate, considering I'd tossed the legal-age illegal one in Mirror Lake.

As we walked inside, Radha leaned over and brushed my hair out of my eyes.

—You shouldn't hide your face, she whispered. —You'll want the best view possible.

Shailly was already doing her thing, as I could tell from the lazy taffy-machine beats being swung-flung round the space. My heart in my throat I immediately began to scan the room for Gwyn and Karsh. I didn't see them anywhere. At a first glance, it felt the room was all Indian, and I wondered at this, as the point had been to mix it up to draw in a wider audience for Karsh. And then I realized it was a handful of non-Indians in saris, swirling their little pink umbrellas, who'd given me that impression. When I glimpsed the trenchman among them, I figured they must be *Flash!* folk. It was confirmed when I recognized a red-headed woman whose picture was on the preview editor's letter on the website (yes, I'd sneaked a peek): Elizabeth "Zeb" Lupine.

Clusters of these draped damsels, and dudes, too, moved along the walls, where I could sideways see stretchy images winking on the brick, probably from the *Flash!* shoots, considering how rapt Zeb in particular appeared: She was pointing out something to an epiphany-eyed guy whose picture I'd definitely seen in *Time Out* or somewhere. She was aiming to be as graceful as possible but was having a little difficulty, as the crisscrossed part of the sari kept shushing down her chest to reveal her tightly bodiced lean mean upper body whenever she waved her spackling cigarette.

Serge Larmonsky caught sight of me and peace-upped me, heading over.

—You're the famous Dimple Lala, correct? he said, while my father nodded proudly, as if *he* were the famous Dimple Lala, and Radha and my mother nudged each other as if I were their combined spawn. —Yeah, I remember seeing you with DJ GJ and Gwyndolyne Baxter Sexton at the desecration gig. You should be very proud—you gotta hear how the Zebster is talking about it. Congrats.

For what? For being seen with DJ GJ and golden Gwyn? I couldn't believe Serge Larmonsky even remembered me. But he was bar-bound before I could say a word.

—Shall we see what this tamasha is all about? my mother suggested, gesturing towards Zeb and company.

—They're shots from the magazine, I explained.

—Not the shots, my mom sighed. —The saris. That one on the titian mission girl is looking particularly nice. Edison?

—Most likely, yaar, nodded Radha.

My parents plunged excitedly over to the buzzing bunch.

—Don't you want to go over and take a look? asked Radha.

I wanted to look for Gwyn first.

—No thanks, I said. —Maybe later.

—Suit yourself . . . but I think you might really enjoy seeing them again.

—Again? *Flash!* isn't on stands yet—I haven't seen any of it.

What was up with her?

—Baapray, Dimple—this magazine is showing a very high quality! my father exclaimed, now conjuring himself up at my side again. —The pictures are fantastical!

—Yeah? I said, surprised. —What did you see?

—All the ones of this hijra, said my mother breathlessly. —I had no idea it was a model. I saw it talking to some people in that corner . . . see . . . over there . . . ?

I couldn't see. Because I was flipping: Someone had already had that idea?

—Now these are the kinds of photographs you should be making one day!

—Those *are* the kinds of photographs she's making, smiled Radha proudly. —They're hers.

We all turned quizzically to her.

—Well, technically speaking, they're *Karsh's* now, but being the generous soul he is, he lent them to the magazine to make repros.

—What are you saying? my father queried.

—The photos. They're all Dimple's. She took them.

She gestured towards the brick.

—All of them!

—*What?* I cried.

—You heard me, yaar, said Radha, grin breaking loose now.

—He did what? I said, flabbergasted. —But how did they decide to—? Why did they—?

—Because your pictures are, as you say, frocking good.

I couldn't believe it. And I couldn't wait! I vaulted into the room to take a look, the Marriage Mafia tagging alongside me.

Except for the space directly behind the stage, where video clips were blinking by like eyes in too much sun, on this side of the club the exposed brick glowed from mortared edge to edge with great glossy images of . . . my own photographs! *Enormous* professionally framed images of *my own* photos.

The supporting wall was so stark these splashes of intense color were like desert water—and a color-therapy bubble bath at that. It was like entering some sort of multimedia installation of my life. And I couldn't believe how enchanting it looked from here: Viewing the images one after another like this, I could see they told a story—where I had once thought was none had been one far more bewitchingly beautiful than I could have ever imagined. And watching people oohing and ahhing over the Zara shots—including, I confirmed now, Zara herself, thronged by admirers (the most truly, of course, PK)—it was as if people were standing inside my head, oohing and ahhing the view from the inside of my eyes, out. As if it was a view, however new to them, they understood.

Clearly, irrefutably, and no less than magically I could now see my life outside myself. And even more magically I could now see my heart in all its motley, melodious complexity, as if it were up on the wall itself.

It was impossible to imagine a time that I had not loved Karsh with every *Dhage na Dhin, Dhage na Dha* of my drumming heart. And the more I simply beheld the thought of him, the more my nerves calmed. The less I doubted, undid, tried to close and control the world in my hand, skin stretching too tight, the more I felt the knots loosen, the drum give, the music play.

I was already walking, running his way.

The club looked the same but different. It was awash in pink light, with a bit of a boudoir ambiance at the moment, which went swimmingly with Tamasha's taffy turntable techniques. No Ravana piñata tonight (as Kavita had explained to me later; Ravana was the ten-headed demon, the enemy in the *Ramayana*), but a whopping prismatic disco ball. And where had been a nearly solely South Asian audience last time was—I realized now, as more and more *Flash!* folk and Lenne Lenape High posse people and Starbucks pals and the usual HotPot crowd and Karsh following filtered in—a rainbow mix. The music had picked up and the foot-tapping, head-nodding business was well under way. I wound among the rainbow tribe, feeling safe in the world, blissfully aware that Karsh hovered somewhere above me.

I slipped behind the bar and swung my bag around to my back and stood there, at the foot of the ladder, trembling slightly before the stained glass wall of bottles and brews, elixirs and quick fixes. My hands quaked and I wondered how I would be able to keep a grip, let alone climb up, up to the club-land firmament. Picturing my mother's dance spear between them, I let my eyes follow my imagination, rung by rung, all the way to that dark opening, sweet and secret as a dug hole.

And a funny thing. My heart grew very still. And slow, an oar through unfathomed water. My breathing deepened and I could hear it clear as if I were swimming.

I felt a wave of calm wash over me. I still wasn't sure what his lips had whispered to the flame as he entered his new year. But my answer was yes.

Before I'd even gotten to the top, a hand reached down to help me up. I climbed the final step to come face to face with him, there in a Nehru jacket and jeans. It was his big night, and he deserved it.

But it was Gwyn's big night, too, and the sight of Karsh was a honeyed one, a pangy sweet like a sad song you love. I felt a flood of unsung tears inside me, tears that followed a receding childhood, tears for everything she had been through, with and without me, for the dust-filled cups of the playhouse and this summer coming to a close. And tears that belonged to a happiness greater than any I'd ever known, too.

He was watching me a little shyly, hesitant. And I realized he looked worried, and it was possibly even because of me, and I was crying then.

—Forgot something? I sobbed, swinging his laced-together shoes towards him.

—Yeah, I suppose I did.

He didn't look too surprised as he took them from my hand and set them on the floor.

—Yeah, well. Me, too, I said.

—Yeah?

And I unwrapped my arms around him, brought my hands to the nape of his neck, sweat and cinnamon, my lips to his left lobe.

—I forgot to do that, I whispered.

His arms were around me, too, now, and I could have stayed there forever. And even pulling me a step into the balcony area he kept me close. Shailly was at one end, multiply eared, perusing the decks like a tarot reader. We climbed over the rooty wires and cords and cables, and around the crates and bags to the other side. In the shadowed corner, he lifted my face, thumbing my tears off my cheeks. He looked at me very seriously.

—Now if I'm allowed to venture a guess about why you're crying, I would have two. The first, a little egocentrically, I suppose, is that you don't know how to tell me you still consider me sunk, and it's putting you through the stress wringer because you aren't used to confronting unfun situations head-on.

—You were never a sunken ship, I said, taking each thumb now in my hands. Both pulsed, as if he had two hearts. —I never—it was all out of context. I'm so sorry.

—It's okay . . . I didn't stay upset about it long, you don't need to apologize. I figured, maybe self-protectively—how could I take it too personally?
You didn't even know me. At least it showed you had a good sense of humor.

—If anything you were a sunken treasure, I said quietly.

He smiled a smile that was at once happy and sad.

—So you talked to Gwyn, he said.

I nodded, stumbling through tears. We sat down now, face to face and
toes touching. Though from here the ceiling wasn't so high and the air was
misted with smoke and sweat, when I closed my eyes, it was easy to imagine
we were on a rooftop edge, close enough to touch the fronded boughs, in the
part of them where they plumed like giant evergreen birds, an occasional
windblown clearing in their feathery mass through which you could just
glimpse the just creased water of Mirror Lake.

—Well, we really had it out, I said, opening my eyes now. —And now she
says she needs time on her own to think about things. But I can't help feeling
I've just lost my oldest friend in the world.

—Dimple, rani, maybe that's the truth: She just needs a little space. A
friendship like yours can't end over something like this.

—Over something like this? I said, poking him gently in the chest.
—I hope you're right, but I think it can. You're pretty out of the ordinary,
Karsh.

—You know, he said, humbly, sincerely. —I don't even think it was me
so much. It's got a lot more to do with you two. You've opened a can of
worms. I'm just . . . sort of symbolic. A catalyst.

I realized then that there were a lot of things besides him that had come
up in the conversation with Gwyn. He was partly right. The fact of him had
triggered an entire set of underlying issues we'd either been ignoring, or
never noticed, or never wanted to deal with.

—Yeah, it's true. The two of us had a lot to talk about, I nodded. —But I
wish we were still talking. You haven't seen her?

He shook his head, and my heart sank in the midst of all this baffling joy.
Happy-sad. It was funny I'd never understood that concept before, that you
could feel two things at once, or maybe even more. Now it seemed this grey
area was the natural, the only, state of things.

—I wish she were here, I said. —I mean, in a way it's her party.

—Well, kudos to *Flash!*, she was certainly the woman to put in charge. After all, she's the one who told them to use you for the visuals.

—What?

—She insisted, Karsh smiled. —Of course, she hardly needed to twist my arm. And once the *Flash!* folk saw the images, they were into it, too.

—She insisted? I said, stunned. I'd always thought she only liked the pictures she was in.

—*Insisted*, he said. —Even when she fully understood my feelings. For you.

I was moved, by both of them, and in spite of myself joy budded in me. I smiled, too, feeling shy, but nicely so.

—I was very clear with her from the beginning, he added. —At least I thought I was.

—She told me she's never been treated with so much love, I said. —At least, by a boy. Maybe she misunderstood. I mean, I even misunderstood what the two of you were about. And until she told me herself I still wasn't sure.

—How could you not be sure? I kept trying to send you signals—leaving the shoes, playing my tablas to you on that tape. When I asked you to dance.

—What?

—At HotPot. And you said your feet hurt. And then I realized maybe it would never work out. You kept pointing out that we were like brother and sister.

—I did? I said nonplussed. —But so did you!

—Well, you do feel like family to me. But not like a sister. Or rather, like a sister . . . but . . . hmmm. Then we'd be getting into contraband thoughts, he winked. —So I never knew how to read you. But I finally figured it would be better to just speak up and say how I feel in case, in case there was any chance . . . rather than regret it for the rest of my life.

Eternal recurrence.

—I know what you mean, I said.

He reached over and took my hand in his, turning it over gently to reveal my palm.

—Look, he said, tracing his finger along a tributary off my lifeline. —It says right here: Everything is going to be all right between the two of you.

—It says that? There?

—Well, it says, um, a current crisis in a friendship may not be its ending but rather the beginning of a new phase, a new sort of happily ever after. . . . See? Right here.

Now he was tracing a second sidestream with one hand, his other holding my own.

—And it says right here that—yes. That a certain someone will be there for you through it all, and will wait for you till you're ready, till you feel fully free. That this certain person, well, it took twenty years for him to find you, give or take—and you didn't even exist for a couple of them! So if it's all right by you, he's not letting you go so easy.

—And what else? I said, nudging him. —What else?

—That's all I'm allowed to read today, he smiled. But he didn't let go of my hand. Looking at our intertwined fingers—knuckles separating the thirty-day months from the thirty-one, counting out a doubled year together—I saw we weren't the same color at all. Gold panned under his skin; umber layered mine. Even brown wasn't merely brown.

—I can't believe we're here like this, I said. —That all this time.

—Yes, all this time. How could you not know?

—So many things. Like that time you came over and out of all the pictures I'd taken chose the one of her for the one you wanted, the one you wanted to keep.

—Dimple, he said, and he looked at me first surprised then very soberly. —Of course I picked that one.

—Of course?

—That was the only one with you in it, he said.

I looked up at him, into his coal and campfire eyes and it was funny, but I think he might have had tears in them, or maybe I did and they were making his look wet. It was bittersweet, but there was nowhere else I'd rather have been than here, and I couldn't believe that this summer journey had led to my being here at all, in the song-boughed sky with him. With him. The most unsuitable suitable boy in my ever expanding universe. Which, as it turned out, suited me just fine.

★   ★   ★

Karsh was on in five, and I came back down to the bar, my bag and spirits lightened somewhat. Kavita was there now, and though not technically on duty tonight, seemed to have been co-opted into lending her expertise. She was at the other end of the bar, standing on a stool rung and gesturing passionately to indicate a more efficient arrangement to the new girl.

The music began to crackle like candy wrappers. She caught sight of me and came over.

—How is it going, cowgirl? she smiled. She climbed on the prattling stool beside me. —The pictures, they are amazing! Looks like you did have a tale to tell after all, isn't it?

—Thanks, Kavity, I said. A zithering dhol dum-dum notched up the air now. —Did you have a good chat with my parents?

—Chat? Those three were guzzling Boozeflash like you wouldn't believe—they hardly had time to talk!

My eyes followed her finger to that risky red fish tank. The name had changed, but the punch looked as potent as ever.

—Oh no! I cried, laughing. I looked out to the crowd, but couldn't see them. Maybe they'd gone on to the restaurant?

Kavita and I ordered a drink, and I caught her up a little on the goings-on of late and above.

We toasted, and by the time I turned around, the music was magnetic, the dance floor was packed, and I couldn't believe it.

—Go Aunty! Go Uncle! Kavita hollered.

My parents were leading a mass of people—including what seemed to be the entire eager-to-be-authentic *Flash!* mass—in that same bhangric Garbhic version of Macarena-meets-Jackson they'd been practicing at home. And it was like the Pied Piper effect: The more they got into it, the more people joined in, till there was literally a mass movement on the floor, rendered hypnotically hungering by the rompy lung-bung thirst-quench sea beat. Razz-a-tazz-*skat*, ba*doomph*-kitschy-grrring, DHA-dhin trika-DUM, bowwow-waah, chitty-*brrring!*—and a voice like a seashell song from a faraway place, brush-breathing you into a curled-upon-itselfness, a resonant hollow emptily full of distant waves and nearer sand.

There was so much life in the song somehow; it was sung and played and sang us like a last breath. A dark underbelly underpinned the music, but a sky soared above it, raining a spangled shower down onto the bass-full flesh. And the tiny convex me seemed to be bobbing in this joyful rain, and you could ride the joy into the scary part and find a strangely safe footing in the center of the fear if you became one with it, like a surfer in the tunnel. I was sitting, but I felt like I was atop a live animal, balanced on the back of a city so dynamic, and that city on a world so wingingly fluxen, that no wonder we needed a little piece of gravity to keep from flying off.

Knowing Karsh was drawing me tidal to the dance floor, I let myself go, right into the heart of it.

And then I was dancing.

Itchy itchy I—ho ho! Once again, the entire place was spilling over. All the boundaries broken, melted away in sweat and song. People leapt on the stage and off, mingling with what seemed like the millions of people flickering on brick and a real tomtomeer and a real sitarista whose strum-thuks blended at times into the music, at others thrusting out like the pages of a pop-up book.

And then *itchy itchy I* again and drums everywhere: above, below, beating in my big toe. Caught like a heart between my legs, inside my throat and emerging, and I was calling *ho ho!* with the chorus of voices, the music dropping out just that moment, and then back in a rush *itchy itchy I* and I was singing with the rest of them *hi hi* I could hear my voice in the mix, a thread unique in a tapestry of sound, and I was dancing with myself and with every motherfrocker on the planet and it was not a lonely number where there was you.

Climbing now, onto the stage and shimmying towards the millions of echoing people, and someone was approaching me from the other side, from the screen side, and I sped up and she did too, both of us skipping now, and I slowed as did she, and then I could see her beautiful black-eyed-bean waves and glittery dupatta and bell bottoms and a trace of her mother's mother's tikka between her smiling eyes, and I was just before her now, close enough to touch, and I was face to face with: myself.

I turned away from the video screen and leapt off into the sea of upturned palms. And as I landed, I began to distinguish one set of hands that stayed upon me, milky-wayed and manicured.

—May I have this dance, supertwin?

I turned. And couldn't believe my eyes. It was Gwyn! She stood before me in some kind of Roaring Twenties number, the blues of her eyes piercing in a face where the hair was swept off and only the mouth was made up, and turned up, too.

—Gwyn! I cried. —You came!

—I wouldn't have missed it for anything, she smiled. —Are you kidding? It's your big night. In a lot of ways.

—But it wouldn't have been without you, I said. —Thank you so much for organizing . . . *all* this. For getting my photos out there.

—Don't mention it, for the pictures. And as far as the party goes, it wasn't my idea, she said. —You know that. But I know a good idea to steal when I see one. Look, I'm so sorry. I—I can't stay away from you, Dimple. I love you.

I pounced upon her, and hugged her close.

—I love you, too, Gwyn, I told her. —Always have. Always will.

She smiled back at me, and I danced in her pupils.

—Listen, I have something for you and Karsh, she said. —To kind of let you know my new position on things. Can we go up right now?

—Go up?

—We're family. Family's allowed, right?

I took her arm in mine and nodded.

—We are definitely family, I said. —Let's go.

★   ★   ★

One hand over the other, I ascended. It felt like the side of a boat, the way the entire club was undulating, and even though I'd been there once already tonight a sense of anticipation laddered higher in me with every step.

Karsh looked happily surprised to see Gwyn climbing up on my tail, and reached down to help her up, too.

—Hey, he said.

—Hey, she said. She took a breath then and faced us, handing each of us an envelope pulled from the beaded pouch gold-chained off her hip. I could feel a small soft shape-changing lump in the paper, wedged in the bottom corner.

—Open them together, she instructed.

He ripped, then I did. I jostled the little mass out into the palm of my hand, beside his hand where one already lay, making two. Two rakhis, like two tiny flower-float rivers coming together.

—You see, a wise woman once told me a story, said Gwyn, and she took one in her hand, unsnarling the thread. She began to tie it around my wrist.

—A story of how she once made it clear to someone that he was like a brother to her.

She was on the second rakhi now, tying it around Karsh's wrist.

—And that she would be like a sister to this person, she said.

She stood back and observed our newly rakhi'd wrists.

—To cut the cord, so to speak. Even though I suppose technically, it's tying the cord. Anyways, Dimple, you're the closest thing to a sister I've got. And Karsh. You're the closest to a brother. And I just want to say I'm sorry about the way I've been acting and all, and I'm not going to walk out on either of you, and I hope you might have room for me now and then in your happiness, and I will be there for whenever that moment might crop up. So happy Rakshabandhan.

—Room for you? I said, and I was crying. I took her in my arms, and Karsh stood shyly back, but we pulled him in and we were in a group huddle.

—Well, you know what I mean, she spoke into my hair. —Who needs a third wheel?

—A tricycle, I whispered back, smacking a kiss on her cheek. —As *another* very wise woman once said.

We held each other for a happy while. And then Gwyn disentangled herself.

—And now that the cord is cut, I've got some business of my own to handle down there, she said, smiling her cavity confessional. —You did say I'm inspiration for a DJ once, didn't you, Karsh? Well, I've got a job to do.

She slid over to descend the ladder, her face disappearing strip by strip over the edge, one pool blue eye winking before vanishing down. And from above we watched her go, stepping over the boxes of records, the tangled wires, the spinning platters to follow her mazey path through the dance floor.

Karsh turned it all up a notch, and she was down there, her gold haloed head swinging in view, turning up the charm and getting down and dirty on the dance floor with anyone and everyone: fast waltzing my father, mirror dancing with Zara, and eventually landing in the center of the energy-dense circle of Trilok (Jimmy) Singh, who was currently breakdancing to his heart's content on a patch of plank. We watched Gwyn wind her way in and get right down on her flapper back beside him, mimicking his moves, and well; the competition mounted, leading them from on-the-back swirlie-whirlies all the way around the world to Russian kickboxing calf-flicks and salsa and sevillanas and strange blends of tree pose and Step moves and the Lindy, and the circle around the two grew to accommodate them.

—I think Tree may have finally met his match, I smiled.

I felt I was looking over the edge of the world. And it was a moment when all was right with the world: The music was all around and inside us. Below, a sea of people were grooving in multiplicitous harmony. All together like this the dancing bodies looked like part of the same organism, the very blood in its veins, and my photos were windows into the multieyed animal; even inanimate objects souled up, chairs jittering to the bass and glasses spinning light.

I had never felt in my whole life like I did then: Zen. Suddenly the Miss America wish for world peace seemed brilliant. Maybe if enough people made that wish we could do huge things, make things happen just from our thoughts and good intentions and all be shiny happy people. And this much was clear now: It was no passive homogenous creature, identity, but rather diversity, a thrashing, grinding, and all-out dirty dancing together. It moved and it grooved and it might even sleep with you before marriage. You were the dancer and the dance, and you could shape yourself through a riff, or a shrug, or an on-the-back spin, adapt to new rhythms without losing a sense of harmony with yourself. And harmony, that was no static thing either, but many different parts coming together to sing the same song.

And the beat, well. The beat you had to follow was your own heart.

These were all ever-changing things, which made people ever-adapting creatures. You could call it confusion on a bad day—or just a call to dance on a good. In any case, I no longer felt confused—well, a lot less confused. And I certainly wasn't confused about The Boy now taking my hand. Standing here, tonight, with Karsh, I had the sense we were at the beginning of our own once upon a time. I had the feeling I was home at last.

—See? he said, tracing that same tributary off my lifeline. —What did I tell you? That she would be back. And that he would wait.

Our eyes met now and we were alone among so many, in a temple all our own.

—You read palms? was all I could manage.

—No, he said, smiling. That smile I so loved now. He hadn't let go of my hand. Below everybody was dancing; he listened for a moment through his phones, and lifted the needle off the record. —But I read lips.

Everybody dancing. And then I couldn't see anything because, finally, his mouth came to mine like a moon winding back into orbit, and there was no place I would rather have been.

We kissed until we tasted the same. Until I couldn't tell where he left off and I began.

It was only when we came up we realized: There was dead silence in the club.

And it was only when we looked over the edge of the world we saw:

Everyone was still dancing.

—Oh, man, Karsh whispered. —I lifted the wrong needle.

He busied himself with a quick save, a low thumping number that crept stealthily up out of nowhere, a humblebee honey-drone becoming a sound of its own, the way the song of an empty room reveals itself upon closer listening, the way the room is not empty at all.

And then Sole Mate was up, to carry through closing. Karsh was set for the night.

—Come on, he said, turning to me. —Do you want to dance?

—I'd love to, I said.

born

It was difficult to imagine summer was already almost officially over. But summer itself didn't seem to think so, hanging on a little longer, hesitant to let go. What had felt like a chill setting in on the tail of the seemingly eternal heat wave of the past months now, after a small period of adjustment, revealed itself to be surprisingly mild weather. Warm enough to swim in, cool enough to wear a sweater.

I slipped one on now, Karsh's blue knit number that he'd left here last night after I'd wrapped up Gwyn's birthday project in the darkening room (which, incidentally, had turned out to be the perfect place to kiss under the same roof as my parents). My bathing suit was on under my jeans when I went out the door for our moon date, a blue moon date with the way I was dressed, and a full one at that.

I passed the playhouse, which Karsh and I had sneaked into earlier to empty of the holy crew—who were now positioned in scrubbed-down shininess just before it—and fill with balloons and presents for Gwyn: a bona fide fringed vintage minidress to equip her for her current flapper phase, a series of some above-ground Asian underground CDs, and a replacement tape for that Dead recording I'd destroyed several weeks before. I'd also just finished a photo collage for her: I'd pasted her oversized bindi'd face from the HotPot shot onto a photograph of a photograph of Marilyn's subway-flung dress. As a final touch, I'd rubber cemented on wide-spanning windbent, light-rent, glitter-veined wings that I'd created from a photo of star-explosion taxi-fast rain in the city one day; they bent up and off the actual page.

Tomorrow she would be seventeen, and we would be the same age again; ever since we were little we'd waited eagerly for that summer-long gap that set us a year apart to seal up, bring us back to supertwin status. And the day was nearly here.

I tucked the treasure hunt clue directing her back to the ovary office into the mailbox now, and continued on through the dried forest floor, across the bridge and to the other side. I went left onto Lake View Road.

Walking down the street now it felt like another planet. Houses had sprung up from the once lunar surface like massive manicured shrubs, gravel paths rattled through grass and marigold, driveways serpentined gardens. The streets were slick and new, no first love fumbling stick etchings in sight. In fact, I had no idea where Bobby O'Malley had written our names that lost summer day. The tar was black and clean as a river, a washed slate.

I'd always thought it would hurt too much to be here, but it was actually all right revisiting the scene of the crime. Because the scene of the crime had changed. And I had, too. It was like the time I went back to visit my elementary school to show Ketan Kaka, and I was amazed at how small everything was—the little desks, the rooms, the building itself—when in my memory my feet had barely reached the ground, the hallways stretched frighteningly far, and the whole place seemed like a labyrinth designed specifically to confuse me.

I was coming around the bend where the last house on Lake View nestled, jutting out to a thin strip of remaining pines that feathered out over the water. This house was cozily tucked half in tree shadow. In the front shone a huge window paved with light, yellow as if it had been rolled on with paint. In fact, the entire place hummed with light. Another house of eternal Diwali.

I was drawn mothlike to this house. As I approached the drive the clack of my footsteps multiplied, as if I'd suddenly sported another pair of feet. I halted. A pause, and then the second set of feet continued padding along, like a lazy echo.

Moving closer, the ghostly stroller grew a bit louder, and I discovered its path: Music strained through the screen in the cracked window, where I could now see two figures. Two women, a shared silhouette swathed in sheer scintillating fabric, spinning and swooshing. Their hair whirled short shadows across their faces and they moved with the intensity of worshippers, all in time to that phantom promenader, those double drums, soft and steady as a heart beating through silk.

The tinkling, twiney window music sounded distantly familiar, like a face you see in passing on a train that speaks to you and is gone. Through it, the drums jabbed out three-dimensional, and they were playing a funky rhythm, offbeat, but still on the pulse—like a photo that clips the cheek but catches the wink.

These drums sounded as if they were being struck underwater; they made me feel I was underwater, too, a pod floating in a safe place. Just then a percussive roll shuddered forth sinuous and thick as a fat fish fin, all scaly light and jelly weight, and tickled my spine. I rose up, buoyant, kicking off my shoes. My feet flipped up as if I were dancing around hot coals.

Dheeta Dheeta Kita Taka Teeta Teeta Kita Taka
Teeta Teeta Kita Taka Dheeta Dheeta Kita Taka

The music was viscous, then liquid. It slaked me, dripped into my fingers and toes and activated me. I began to sway, dancing in the dark with my secret partner. I forgot myself; I recognized myself.

Dhage na Dha Teeta Dhage na Dhage Tin na Gi na
Tage na Ta Teeta Dhage na Dhage Dhin na Gi na

I found myself dancing with and without the silhouetted window genies, spinning an invisible Hula Hoop around my waist, plucking fruit from imagined trees, twirling my hair, insouciant, off my face.

Dhage na Dha tira kita Dhati Dhage Tin na Gi na
Tage na Dha tiri kita Dhati Dhage Dhin na Gi na

I was closer now.

One woman slowed, and the other bent to touch something. The music faded. Window shut, lights dimmed. And the drums kept going.

Wishing pennies blinking in a lake.

They seemed to move the very clouds, which were scuttling off the moon.

And that's when I saw him. Up on the roof, the figure hunched in the shadows, thighs squeezed around the tablas, swathed in white. And if I could see him—I realized as the last cloud peeled off, fully untucking the moon—he could see me.

Light flooded the street like a cosmic river. The player's face shone with sweat and he was staring right at me.

—Hi, you, he said.

—Hi, I smiled. And I realized: This had never been the last house, but the first.

★   ★   ★

Moments later, Karsh was in the driveway, a very punctual moon date indeed. He smiled and brushed my hair up off my forehead and kissed me there, smack upon my third eye, where the bindi would be. He wove my hand in his and we made our way back, retracing my steps.

On the bridge, he glowed slightly, the triangle of flushed mooncast light on the black-wine water ricocheting up to his figure and then onto me.

—Are you sure you want to do this?

—Never been more, I said.

We walked, stumbling and grass grasping down the rocky side slope that led to the water. I shed my jeans and chappals on the bottom of the bank, skin melding effortlessly into sky. His T-shirt was off, and then we were holding hands, wading into the inky gold-tipped liquid.

Once we'd moved away from the water sifting through to the other side of the bridge, the only sound in the universe was us, the summer cicada symphony on hiatus. First the pushed trickle-drip as we walked as far as we could go, calves creasing, knees cutting water, and then the slosh of thigh and waist till the drowned silence grew chest deep, then neck, and we could walk no more, thin plinks coming off the lashes, caught by cheek drops before the fall, nearly noiseless, like rain joining rain, the doubled drop tadpoling with accumulated speed down a windowpane.

And then the music of our staggered strokes as we began swimming, and the water lifted us, heels out of mudsuck and wet sand, now feet not touching ground; it was safe and secret at the same time. We swam up through gilded crests that looked like a blown glass dawn till you touched them and they gave without breaking, out towards our makeshift ship, our titanic romance.

When we got to the raft, I clutched the wet dark rail of the ladder dropping down and disappearing to that imaginary doused dance floor, and felt the raft tip towards me. This used to frighten me, the tilting, but tonight it felt as if it might be leaning in to help me up, and I climbed a glistened way to the deck, rungs rolling their shape achily into the soles of my feet and Karsh a moment behind me, creating an even greater tilt and then an even greater sense of balance.

We crouched there a moment, till the rocking subsided. He pulled me in a squatting fetal position into his warmth. Before we'd touched, I'd always thought the electricity lay in the thin space between us. But touching, it was galvanized, a drowned current.

—Now you told me you knew once how to do it, he said.

—It's just when I started thinking about it too much, I explained. —I was terrified by the whole idea of my feet being where my head was.

—But think of the upside-down chandeliers, he told me in the secret cove of my ear. —How they turned to flowers. And know that you won't be alone now. You're not alone. At least not in a scary way. Trust your body to protect you—everything you need to know is inside you already, rani. Always has been.

I turned and rested on my knees and lay both my hands on his cheeks, so his face was a prayer between them, stroked his fiery damp eyebrows. I was rocking gently in the centers of his eyes, in the openings that dilated, led straight into him.

—Are you ready? he whispered.

—I'm ready.

I rose and stepped onto the base of the board. Slowly I walked out to the edge of it, pulsing down a little with my heels on the way, to get a sense of spring in them. I hung my toes just over and looked down. The moon was out full force now, mirrored in the water, upside down and right side up and something else altogether at the same time.

The water wasn't far—a short space to get head over heels. But one summer was a seemingly short space, too. And that was all it had taken for me to get as head over heels as you could without walking through the world on your hands. Now I knew firsthand that having my universe turned upside down didn't have to be a bad thing: He'd already done that to me; I'd already done that to me.

I turned back and he was on the edge of the raft, feet in water, at the ready and nodding at me. Yes.

And I dove.

Slow-swimming mermaid percussions . . . mirror slake deep diving . . . shellfish sunken treasure song . . . bubble drunk . . . stone-skip water-ringing . . . wishing pennies lake blinking.

Dha Dhin Trika Dha Dha Dhin Trika . . . Ta Tin Trika Dha Dha Dhin Trika . . . Dha Dhin Trika Dha Ti Dha Ge Tin Na Gi Na . . . Ta Tin Trika Dha Ti Dha Ge Dhin Na Gi Na . . .

A reverse birth, my ears filling up, breathing percussive; I could hear my heart here. Winging down, down to run my hands in the seaweeden rock-ridden sand at the bottom before kicking off and then rising up, effortlessly, following my heard stream of bubbles, up up, and, with a surge of sound, like the disco filter effect he'd played me today: into air.

I gasped. And Karsh was already in the water beside me.

★　★　★

We were lying on our backs on the raft now, staring at a sky with too many stars to count. It was hard to believe it was September. Karsh's hand rested gently on my belly; it made a safe place there and I watched it rise up and down with my breathing.

Tomorrow would be my first day of senior year. It was funny imagining it: the same building, bustling with the same teachers and pretty much the same group of kids—but after this summer I had no doubt it would be an entirely new place. A place where Jimmy (Trilok) Singh would be Trilok (Jimmy) Singh and I would join him for lunch and maybe even bring along my own (defrosted) samosas. Where I might take a different route through the corridors to a new class, where I might take the bus or even walk. And sometimes my boyfriend—no, perhaps my jeevansaathi—would meet me after in his midnight Golf with my bindi riding over his mirrored eyes and we would merge into the city and look at where we'd been from the water's second side. It would be a place where a postcard on a locker door would have a story behind it and my best friend in the world would be a somewhere glued together and I would love her all the more for the cracks we'd allowed, then sealed.

And I would keep Chica Tikka with me at all times, and I would have someone to share all these pictures with, these bits and pieces of so many lives. Of my own life. I was eager to see what the tale would be. It was a lot like the darkening room—the same way the pictures floated up, there, coalescing element by element, the way you never really knew what story you were telling till you filtered and heightened its color, dodged its shadow, shifted its light, and with your own hands. Everyone had a story. Everyone was making a story, all the time. And this was only the beginning of mine.

I remembered that rainbow I had seen once as a girl, that nearly full-circle Ferris wheel arching its array of breathtaking color over this pond and disappearing somewhere secret on the other side, bringing what had seemed then to be two different and distant lands together.

I knew where it ended now.

He was spinning his finger, making a deepening circle in my belly button.

—They say it's going to be an Indian summer, he said.